JOSEPH PAUSED FOR A MOMENT as something attracted his eye. It was a glimmer of light, and it came from a narrow slit in the stone at the far end of his cell. . . . It must have been that the sun, as it dropped lower on the horizon, lined itself up perfectly with the opening, allowing a brilliant stream of light to shine suddenly through and fall at his shackled feet. It was a small thing. Some would have dismissed it as mere coincidence. But Joseph saw it as an answer to his prayer. If light could somehow penetrate the gloomy depths of this prison, the power of God could reach him here as well. The Lord was aware of his distress and would help him through this abysmal time of darkness.

Comments from readers

Joseph and Asenath

I loved *Joseph and Asenath*. It is a powerful novel of Joseph, the lost son of Jacob who was sold into Egypt. This beautiful love story grips you from the first page. As Chappell taps into the lives of Joseph and Asenath and the love they shared with one another, he uncovers the dangers they faced and overcame by magnifying their faith in God. This remarkable book should be on everyone's must read list.

Karen C.
Pleasant Grove, Utah

Praise for other books by Alex Chappell

A Rod of Iron

Our family really enjoys Alex Chappell's books. *A Rod of Iron* gives a unique insight on how things would have been at the time of Nephi. The book brings to life the story of Nephi and his family and makes it easier to understand and relate to without detracting from the gospel principles and spiritual teachings of the Book of Mormon. We look forward to reading his next book.

Guy and Jane Wann
Ojai, California

More Precious Than Gold

This book is a gem. I wanted the book to continue! It is inspiring and should be hailed as a classic love story. The author should be commended.

Emeline M. Parr
Massillon, Ohio

Joseph & Asenath

ALEX G. CHAPPELL

Published and Distributed by:

Granite Publishing and Distribution, LLC
868 North 1430 West
Orem, Utah 84057
(801) 229-9023 • Toll Free (800) 574-5779
Fax (801) 229-1924

Cover Design by: Tammie Ingram
Page Layout and Design by: Lyndell Lutes

ISBN: 1-932280-86-3

Library of Congress Control Number: 2005933236

First Printing October 2005

10 9 8 7 6 5 4 3 2 1

Printed in the United States of America

Acknowledgments

THE AUTHOR WISHES TO GIVE SPECIAL THANKS to each of the following individuals: Thanks to Joyce Fife, John Jones, and all the staff at Granite Publishing for their invaluable suggestions and insightful recommendations. Thanks also to Ken and Lyndell Lutes for their careful editing and typesetting of the manuscript. A final thanks to Laurie Tenny for the beautiful artwork that graces the cover of this novel and to Tammie Ingram for her work on the cover design. The support of these talented individuals as well as that of numerous family members and friends has been greatly appreciated.

Map of Egypt and Canaan

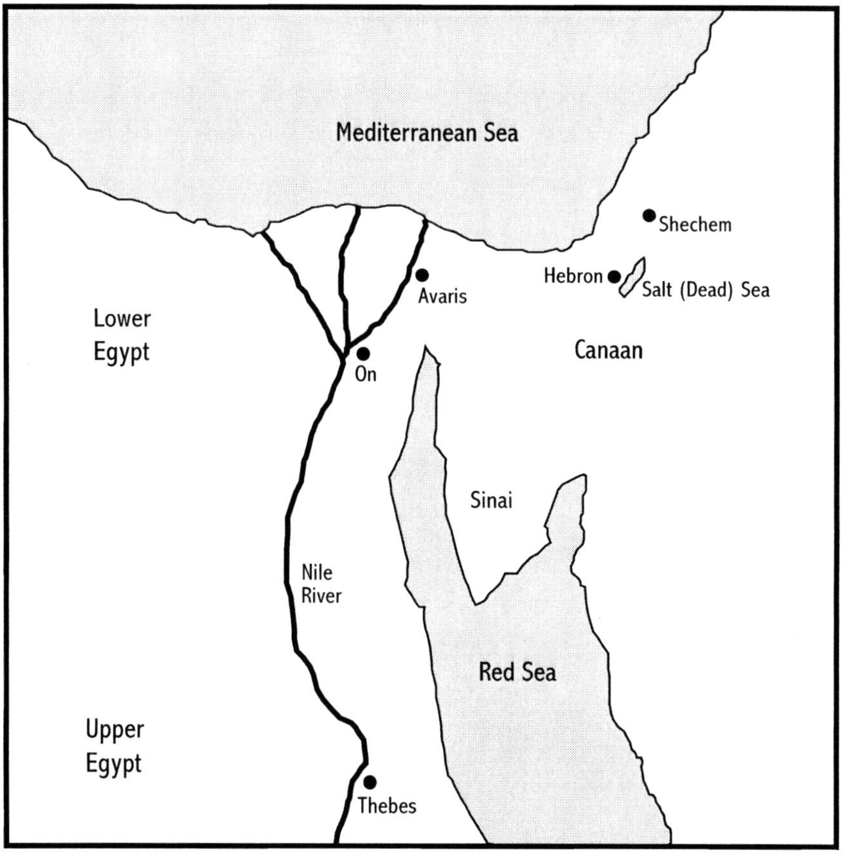

Mediterranean Sea

● Shechem

● Avaris

Hebron ● ◊ Salt (Dead) Sea

**Lower
Egypt**

● On

Canaan

Sinai

Nile
River

Red Sea

**Upper
Egypt**

● Thebes

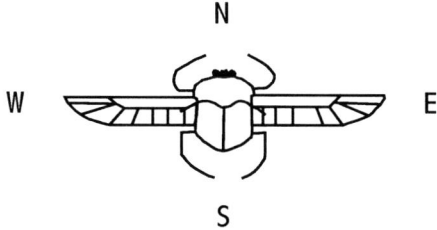

N

W   E

S

Cast of Characters

CHARACTERS MARKED WITH AN ASTERISK (*) are historical figures in the book of Genesis whose actual names are not known. Characters marked with a double asterisk (**) are fictional characters not mentioned in Genesis. Khyan, Nebireyeraw, and Sebekamzaf are historical figures who may or may not have lived at the time of Joseph.

Household of Jacob

Jacob, *also known as Israel*
Leah, *first wife of Jacob*
Reuben
Simeon
Levi
Judah
Issachar
Zebulun
Dinah
Zilpah, *Jacob's concubine and Leah's handmaiden*
Gad
Asher
Bilhah, *Jacob's concubine and Rachel's handmaiden*
Dan

Naphtali
Rachel, *Jacob's second wife*
Joseph
Benjamin

Household of Potipherah

Potipherah, *high priest of On*
**Seshep, *wife of Potipherah*
Asenath, *daughter of Potipherah*
**Nesmut, *servant in the house of Potipherah*

Household of Potiphar

Potiphar, *captain of Pharaoh's royal guard*
*Neferset, *Potiphar's wife*
**Pekhti, *chief groom*
**T'chet, *chief steward*
**Amakh, *keeper of the flocks*

Household of Setmosis

**Setmosis, *chief priest in the temple of Seth at Avaris*
**Ari, *wife of Setmosis*
**Mera, *oldest daughter of Setmosis*
**Netchem, *youngest daughter of Setmosis*

Household of Pharaoh

Khyan, *Hyksos king of Egypt*
*Ta, *chief baker*
*Thet, *chief butler*
*Aten, *royal advisor*

Additional Characters

*Anebni, *keeper of Pharaoh's prison*
Nebireyeraw, *vassal king of Thebes*
Sebekamzaf, *prince of Thebes*

PART ONE

Now Israel loved Joseph more than all his children,
because he was the son of his old age:
and he made him a coat of many colors.

Genesis 37:3

ONE

As he approached the pasture, Joseph's stomach twisted into a cold, hard knot, and his fingers tightened around the shepherd's staff in his hand. They would be waiting for him. They would be waiting near the sheep, watching for an opportunity to torment him. It had been happening since he was a little boy, and he had come to expect it as surely as he expected the sun to rise in the morning. But he knew that today was going to be worse than usual. It was the first time his father, Jacob, had asked him to watch the flocks since the day Joseph reported the murmurings of his brothers to his father, and the sons of Bilhah and Zilpah had been watching Joseph with angry eyes ever since then. They'd been biding their time—anticipating the opportunity to catch him away from the watchful eyes of their father. They'd been patiently waiting for revenge, and now it seemed that their chance had finally come.

He'd thought about asking his father to let him tend the flocks alone instead of having to guard them with Asher, Gad, Dan, and Naphtali; but that would only postpone the inevitable. Somehow— some way—they would find the means of catching him alone. Better to get it over with now while he was prepared for it than to have it happen when he wasn't ready.

At the current moment, everything seemed unnaturally serene and normal. The scene before him was as peaceful as any he had ever experienced. But he knew his brothers well enough not to let his guard down now. He was instantly wary when Dan and Naphtali came into sight.

The two were already here watching Jacob's largest flock. Their backs were to Joseph, and Dan was gesturing with his arms while Naphtali nodded his head, agreeing with whatever Dan was saying. Joseph wondered if they were talking about him—deciding what they would do to him when he showed up. But at least Gad and Asher were nowhere in sight. He might be able to hold his own against two of his brothers, but four would be more than he could handle. Comforted a little by this great good fortune, he straightened his shoulders and moved more confidently down the path. He was almost to them when a mysterious object snaked out of the dry, yellow grass, catching him unexpectedly around one ankle.

A cry of surprise escaped Joseph's lips as he tumbled to the ground. Before he could figure out what was happening to him, two figures rose out of the grass, rolled him roughly to his back, and pinned him against the sun-baked earth. One of these attackers, Asher, pressed a shepherd's staff hard against his neck and dug both knees into his biceps while the other held his legs so that he couldn't kick. He struggled for a few moments to escape them, but Asher jammed the staff even harder against his Adam's apple, and Joseph realized that further resistance would only result in more pain.

"Look what we have here," Asher said, turning his head to grin at Gad. "What do you think it is?"

"I don't know," Gad said, scratching the stubble on his chin as if he were perplexed. "I've never seen anything quite like it. I think all those bright colors are going to blind me."

"Do you think it's dangerous?" Asher asked. He took one hand off the staff to pull at Joseph's coat, and Joseph quickly gulped a breath of air.

"All right," he gasped, his throat still hurting. "You've had your fun. Now let me up. You're hurting me."

"Not a chance," Asher said. A snarl curled the corner of his lip, and he again pressed the staff against Joseph's neck. "The fun is just beginning, little brother. But this time it's going to be all ours!"

"Careful, Asher," Gad warned in a mocking tone. "I've finally figured out what we've got here. Look at all those bright colors. It must be a bird. It's the kind of bird that will fly to Father's tent and start squawking the instant we let it go. Maybe we should put it in a cage to keep it quiet."

"Or maybe we should wring its neck," Asher growled. "That would solve all of our problems. Don't you think?" Asher moved to put more of his weight against the staff, and Joseph felt as if his windpipe would be crushed. But the sudden shift in Asher's weight gave him an opportunity to get one arm free, and he used this sudden advantage to fling Asher to the ground while kicking Gad away from his feet.

Asher's reflexes were like a cat, but Joseph's were quicker. In one fluid motion, he rolled into an upright position and staggered away from his angry brothers. Asher followed, raising the staff above his head as if he would strike his younger brother with it, but Joseph's fists came up, prepared to strike back.

"Are you going to fight me?" Asher demanded. "Do you think you're big enough now to handle your older brother? Is that what you think?"

Joseph didn't answer, but he locked eyes with Asher and kept his fists where they were. Although fighting wasn't his way, he wasn't about to let Asher hurt him again.

By this time Dan and Naphtali had come to join the fray, and Joseph realized just how badly he had underestimated their anger. Their eyes were looking for blood, and they eagerly egged Asher on.

"Hit him!" Dan said, a gleeful grin on his face. "He won't hit back. He'll be too worried about what Father will think about him fighting."

"And he wouldn't want to soil that beautiful coat of his," Naphtali chimed in. "Even if he does have a little bit of fight in him, he'll be too busy protecting that precious coat to find time to defend himself."

"I hear the daughters of kings have coats like yours," Gad taunted. "Are you a princess, Joseph? Or are you just pampered like one?"

They all laughed, but there was no smile on Joseph's face. He took a quick step backward as Asher jabbed the shepherd's staff at his face, and he swatted the tip of the weapon away.

"What's the matter, little brother?" Asher asked. "Are you afraid you might get blood on that coat? Is that why you won't come close enough to fight me? Or is it just that you're a sniveling, little coward?"

He was only seventeen, but Joseph was large for his age. He could take down any one of his brothers in single combat. All of them knew that, which was probably why they had planned this attack together. If there was any cowardice here, it could be found in his brothers' actions. But it probably wouldn't be wise to mention that right now.

"Fighting among brothers is displeasing to the Lord," Joseph said instead. "I have no desire to fight any of you."

"Then this isn't your lucky day, is it," Gad taunted, "because we want to fight *you!*"

There appeared to be no way out of this. His brothers cared nothing for the will of the Lord. They never had. But Joseph found sudden salvation from an unexpected source.

"Asher! Joseph! What's going on here?"

Both turned in surprise as their father's voice rang sternly in their ears; and Dan, Naphtali, and Gad moved quickly away from the two combatants. Asher lowered his staff as Jacob approached, and Joseph put his fists down; but it was apparent that their father had seen enough to realize what was going on.

"Asher and Joseph were just practicing a little self-defense. Weren't you?" Gad said. "We want to be prepared in case robbers fall upon our flocks."

"That's right," Asher said, picking up immediately on Gad's ploy.

He moved forward to give Joseph a good-natured slap on the back, and he nodded his head. "You never know when something like that might catch us unaware."

Jacob stroked his thick, white beard which looked even whiter than usual against his angry, red face. But his voice was low and calm when he spoke.

"All of you follow me," he said. "We have some important things to discuss. By the looks of things here, the sooner we discuss this the better."

Asher shot Joseph a venomous stare, then turned his eyes back to Jacob. "What about the flocks?" he demanded. "Who's going to watch them?"

"They're close to our tents," Jacob replied. "And they seemed to be just fine while you had your backs to them practicing your 'self-defense.'" He gave Dan, Naphtali, Gad, and Asher a severe glare, and they all lowered their eyes. "Come. This will only take a few minutes."

Joseph searched for his staff which had fallen to the earth during the struggle, and then he straightened his cloaks and rubbed his still aching neck. His father had shown up just in time, but he feared this sudden rescue would only make things worse for him in the end.

Jacob bowed his head and remained silent for several long moments. He didn't like the idea of sending his sons so far away from Hebron, but there were advantages to what Reuben and Judah had proposed to him today. In fact, after what had happened between Reuben and Bilhah, it might be good to put some distance between those two. More importantly, it would give Joseph a rest from the baleful glares and uncivil tongues of his older brothers. Jacob wasn't sure what had been going on near the pasture, but he was certain that he'd shown up none too soon. With resolve, he lifted his head and addressed his sons.

"The land of Shechem is several days journey from here," he said, "and Simeon and Levi have made enemies in that region." He paused for a moment to give each of them a meaningful glance. "But I agree with Judah and Reuben that we need to find new pastures for our flocks. Because of this drought, there's not much grass left for our animals to graze on. We have to do something, and their plan seems to be our only option. You will all depart for Shechem tomorrow. Our flocks will certainly perish if we keep them here."

A triumphant smile broke through Judah's heavy, black beard, and he puffed out his chest with pride. "We'll start packing our provisions today," he said in a deep, commanding voice. "We'll make our departure at dawn."

"Wait a second," Simeon interrupted. "I don't remember anyone casting lots and choosing you as our leader. Who said you got to tell us what to do?"

"*I* did," Judah replied. "And I don't need your vote to put me in charge. It was mostly my idea. That automatically makes me the leader of this little expedition."

Both men gave each other dangerous stares, and Jacob opened his mouth to stop the fight before it started. But Naphtali jumped in before Jacob got his chance to speak.

"Why don't we let Joseph settle this," Naphtali said. "He's our true leader. Isn't that right, Joseph?"

All eyes turned suddenly to the youngest brother present, and snickers filled the tent.

"That's right," Judah said, his eyes widening in mock dismay. "I almost forgot about that. Let's see . . . How did it happen? Did God tell you in a dream that you were to rule over us? That's right. That's what it was. Forgive me, Mighty King of Dreams!"

"Enough of this!" Jacob snapped. "You're brothers. I'm tired of this constant bickering. There will be no more arguments. There will be no more ridicule. Do you understand?"

His sons lowered their heads and lapsed into silence, but he didn't miss the covert smirks that passed between them. Joseph was silent as well, his eyes lowered, and Jacob could tell that Judah's and Naphtali's comments had stung him.

"Judah will be in charge," Jacob said, a deep frown creasing his weathered face, "but I will hold you all equally accountable for the welfare of our flocks."

"Good," Judah said, folding his arms smugly across his chest. "And now that the question of leadership is settled, I'm ready to make my first decision. The first one is for you, Joseph. I want you to leave that rainbow-colored coat behind. I wouldn't want you to soil it and dim its radiant colors. Besides that, our enemies will be able to spot it from miles away." There were snickers again, and Judah met Jacob's scowl with a wide-eyed look of innocence. "What?" he asked. "I'm only trying to give some friendly, brotherly advice. Can't I help my younger brother preserve his own life?"

"Joseph won't be going with you," Jacob said, continuing to give Judah a piercing look, "so it won't be necessary for you to give him any advice. I can't have all my sons gone at once. I need at least one around to help me here. Benjamin is still too young, so Joseph will have to stay in Hebron."

No one said anything, but the looks that were cast in Joseph's direction were unmistakably malicious. It only made Jacob that much more certain that it was the right thing to keep Joseph home.

"There's much to be done before you leave tomorrow," he said, motioning with one hand to indicate that the meeting was over. "Speak with Zilpah and have her get you any provisions you think you might need. You can also take some of the extra tents and two of the pack animals."

The boys uncrossed their legs and got slowly to their feet. As they began to file out of the tent, Judah paused, turned to Joseph, and made a deep, regal bow. "Look, Joseph!" he exclaimed. "It's already beginning to happen. Your dream is coming true!" The others burst into loud, mocking laughter; but they hurried outside before their father could chastise them again. Even in the dark interior of the tent, the pain in Joseph's eyes was all too evident.

"Stay here for a moment, my son," Jacob said before Joseph could follow Judah out of the tent. "I have a few words to speak to you."

Joseph nodded and dutifully returned to the sheepskin rug where his father was still seated. When Jacob motioned that Joseph, too, should sit down, the youth lowered himself into a kneeling position.

"I've been thinking," Jacob said, "about your dreams—"

"I'm sorry," Joseph blurted out. "I didn't mean any disrespect to you or mother or to my brothers. I couldn't remove the dreams from my mind. I thought it would help if I told somebody about them."

Jacob raised a hand, palm outward, causing the boy to lapse into silence. "It wasn't wrong for you to tell me the dreams," he said. "I've been pondering and praying about your dreams for several days now, and I believe they were given to you by God. It may be that you have a gift—a spiritual gift—that entitles you to such inspiration. But, in the future, it would be wise if you tell these dreams only to me and not to your brothers or your mother."

"Yes," Joseph agreed. "I should have thought of that. I should have known it would upset them."

"You're a good boy," Jacob said, reaching out to clap a hand on Joseph's shoulder, "and highly favored of the Lord. Don't let the actions and words of your brothers make you feel badly about yourself."

Joseph nodded, but his clear, brown eyes were still darkened by the hateful words of Judah and the laughter of the others. Those warm, honest eyes reminded Jacob so much of Rachel. His heart ached for a moment as the memory of her beautiful, smiling face wafted briefly through his mind. He missed her still, and he would miss her until he died. The day that he watered her grave with his tears, he'd felt as if his heart could never experience joy again. But he managed to find some solace in the two children she'd left behind. Joseph and Benjamin were so much like her—cheerful and forthright and determined. Jacob went on living for these two sons. They were the pride and joy of his life.

"Go find Benjamin and make sure he's not wandering off into trouble again," he finally said, turning his head so that Joseph wouldn't see the tears glittering in the corners of his eyes. He motioned for Joseph to go, and the youth departed silently from the tent. Once Joseph was gone, Jacob rose from the rug and roughly wiped the tears from his eyes.

He was partly to blame for the animosity his other sons felt toward Joseph. Because of his deep love for Rachel, he had a special bond with his youngest two sons that he didn't have with the older ones. He knew this had helped to alienate the sons of Leah, Bilhah, and Zilpah; but he couldn't seem to help himself. If there was any part of his life he wished he could change, it would be to strive harder to better show his love for all his family. He was trying, but he knew it would take time for those who felt slighted to let go of old grudges and allow emotional wounds to heal. Sorrowfully, he shook his head then looked up, startled, as Leah stepped unannounced into the tent.

"I've come to clean up the meal," she said, motioning to the empty bowls and platters that littered the floor. "If I'm disturbing you, I can leave."

"No. Don't go." He moved forward, tenderly grasped her hands in his own and saw a surprised look enter her lovely, gray eyes. "I gave our sons permission to go to Shechem," he said.

"I know."

"And I know how you feel about them going. But I think it will be a good thing for them to get away for awhile."

Leah nodded then pulled her hands from his grasp and stooped to gather up the wooden platters. He had been meaning to get her the copper utensils she'd been asking for—she'd asked again only a few days ago if he would purchase a copper bowl at the market—but the troubles with the flocks and the disputes between their sons had kept him too busy to find the time to travel into the town of Hebron.

"You're still upset about the coat, aren't you?" he asked.

Leah stiffened, but she continued with her task.

"I *had* to give it to Joseph," he said. "I had to send a clear message to the rest of my sons."

"And what message was that?" she asked, keeping her eyes focused on the platters she was collecting into her arms.

"That the birthright belongs to Joseph," he replied. "That it can only be had by one who strives to keep the commandments of the Lord. I want them all to understand how important it is to keep the covenants we've made with God."

Leah didn't say anything, but Jacob knew she had known what he would say before he even said it. Just like his sons, she knew the meaning of the coat the moment he handed it to Joseph. It was a magnificent coat. A coat of many colors. One fit to be worn by a prince or a king. It was the type of coat that noblemen and the children of kings so often wore, a garment with long sleeves that reached to the wrists and a hem that extended to the ankles. It was the outward symbol of the birthright which Reuben had lost because of his immoral act with Bilhah.

"What Reuben did was an abomination before God," Jacob said. "I had no choice but to take the birthright from him. You see that, don't you? He forfeited it through his sinful actions, and I had to give it to another. Joseph is Rachel's oldest son. That makes him the next legal heir." He could tell that Leah didn't agree with his interpretation of the law of inheritance; but, in this instance, she kept that particular opinion to herself.

"You don't have to defend your decision to me," she said. "You've always strictly followed God's laws. I'm sure you did what you felt was right."

"Some decisions are forced upon us," Jacob said. "We don't do it because we like it. We do it because we have to. In this case, I did what I believed God would have me do."

Leah stood up now, her arms full of platters and bowls, and she walked to the opening of the tent. Jacob moved toward her, hoping to soothe her with some tender act of affection; but she avoided his touch and pushed open the flap with one elbow.

"I wish you would reconsider," she said. "About sending the boys to Shechem."

"It gives me no pleasure to send them there," he said. "But there's not enough grass here for the animals. If we want our flocks to prosper, we have to send them where the grass is plentiful and green." He fell silent for a moment and nervously stroked his beard. It took several moments before he could bring himself to raise his eyes and look at Leah. "How does Dinah feel about what's going on?"

"She's still afraid of her own shadow," Leah replied. "All this talk about taking the flocks and the herds back to the land of Shechem is bringing back old, terrifying memories. I don't know what would have become of her if Simeon and Levi hadn't rescued her from Prince Shechem and his men."

Jacob nodded. The abduction and rape of their daughter had been a horrible ordeal for the entire family. Simeon and Levi were particularly outraged by it. But, no matter how justified their anger might have been, he couldn't condone the deceitful way in which they had made possible the slaughter of an entire town. Dinah was safely back home. That was an undeniably good thing. But luring an enemy into the covenant so that he and his men could be easily murdered was an act of wickedness as abominable, if not more abominable, than Shechem's. It was displeasing to God; therefore, it was displeasing to Jacob.

"Simeon and Levi just did what had to be done," Leah said, seeming to read her husband's thoughts. "They only did it to save their sister. There was no other way."

"They did it to satisfy their own rage," Jacob replied, sadly shaking his head. "And they didn't allow God the time to show us a better way."

Leah looked as if she wanted to answer that, but she stopped herself and angrily shook her head.

"I'd like to prepare a farewell feast for our sons' departure," she said. "Can you have one of them slaughter a goat or a sheep for our dinner?"

"I'll have Joseph do it."

She nodded, moved out of the tent, and let the flap fall shut behind her. In the semi-darkness, Jacob remained alone with only his thoughts to keep him company.

Life seemed to get harder the older he became. No matter what he did now, he would never please the people he loved most. He only hoped he could please God better than he'd managed to please his own family.

Chapter Notes

1. The Septuagint, or Greek version, of the Old Testament indicates that Joseph's coat was an actual "coat of many colors." However, the original Hebrew word—*ketohnet*—merely indicates a tunic or linen garment that may or may not have been made of many colors. Descriptions in this chapter are based on the more familiar Septuagint translation.

2. The opening paragraphs of this novel refer back to Genesis 37:2 where it is stated that Joseph "brought unto his father" the "evil report" of Bilhah's and Zilpah's sons. The Hebrew word *diba* can mean either 'evil report' or 'whispering.' In other words, Jacob's sons were murmuring against him.

3. *Shechem* from the story of Dinah is both the name of a place and a man. The man named Shechem was a son of Hamor who was a prince or ruler over the land of Shechem. Hamor's son most likely derived his name from the town his father ruled over.

TWO

"MY LEGS ARE TIRED," Benjamin complained. "Do we have to walk much farther?"

Jacob turned with an indulgent smile on his lips; but Joseph, who had always been protective of Benjamin, was already going to the little boy's aid.

"Here you are, Benjamin," he said, reaching down to lift the child easily into his arms. "Our old donkey doesn't have much to pull today. I'm sure she won't mind if you ride along."

Benjamin giggled happily as Joseph deposited him in the cart. A moment later he had forgotten about the length of their journey. He turned his attention instead to the contents of the cart and bounced with childlike glee atop a soft pile of rolled up sheep skins. Jacob smiled. He was enjoying these moments with his two youngest sons. It would have been a perfect moment if not for the small twinge of guilt he felt knowing that this was only made enjoyable because of the absence of his older sons. Things had been so much easier when all his children were the age of Benjamin. There had been so much less contention and the problems had been so much easier to solve. His children's hearts and minds were still pure at that age. How he wished that more of a child's innocence and innate goodness could last into adulthood.

"Father?" Joseph said, interrupting Jacob's thoughts.

"Yes?"

"How long do you think it will be before Reuben and Simeon and the others return with the flocks?"

Jacob tried not to appear troubled by this question, but Joseph was as perceptive as he was honest. He spoke again before Jacob could answer.

"I can travel to Shechem if you'd like. I can check on them and bring back word."

Jacob emphatically shook his head. "No. It's much too far. We'll wait a few more days to see if we receive any news of them. If there were trouble, I'm certain that Judah would have sent Issachar or Zebulun back to tell us."

Joseph nodded and kicked a small pebble so that it bounced up the path ahead of them. Something else was on his mind, and Jacob waited patiently until Joseph offered his thoughts of his own accord.

"Do you think they'll ever accept me?" the boy asked. "Do you think they'll ever stop hating me?"

Jacob looked away, uncertain how he should answer. "'Hate' is a strong word," he said. "They may resent the fact that you've been favored because of your righteousness, but that doesn't mean they hate you."

Joseph stared at him. He knew. They both knew. They both knew that Jacob's other sons were filled with hatred toward Joseph. But, for some reason, Jacob couldn't bring himself to verbally acknowledge it.

"What if you give the birthright to one of the others instead of me?" Joseph asked. "What if you give it to Dan or to Gad? They were the firstborn sons of their mothers. Wouldn't it be possible for me to relinquish the birthright to one of them?"

Jacob didn't answer for several long moments. When he did, his voice was weary.

"Your birthright is more than a mere physical inheritance," he said. "Giving your birthright away isn't going to solve this problem.

The birthright is a spiritual as well as a physical one. Under the covenant which my fathers and I have made with the Lord, the firstborn of all our flocks and the firstborn of our children belong to the Lord. God intended for you to have this birthright. It's not His will for you to give it away."

"Then what do I do?" Joseph asked. His voice was filled with pain, and Jacob couldn't bear to look into his eyes. He also couldn't bear that he had no solution to offer.

"I don't know," he said. "I constantly pray that the Lord will soften the hearts of your brothers. I constantly pray that they will repent of their wickedness and treat you like a brother instead of an enemy. But my prayers have remained unanswered, and I don't know why. All I know is that God can even turn the angry feelings of your brothers to serve His wise purposes. I wish I had something more comforting to tell you, but I don't."

Joseph nodded and lapsed into silence for several long minutes. He appeared to be struggling within himself, but finally seemed to come to some conclusion and spoke again.

"I should have never told anyone about my dreams."

"Your brothers resented you before that. Your dreams have nothing to do with their behavior."

Joseph stared at him again, and Jacob remembered how he had first reacted when Joseph recounted the dreams to him.

"Your dreams only confirm that God wanted you to have this birthright," he quickly tried to explain. "I should have realized that the moment you told me about the first one. I . . . I . . . apologize for the things I said, Joseph. I . . . "

"I didn't ask for the birthright," Joseph said, staring absently off into empty space. "I wasn't even seeking it. They think I tried to steal it out from beneath them. I never asked to have it."

"I know that."

"Why don't they know it?"

"I suppose it's because they don't want to. I suppose it's because they would rather blame you for their lost blessings instead of recognizing their own faults."

"That's not going to change when the inheritance is divided among us," Joseph said. "They'll still resent me. They'll still hate me. What will become of me then?"

"Do you remember your dream?"

Joseph looked uncomfortable. It was obvious he didn't want to think about that now. But he finally nodded his head.

"In your first dream, you were binding sheaves in the fields and beheld your brothers sheaves standing around your own. What happened after that?"

"My brothers' sheaves bowed before my sheaf," Joseph slowly answered.

Jacob nodded. "And what happened when the sun, the moon, and the eleven stars appeared to you in a second dream?"

"They made obeisance to me as well."

"Somehow, God will humble your brothers enough that they will bow down to your authority," Jacob said. "This is what He has promised you through your dreams. Have faith in God. He will uphold you and give you strength to accomplish His will."

Joseph pondered that for a few moments. There was still pain in his eyes, but Jacob's words seemed to have strengthened him. If only all of Jacob's sons would listen to his counsel.

"Look!" Benjamin suddenly cried out, pointing a finger up the path before them. "Hebron! We're almost there!"

"Indeed we are," Jacob replied, reaching back to tussle the young boy's hair. "And there will be more things to see than you can possibly imagine."

Benjamin bounced with enthusiasm as they passed from the low, vine-clad hills into the town, and Jacob worried that his youngest son would bounce himself right out of the cart. But Joseph, ever watchful where Benjamin's safety was concerned, moved back a few steps to prevent his smaller brother from losing balance and falling.

The market, when they reached it, was a feast for all five senses. The odors of spiced chicken, incense, cinnamon, and fragrant oils wafted temptingly to their noses. There were fruits, meats, and vegetables to be tasted; colorful, exotic fabrics that appealed both to the eye and to the hand; and, above all, the clamor of men's and animals' voices added a sense of busy excitement that made Benjamin's sparkling, brown eyes open wide with wonder. Joseph lifted Benjamin from the cart and placed him high atop his own broad shoulders. Together, father and sons scanned the wares that were on display.

It was a busier day than usual, probably because of the arrival of a caravan of Midianites who had passed by Jacob's camp earlier in the day. Hebron lay along a major trade route that stretched from the south end of the Dead Sea across the forbidding—and mostly desolate—reaches of Edom. The route led to such distant and exotic lands as Nubia and Egypt and was frequently traveled by the Midianites. Jacob could see by their wares that they had indeed come by way of Egypt. Most of their merchandise was of Egyptian workmanship. It would be a good day for trading. It would also be a good day to see how much Joseph had learned from earlier trips into the city. Someday it would be his responsibility to care for the family. He needed to practice the fine art of trading while he was still young.

"Your mother asked me to get her a copper bowl," Jacob said. "You've watched me trade before. Why don't you try your hand at it today?"

Joseph glanced around at the different stalls but hesitated.

"Try it with that merchant," Jacob said, nodding encouragingly and motioning toward one of the Midianites. "I'll wait here at the cart with Benjamin. You'll do fine."

Joseph again looked uncertain, but Jacob waved his hands in the direction of the stall until Joseph set Benjamin on the ground so he could move toward it.

Jacob gave one last encouraging smile and watched to see what would happen.

Joseph picked up a bronze pot, turned it carefully over in his hands, and examined it. It felt good to be trusted by his father. He wanted to please him. But he was still troubled by the uncertainty of his future. And there was more to his situation than just the bad feelings of his brothers.

After Rachel died, Leah had assumed the role of mother in Joseph's and Benjamin's lives. Jacob had instructed Joseph, only twelve years old at the time, to honor Leah as he would his own mother, and he tried his very best. He desperately wanted to win her love, her approval, and her acceptance. But no matter what he did, he always sensed that Leah, too, resented him. It had only gotten worse when his father gave him the coat of many colors.

Leah had been distant before. She became positively cold whenever she saw Joseph wearing his colorful new coat. She was polite to him—and fair—but the warmth he saw between her and her own sons, or even between her and Benjamin, was noticeably lacking when she spoke to him. He couldn't bring a smile to her face the way Benjamin did, and he couldn't please her the way Reuben or Judah could. And, oddly enough, it seemed that the more obedient and helpful he tried to be the more withdrawn she became. Maybe it was because he was a reminder to her that her own sons had lost favor in Jacob's eyes. Maybe he was a reminder that she herself had been displaced by her own sister, Rachel. It wasn't his fault, and he was sure she didn't deliberately treat him differently from the others. But there was a chasm between them that couldn't seem to be bridged.

Much of the jealousy and envy within the family was a direct side affect of Jacob's plural marriages. His father tried to be fair; but, as righteous as he was, Jacob was only human. Even Joseph knew that Rachel held a special place in his heart that none of his other wives could ever take. And where more than one woman had to vie for the attention of the same man, there seemed bound to be jealous competition. Joseph couldn't imagine how difficult that balancing act must be. Plural marriages were common among his people, but he himself had no desire to enter into such an arrangement. If he could, he would find one woman to marry—one woman whom he could love and cherish and give his undivided attention to.

"It's a fine piece of workmanship, isn't it?"

Joseph jerked his eyes away from the pot and looked up in surprise at the bearded Midianite who had just addressed him.

"Yes. Yes, it is," Joseph said.

"If it pleases you, perhaps we can settle on a price."

"Actually," Joseph said, knowing that Midianites never kept their best merchandise out in the open, "I'm looking for something very special. Something of the highest quality."

"Then you've come to the right place!" the Midianite exclaimed. The whiteness of his teeth contrasted sharply with the darkness of his beard, as a huge, friendly grin split his face. "I deal in nothing but items of the finest quality. Here! Let me show you something extraordinary!" He reached to snatch a wooden object from the midst of several bronze figurines and proudly displayed it a few inches from the tip of Joseph's nose.

Joseph peered at it through squinted eyes and realized it wasn't really wood at all. It was ivory—delicately carved into an object of exquisite beauty. The top was curved, like a flattened crescent moon, and a rounded pillar extended from the center of the curved piece to attach to a polished, block-shaped base. Egyptian hieroglyphic characters danced down the pillar in vertical lines, and Joseph noted with interest how they had been etched into the ivory then painted to add to the already compelling beauty of the piece.

"It's wonderful," he finally said. "What is it?"

The Midianite studied Joseph with surprise, then he burst into loud, belly-shaking laughter. Joseph blushed at his own ignorance, but the Midianite reached out and patted him on the arm in a jovial fashion.

"I suppose you wouldn't have need of such an object in a

shepherd's tent, would you?" he said, wiping a mirthful tear from the corner of one eye. "I have to admit, I'd prefer a rolled up blanket or a sheepskin over this."

"It's for sleeping?" Joseph asked, looking skeptically at the object before him.

"It's an Egyptian headrest," the Midianite replied. "The finest money can buy."

"And what does this mean?" Joseph asked, pointing to the decorative hieroglyphs.

"It's a prayer to Nephthys, goddess of the night. I've been told these are very comfortable, but I would imagine it would take a special prayer to help *me* rest on such a thing. I see now that this is not the item for you. What is it that you *are* looking for, my young friend?"

"A bowl," Joseph said. "Of Egyptian copper. Do you have any?"

The Midianite raised a finger, signaling Joseph to wait a moment, and he turned to locate something hidden at the back of the pavilion. When he turned back again, there was a stack of large, copper bowls in his hands, and he set them out, one by one, for Joseph to view. "The finest bowls from the finest Egyptian copper," he said, waving an open hand across them. "Do you have gold or silver? Or have you come seeking to make a trade today?"

"I've brought things to trade," Joseph said.

"Wonderful! I knew you were a man after my own heart."

"My things are in the cart," Joseph said as he quickly selected a bowl and mentally calculated its worth. "Let me show you what I have."

At the cart, Joseph selected a blanket and tucked it, along with two sheepskins, under his arm. He was determined to get the best of those six bowls. Leah herself had spent many weeks carding, spinning, and dying wool and then many more weaving it all into this blanket. He couldn't let it go for anything less than the very best. He refused to return home only to see disapproval written in his foster mother's eyes. Today, at least, he would leave her no room for any-thing but grudging respect.

Joseph placed a sheepskin next to a bowl. He knew it wasn't even near the actual value of the bowl, and he also knew his father had taught him to be honest in his dealings with others—to trade worth for equal worth—but this was the manner of trade among his people. Both he and the Midianite knew that the blanket was the real object of payment. The Midianite was already glancing at it with interest, but first they must dicker and barter so that both could feel they had gained the most from this trade.

"This sheepskin for that bowl," Joseph said.

"Surely you're joking with me!" the Midianite exclaimed, his face a picture of dismay. "I could not part with this excellent bowl for even ten of those skins."

"I would consider giving five," Joseph returned, "but no more than that." He put an index finger and thumb thoughtfully to his chin. "If this bowl is that valuable to you, I guess I'll have to settle for one of lesser quality." Joseph set a second sheepskin next to the first and pointed to the largest bowl—the one at the end. It was a bur-nished, less ornate bowl, yet it was obvious to even an inexperienced trader that it was the best of the six.

The Midianite twisted his face into an expression of horror. "Only two sheepskins for something as wonderful as this?" He pretended to be offended. "This isn't just a bowl. This is a work of art!"

"Then let me trade you one work of art for another," Joseph said. At this point he removed the blanket from beneath his arm and unrolled a portion of it for the Midianite to examine. Expert fingers reached out to feel the texture of the blanket's fabric, and shrewd eyes traced the richly colored, intricately woven patterns. The Midianite was silent for several long moments before finally nodding his head in approval. "The blanket and both sheepskins for the bowl," he said.

But Joseph wasn't yet done with his negotiations. "My mother made this with her own hands. How can I insult her by bringing home only one simple bowl?"

"Your mother, you say?" The Midianite lowered his head and scratched his bearded chin.

"I shouldn't do this," he mumbled. "I'm a fool to do this. A sentimental fool. But a boy should never have to disappoint his mother. I'll give you this bowl and this mirror for the blanket and the skins." Next to the bowl, he placed a mirror—one made from the same Egyptian copper as the bowl—its surface polished so carefully that Joseph could clearly see his reflection in it. Some might have agreed on the trade right now, but Joseph had seen the way the Midianite admired Leah's blanket. He knew he could get more. So he paused for a moment and examined the contents of the pavilion.

A bowl for Leah. A mirror for Zilpah. Now he needed something for Bilhah. And then his eyes fell upon it. A small, golden comb. He turned his eyes back to the Midianite, ready to close the deal.

"The blanket and one sheepskin for the bowl, the mirror, and that comb," he said. "It's the best offer I can make."

"I'll be begging in the streets," the Midianite complained. "My children will be forced to go without bread!"

"Then the blanket and both sheepskins. But I'll give you no more."

"I accept your trade," the Midianite said, shaking his head as if he had just been robbed. "I can only hope that I make up for today's losses when I and my brethren reach Gilead."

Joseph smiled as he placed the blanket on the table and gathered his purchase into his arms. He had received fair compensation for the blanket and the sheepskins, and the pride reflected in his father's eyes made him feel warm inside. But he still worried that Leah might somehow find fault in all or part of this transaction. Even his best intentions often brought a frown of disapproval to her lips.

"I'll have to let you do more of our business dealings," Jacob said as they slowly moved away from the pavilion. "I could have done no better myself."

It was a high compliment, particularly since it came from a man in whose hands all things seemed to prosper. It was good to please his father. It would be even better if Joseph could manage to please the rest of his family. Hopefully that day would not be long in coming.

THREE

"IS SOMETHING WRONG, MY PHARAOH?" Potiphar brought his own chariot alongside Khyan's, and his brow furrowed with concern. The pharaoh had brought his chariot to such an abrupt, unexpected halt that it had taken all of Potiphar's skill as a charioteer to avoid a collision with his king. Now Pharaoh was gazing across the sands with stern, calculating eyes, watching the walled city of On as it shimmered like a waking vision in the hot, rippling air. He didn't answer Potiphar's question for several long moments.

"It's a beautiful city, isn't it," Pharaoh finally said.

"Yes," Potiphar agreed. "A magnificent city. A jewel in the crown of your kingdom."

"But what do you think of its high priest? Is the high priest of On loyal to me? Or do Potipherah's loyalties lie elsewhere?" At this point, Pharaoh's eyes locked with Potiphar's, and Potiphar paused for a moment to carefully consider the question.

"You have many enemies in Upper Egypt," he answered. "The sons of the original pharaohs would like nothing better than to drive us back into Canaan where our ancestors once dwelled."

"They still call us *heqa-khasut*—rulers of foreign lands—don't they?" Pharaoh said, his eyes darkening with anger. "We speak the language of Egypt, we follow the customs of Egypt—we even worship the gods of Egypt—yet the old Egyptians still plot against us."

"They'll plot against our people until either we or they are driven out of Egypt," Potiphar said. "But the high priest of On is of the same Hyksos lineage as we are. He won't ally himself with your enemies in Upper Egypt. They wouldn't trust him."

"And neither do I," Pharaoh said, shaking his head dubiously. "But Potipherah and his priests are at least as cunning as they. The priesthood of On also wields great power. The great god Ra is popular among all Egyptians—both those of Hyksos blood and those who are not. As high priest of Ra, Potipherah has influence among the people of this region to sway them if he can. I don't expect a direct military attack from him, but he would remove me from my throne if it served his purposes."

"He would be a fool to try," Potiphar said. "As powerful as he is, you are ten times more powerful. The blessings of the storm god, Seth, are upon you. Potipherah could never hope to defeat you in battle. Even if he stirred the people of On up to anger and allied himself with the princes of Thebes, he could never overcome our defenses at Avaris."

"Whatever he intends," Pharaoh said, scowling, "he will find a devious means of getting what he wants. But I'm even more devious and cunning. We're here today because I've prepared something that will serve to remind him of where his allegiance must be."

Potiphar was curious, but he knew better than to question his king. Pharaoh would reveal his plans when it suited him to do so—not a moment sooner.

Without warning, Pharaoh snapped the reins over the backs of his horses, and his gilded chariot shot forward. Potiphar quickly raised one fist, brought it abruptly down in front of him, and the entire column of chariots followed Pharaoh toward the double-bricked walls of On. It took only a few minutes to reach the great, walled compound of the Temple of Ra—walls that loomed imposingly above their heads.

Pharaoh's display of military might was impressive, but Potiphar felt a tingle of fear run up and down his spine as the shadow of the temple touched his skin. Pharaoh wielded the power of spears, bows, swords, and chariots; but the priests of On wielded the power of the gods. One never knew how the will of the gods might change. On a whim they could remove Pharaoh from his throne. Potiphar hoped Khyan had a good plan. And whatever Khyan did, Potiphar hoped it wouldn't anger the gods.

"Why wasn't I warned that Pharaoh was coming!" Potipherah stalked across the stone floor of the temple and swept off his outer robe so that it fell to the polished tiles. "You've been told to warn me of such things in advance!"

"We only learned of his coming a few moments ago," the lesser priest replied, his eyes lowered as he bowed before his superior. "The watch guards informed us of his arrival the moment they spotted his procession, but he was already entering the city before I could get to the temple. He's waiting for you at the front gate now."

Potipherah's eyes flashed with anger, but the beads of perspiration on his shaved head betrayed his inner nervousness. Could Pharaoh have learned of his secret meetings with the princes of Thebes? Could he already know of the hidden alliances Potipherah was forging? Whatever the purposes for Pharaoh's unexpected visit, Potipherah's anxiety increased tenfold when he reached the huge, rounded columns that marked the main gate of the temple. The street beyond the temple compound was crowded with chariots and soldiers, and Pharaoh's eyes sparkled more dangerously than usual. This was no ordinary visit. Khyan was sending the city a message, and Potipherah thought he knew what it might be. But, despite the inner tension he was experiencing, he forced a placid smile to his lips and moved quickly to greet Egypt's king.

"My Pharaoh," he said going down to one knee and bowing his head with just the right amount of reverence and respect. "To what do I owe the pleasure of this unexpected visit?"

"I've come to reward you. Reward you for your loyalty to my kingdom and the gods." Pharaoh gestured for Potipherah to rise, then removed the tall hat that was the symbol of his kingship and smiled as he placed it in the crook of one arm. "But first things first," he said. "My men are tired and hungry. Arrangements must be made to attend to their needs."

"Of course. I will send one of my priests to notify the nomarch of your arrival," Potipherah replied. "And I would be honored if you would accept the hospitality of my own humble home. I'm sure that you, too, are tired and hungry after your journey."

"Yes, I could stand a little rest and refreshment," Pharaoh replied. He was still smiling, but his eyes were free of all emotion. There was nothing in his demeanor that would betray any of his inner thoughts.

Perhaps Potipherah had underestimated this pharaoh. Perhaps Khyan was shrewder and more dangerous than any of his enemies had imagined. But Potipherah would weigh the situation carefully before he came to any conclusions. If he wasn't yet discovered, it would be foolish to reveal anything now.

"If you'll allow me a few minutes," Potipherah said, "I will go ahead of you and have my servants prepare a feast in you honor."

"There's no need for that," Pharaoh said, waving the suggestion aside. "I won't be here long enough for that. A light meal and a little rest will be all I need. We shall walk together. It will give us a few moments to discuss the affairs of this great city."

Potipherah nodded. What else could he do? But he was uncomfortably aware of how closely Potiphar watched him as he, Pharaoh, and several members of the royal guard crossed over from the temple to the priests' quarter on the opposite side of the street.

Potiphar was the captain of Pharaoh's royal guard, and he was also much more than that. His official Egyptian title was 'chief of the slaughterers,' and it was that title that struck fear into the heart of even as mighty a man as the high priest of Ra. Among Potiphar's many important duties was his command over the royal execution- ers. If Pharaoh had discovered Potipherah's treachery, it would be Potiphar who carried out the orders to perform the execution. As he thought about this, the high priest did his best to hold back an involuntary shudder.

The short walk to his palatial home seemed to last much longer than usual. Pharaoh chatted pleasantly about the collecting of tributes and asked many questions about the day-to-day affairs of the city, but Potipherah could tell he was holding something back. By the time they reached the house, he was certain a squad of executioners must be waiting inside to slay him the moment he crossed the threshold. But there were no executioners waiting for them. There were only the cool interior of the house, a few scurrying servants, and Potipherah's own daughter, Asenath, her eyes wide with both surprise and delight to see her father home so early.

"Father!" she called out, rushing forward to greet him. But then she recognized who her father was with, and she dropped quickly to her knees.

"This is my daughter," Potipherah said, as Pharaoh acknowl- edged her with a slight nod of his head before motioning to her that she could rise. "Her name is Asenath."

Even at such a young age, Asenath was already more beauti- ful than a lotus blossom and more graceful than a gazelle. She was Potipherah's only child—the pride and joy of his life—and nothing brought him more joy than to be greeted by her perfect, white smile and flashing, blue eyes. She promised to be a stunning beauty when she finally blossomed into womanhood, and Potipherah was pleased to note that even the king of Egypt was not immune to his daughter's beauty.

"You have a lovely daughter," Pharaoh said. "I imagine that she has turned the heads of many young men."

"She has," Potipherah admitted, trying not to glow too much with pride. "But I'm in no hurry to get her married. She's the only child I have, and there's time enough to spare."

Pharaoh's smile broadened, but he turned his attention to the house around him before Potipherah could determine what that larger smile might mean.

"Your home rivals the palaces of some kings," Pharaoh said. "It's a testament to your power."

"My earthly possessions are of little importance," Potipherah quickly replied. "My service to Ra is what truly matters."

"Yes," Pharaoh mumbled. "Yes, of course."

"Asenath," Potipherah said, trying to disguise the nervousness that caused his voice to tremble. "Will you please inform the servants that Pharaoh and several members of his royal guard are our guests? Tell them to prepare a light meal and bring it immediately to the garden porch."

Asenath nodded, cast one last curious glance at Pharaoh, then hurried off to the kitchen. Potipherah waited for her to disappear from sight before addressing Pharaoh again.

"I must apologize in advance for the meager fare we have to offer you today," he said. "If only I had known in advance of your visit to On, I could have treated you to the hospitality you so rightly deserve."

"This visit isn't about what I deserve," Pharaoh said, clapping a hand on Potipherah's shoulder. "I came here because of what *you* so rightly deserve."

Beads of sweat began to form again on Potipherah's clean-shaven head, and it seemed that he could see laughter dancing in Pharaoh's eyes. It was obvious that Pharaoh was aware of his discomfort, but whether or not he knew the cause, Potipherah could only guess. Potiphar, for his part, was drumming his fingers against the hilt of his sword—a sword that was meant, perhaps, to take Potipherah's life. And he began to think that Pharaoh must suspect everything.

"If you'll follow me," Potipherah said, licking lips which had suddenly gone dry, "we can sit in a restful place while you explain the purpose of your unexpected but very welcome visit."

Trembling now, he led Pharaoh and Potiphar through a home that usually made others tremble. It was an intimidating edifice. They walked through a wide hall across red quartzite tiles and passed between tall, square pillars that supported the crushing weight of a stone slab roof. Imposing statues of the gods stood watch over doorways both to the left and to the right, and murals depicting the lives and deeds of the gods adorned the thick stone walls. The home was lavish even by royal standards—not so richly constructed as Pharaoh's palace, but palatial in its own right. The crowning jewel, however, was the walled garden adjoining the living quarters. Two guards under Potipherah's employ stood constant watch over the garden's entrances, allowing only Potipherah's family, or guests of the family, to enter. The walled enclosure was filled with date palms, fragrant flowers, and pomegranate trees. These and other plants flourished around a large pool of water that served both as a cool place to swim in the heat of the day and a cistern to water the plants. Potipherah led Pharaoh and Potiphar to a covered, stone porch that overlooked the garden, and he motioned toward a set of low, curved chairs around a small, wicker table. Pharaoh accepted the invitation to sit. But Potiphar took a position off to one side where he could watch both Potipherah and the garden sentries.

"I suppose you're eager to find out why I made this sudden trip to see you," Pharaoh said.

"Yes. I'm very curious." That was an understatement. At this very moment he was fighting down a stomach-churning wave of panic. He didn't want to look any more guilty than he was already feeling, but he feared that Pharaoh could see right through him.

Pharaoh removed a tube-shaped leather pouch from his belt—a pouch Potipherah hadn't noticed until just now—and he opened it to remove a long, papyrus scroll. With great ceremony, Pharaoh unrolled the scroll across the wicker tabletop. "Read it," he commanded, thumping the table with a fist and pushing the scroll toward Potipherah.

Potipherah read. And then his face lost all its color. His voice trembled when he looked up to respond.

"I-I don't understand. I—"

"There's nothing for you to understand," Pharaoh interrupted. "The great god Seth has chosen to honor your household. That's all you need to know."

"My household is unworthy of such a great reward," Potipherah stammered, feeling both horror and hopelessness as he realized what was happening. "Our greatest reward is to know that we are servants of the pharaoh and the people. I and my family need no other reward than that."

"Nevertheless, you *shall* be rewarded," Pharaoh insisted. He stood up, turned his back to the high priest, and paced away from the table. When he turned back, the smile on his face was gone. "I trust that you can make things ready before I depart?" As he said this, Pharaoh's face became suddenly hard. There was no mirth in his cold, dark eyes now.

"This will take affect *today?*" Potipherah asked, barely able to find his voice. He felt his strength—his very being—beginning to drain from his body.

"This takes affect *now*. You don't intend to deny the great god Seth his wishes, do you?"

"N-no. Of course not."

"Good. Then see that this is attended to. I leave for Avaris after I meet with the nomarch. There must be no delays. I want your family ready when I return to your house."

Potipherah weakly nodded his head. The king of Egypt exacted a high price for treachery. A high price indeed.

Chapter Notes

1. The Hyksos were a group of Semitic people who conquered and ruled Egypt sometime around 1640 B.C. Evidence suggests, however, that their migration into Egypt began at an earlier date. Although they were economically and culturally less advanced than the Egyptians, they possessed much more sophisticated weapons, and this explains, in part, why they were able to conquer and control so much of Egypt. Scholars credit the Hyksos with introducing to Egypt improved bows and battle-axes, advanced fortification techniques, and horses and chariots. During their relatively brief rule over the region, they also attempted to blend into Egyptian society by adopting the religion, customs, and language of the land. Unfortunately for them, their dynasty was doomed to eventual defeat and expulsion. In 1521 B.C., a Theban revolt finally ended the Hyksos dynasty. Some scholars believe that Ahmose, who drove the Hyksos from power, is the Pharaoh who "knew not Joseph" (Exodus 1:8); and the placement of Joseph during Hyksos rule would explain why the new pharaoh would bring the Israelites, the allies of the Hyksos, into bondage. Because the succession of Hyksos rulers and the dating of their individual reigns is inconclusive, it is impossible to know exactly which Hyksos pharaoh ruled when Joseph was promoted to grand vizier, but this story assumes that it took place during the reign of Khyan. By Khyan's time, Hyksos power was firmly established and Hyksos influence extended well beyond the bounds of Egypt. It is hoped that this setting will provide the reader with a glimpse of what Egypt might have been like in Joseph's day.

2. *On* (also called *Iunu* and *Heliopolis*) was an important city both religiously and politically. It was the center of the worship of Ra, the sun-god, and a high priest of On such as Potipherah would have wielded great influence. It is interesting to note that the name Potipherah means either *devoted to the sun* or, as some scholars suggest, *gift of the sun-god* (from Egyptian *Pa-tu-pa-Ra*). Either way, Potipherah is a suitable name for one who devoted his life to the service of Ra.

3. *Asenath*, daughter of Potipherah, is mentioned only a few times in the Old Testament, and little information is given about her there. "The Story of Asenath" (also called "Joseph and Asenath") is a Greek text of the Pseudepigrapha, the non-canonical Jewish writings from the period of 200 B.C. to 200 A.D., and it describes Asenath as being "tall like Sarah, beautiful like Rebekah, and as fair as Rachel." It also claims that she appeared more like "the daughters of the Hebrews" than like "the daughters of the Egyptians." Although the text is obviously a fictional account intended to exaggerate and glorify the characteristics of Asenath and Joseph, there may be one element of truth in its descriptions. If Asenath actually was a woman of Hyksos blood, she would have descended from the same Semitic lineage as Joseph

and thus physically resembled "the daughters of the Hebrews." The name Asenath probably means "one belonging to the goddess Neith," but some have suggested the alternate meaning "she belongs to her father."

4. In the original Hebrew text of Genesis, Potiphar is referred to as Pharaoh's *sar hatabakhim*. The word *sar* is used to refer to an official, a leader, or a captain, and the term *tabakhim* has been translated by different scholars as meaning "butchers," "slaughterers," or "bodyguards." These are the words used when Potiphar is called "an officer of Pharaoh, *captain of the guard*" (Genesis 39:1, italics added) and are found again when the chief butler speaks of being placed in ward "in *the captain of the guard's* house" (Genesis 41:10, italics added). It's possible that Potiphar was both the commander of Pharaoh's royal bodyguards and the overseer of the imprisonment and execution of Pharaoh's enemies.

FOUR

JOSEPH SHIELDED HIS EYES against the glare of the sun
and scanned the valley below him. There were a few withered trees to
shade the ground, a flock of sheep searching for grass, and a collection of scattered boulders that shone like bleached skulls in the sun;
but there was no sign of the errant cow Joseph sought. This worried
him. Other than the cow, they only had one goat to provide their
family with milk. The rest of the cows and goats were in Shechem
with Jacob's older sons. If anything bad happened to this cow, the
favor Joseph had gained by bringing Leah the copper bowl would
quickly be lost.

"I don't know," he muttered, shaking his head with frustration.
"I don't see it anywhere. How about you, Benjamin? Can you see
something I can't see?" He tilted his head to one side and glanced up
at his younger brother who was riding on his strong, broad shoulders;
but Benjamin just shrugged and frowned. "That's all right," Joseph
said. "That silly, old cow can't be too far from here. We'll find it if we
keep looking."

Carefully, so that he wouldn't stumble and injure either Benjamin
or himself, Joseph started down the side of the hill toward the valley
floor. He wound his way between boulders that were usually half
overgrown with lush, green grass. But this season the ground around
them was parched and bare, and it was easy to keep his footing. Any

blade of grass that did manage to push its way through the earth was either scorched to death by the sun or nibbled to the root by a roving cow or sheep. Joseph decided it was a good thing Jacob's sheep and cattle had been removed to Shechem. It was hard enough to find fodder for the one cow and two goats that had been left behind to provide milk for those here in Padan-aram. The rest of the animals would have most likely starved to death if they'd remained here under these uncharacteristically dry conditions. What worried them all was the fact that the entire family might have to move out of Hebron if the weather didn't change soon.

"I hear something," Benjamin said, patting Joseph's head with both hands to get his attention.

"You do? What is it?"

"Listen. It's over there."

Joseph stopped and heard only the soft rattle of a few pebbles that had just been dislodged by his feet. But in a moment he, too, heard something. It was the deep, desperate lowing of a cow, and it was coming from behind a wilted stand of trees.

"I think you've found our lost cow," Joseph said, patting Benjamin's knee. "It's a good thing I brought you along, isn't it?"

"I told you I was a good helper."

"Yes, you certainly did. Now let's get that stubborn animal and take it back home."

They finished the descent to the bottom of the hill then moved at a slow trot toward the trees. It felt good to pass through the cool shade cast by their leaves and branches. But Joseph immediately forgot his own discomfort when he saw what was on the other side. About a stone's throw away, the soil was darkened by a small, muddy bog. In an otherwise thirsty place, this patch of earth was moistened by some unseen source of water—probably an underground stream that was seeping to the surface at this slight depression in the valley floor. The bog was about as big around as one of Jacob's larger tents, and the family's errant cow was wallowing helplessly in the middle of it.

"This isn't good," Joseph said, stopping in his tracks to stare in dismay at the cow and the bog that trapped it. "How about if I put you on the ground now, Benjamin? Just while I try to figure out what to do about this new problem."

"Why don't you just lift the cow out of the mud?" Benjamin asked, as Joseph removed him from his shoulders.

Joseph laughed. "I'm glad you think I'm strong," he said, "but lifting a cow isn't quite the same as lifting you. It's going to take more than just my muscles to get an animal that large out of this mess. Maybe we'll have to go back to the tents and get some help."

As if sensing that they were about to leave it alone, the cow struggled anew. It lifted its front hooves from the mud and pawed frantically at the wet, gooey surface. But its efforts achieved the opposite effect of what it was hoping for. Now, with a sharp sucking sound, the mud began to pull the beast deeper. It was obvious that Joseph couldn't leave. If he did, the cow might sink beneath the surface and suffocate before he had a chance to save it. What he really needed was some rope. If he had a short length of rope and tied it around the cow's horns, he might be able to provide the extra leverage the cow needed to get itself out of the mud. He would have sent Benjamin back for some if his younger brother was a little older, but that was out of the question at this time. There was nothing left now but to go in after the cow himself.

He'd just have to use caution so he didn't get stuck in there, too.

"I want you to wait right here at the edge of the mud," Joseph said, unlacing his sandals and setting them in the dry dust next to Benjamin. "Do you understand? Mother will be furious if you get any of this mud on yourself." Benjamin nodded, and Joseph tussled his hair. "But I have an important job for you," he continued. "I need you to hold my coat so it stays clean. Do you think you can do that?"

"I can do it. I'll keep it safe."

"Good. Now wait for me here."

Joseph carefully folded his coat of many colors and placed it in Benjamin's arms. Then he walked to the edge of the bog and stepped gingerly into the mud. He grimaced as it squished around his toes, but he waded into the bog until the mud was almost up to his waist.

The cow's eyes were wide with fear, and froth had formed around its mouth. He had no idea how he was going to get such a large animal out of such a deep mud pit, but he still had to try.

"It's all right," he said in a soothing voice as the cow stirred uneasily and snorted at him. "I'm here to help you. Just let me get a grip on you, and we'll see if I can pull you to the edge." He reached out and firmly grasped both horns; but, the moment he did so, the muscles rippled in the cow's neck, and it whipped its head around, throwing Joseph backward. He hit the mud with a loud splat and was wet and muddy from head to toe by the time he managed to struggle back to his feet.

"Mother says not to play in the mud," Benjamin said, giggling. "You're going to be in big trouble, Joseph."

"You're probably right," Joseph said, laughing despite himself. "But this cow will be in even worse trouble if I don't find some way to get it out. What do you think we should do?"

Benjamin shook his head then stopped, his eyes lighting up. "We should say a prayer," he answered. "Father says we should pray whenever we need help."

"You're right. Thank you, Benjamin. I should have thought of that before we even left to look for this cow." Joseph sloshed to the edge of the bog and paused to shake the mud from his arms and hands. Then he walked up the bank and knelt next to Benjamin in grass that had been cropped close to the earth by grazing animals. "How about if we say a prayer together?" he said. "If anyone can get a cow out of this mud hole, God can."

Their prayer was short and simple, but it was a prayer filled with trust. Joseph was praying to a God with whom he was well familiar. It was the God of his fathers—the same God who had appeared to Jacob at Bethel and given him the new name Israel—and Joseph got back to his feet fully expecting to receive some answer.

"There has to be something around here that we can use," he said, casting his eyes around. "Maybe if I can find a big enough, long enough branch, I can put it under the cow and pry it out of the mud. Or maybe—" He stopped in mid-sentence, his face brightening. While he and Benjamin were praying, the cow had moved to a new position. It had managed to raise its head a little higher above the mud and Joseph saw something he hadn't seen before. Still looped around its neck was the rope which had been used to tie it behind Leah's tent. There was rope here after all! He just hoped it was long enough.

"Our prayer has been answered," Joseph said, turning with a triumphant grin toward Benjamin. "You were right Benjamin. A prayer is what we needed. Wait here again while I find the other end of that rope."

Not quite so carefully this time, Joseph slogged back into the mire. It took him only a few moments to fish out the end of the rope and only a few moments more to get back to solid ground at the mire's edge. With firm soil once more under his feet, he leaned back and pulled with all his might.

At first, nothing happened. He might as well try to budge a mountain as to get so large an animal out of so deep a place. But Joseph had never been one to give up easily. Gritting his teeth with raw determination, he pulled and strained until the biceps in his arms hardened and bulged. The mire sucked at the thrashing cow, unwilling to release its captive; but Joseph backed slowly across the earth until, finally, the cow had enough footing to stagger wearily out of the mud.

"God was with us today," Joseph panted, leaning over to place both hands against his knees as he gasped for breath. "There's no way anything could have come out of that mire without some added help from above." He straightened his back now and looped the muddy rope through one of his fists. "Come on, Benjamin. We should say another prayer—this one to thank God for His help. Then we should be getting back home. Mother and Father will be worried if we're gone too long."

A short time later—weary, muddy, and grateful to be home— Joseph stumbled back into his father's camp with Benjamin at his side and an exhausted cow in tow. He saw his father standing before Leah's tent, watching him with surprise and then amusement. Joseph waved and smiled back. But the smile on his lips faded when Leah stepped out of the tent and looked at him. She, too, seemed surprised; but her face lacked the amusement that was so apparent on Jacob's. As she observed the drying mud that caked Joseph's body and clothes, a disapproving frown crossed her lips. She shook her head with disgust and disappeared back into the tent before he could even open his mouth to explain.

"I . . . I had to pull the cow from a mire," he said, turning help-lessly to his father. "The cow knocked me over and—"

"I understand," Jacob said. He moved closer and patted Joseph on one of his muddy shoulders. "Thank you for bringing back the cow. Tie it to one of the trees and then clean yourself up. I need to speak with you about something important."

"What is it?" Joseph asked, forgetting his own problems for a moment as he noticed the troubled look in his father's eyes. "Is some-thing wrong?"

"No. Nothing is wrong. Wash yourself and put on some clean, dry clothing. This can wait until you're comfortable and ready to come into the tent."

Joseph nodded then led the cow to one of the nearby trees. His muscles ached and his feet were sore. It would be nice to be clean and dry again. He just wished he knew what was bothering his father. That look only came into Jacob's eyes when something troubling or important had happened. Joseph hoped it wasn't something he had done. He only wanted to please his family. Unfortunately, he seemed doomed to always be a miserable failure at that.

FIVE

"You're back early," Ari said, smiling with pleasant surprise as she moved into the antechamber to greet her husband. It wasn't often that he came home early. As chief priest in the temple of Seth, Setmosis was almost as busy as Pharaoh. But one look at his tired face warned her of a specific reason for this unexpected return. "You also look troubled," she said. "Is something wrong?"

"No. Nothing is wrong." He handed his outer, leopard-skin robe to a waiting servant and shook his head, but Ari wasn't convinced.

"Something's bothering you. Don't try to hide it from me. I can read your face like a scroll. What is it?"

Instead of answering, Setmosis wrapped an arm around his wife's waist and glanced around the room. "Where's Netchem?" he asked. "Isn't she back from the temple yet?"

"No, not yet. She's almost as bad as you. She spends every spare moment in that place. I think she does it to please you, but I hardly get to see my own daughter anymore because of it."

"Be grateful that you get to see her at all. There are some mothers who aren't so fortunate."

Ari looked at him curiously; but, if he noticed the look, he didn't acknowledge it. He seemed to withdraw suddenly into his own inner thoughts, and she realized she'd have to drag this out of him if she was ever going to find out what inspired such curious comments. "Something important is happening," she said. "What is it? Is it bad? Has someone important died?"

"No. It's nothing like that. But there are things other than death that can take a person unexpectedly away."

"You're starting to frighten me. Tell me. What's wrong?"

Her husband met her gaze now, and he spoke with a weary voice. "Pharaoh suspects the high priest of On to be in league with the princes of Thebes," Setmosis said, "and the other day, when he visited On, he decided to do something about it. Because of what happened there, we're about to gain an extra daughter while another set of parents loses theirs."

"I don't understand you at all. What are you trying to tell me? Are you telling me Pharaoh has stolen a child away from her family? Stolen her to give her to us? What could that possibly have to do with the high priest of On and the princes of Thebes?"

"It has everything to do with them," Setmosis explained. "To assure that Potipherah doesn't make any rash decisions to ally his city with Thebes, Pharaoh has decided to bring his daughter, Asenath, to On. She's at Pharaoh's palace now, and she'll be showing up here soon. Pharaoh has selected us to be her foster parents."

Ari's eyes went wide, and her mouth dropped open. It was several moments before she could find her voice to speak. "She's a political hostage then? And we're her prison keepers?" She paused to ponder what she'd just said then shook her head violently. "No! I won't do it! Pharaoh can't just go around taking children from their families. I won't be a part of such wickedness."

"We have no choice in the matter," Setmosis said. "The girl has been brought here to serve in the temple of Seth as one of his priestesses. Pharaoh has decreed that Potipherah's daughter will train side by side with our own daughter. We cannot ignore a decree from Pharaoh. I know this will place an extra burden on you, but—"

"It's not the burden on us that bothers me," Ari interrupted.

"It's the awfulness of what Pharaoh is doing to this poor girl and her family. It infuriates me! Isn't there something you can say to him? You're the chief priest. He respects you. There must be something you can say that will soften his heart."

"There's nothing I can say," Setmosis answered, lowering his head and shaking it. "I don't agree with Pharaoh's tactics, but desperate times do call for desperate measures. Pharaoh has to quell the seeds of rebellion wherever he finds them. It's unfortunate that an innocent, young girl has been caught up in the middle of this, but she can thank her father's misguided ambition for her captivity."

"It's wrong! It's wrong and you know it!"

"I already told you we have no choice in the matter. The girl will remain in Avaris and we will be her guardians. Eventually, Pharaoh will choose a husband for her—a husband who is loyal to him—and then she will be free to go. But until that time . . . " He allowed his voice to trail off and shook his head helplessly.

"What did you say her name was?" Ari asked.

"Asenath."

"And how old is she?"

"The same age as Netchem."

"Then I'll send a servant to bring Netchem home from the temple. Asenath is going to need a friend, and, for a while, Netchem might be the only one she has. I want her to have a warm reception when she gets here. She's going to need that, too. The poor child has just been ripped from her family and home. She must be terrified."

"She'll be all right. Once she gets used to us and her new life, everything will be fine."

"Perhaps. But what if she distrusts us instead? What if she hates us because we're the instruments of Pharaoh's cruel plan?"

"The gods will provide," Setmosis answered, pausing to tiredly shake his head. "We have to trust in that. That's the only thing we can do."

"No. We could do more. At least you can. You can speak to Pharaoh.

You can try to convince him to free her."

"I'll do what I can," Setmosis said, turning his eyes away so as not to be forced to meet Ari's fierce gaze. "But I can guarantee nothing. Pharaoh has made up his mind, and I'll fall into disfavor if I push the matter too far. Put Asenath in Mera's old room for now. We need to prepare for this as if it's going to be a long-term situation rather than a short one. I don't foresee Pharaoh changing his mind any time soon."

Her father always told her that the future of Egypt rested in the hands of the ruling families of Thebes.

"One day those of true Egyptian blood will rise up against us and drive us back into Canaan and Syria where our ancestors came from," he said. "Only those Hyksos who ally themselves with the royal families of Thebes and marry into them will remain when the inevitable reversal of power comes."

Asenath didn't know if this was true or not, but she realized now that her father wasn't as invincible as she'd always imagined him to be. If he were, she wouldn't be here now. She wouldn't be far from home with no power to return to her family.

Pharaoh's capital was an imposing city. Avaris crouched like a hungry lion on the bright sands of the Nile River Delta, and it seemed that the desert itself must have spawned this mighty collection of buildings, beasts, and men. Towering walls of beaten earth formed a defensive barrier around the city, and the entire place seemed built to intimidate the enemies of the Hyksos kings. It successfully intimidated Asenath. Even now she trembled when she thought about her first view of Avaris. How could the walls of this place ever be brought down? How could the Hyksos who had conquered Egypt with their chariots, bows, and battle-axes ever be driven from the land? Perhaps her father was making allies with the wrong people. And perhaps she would suffer here until the end of her days because of it. A cold wave of despair began to wash over her, and then the chariot she was riding in stopped with a jolt, shaking her away from her unhappy thoughts.

She was in the street before the Temple of Seth, patron god of Avaris; and a statue of Seth—five times her size—stared malevolently down upon her. She felt herself grow cold inside as its sightless eyes drilled holes into her soul.

"Pharaoh instructed me to leave you here," the charioteer said. "You are to enter and ask for Setmosis. He is chief priest of the temple, and you'll be staying with his family while you train to be a priest-ess."

Asenath silently nodded her head and gathered into her arms the small, wooden box that contained all the earthly possessions she'd been allowed to bring with her to Avaris. She stepped down from the chariot and took several halting steps toward the temple, but the charioteer stopped her when he realized where she was going.

"Not there," he said. "Here."

She turned to follow his pointing finger and saw a large, mud-brick house that faced the protective outer walls of the temple. But before she could ask if this house was where she should enter, the whip of the charioteer cracked loudly over the horses' heads and the chariot disappeared in a choking cloud of dust.

She was alone now. Alone and entirely uncertain about what she should do. She could try to escape. She could flee beyond the city's earthen walls and attempt a perilous journey back to On. But she was the daughter of a high priest and expected to act as such. As frightened as she was, she managed to draw in a thin, shaky breath before cautiously approaching the front gate of Setmosis' house.

Although smaller than her own, this house was not that much unlike her family's. A wall surrounded the main house and its outbuildings, and she could see the branches of garden trees hanging over one edge of that wall. There was also a guard at the front gate—just as there would be at her home in On—and this one seemed to watch her with amusement as she approached.

"My name is Asenath," she said in a voice that wasn't nearly as strong as she'd hoped it would be. "I—"

"Go through here, enter the antechamber, and announce to one of the servants that you've arrived," the guard instructed her. "The master and his family are waiting for you."

Asenath nodded, straightened her shoulders, and swallowed the hard lump that had lodged itself in the center of her throat. It hurt going down, and it reminded her how close she was to tears. But, clutching her box of belongings more tightly against her breast, she forced her feet to carry her bravely through the gate.

It was dark inside the house, and it took several moments for her eyes to adjust from the harsh brightness of the Egyptian sun to the cool shadows of Setmosis' home. When she could finally see what was around her, she jumped back in sudden surprise.

"I'm sorry. I didn't mean to scare you."

She was staring into the warm, brown eyes of a girl who must have been about her own age. The girl smiled at her, but her heart was still racing too fast for her to regain her composure and smile back.

"Hello. My name is Netchem," the girl said. "Are you Asenath?"

"Yes."

"Follow me," Netchem said, smiling even more brightly. "My father said to bring you to the great hall as soon as you got here."

Netchem grasped Asenath by one of her hands and towed her quickly from the dim antechamber to a large, spacious room beyond it. She was now in the main hall—a place of tall, wooden pillars and polished, tile floors. It was smaller than the great hall in her own home, but there was every indication here that this was the residence of an affluent family.

The walls of the room were covered with pleasant scenes of delta marshes and flying birds. Reeds, papyrus, fish, and fowls of the air decorated the painted pillars that supported the vast ceiling above her, and both the ceiling and floor were colored the deep shade of blue that Egyptians—especially the wealthy ones—were so fond of.

There were also brick platforms along the walls, and these were covered with soft skins of exotic animals, providing comfortable places for the family and their visitors to sit. As if she didn't already have proof enough of Setmosis' wealth and power, her eyes now discovered a large collection of low, backless, ebony stools which were scattered here and there across the hall. Chairs were a luxury item in Egypt. A lesser family would never have been able to afford them.

At the far end of the hall, a tall man and a slender, graceful woman waited for Asenath and Netchem. The man's head was shaved in the manner of priests, and there was an aura of power about him that made a tingle of fear go up and down Asenath's spine. He wore gold bands around his wrists, bands of lapis and gold around his biceps, and a broad, golden collar over his upper chest and shoulders. This must be the chief priest in charge of the great temple complex of Seth. No one else would carry himself with such dignity and authority. He reminded Asenath a little of her own father.

The petite woman standing at Setmosis' side was wearing a simple linen *kalasiris* and an *usekh*—a traditional necklace which extended from her neck to her waist. She had the same warm, brown eyes as Netchem, and it was obvious that Netchem received her grace and beauty from her mother. They seemed like the type of family her own family associated with in On, but this only slightly put her at ease.

"You must be Asenath," the woman said. "We've been expecting you."

Asenath nodded but didn't speak. She wasn't sure whether she should nod, bow, or extend the hand that Netchem had finally released. She was still wondering about it when Setmosis made his introduction.

"Welcome to our home," he said. "We hope you'll find everything here to your liking. My name is Setmosis. This is my wife Ari. And Netchem has obviously already introduced herself to you."

Asenath timidly nodded her head and finally managed to force some words past her lips. "I'm pleased to meet all of you," she said while she stared uncomfortably at her toes.

"This is a difficult situation for you," Setmosis said. "We know it is. We also understand that you're here against your will. You have the freedom to go anywhere you wish within the boundaries of our estate and home—we want you to feel welcome here. But, as you've probably already been told, Pharaoh has strictly charged me not to allow you to travel any farther than the edge of the temple complex without one of us nearby to accompany you. At the temple, Netchem will be your constant companion. She'll help you while you adjust to your new duties there. And here in the house—"

"I'm sure we'll have plenty of time to discuss all these things later," Ari suddenly interrupted. Asenath watched in puzzlement as Ari gave Setmosis an angry scowl, then Ari smiled again at her and asked, "Is there anything we can do for you now? Perhaps you'd like something to eat or to drink?"

She knew Ari was trying to put her at ease—trying to lessen the impact of the harsh new reality of her imprisonment—but all she really wanted was to be left alone. If she could, she'd already be hiding in a corner, crying.

"I'm not very hungry," she managed to get out. "I think I'll feel much better if I just rest for a while."

"Of course," Ari replied. "These past few days have probably been very long and tiring for you. I'm sure that Netchem will be happy to show you to your room."

Netchem nodded, took Asenath once more by the hand, and cheerfully led her from the hall. Asenath followed meekly behind, feeling like this was all some strange kind of dream rather than the harshly real situation it actually was.

"My bedchamber is here," Netchem said when they reached the living quarters at the back of the house. "This one across from mine is yours."

In the Egyptian tongue, the word *netchem* meant "pleasant," and it was a perfect name for such a cheerful person as this. But it didn't matter how pleasant or cheerful Asenath's jailers were. Though this family seemed nice enough, she couldn't help but remember her father's last, whispered words as Pharaoh's men took her away from On. "Pharaoh will place you in the home of some influential Hyksos family of Avaris," he'd said. "Whatever you do, my daughter, don't trust them."

This message ringing again in her ears, the first thing Asenath's eyes drifted to as Netchem led her into her room was the barred window at the top of one wall. There was a high window like this in her own room back in On. The iron bars were actually there to keep intruders out while allowing the cool, evening breezes in. But her window at home had never made her feel trapped the way this one did.

It seemed to be a comfortable prison cell. The room was furnished with a small table and an oil lamp. A low bed with a curved headrest provided a place to sleep, and there was a handsomely carved, wooden chair in one corner if she needed a place to sit. Netchem let go of her hand at this point and grinned.

"It's nice, isn't it?"

"Yes. Very nice."

"It was my sister's room before she married and left the house. We didn't have much time to get it ready for you; but when the servants came in to clean it, I told them where to put all the furniture." She reached for the box of Asenath's possessions, not noticing how reluctantly Asenath let it go, then placed it on the room's single table.

"We didn't even know you were coming until today," Netchem said. "This was a big surprise to us. I bet it was a surprise for you, too."

"Surprise" wasn't a word Asenath would use to describe this situation. To her a surprise was something pleasant—something to be enjoyed. There was nothing enjoyable about this. Her world had been turned completely upside down, and not even her father was powerful enough to stop it. But she nodded her head, agreeing with everything, and her foster sister beamed.

"I'll let you rest now," Netchem said. "But if you need anything, send one of the servants to find me. All right?"

Again Asenath nodded. She realized she was doing more nodding than speaking, but she didn't feel strong enough to form words. She was too afraid she'd break into tears, and she knew her father would be displeased with her if she showed weakness before his enemies. Summoning all the self-control a young girl her age possessed, she waited until Netchem had left the room and shut the large, wooden door behind her before allowing herself to sink into a miserable heap on the floor.

She was the daughter of Potipherah, high priest of On. She was soon to be a priestess in a temple. That meant she had to be fearless and strong. But she felt neither fearless nor strong today. All she felt was frightened and alone; and a series of violent, choking sobs broke free from her throat.

If any of the gods were merciful—if any cared about the plight of an unhappy young girl—one would step forward now and provide an avenue of escape. But the gods were as distant and uncaring now as they had always seemed to be.

Maybe it was Asenath's fault that they gave her no help. Maybe they knew that she sometimes doubted their existence, and they were now punishing her because of it. A cold chill went up and down her spine as this frightening thought occurred to her.

"I'll do better," she whispered. "I'll do better if you save me. I won't doubt you anymore."

But her words felt hollow and useless. She was under the power of the dark god Seth and only a much more powerful god could set her free. Where could she ever hope to find a god such as that?

Chapter Notes

Avaris, the capital city of the Hyksos kings, was located in the Delta region of Lower Egypt near Qantir at Tell el-Dab'a. The earthen defensive walls and the temple of Seth are both known to have existed, but most of the details in this chapter are fictional descriptions of a long-dead city.

SIX

"CAN YOU SEE WHO IT IS?" Reuben asked, drumming his fingers nervously against the hilt of his sword. Though the rest of his brothers wouldn't say it, he knew they, too, were apprehensive about the approaching stranger. Swords had constantly been near at hand from the moment they brought their flocks to Shechem; and, even here in Dothan, there was always a worry that enemies might spring a sudden surprise attack on them. Reuben could see Simeon, Levi, Judah, and the others half unsheathing their swords as they crouched silently in the grass beside him. Everyone was tense.

"I can't see him very well yet," Zebulun said, squinting his eyes and shading them with one hand. "He's still too far a . . . Wait! I do see who it is! I would recognize that rainbow-colored coat anywhere. It's Joseph!"

A collective sigh of relief escaped from ten throats at once, and Jacob's sons rolled from bent-kneed, crouched postures to more comfortable positions in the grass. Judah, however, got immediately to his feet, the tenseness on his bearded face fading to be replaced by hard, angry lines.

"So the Master of Dreams comes to grace us again with his presence," he said with a sneer. "Do you think he's come so that we can bow down before him? Or does he have another dream he can't wait to share with us?"

"The artful pretender must think he can deceive us with his lies the way he's deceived our father," Levi said. "Maybe this time our brother, the great dreamer, thought he saw us putting a crown on his head and a scepter in his hand. We should kill a fatted calf to celebrate the arrival of our future ruler!"

The others laughed at Levi's barbed insult, but Judah didn't join in. Instead, his already dark eyes grew darker, and his voice was cold when he spoke. "I have a better idea," he said. "Forget killing the fatted calf. I say we kill *him*."

All were silent for several moments. Then the corners of Simeon's mouth curled into a sneer, and he added his own thoughts to Judah's. "Joseph has been nothing but trouble to us," he said. "He sits home in Father's tent while we tend the animals and risk our lives in the lands of our enemies. We do all the work, and he receives all the profit of our labors. And the most insulting part of it all is that once Father dies, the birthright will give Joseph a double portion of everything *we've* worked so hard to build."

"Joseph!" Judah said, spitting out the name like it was something rotten or foul. "It makes me sick to hear that name. Father gives him the feast while we inherit the crumbs. We're treated no better than dogs just because we were born to the wrong mother!"

"Let's slay him, cast his body into some pit, and be done with it!" Levi said as the air around them grew thick with rage. "One of Dothan's wells is less than a stone's throw away from us. We can put his body there, and then we'll tell Father that some evil beast has devoured him. It's quick. It's simple. It will solve our problem once and for all."

"We'll see what comes of his dreams then!" Naphtali laughed, slapping Levi heartily on the back. "Won't we!"

Reuben had been listening to all of this in silence. He hated Joseph as much as any of them but knew he had to say something before things got out of hand.

"Have you all gone mad?" he asked. "I can't believe you're actually considering this."

The laughter faded. Angry eyes turned to stare at him.

"You have a problem with this, Reuben?" Judah asked, his voice low and dangerous. "I would think that *you* of all people would have the most to gain from Joseph's untimely demise."

"I don't like the special treatment Joseph gets," Reuben replied. "I agree with you that something should be done about it. But I do have a problem with getting his blood on my hands. There are other ways to go about this without actually shedding his blood."

"Really?" Judah sarcastically demanded. "Like what?" His voice was still hard, but the flames of his anger seemed to be dying down just a little.

"I don't know," Reuben hesitantly admitted. "I just think we need to give ourselves time to think about it. Except for the part about killing him, we could do as Levi suggests and throw him into this pit." He paused to gesture toward the nearby cistern. "It's empty now because of the drought, and it will be impossible for him to climb out of it. It will make a perfect prison until we can all come to an agreement about what to do."

"Enough of this senseless chatter!" Simeon growled. "I say we just cut his throat and be done with it! We've already had years to think about this. The time for thinking is over, and the time for action has come." He unsheathed his sword for emphasis and allowed its blade to glitter menacingly in the sun, but Judah raised one hand and shook his head.

"It was one thing for you to run off like a madman and spill the blood of Shechem and his men," Judah said, stroking his thick, black beard with one hand, "but this is different. If we decide to kill our own brother, we have to do it right. The last thing we want is for news of his death to get back to Father and for it to look like we had something to do with it. For now, I say we throw him in the pit like Reuben suggests. We can argue about what to do with him when we actually have him in our hands. Everyone except Zebulun hide in the grass. Zebulun, you distract Joseph before he reaches us. We'll take care of the rest."

Zebulun nodded and Simeon glowered, but everyone dropped into the grass like Judah had commanded. Somehow Judah always seemed to get his way when he wanted it badly enough.

One way or another, Joseph was probably going to end up dead. But at least Reuben could now honestly say that he'd tried to save his younger brother. Jacob couldn't find fault in him for that. If only . . .

No. It was a crazy idea. Judah would kill him if he tried to pull it off and failed. But what if he could convince his brothers to leave Joseph alive in the well? What if he could do that and then come back later and pull Joseph out?

If there was any chance of winning his birthright back, this might be it. Reuben would be favored above all the other sons of Leah, if he somehow managed to snatch Jacob's favorite son out of the hands of his older, bloodthirsty brothers. It was a risky idea, but it could just possibly work.

He struggled now to keep a smile off his face. He'd have to be cautious. He'd have to be crafty. But the more he pondered it, the better he liked his odds.

Say goodbye to the birthright, Joseph, he thought happily to himself. *When I bring you safely back home and explain everything that happened here today, Father will be so overjoyed that he'll give back to me what was already rightfully mine.*

Joseph's shoulder was the first part of his body to strike the ground. His head was next. Dazed, confused, and disoriented, he tried to lift himself to his feet but couldn't. The best he could manage was to roll onto one elbow while he tried to clear his vision and figure out who had just attacked him.

His assailants had seemed to come from out of nowhere. One moment he was greeting Zebulun and the next he was being assaulted by a band of shouting men. They had kicked and pummeled him, stripped away his coat, then thrown him. He didn't know why it seemed so long before he hit the ground or why everything was now spinning crazily around him, but he felt a moment of panic as he realized that they must now be attacking Zebulun.

He should get up to help his brother. He should at least shout for aid. But his temples were throbbing, and he couldn't seem to make his eyes focus. Although he blinked again and again, the world kept spinning around him in a dizzying fog, leaving him in a murky mess of confusion. He wasn't sure how long it took for his eyes to clear so that he could cautiously survey his surroundings; but, when he could see, he discovered why it had taken him so long to strike the ground. He was alone at the bottom of a deep, dry pit, and his attackers were watching him from above. A stone, dislodged by one of the men, landed with a thud next to him; and he backed quickly to one side, protectively shielding his aching head from the falling debris.

"Is he dead?" the voice of an enemy echoed down from above.

"No, he's still alive. I think I see him moving down there."

"Too bad," a third voice that sounded oddly like Simeon's echoed down to him. "I was hoping the fall would kill him."

"Joseph! How is it down there?" a fourth voice—one that sounded like Asher's—said.

Joseph stared in disbelief at the circle of faces above him. They were all there—from Reuben on down to Zebulun. They were standing around a low rock wall that encircled the pit, and they were watching him with malicious smiles on their lips.

"It . . . it was you? You did this to me?" Joseph's voice came out in a faint croak of disbelief, and he rubbed his eyes to make sure they really were working.

"Don't sound so surprised," Simeon called down to him. "You've had this coming for a long time now. And look. You forgot something up here." He dangled Joseph's coat tauntingly above the pit, and all the other brothers laughed. "But don't worry," Simeon continued in a falsely comforting voice. "We know how much this means to you. We'll make sure it gets safely back to Father even though you probably won't."

Suddenly it all registered in his brain. He understood what was happening. His own brothers had laid a trap for him, and now they intended to leave him in this pit to die. He looked around himself again, trying to decide just how bad his situation really was, and realized it couldn't get much worse. He was in a dry well—probably one of the two wells from which Dothan got its name. It was wide at the bottom, but it tapered to a small opening at the top. It would be virtually impossible to climb out of it on his own.

"Please!" he called out, realizing even as he did that his plea would most likely fall on deaf ears. "Don't leave me down here! Whatever our differences are, it doesn't need to come to this! We're brothers, not enemies. You have to listen to what I have to say."

"Don't expect anyone to bow to you while you're down there," Gad taunted. "And don't think you can talk yourself out of this. Father isn't here to save you this time. You're finally going to get what you deserve."

"That's right," Simeon said. "But don't give up hope just yet. You'll still become a ruler. In a few short days from now you're going to become king of the worms."

That remark prompted another raucous round of laughter, and Joseph felt his stomach tighten with fear.

He'd always known his brothers hated him, but it wasn't until this moment that he realized just how deeply that hatred ran. He could see it etched in all its ugly intensity across their sneering faces. He could see it in their eyes and hear it in their voices. It was completely undisguised now that Jacob wasn't near to see it.

"Please," Joseph tried once more. "If ever I've done anything to offend you, I beg you now to forgive me. Give me a chance to make things right with you."

"Maybe you didn't hear us the first time," Judah said. "We don't fall for your false righteousness like Father does. Your powers of persuasion have served you quite well up to now, but that's all about to end."

Joseph felt his heart sink lower within him. They didn't see him as a brother. They saw him as an enemy. And they intended to eliminate him as surely as Simeon and Levi had eliminated Shechem. They left him alone now, but he could hear their jubilant laughter as they moved slowly away from the pit. Suddenly he knew the true meaning of hopelessness.

The temples of Egypt were not places of public worship. They were "mansions" for the gods and, as such, were rarely entered by anyone but the priestly caste. Though she was daughter to the "chief of seers"—the great high priest of On himself—Asenath still trembled when Netchem led her toward the massive, fortress-like walls of Seth's temple. In the past, her only glimpse into any temple had come during the Sed festival. It was a new and frightening experience, therefore, to actually cross between the mighty pylons at the temple entrance to step into the forbidden world beyond.

"Do you see the wavy pattern on the outer temple walls?" Netchem asked.

"Yes. They're very pretty."

"My father says they represent the first stage of creation," Netchem explained, "the 'primeval waters' upon which Egypt floats like a giant bowl of clay. The outer walls are supposed to be a defense against the forces of chaos and evil."

Asenath nodded. Her own father had already explained much of the symbolism of Egypt's temples to her.

"The Hyksos people observe the outward traditions of Egypt," he often told her, "but there are few among us who truly understand the culture we try to call our own. You, however, need to understand it all. One day, you will marry a prince of Thebes, and then—when our family is merged with an old family of Egypt—we will finally become the true Egyptians we deserve to be."

The memory faded, and a heavy cloud settled over Asenath's soul. Netchem was still chattering about the temple, but she didn't hear much of what her new foster sister was saying. Instead, she was lost in muddled thoughts of her own.

What did her father mean exactly when he spoke of her family one day becoming "true Egyptians?" Were they not already Egyptian enough? And was there something wrong about being Hyksos? She felt so lost and confused, and she felt even more confused when she saw what waited for her beyond the imposing, mud-brick walls that protected the inner courtyards of the temple.

She'd expected to find something intimidating and majestic when she entered the temple grounds, but what she actually found was rather disappointing.

The Hyksos had changed the name of their own god to the name of a similar local deity. They had adopted the dress, language, and customs of Egypt. But the temple of Seth retained the distinctive mark of the Canaanite land Asenath had never known. This was not an Egyptian temple like the great temple of Ra in On. This was a temple of a Semite rather than an Egyptian people.

"It's beautiful, isn't it," Netchem said, glowing with pride. "Follow me. It's even more beautiful on the inside."

Together, the two girls climbed up the front steps of the temple where two menacing statues of Seth stood guard. Asenath couldn't help but shudder a little as she passed beneath the ugly, stone sentinels. Seth had the body of a man, but his head was the frightening visage of some dog or jackal-like beast. She knew these statues were only lifeless representations of Seth, but she still had the uncomfortable feeling that they might move from their posts and seize her if she turned her eyes—even for a moment—away from their dark, stony faces. The feeling remained with her until she and Netchem made it past the idols into the cool interior of the temple.

It was a surprisingly simple structure. It consisted of nothing more than a court, an open porch, and this broad, smoky room. But, now that she was inside, she realized it was still large enough to make even a tall girl like herself feel small. The smoke was coming from two censers of smoldering incense set on cylindrical stands at the base of a short flight of steps. At the top of those steps was a huge, stone altar and, behind it, cast in bronze and shown in a seated position, was a large statue of Seth. Asenath shuddered again as she stared at the unfriendly god.

"One of our jobs will be to keep the incense burning," Netchem said. She spoke in a hushed voice and pointed to the wisps of smoke that curled eerily towards the ceiling. "We will learn and recite prayers; and, when we are ready, we will help to teach the daughters of Pharaoh in the temple school."

It seemed like a meaningless existence, but Asenath didn't dare say so in the presence of Seth—even if it was only his statue. Better to keep such thoughts to herself while she waited patiently for her father to somehow arrange her release.

"Come," Netchem whispered. "I'll take you to the scriptorium. We'll probably be spending many hours there together. There are stacks of temple texts to be memorized and other important study to be done."

Netchem seemed to believe this would inspire Asenath; but, if anything, it only made her more depressed. Although her father had promised he would sway Pharaoh to secure her release, every new minute she spent in Avaris made her doubt that promise more and more. She might be here for years. She might be here for the rest of her life. She could see no avenue of escape.

None at all.

"It's kind of scary the first time you see it," Netchem said, placing a comforting hand on Asenath's arm when she noticed the troubled look on her face. "But you'll get used to it. It's really not all that bad once you learn your daily duties."

Asenath nodded. She didn't figure it would do any good to say what was really bothering her. It was apparent that she'd have to find a way to suffer through this on her own. Her father couldn't help her and the gods wouldn't. This was going to be her permanent home.

The round, flaming orb that was the sun was directly over the pit now, illuminating its depths with warm, bright light. It took Joseph several long moments to figure out where he was and then several more to realize it was the frayed end of a rope, brushing persistently against his face, that had aroused him from his fitful sleep.

"Wake up, dreamer!" Dan's voice echoed down to him. "We've decided to pull you out. You don't want to stay down in that pit forever, do you?"

With a groan, Joseph staggered to his feet. He'd been certain that his brothers would leave him down here to die, and relief washed over him as he tied the loose end of the rope around his waist. Perhaps the Lord had listened to his prayers and softened his brothers' stony hearts. But then another thought—an unpleasant one—occurred to him. What if they really hadn't changed their hearts at all? What if they were only bringing him up to kill him faster and avoid the possibility that someone from Dothan might unexpectedly find and rescue him?

He could try to undo the knot he'd just tied and drop back to the bottom of the well again; but that would only mean a prolonged, agonizing death of thirst and starvation. He had no chance of survival down there. At least he could fight for his life the moment they finished hoisting him to the top.

A quick, whispered prayer left his cracked lips as he came nearer to whatever fate awaited him. Throughout all the long hours of his captivity at the bottom of this pit, he had been praying for deliverance. He would just have to put his trust in God and believe that this would all work out for the best.

There were no welcoming smiles to greet him as Gad reached

out a free hand and helped him over the low, rock wall. There was also no time to ask his brothers what they intended to do with him. While Gad and Asher held his arms, Issachar swiftly looped the rope around his wrists, binding his hands together. He forgot his original intention to fight as this new indignity was forced upon him. He was much too exhausted and weak to do anything about it, anyway. In silence, he suffered it all as Issachar took the loose end of the rope and led him to the place where the rest of his brothers were standing. Only Reuben seemed to be missing from the group.

Not far away, a long row of heavily laden camels was grazing next to his own family's flocks. Judah and Simeon were speaking to the owners of those camels—a group of Ishmaelites—and, by the style of their flowing, desert robes, he guessed that these men were from Midian.

"It's all here," Judah said, nodding to Simeon and displaying something in one of his cupped hands. In the glare of the noonday sun, Joseph thought he caught the flash of silver. His guess was confirmed as Judah dropped the money with a jingle into a small, leather pouch tied at his waist. "Twenty pieces just as agreed on," Judah said. "Did you get him out of the pit?"

"He's right here." Issachar stepped forward, held up the end of the rope that bound Joseph's wrists, and Judah smiled.

"Excellent!" he said. "My friends, it looks as if you now have yourselves a slave."

"Make sure you sell him to an Egyptian who will give him lots of hard, backbreaking labor," Simeon said.

"That's right," Issachar chimed in. "He's already had the benefits of a soft, lazy life. It's time he learns to work for his keep."

Slave? Egyptian? Joseph felt the blood drain from his face. His brothers had decided not to kill him after all; but that, it seemed, was only so that they could make a profit off his humiliation and suffering. He'd been saved from death only to be sold into a miserable life of servitude.

"Enjoy Egypt," Dan, who was standing behind him, whispered

into his ear, "because you're going to be spending the rest of your life there."

"Come on." Asher grunted. "We don't have all day. Your new masters are waiting for you, and we know you won't want to make a bad impression on them." He pushed Joseph roughly forward, and there were smirks on his brothers' faces and laughter in their voices as he hung his head in sorrow. Unceremoniously, he was half shoved half dragged to the group of Ishmaelites who stood with Judah and Simeon. The one who appeared to be the leader reached out a weathered hand to lift Joseph's chin, and his large, white teeth shone in a smile through his greasy, black beard.

"The boy looks young and strong," he said. "We should make a good profit on the sale of this one." He glanced over now at two of his own men, pointed to Joseph, then jerked a thumb toward the camels. The two burly men carried Joseph to the nearest of the camels and plopped him heavily on its back.

"Don't try to escape," one warned as the other removed the ropes from Joseph's wrists to replace them with metal shackles. "Or else . . ." The Ishmaelite paused to draw a finger quickly across his neck, and he made an unmistakable, cutting noise in the back of his throat. Joseph got the picture.

While he waited, a few more words passed between his brothers and the leader of the caravan; but he was too tired and too stunned to catch much of what was said. His last memory of his brothers would be the sight of them, laughing and mocking, as the Midianite caravan carried him away to Egypt.

Chapter Notes

1. The Biblical town of *Dothan* was situated on an important ancient trade route at the southern end of the plain of Jezreel. *Dothan,* or *dothayin,* is a Hebrew or Aramaic word meaning "two wells." The pit mentioned in Genesis 37 could very well have been one of these two wells. The wells can be visited today at Tell-Dothan.

One of them is named *Jubb Yusuf*—the Pit of Joseph.

2. The *Midianites* were a wandering group of Arab people. Although they were actually descended through Midian, the son of Abraham's concubine, Keturah, they came to be viewed as part of the Ishmaelite tribe. Jacob's family and the Ishmaelites shared in common the West Semitic language of Canaan.

3. When the Hyksos first entered Egypt, they brought the worship of their own god, Sutekh, with them. Because of similarities to Egypt's native storm god, Seth, Sutekh soon became associated with him. Avaris was the main center of the worship of Seth and, according to one ancient stela, important Egyptian officials such as Seti, the father of Ramses II, came to pay their respects to him even after the Hyksos had been ousted from power. Seth (also referred to as Set) was the brother of Osiris, Isis, and Nephthys and was the father of Anubis. There were brief periods of time—such as during the Hyksos era—when he was respected as a great, benevolent god. But throughout most of Egypt's history, he was regarded as a dreaded god of evil.

SEVEN

"You're a long way from Hebron. How did you fall into the hands of those men?"

Joseph, groggy from the heat and the ordeal of the day, snapped his eyes open and turned to face the Midianite who had addressed him. His eyes opened even wider when he recognized the speaker. It was the trader from the market at Hebron, and he had brought his camel up next to Joseph's.

"My father sent me to check on my brothers," Joseph answered, eyeing the man carefully. "I went searching for them in Canaan and was told by a man there that they had moved their flocks to Dothan."

"I see." The Midianite nodded his head. "It's a shame you didn't find your brothers before these men found you."

"Those men *were* my brothers."

The Midianite was shocked for several long moments into silence. His voice was sympathetic when he spoke again. "I'm sorry. I don't know what to say."

Joseph shrugged. What appropriate thing was there that anyone could say?

"My name is Elan," the Midianite finally said. "Tell me, boy, what is yours?"

"Joseph."

"I would set you free, Joseph. But Ishdaah would slit my throat if I did." Elan glanced meaningfully at the leader who rode ahead of them. "He purchased you for a third less than the normal asking price for a slave. He intends to sell you in the markets of Egypt for much more than that."

Joseph nodded and swallowed hard. A lump was forming in his throat, but he didn't want to weep in front of these Ishmaelites. He fought with all his might to hold back the despair that threatened to force itself to the surface.

"You're a good trader," Elan said. "Fair and shrewd. I respect that. Because of this, I'll do my best to make your journey comfortable and safe. I wish I could do more for you, but I can't."

"Thank you," Joseph said, unable to maintain eye contact. "I appreciate your kindness."

"If you get hungry, let me know. If you're thirsty, call for me. But don't try to run. Ishdaah won't kill you. He'd lose his investment if he did. But he won't think twice about making you wish he'd killed you."

"I understand."

Ishdaah suddenly glanced back at them, his eyes filled with suspicion, and Elan brought the conversation to an abrupt end. He allowed his camel to drop back to the end of the caravan, leaving Joseph alone with his troubled thoughts. They had left the fertile, green plain of Jezreel behind them now and were headed west toward the coast of the Mediterranean Sea. Had his captors chosen instead to take the trade route through Hebron, there might have been hope that Jacob would learn of Joseph's capture and set him free. But there was no hope now. The Midianites would follow the coast to the Nile Delta, and Joseph's fate would be sealed.

It was a struggle in this situation to maintain faith in God. He wanted to understand God's wise purpose in all of this, but at the moment he could find none. The blackness of his despair nearly choked him. He was trapped in a nightmare. That's what this was. If he would just wake up, he could escape it.

But it wasn't a nightmare. It was real. And had he known how long it was actually going to last, the despair would have probably crushed him.

"How do you like it so far?"

"How do I like what?" Asenath stopped walking and turned toward Netchem with a puzzled expression on her face.

"Your duties as a priestess. Are you enjoying yourself now that you've had a few days to settle in?"

"Is it always like this?" Asenath asked, ignoring the question.

"Is it always like what?"

"So boring." Perhaps she shouldn't have been so blunt. She watched Netchem's eyes flicker nervously toward the watching statues of Seth, and the girls's face turned slightly pale. But Asenath's initial timidness had begun to wear off. Now that she was becoming familiar with these new surroundings, more of her natural assertiveness was starting to come to the surface. "We do the same things all day every day," she said, her boldness growing. "Prayers, ablutions, spells. Isn't there anything interesting or useful to do here?"

"You mustn't talk that way," Netchem cautioned. She came closer to Asenath and shook her head in warning. "You might anger the great storm god. These things are what we do. What all priests and priestesses do. It's not our place to question why."

She understood Netchem's fear. All her life Asenath, too, had been taught not to question the religious beliefs or the gods of Egypt. But today she wasn't satisfied with blindly accepting her people's ways. Perhaps this dangerous boldness came from being so far away from her father and her home city of On, but she was going to speak her mind.

"We're taught to look forward to and prepare for death, right?"

"Yes." Netchem still looked uneasy, and she was watching Asenath with cautious eyes.

"We're taught that the next life will be a better version of the one we're living now. But do you enjoy the life of a priestess? Do you want to live this way for the rest of eternity?"

"I-I don't know," Netchem stammered, beginning to squirm. "But I'm sure it could be worse. We could be the daughters of farmers or tomb builders. You wouldn't want to live that life forever, would you?"

"Have you ever wished that you could choose your own destiny?" Asenath asked, ignoring Netchem's answer. "Instead of having your family or the gods choose your place for you?"

"We really should go somewhere else to talk," Netchem said. "Our duties here are finished."

Asenath nodded and followed Netchem. They moved beyond the walls of the temple enclosure, crossed over to the house of Setmosis, and went to the shaded garden behind it. Netchem looked visibly more relaxed now that the statues and the incense and the priests were nowhere near them. Her shoulders, which had been stiff and tense, loosened and some of the color returned to her face. But it was obvious she was still far from comfortable with Asenath's questions.

"I think Ptakh likes you," Netchem said in a blatant attempt to leave the earlier topic of conversation entirely behind them.

"What makes you say that?" She really wasn't interested at all in what Ptakh thought of her, but it was probably best not to push Netchem any farther than she already had.

"He hinted to me the other day that he likes you," Netchem replied, grinning sheepishly. "He says your eyes are as blue as the eyes of Isis, and your skin is twice as fair. Don't tell him I told you. I wasn't supposed to say a thing."

"I won't tell," Asenath quickly promised.

"So?"

"So what?"

"So do you like *him*?"

"He seems nice enough. But it doesn't matter who I like."

"Why is that?"

"Because, when I'm old enough, Pharaoh will choose my husband for me. My entire life is already decided. I don't have any say in it at all."

"I didn't know that," Netchem whispered. "I'm sorry."

Asenath shrugged her shoulders, and the momentary wave of anger she'd felt gave way to cold depression. "Even if Pharaoh didn't choose for me," she said, "my father would. So it doesn't matter who I end up marrying. I've always known that the choice was never mine to make."

"My father is training Ptakh to be the next chief priest of the temple," Netchem said. "Maybe Pharaoh will end up choosing him to be your husband. I'm sure your father would approve of that."

"My father has other things in mind," Asenath replied, shaking her head. "He wants me to marry a nobleman—a future pharaoh. He already has a family picked out for me in Thebes."

"The Thebans are rebels," Netchem said, her brow furrowing. "They don't even honor Seth. They think he's an evil god instead of the kind protector of our people. Why would your father want you to marry one of them?"

Asenath realized too late that she'd probably said more than she should. Now it was her turn to deflect the conversation in a different direction. "It's hard to explain. But what about you? Is there someone *you're* interested in?"

Netchem, so prone to blush, turned a bright shade of red, and Asenath smiled.

"It's Yeptah, isn't it?"

"Yes, . . . but how did you know?"

"I could tell by the way you look at him when you don't think anyone is watching."

"You don't think other people have noticed, do you?" There was a hint of dismay in Netchem's voice, and Asenath's smile grew.

"No," she lied. "I think your secret is safe. But I could ask him what he thinks of you if you'd like."

"No!" Her response came quickly. "Don't say a thing! He might figure out that I like him, but he might not like me back. That would be humiliating!"

They were silent for several moments while Netchem blushed and stared at her feet. Then Netchem said, "I'm sorry Pharaoh is forcing you to stay here. I wish you were here because you wanted to be. I guess you'll never want to be my friend as long as you're forced to stay here."

Asenath didn't quite know what to say. Even though she'd been here only a few days, she had felt an unexpectedly growing fondness for Netchem. She'd never realized that Netchem might like her, too.

"I . . . I'd be glad to be your friend," Asenath said after several awkward moments of silence had passed. "It's not your fault that I'm here. Thank you for being a friend to me."

"I should let Mother know that we're back from the temple," Netchem said, grinning. "Maybe she'll get one of the servants to prepare some fresh melon for us. Would you like that?"

"No, thank you. I think I'll just go to my room and rest for awhile."

"All right. I'll come and find you when it's time to recite prayers at the temple again."

Asenath gave Netchem a wry smile. "More prayers," she mumbled. "I can hardly wait."

"It will get better," Netchem assured her. "We're only in training. We'll be given more interesting things to do once we're full-fledged priestesses."

"Of course," Asenath said. "It can only get better."

Netchem, missing the deeper meaning of what Asenath had just said, gave another smile then hurried away, leaving Asenath alone with her troubled thoughts and emotions.

It would be nice to have at least one friend here in Avaris. She knew her father had warned her not to trust these people, but it couldn't hurt to befriend another girl her own age. Perhaps it would take away some of the loneliness if she had someone to confide in and entrust with the secrets of her soul. At any rate, whether or not she was friends with Netchem, her father would never know.

Asenath paused for a moment as she reentered the cool interior of the house, and she let her eyes idly wander over a mural that decorated one of the walls. It was a vivid, colorful scene showing Seth as he benevolently restrained a desert storm, protecting his Hyksos worshipers from its wrath. Should she put her heart into the worship of this Hyksos god as Netchem and her family did? Or was it a betrayal of her father and all that he wished for to do this?

Slowly, she turned away and put her hands to her head. It was such a difficult thing to live among a people who recognized so many different gods. How was such a young girl as her to know which god she should love and serve? Her father, on one hand, claimed that Ra was the greatest of all the gods. The Pharaoh and the family of Setmosis worshiped Seth. But Asenath's own heart gave her no clear answer as to which god or goddess she should serve.

For now, it seemed, it would be best to serve Seth. She would learn his prayers and practice his rites. Yet, even as she thought this, something deep inside her heart told her there was a God other than Seth who watched over her. Perhaps one day this God would reveal Himself to her. Perhaps then she would understand what her destiny was meant to be. Until that time, she could only wait. She was helpless to do anything more than that.

"Where is he!" Reuben demanded. His face was ashen and his eyes were wild with distress. "You were supposed to leave him in the pit! You weren't supposed to kill him! Joseph is dead, and now where am I supposed to go? Father will banish me from his presence when he finds that I left Joseph in your hands to be killed!"

"Calm down, Reuben," Judah commanded. "He's not dead. Killing him would have profited us nothing. But we found a way to get rid of him and make some money in the process." While Reuben stared at him in bewilderment, Judah removed a small, leather pouch from his belt and motioned for Reuben to hold out one of his hands. As soon as he did, Judah poured a small pile of silver coins onto his open palm.

"We sold him to a traveling group of Midianites," Judah said, grinning as if he were pleased with himself. "Are you going to enjoy your share of the silver now, or are you going to wait until you're done grieving?" There was a slight tone of sarcasm in his voice, but Reuben was still too bewildered to be angered by it.

"What are you saying? You're telling me that you sold him? You sold our own brother?"

"Yes, we sold him. Sold him to a caravan traveling to Egypt. And I suppose they'll sell him to some rich Egyptian once they get there. At any rate, we'll never have to worry about the King of Dreams again."

"How is this any better than if you had actually killed him?" Reuben demanded. "Either way, he's gone; and Father will suspect that we had something to do with it."

"The old man won't suspect a thing," Judah replied, dismissing Reuben's fears with an unconcerned wave of his hand. "We've already figured out how to handle this. If nobody tells him what really happened, Father will think Joseph is dead, and he won't blame any of us for it."

"And how do you expect to keep this from him?"

"We still have Joseph's coat," Simeon said. He was standing a short distance away; and, with a grin, he held up the coat for Reuben to see. It was ripped and mangled—reminders of the brief but fierce struggle before Joseph was thrown into the pit—but it was still intact enough to clearly identify what it was. "A few more rips, a little blood, and what do you think Father's first thoughts will be when he sees it?" Simeon continued.

"He'll believe that we killed Joseph!" Reuben exclaimed. "He'll blame us for what happened!"

"Issachar and Zebulun will take the coat ahead of the rest of us," Judah said, his patience with Reuben clearly beginning to run out. "The two of them will tell Father that they found it on their way home. They'll act worried and ask him if it's Joseph's coat. There are wild animals out there. One of them must have pounced on Joseph and killed him. Do you understand now?"

"I don't know," Reuben said, shaking his head. "It might work. But—"

"It *will* work," Judah insisted. "Father will be so grief stricken, he won't suspect a thing."

"And what if one of us decides to tell him the truth?" Reuben demanded. "What if someone tries to use the truth to get in Father's good graces?"

"I'll personally slit the throat of anyone who tries it," Judah said. His eyes burned like angry, red coals as he fastened them on each person, one brother at a time; and Reuben shivered a little. As he looked into those eyes, he had no doubt that Judah really would follow through on his threat.

"Dan . . . Naphtali . . . ," Judah said after he had allowed several moments of silence to pass by so that his words could sink in. "Go kill one of the kid goats. Smear its blood on the coat and make it look like something vicious attacked the person who was wearing it."

"I guess that leaves just one last thing, doesn't it," Simeon said.

"And what is that?" Judah asked.

"Dinner. What will it be? A feast of *goat* perhaps?"

Everyone laughed. Everyone but Reuben. He had the odd feeling that the events of this night were going to come back to haunt him. No. Not just him. To haunt them all! But there was nothing he could do now to change it. Nothing at all.

EIGHT

THE MARKET PLACE OF AVARIS was a confusing milieu
of activity unlike anything Joseph had ever before witnessed. Everywhere he turned there was activity and noise. His great-grandfather,
Abraham, had sojourned in this land; and Joseph had heard many
second and third-hand accounts about it. But nothing could have
adequately prepared him for the mind-boggling reality of the experience. He almost forgot that he had been brought here against his will
until a sharp cuff to the side of his head reminded him of that harsh
fact.

"You aren't here to view the sights!" Ishdaah barked at him. "Get
that camel unpacked. I have goods that need to be sold!"

One of those "goods," Joseph realized, was himself; but he did as
commanded and carried the merchandise to the pavilion of his Ishmaelite masters. He quickly unloaded bags of spices from Asia; sacks
of myrrh, nuggets of dark gum-resin that were the rarest and most
costly of all incenses; and containers of balm, a highly coveted product from Gilead. When the task was done, he slumped tiredly against
a wooden pole hoping for a moment of rest. But Ishdaah would have
none of that.

"What do you think you're doing, boy! You're not going to loll
around here all day. It's time to collect on my investment. Come with
me."

The big Ishmaelite grabbed Joseph roughly by the arm and jerked him into an upright position. Now that his shackles were removed, it would have been easy enough for Joseph to fight his way free from his surly captor. But one glance at the flashing swords of the other Ishmaelites convinced him of the folly of that course. For now, at least, he would have to endure the abuses with patience. God would provide an avenue of escape when the time was right. He desperately tried to hold faith in this thought.

Once again Joseph's hands were bound, this time with a braided rope of camel's hair; then Ishdaah led him through the crowded street like a goat on a tether. In the same humiliating manner that his brothers had brought him before the Ishmaelites, Ishdaah now dragged him along to the slave market. A large crowd had assembled there, and Joseph, who was tall for his age, peered over the heads of the spectators to catch a glimpse of what awaited him. What he saw didn't make him feel any better about his situation.

The crowd was standing in a semicircle around a large, stone block where a wretched man stood on display. His head was hanging so that his chin rested against his chest, and two men with spears—one on each side of him—made sure he didn't move from the spot. A fourth man—a vile, greasy little fellow—stood in front of the block. He was speaking to the crowd in rapid, eager Egyptian, gesticulating with his hands at the unhappy man behind him.

Joseph watched with morbid fascination as the auctioneer stirred up the crowd in a poorly concealed attempt to get bids. But he wasn't allowed to watch long. Ishdaah, suddenly noticing that he'd slowed, gave the rope a sudden, vicious yank that nearly sent Joseph sprawling to the ground.

The fibers of the rope cut painfully into the flesh around his wrists, but he wasn't about to give Ishdaah the satisfaction of hearing him cry out in pain. He bit back an unwanted yelp, and marched behind his Ishmaelite master in the most dignified manner possible to him under such clearly undignified circumstances.

"Stand over here!" Ishdaah snarled, as they came to a line of very unhappy looking slaves. "Hopefully, it won't be long now before you find yourself with a new master."

Without bothering to see if Joseph did as told, Ishdaah stalked over to a small table where a scribe was writing something on a scroll. The two spoke with each other for several moments, Ishdaah pointed at Joseph, the scribe nodded, and then Ishdaah walked off to the other side of the slave market.

For the moment, Joseph was free from the harsh treatment of his surly captor; but there was little chance of escaping whatever new fate was about to come. A band of armed soldiers stood near at hand to prevent slaves from fleeing, and there was nothing left for Joseph but to stand in awkward silence while he waited to be sold.

He was the last in a long, straggling line of men, women, and children. A tall, powerfully built Nubian stood directly before him. And a few more steps ahead stood a pale, trembling girl—a fair-skinned, blue-eyed Amorite—whose people inhabited the Shephelah near Joseph's own home in Hebron's rolling hills. He wondered what circumstances had torn these two from their homes and families, and felt an immediate sympathy for their plight. But his own plight currently weighed most heavily on his mind.

He was numb with misery, fear, and despair. He was also confused. How could a simple shepherd boy from Hebron find himself thrust so suddenly and unexpectedly into the heart of an Egyptian slave market? He'd tried to live a righteous life, so what was it that he'd done to offend God and forfeit the blessings and protection of heaven? He tried to understand the meaning of this. He really wanted to have faith and courage. But, at the moment, he felt utterly abandoned by his God.

He wasn't sure how long he waited in line. It seemed a short eternity. The eternity was made even longer by the occasional wealthy Egyptian—frond-waving entourage of servants in tow—who would walk up and down the line, looking over the slaves with a discriminating eye. If the Egyptian liked the look of a certain slave, he might grasp that slave by the chin, turn his or her head from side to side, and walk several times around the slave, nodding his head with approval. This happened to Joseph more than once, and then the potential master would disappear into the crowd, waiting for Joseph's appearance on the auction block.

One of these interested parties was a tall, broad-shouldered man with stern, gray eyes. The armed soldiers who stood watch over slaves seemed to treat this particular man with great deference, and Joseph guessed by this and by the heavy, golden collar covering his shoulders and chest that he was a man of some importance. Unlike the other potential buyers, this man brought with him only one servant instead of many. The waving fronds and fly switches were also noticeably absent. But the master frequently consulted the servant almost as one would speak to an equal. The pair spent several minutes standing off to one side, speaking in low voices; but finally they, too, disappeared into the noisy crowd of buyers.

Joseph was young and strong. Perhaps that was the reason behind the interest in him. But he felt humiliated by this attention rather than pleased. The longer he stood there and the more he was scrutinized, the greater became the sick feeling of despair in the pit of his stomach.

There was no way to know for sure how long he actually waited to receive his humiliating turn on the auction block, but finally his turn came. He didn't fight against it when a spear-toting soldier came to lead him to his fate.

He felt the weight of a hundred or more eyes resting upon him as he stepped up onto the stone pedestal, and the short, greasy man spoke excitedly in words he couldn't understand. For just a moment, he wished he could know exactly what was being said about him, but then he reconsidered that wish. It was degrading enough to understand that he was being bartered over like a cow or a sheep in the marketplace at Hebron. He didn't need to know all the humiliating details of this transaction.

The bidding went on for several minutes, and the auctioneer's voice raised a pitch as the competition over Joseph became more fierce. Joseph was tempted to raise his eyes to see which members of the crowd were so eager to make him their slave, but the shame of it all convinced him to keep his eyes focused on his feet. When this part of the ordeal finally came to its end, he was led to an open area at the other side of the auction block where a grinning Ishdaah waited near a pompous pair of slave market officials. Even though he hadn't looked up to see who finally won the right to purchase him, Joseph wasn't entirely surprised to see the gray-eyed Egyptian and his servant appear from the edge of the crowd.

"You've been a better investment than I ever dreamed you would be," Ishdaah chuckled as one official collected money from Joseph's new master and the other recorded the transaction on a papyrus scroll. "In fact, you may end up being the most profitable part of this journey."

Joseph didn't answer. There was really no appropriate response for a comment like that. His liberty had been taken from him, and he'd now been made the property of another man. What was he supposed to say about it?

Ishdaah quickly collected his earnings off the sale and just as quickly disappeared with it. Joseph waited nervously for the gray-eyed Egyptian to step forward and claim him; but, to his surprise, the master walked off in another direction and the servant approached him.

"Over this way," the servant called out, startling Joseph by speaking to him in his own language. "The master has other business in the city, and I'm to take the two of you back to the estate."

The two of you? He thought he must have heard wrong but then saw the tense, pale face of the Amorite girl who had gone to the auction block a few minutes before him. Her eyes were darting back and forth like the eyes of a frightened animal, and she stayed as close to the servant as she could without actually bumping into him.

"You've been brought here from Canaan, haven't you?" the servant said, coming up to Joseph and placing a friendly hand on his shoulder.

Joseph answered with a slow nod of his head.

"I thought you were." The man grasped the rope that bound Joseph's hands, took a few moments to remove it from his wrists, then cast it to the ground. "I told the master that Canaanites are hard workers," he said, motioning for Joseph to fall in step behind him. "You have been purchased to work for me in the master's stables. And you'll be glad you now belong to Potiphar rather than any of those other men who were bidding on you today. Potiphar is a just master. If you work hard, he'll treat you well and you'll have a good life on his estate."

"You speak my language," Joseph mumbled, realizing suddenly that he understood everything which was being said to him. "How do you know my language?" Perhaps it wasn't the most appropriate question for a newly acquired slave to ask, but the man just smiled and laughed.

"Before Potiphar hired me to work on his estate," he said, "I was a *suten hemu*—a royal workman—who supervised a crew of Canaanite slaves. The slaves taught me their language, and I taught them mine. You won't find many people here who can speak with you in your own tongue, but that soon won't matter. Eventually you'll learn enough Egyptian to get along."

Joseph nodded. But secretly he hoped the Lord wouldn't leave him here long enough for that to be necessary.

"My name is Pekhti," Joseph's guide said as he led Joseph and the Amorite girl from the market to one of the surrounding streets. "This . . . " He paused to nod toward the girl. " . . . is Ketra. She comes from Lachish in your land. Since you'll be working with me in the master's stables and she'll be a maidservant in the house, you probably won't see much of each other. But, when you do, you'll each have someone you can converse with in your own language."

Ketra smiled timidly at Joseph, but she quickly lowered her eyes again to stare at her moving feet.

"Do you have any experience caring for horses?" Pekhti asked, turning his attention once more to Joseph.

"My family raises cows, goats, sheep, and camels," Joseph replied. "But I don't know much about horses."

"No matter," the man replied, smiling in a good-natured way. "As long as you know how to work, I can quickly teach you everything you'll need to know. I'll show the two of you your places in the slaves' quarters, and then I'll take you to the stables . . . " He nodded at Joseph.

" . . . and you to the house." He turned now to nod at Ketra. "The transition will be easier for both of you if you jump right into your work."

The man spoke easily to them as if it was a commonplace thing for him to lead two humans who'd just been sold into slavery to their permanent place of bondage. Joseph became suddenly aware of how easy it would be to dart away down a side street and take his chances at regaining his freedom. But somehow he couldn't do that to a man who seemed to trust that he wouldn't. Instead he followed obediently and listened as Pekhti began to speak with pride about the excellence of Potiphar's horses, the quality of his chariots, and the joys of working for such a great and generous man. Joseph only listened to half of what Pekhti said—it was hard to concentrate on pleasant conversation when his heart was in turmoil and a leaden despair was sitting heavily in the pit of his stomach—but he gave the man his complete attention once they came within sight of Potiphar's house.

"Welcome to your new home," Pekhti said. "Potiphar's estate is the large property, next to Pharaoh's prison, and Pharaoh's palace is the complex of buildings you see just beyond that."

The palace complex was enormous. But the home of Joseph's new master was far from insignificant itself. In fact, if not for its near proximity to the palace, Joseph might have mistaken Potiphar's home for the palace of a king. Whatever it was Potiphar did for Pharaoh, it had obviously made him a very wealthy and highly favored man.

"The slaves' quarters are at the rear of the building," Pekhti said, once they had arrived at the property and passed through the outer wall surrounding it. "We'll go there first. But let me explain a few rules to each of you, because it will be important to know what the master and the mistress expect. One thing, of course, is that you never try to escape. Potiphar requires an oath from each of his slaves that they won't do it. In return, he will treat you with fairness and kindness, but the consequences will be severe if you break your oath. Do each of you swear not to flee from your service to your new master?"

Ketra timidly nodded, but Joseph hesitated. A life of slavery was something he'd never anticipated. He had been taken against his will from his home and his land, and he didn't at all like the feeling of being the property of another person. An oath was a solemn promise that could never be broken, and to swear one now would be to bind himself with invisible chains stronger than any physical ones his new master could ever place upon him. He didn't want to make this oath.

"You'll never make it across the desert alive," Pekhti said, seeming to read Joseph's mind. "That alone would make fleeing an act of foolishness. But the master is also the captain of Pharaoh's guard— the chief of the executioners—and if the desert doesn't destroy you, Potiphar will."

Joseph pondered his limited options then wearily nodded his head. "I give you my solemn word," he said. "I will not attempt to escape." Now he truly was a slave. Only God could release him from this oath. Only God could save him now.

"You've made the only wise choice you could make," Pekhti said, warmly thumping a broad hand against Joseph's back. "And you'll find that your life here will be more pleasant than you might think. Potiphar gives his slaves a certain amount of freedom that other master's don't give. But he expects your loyalty in return. I sense that you're a young man of honor. You'll do well in the household of Potiphar."

Joseph nodded, but he was filled with despair. He knew he had to trust in God and make the most of whatever circumstances God chose to place him in, but he still didn't understand why all of this was happening to him.

Things weren't supposed to happen this way when you were striving to live a righteous life. Where was God's justice and mercy now that he needed it? None of this made any sense at all.

Asenath rubbed the sleep from her eyes, stretched, yawned, then reluctantly got out of bed. It grew harder and harder to force herself up each morning. Not because she was so tired, but because she had so little to wake up to. Sleep was her only escape from the mundane life Pharaoh had sentenced her to; and, even in her deepest sleep, she often found her dreams invaded by visions of Seth and his accursed temple.

But the dreams of the past few nights had been different. Actually, it was only one dream, and it kept repeating itself. Every Egyptian priest and priestess knew that repeating dreams foretold the future or conveyed important messages from the gods to their servants. She sensed symbolism in this particular dream—she remembered oxen, heads of wheat, and the Nile—but she had no idea what any of it meant.

Perhaps Setmosis would know. He was chief priest of the temple and one of those who Pharaoh consulted whenever he received a dream or omen from the unseen world. But she wasn't keen on the idea of sharing something so personal with the man who served as her chief captor.

While these thoughts passed through her head, Asenath dressed, lined her eyes with *kohl,* then carefully combed out her long, black hair. She stayed alone in her room until it was time to meet Netchem to make their daily trip from the house to the temple complex.

"You didn't come to have breakfast with me this morning," Netchem said, a hint of concern in her voice as they crossed the street together. "Are you not feeling well?"

"I'm fine. I just wasn't hungry."

"You're never hungry. You're going to waste away and die if you don't start eating more."

"Is death such a bad thing?"

She didn't really mean what she said. She only wanted to escape Avaris, not life itself. But it left her mouth before she could stop herself, and she saw Netchem's eyes darken with worry.

"My father is going to let us start carrying the incense for the sacrifices," Netchem said. Her voice was filled with a false, hollow cheerfulness, but Asenath could see that her words had disturbed her friend. "That ought to be more exciting than memorizing and reciting prayers, don't you think?"

"Yes. I'm sure it will be."

She had no desire to drag Netchem down into the black gloom that enshrouded her own life, but this morning for some reason Asenath just couldn't seem to force a false smile to her lips. Misery had her in its iron grip, and she no longer had power to break free.

What good did it do her to feign happiness when the light of joy had been utterly extinguished from her life? Let misery have free reign over her. Today she just didn't care.

NINE

"WE HAVE SERVANTS TO DO THAT."

Ari looked up from her work and smiled. She was in the corner of the courtyard that served as the household kitchen, crouched next to a large bowl, and slicing onions into it. A three-legged table stood next to the kitchen's cone-shaped, clay oven; but that was used mainly for cutting fish and other meat. So, like most other Egyptian women, she usually prepared the family's food while sitting or crouching on the floor. This was how her mother had taught her to do it. This is how it had been done for centuries. But it always seemed to bother Setmosis to see her doing it.

"I like to cook," she said, explaining it to him like she'd already explained a thousand times before. "My mother cooked for my family. I choose to do it for ours."

"But your mother didn't have a small army of slaves to do it for her. I don't know why I pay for kitchen servants when you try to do all the work yourself. If you won't let me get rid of some of them, I wish you'd at least let me purchase a slave. A slave doesn't get paid a daily wage to sit around and do practically nothing."

"Our servants don't sit around and do nothing," Ari replied, laughing and shaking her head. "There's plenty of other work in this enormous house to keep them busy. And I do use them in the kitchen sometimes. At least twice a month you bring in some priest or dignitary to enjoy the hospitality of our table. I need skilled cooks here to help me with that. Besides, you already know how I feel about taking someone's liberty away to make them a slave . . . " She allowed her voice to trail off and gave her husband a meaningful glance.

"You're the wife of the chief priest of Seth," Setmosis said. "A woman of your status shouldn't be doing menial labor in the kitchen. What if someone important showed up unexpectedly at the house and found you cooking or cleaning or—"

"Would you rather that I become one of those mindless, idle wives like the women most of your priests are married to?" Ari asked, setting aside the knife she had just been using. "I'm sure I'd go mad with boredom if I lounged around my home, all day the way they do in theirs. Allow me to oversee the affairs of my home and you see to the affairs of your temple. I know what's best here just like you think you know what's best there."

Setmosis shook his head and tried to look irritated, but she knew he was actually amused. She hadn't been raised in the home of a priest or a high official the way most wives of the priestly class were. She was the daughter of a simple stone cutter and a living example of the independence enjoyed by Egyptian women. That independent nature was part of what Setmosis had fallen in love with, and she wasn't about to change it.

"Fine," he finally muttered. "Keep your servants and do all of the work yourself. See if I care. But don't complain if I begin to enjoy your cooking too much and one day refuse to let you retire from the task."

Ari smiled, picked up the knife again, and resumed her interrupted task. Setmosis leaned against the unlit oven and watched her.

"How is Asenath adjusting at the temple?" she asked after he had stood there a few moments in silence.

"The girl seems to be learning her duties well. And she and Netchem have become fast friends. They don't have to be supervised much. They're both very dependable."

"Is she happy?"

"Netchem? Or Asenath?"

"You know which one I'm asking about."

"Does Asenath have reason not to be?"

Ari stopped what she was doing and turned her head to scowl at him. He tried to act as if he didn't notice the disapproving look on her face.

"Besides the fact that she can't return to be with her family, she seems to be adjusting quite well," he said. "I would send her home myself if I could, but Pharaoh doesn't seem inclined to change any of his plans for her future. It's been two months already, and he's content to leave things as they are. She'll have to endure the separation from her family the best that she can."

"It's an evil thing that he's doing," Ari said, shaking her head angrily. "It can only lead to sorrow and disaster. If his actions don't anger Seth, they will surely anger Ra. Either way, it will lead to misfortune for the pharaoh."

"Pharaoh is a god himself. I don't think he's concerned about angering the other gods."

"He should be concerned! His conscience should sear his soul for what he's doing to an innocent girl! This is hurting her more than it's punishing her father. I'm sure that Potipherah suffers from the lack of his daughter—and I can't imagine what his poor wife must be going through—but it isn't going to change Potipherah one way or another. Asenath is suffering. And her suffering is beginning to trouble our own daughter as well."

"Why? Is there something going on that I don't know about?"

Ari paused, unsure if she should tell him what Netchem had told her just a few days earlier. He was a strict man when it came to observing the traditions of the gods, and she wasn't so sure he would be as understanding about a young girl's confusion as she was.

"Asenath has doubts," she finally said.

"Doubts? Doubts about what?"

"About the gods. And about her place in society."

"Doubts about the gods? That's absurd! I'll talk to the girl about this. Someone has to set her straight."

"That someone isn't going to be you."

"What do you mean it's not going to be me? Pharaoh has charged me with keeping watch over the girl and her welfare. It's my duty to set her straight!"

Ari gathered the bowl of onions into her arms and got slowly to her feet. She set the bowl on the table then turned boldly to face her angry husband. Setmosis was a great and powerful priest, and he struck fear into the hearts of most other men and women. But he was just a man to her. She had no trouble defying him when such a thing became necessary.

"Asenath has been yanked from her home, thrust into the service of Seth, and told that she has no say in her future destiny," Ari said. "*Any* girl would be confused and upset if that had happened to her. The last thing this girl needs is for an irate priest to come storming up to her to command her to repent and bow herself down to the will of the gods. It's been two months now, and she's said nothing more about it. I'm certain she'll find a way to come to terms with her feelings if she hasn't already."

"What exactly did she say to Netchem? Doesn't she know she could bring the wrath of the gods down upon herself and upon our household?"

"If it will make you feel better," Ari said, not answering his question, "I'll talk with her about it. But you're to stay out of this matter. Is that understood?"

"Sometimes I wonder who the true lord of this house is," Setmosis muttered, shaking his head in frustration. "It annoys me that you always know everything before I do. I'm supposed to be a seer and yet I can't see what's going on right beneath my own nose."

"Sometimes the things closest to us are the hardest things to see," Ari said. "You should have learned that by now after raising two daughters of your own. And now the gods have seen fit to give you a third. Perhaps you didn't learn the lesson well enough with only the two."

"Why cannot the gods send me boys!" Setmosis lamented. "They're so much easier to understand than girls. So much more predictable!"

"That's the very reason why you didn't get sons," Ari said. "It's because you need to learn patience. The gods are trying unsuccessfully to teach it to you."

"Then I pray they give me added strength to go through with this trial," Setmosis replied, "because I sense that it's going to be a long one."

"We'll all need strength and patience. Asenath most of all."

At this point, their conversation had to come to an abrupt end. Netchem and Asenath appeared unexpectedly at the far end of the courtyard, and Ari quickly put a cautioning finger across her lips.

"Are the afternoon libations already completed?" Setmosis asked, a strained smile on his lips.

"Yes," Netchem replied with a weary smile of her own. "The great god has received his food and drink. Now we've come home to receive ours."

"I'll have a meal prepared in a few minutes," Ari said. "It's a beautiful day, so I think we'll all dine in the garden."

"I think I'll rest until it's ready then," Netchem said, stretching both arms above her head and yawning. She turned to leave, and Asenath began to follow; but Ari spoke quickly before Asenath could go.

"Asenath, has your mother taught you much about preparing meals?"

"No," Asenath replied. "We had servants to do that."

"So do we," Setmosis said, rolling his eyes. "But my lovely wife chooses to do it all herself."

"Every person who puts food in his or her mouth should know at least a little about preparing it," Ari said. "Will you stay for a minute and help me, Asenath?"

Asenath glanced uncertainly at Netchem, and Netchem walked back to join her. It wasn't exactly what Ari wanted.

"I'm not all that tired," Netchem said. "I can stay and help, too, if you want."

"No. You go and rest. Asenath's help will be enough."

Netchem looked again at Asenath, saw that her friend was uncomfortable with this, and opened her mouth again to speak. But Ari give her a quick glance along with a subtle tilting of the head toward the door, and Netchem seemed to finally get the unspoken message.

"Mother's the best cook in all of Egypt," Netchem said. "You'll like learning from her. I think I'll go and rest after all. I'll meet you in the garden later." She gave Asenath an encouraging smile and quickly exited the courtyard. Setmosis, realizing now what was going on, wasn't far behind.

"I have some business of my own to attend to," he said. "Send one of the servants for me when it's time to eat."

The moment the others were gone, Ari turned to Asenath, speaking as casually as possible. "Can you reach that copper bowl on the top shelf, dear? I'm going to need it for the last course of this meal."

Asenath nodded and retrieved the large bowl. Now came the tricky part. Ari knew what the two of them had to discuss, but she didn't want to alienate her foster daughter in the process. Asenath was in a difficult enough situation as it was and didn't need Ari adding to it. But something had to be said to her. Something had to be done. With her own mother absent, Asenath needed another woman to fill that role. Ari could only hope that the gods would show her the way.

"He's been like this for weeks now," Reuben said. His face was dark, and his voice was filled with nervous agitation. "Someone has to tell him what *really* happened to Joseph. Even Mother and Benjamin can't comfort him. This is going to put him in his grave unless someone tells him Joseph is still alive."

"Nobody's going to tell him anything," Judah said. "We've already been over this a million times before, Reuben. Just keep your mouth shut and everything will be fine."

"Fine? Everything will be fine? He's been grieving for two months!" Reuben exclaimed. "He's still wearing sackcloth and covering himself in ashes! I don't care if you do try to kill me, Judah. I'm going to tell him! I'm going to tell him exactly what you and the others did!"

"Lower your voice!" Judah hissed. "Someone is going to hear you, and you'd better consider the consequences before you let that happen."

"I already told you," Reuben said, his lower jaw jutting out in stubborn defiance. "I don't care how you threaten me. The truth has to be told."

"The truth? And what exactly is the truth, Reuben?"

"Why are you asking *me* that question? You have a conscience, don't you? Or wasn't it working when you and the others decided to kill Joseph? He'd be dead right now if it weren't for me."

Judah burst into sudden laughter, and Reuben stared at him in surprise. But he only stared for a moment. His surprise quickly turned to annoyance, and that rapidly became anger.

"Don't laugh at me," he growled, placing one hand threateningly on the hilt of his sword. "I'm going to be the only one laughing once Father finally learns the truth."

"Yes, Reuben. You're a real hero, aren't you? Father will be so happy when he finds out that Joseph is still alive that he'll probably give the birthright back to you. At least that's what you're hoping for, isn't it? You thought it would happen anyway once Joseph was out of the picture. That's why you didn't say anything before now. But not even Benjamin has received it. So you're going to make one last attempt to win back Father's favor."

"When he finds out that Joseph isn't really dead, my personal motives will be the last thing on his mind," Reuben said.

"Wake up!" Judah snapped. The smile on his face suddenly twisted into a cold, angry snarl, and his eyes drilled holes through Reuben. "You had more to gain by Joseph's disappearance than any of us. You've resented Joseph from the moment he received your birthright, and Father knows that."

"So? What is this elusive point that you're trying to make, Judah?"

"If anyone had a motive to kill Joseph, it was you. If anyone had a motive to sell him to a passing caravan, it was you. It's going to seem very strange to Father that you said nothing for two months and then suddenly come to him proclaiming that you did your best to keep Joseph alive. It will seem even more strange when the rest of us deny knowing anything about it and put the idea into Father's mind that perhaps you were the one who killed him and that you left Joseph's coat where you knew we would find it. Are you ready to answer all the hard questions Father will undoubtedly have for you then?"

"That's not what happened! He'll know you're lying. You . . . you wouldn't!"

"No?" Judah raised his eyebrows questioningly and an evil smile spread across his lips.

Reuben stared at the dry earth now, and his mind sought desperately for an answer to Judah's threat. Behind him, the leaves of a tree rustled in a hot breeze, and the plaintive baaing of a sheep disturbed the temporary silence. But no sound escaped Reuben's throat. He had no response for this, because Judah was absolutely right. If he spoke up, he would look guiltier than any of them and would probably end up paying the penalty for all.

"So what do we do?" he finally grumbled.

"Wait," Judah replied. He plucked a long blade of grass from the ground, put it in the corner of his mouth, and chewed on its woody stem. "We simply wait. Father won't live forever. One day he'll die, and then we'll inherit everything he has. And the best part of it all is that there will be one less son to take a share of that inheritance."

Reuben slowly nodded his head. Judah was right. Reuben may not have the birthright back—he would probably never get it back—but he *would* get more inheritance with Joseph out of the way than he would with Joseph here.

"A wild animal must have killed him," Reuben said. "Father's fear was correct. There's no other logical explanation for Joseph's shredded, blood-soaked coat."

"That's right," Judah said, nodding and smiling. "And we'll never see or hear from Joseph again. Will we."

There was confidence in Judah's voice, but Reuben had lingering doubts. What if Joseph unexpectedly showed up at Jacob's tent one day? What if the truth eventually did find a way to reveal itself? He attempted a confident smile of his own, but it felt weak. It reflected his own inner fears and guilt. No matter. He had to remain silent now. Judah had left him with no other choice.

This wasn't his fault. Surely the Lord couldn't blame him for his part in this messy affair.

"What is the name of that new male slave we purchased just a few months ago?" Potiphar said. "The one who works with you with my horses."

"Do you mean Joseph?"

"Yes. That's the one. T'chet has been complaining to me about him, and I want to know what you know about the situation."

Pekhti looked up from the pair of horses he was harnessing to Potiphar's best chariot. There was a half surprised, half confused look on his face.

"I'm not sure what you're talking about, Master. I never knew there was a problem with Joseph. He's the hardest working slave on my crew."

"T'chet has been telling me that this slave, Joseph, is never in his place when the hired servants come to roust the slaves out of their beds in the morning. Where is he so early in the morning? You're his overseer. What is it that he's up to?"

The concerned look on Pekhti's face faded to be replaced by a relieved smile. If he had detected the dangerous hint of anger in his master's voice, he didn't seem worried by it any longer. His voice was pleasant when he answered.

"You don't need to worry about Joseph, Master. The reason he isn't in his bed when the slaves are made to get up in the morning is that he's already here in the stables, working, at that time. He gets here before even I do. He starts his work before the sun even rises."

Potiphar looked skeptically at his chief groom. In all his experience he'd never met a slave—male or female, young or old—who went to work any sooner than he or she was required to do. Even the oldest, most faithful servants didn't get out of their beds early to start work before the rest of the servants.

"I've never met a slave quite like this one," Pekhti said, apparently seeing that Potiphar still wasn't convinced. "He's not afraid of hard work. He's not afraid to bend his back over a task or get his hands a little dirty. I'd rather have one of him than ten of any other slave on this property. He's worth his weight in gold."

"He impresses you that much?" Potiphar said, amused now more than concerned or angry.

"The stalls have never been cleaner. Your horses have never been healthier. My greatest worry about Joseph is that you'll see how well he supervises himself and decide you have no more need of me."

Potiphar laughed. "I don't believe in leaving slaves unsupervised—no matter how self-motivated they are," he said. "Finish preparing my chariot, Pekhti. I think I'll have a look around for myself, and then I'll decide if he's really everything you claim him to be."

Pekhti nodded, and Potiphar made his way into the stables.

Potiphar's stables were more like a palace for horses than a simple structure for sheltering animals. Ornately carved pillars depicting scenes from Egypt's mythology supported the protective stone roof. Each horse had its own individualized stall, and each stall was decorated with vivid murals of generals and kings riding their chariots into glorious battle. When the business of the Pharaoh wasn't keeping Potiphar away, he lavished more of his time and his wealth on his horses than anything else on his property. He spent so much time with them, in fact, that Neferset, his wife, complained that he loved his horses more than he loved her. Perhaps he did spend a little too much time hunting in his chariot in the delta. But it was a necessary release from the stress of his official duties. He'd already commissioned another expensive piece of jewelry for Neferset. That would quiet her for a while once he brought it back from Thebes and presented it to her. He smiled a little as he anticipated the excitement on her face when she received another treasure for her growing collection of trinkets and jewels, then he turned his attention back to the stable around him.

Apparently, Pekhti's glowing report about the new slave was not an exaggeration. The duties of the kingdom had kept Potiphar away from his stables for longer than he would have liked, but nothing had suffered due to his absence. Every harness was in its proper place. The floor tiles and pillars had been scrubbed until they shone. And the horses were groomed to such perfection that their hides sparkled with a healthy, lustrous sheen. Someone who gave meticulous attention to detail was keeping these stables in order—someone who loved and respected animals almost as much as Potiphar himself.

He wasn't quite sure what to do when he came up behind the young, muscular slave who was shoveling manure from a stall, but he was pleased to find one of his slaves working so well even with no overseer in sight. He'd wondered more than once if it was wise to spend so much money when bidding on this Hebrew at the slave market. If Joseph worked like this all the time, it appeared that Potiphar's money had been well spent.

Joseph leaned the wooden shovel against a pillar, straightened his body, and rubbed his lower back with one hand. The upkeep of the stables required a great deal of hard, physical labor. Hard work was nothing new to him, but he drove himself to work harder now than he'd ever worked before. There was a reason behind his increased exertions, and it wasn't entirely because he wanted to please his new master and overseers. He worked so hard because he found it to be the only way to even slightly deaden the inner turmoil and pain he was suffering through. Unfortunately, even hard labor couldn't take his mind entirely away from his troubles.

He missed his family. Especially his father and Benjamin. And the longer he was here, the less likely it seemed that he would ever see them again.

When he was a little boy, Joseph remembered being taught that the Lord could offer him solace and comfort if he approached Him humbly in prayer. All he needed was to have enough faith, and God would provide answers to his problems. It was relatively easy to put his trust and faith in the Lord when a faithful prophet-father was right there beside him to give encouragement, wisdom, and support. But all of that had changed when his brothers sold him into slavery. He was alone now. He had no father here to shield him from the worst of life's problems. All he did have were his own faith and inner-strength; and, at the moment, both seemed woefully inadequate to sustain him.

He loved the Lord. The Lord had watched over him and spared him when his brothers wanted to kill him. He felt a great debt toward God that he could never repay. But he also fought with feelings of neglect and abandonment. Thus far, every prayer he'd offered asking for his freedom had gone entirely unanswered. The more he prayed, the more desperate his prayers became; and the more desperate he grew, the more he experienced the sinking feeling that God had no intention—no immediate intention at least—to grant his pleading wishes.

"You should always accept the Lord's will," his father had taught him. "The Lord only refuses our righteous requests when it's in our best interests for Him to do so." It made logical sense at the time. The Lord, after all, had more wisdom than Joseph did, and who was he—a simple boy—to doubt the judgment of the God of his fathers? But when he was being taught this principle, he wasn't far from his family, languishing alone in the bonds of slavery. How was he supposed to faithfully accept God's will if that meant he was to remain in Egypt, the property of another man?

Conflicting feelings of faith and despair were tearing Joseph apart inside. Prayer had always been a pleasant experience for him in the past, but now it sometimes seemed like a torturous exercise in agony. He wanted comfort. He wanted to be back in Hebron where he belonged. But it apparently wasn't what God wanted for him.

"You seem to be taking very good care of my stables."

Joseph jumped. The voice came from directly behind him, and he whirled in confusion to face a tall, powerfully-built man who wore a gold, sunburst collar about his neck and shoulders. It took only a moment before his mind registered that his work was being observed by Potiphar, the lord of these stables.

"I-I try to complete my duties in a way that will please you," Joseph nervously stammered. "I hope my efforts meet with your approval."

"You're already speaking Egyptian," Potiphar said, lifting his eyebrows in surprise. "I wasn't sure that you'd understand me. Your progress with the language is as remarkable as everything else Pekhti has been telling me about you."

"Pekhti and the other servants are teaching me," Joseph said. "And I practice by speaking to the horses while I work." He could also have mentioned that he prayed silently in Egyptian in an attempt to master the language of his new home. But he quickly decided against that. He had learned early on that his Egyptian masters weren't interested in anything that was a part of his past. As far as most of them were concerned, a slave's history began when he was purchased and ended when he was sold or died. Any information beyond that seemed to make them uncomfortable.

"You speak our language and you know how to care for my animals," Potiphar said. "Do you also know how to handle a chariot?"

"No," Joseph replied. "Pekhti takes care of the chariots himself. I only feed the horses, groom them, and keep the stables clean. Occasionally, I oil harnesses and straps. But Pekhti looks over your chariots."

"Of course . . . of course . . . ," Potiphar murmured as if that made all the sense in the world. I suppose it wouldn't do to have a slave preparing chariots. It would just be providing him with a temptation to try to steal one and escape."

"I would never steal another man's property," Joseph blurted out. He'd spoken before he took the time to think about what he was saying, and he recognized his mistake as a look of displeasure suddenly darkened Potiphar's face. It wasn't the place of a slave to contradict his master. It wasn't acceptable for a slave to be so bold.

"Are you telling me you wouldn't seek to regain your freedom if you thought you had a chance at success?" Potiphar asked.

Joseph paused. He had asked this question to himself a thousand times since coming here, but he always came up with the same answer. "No," he quietly replied. "I made an oath that I wouldn't, and it would displease the God of my fathers if I broke that oath. I will never do anything to displease my God."

Potiphar stared at Joseph as if he were sizing him up, and then he nodded his head. Some of his sudden anger seemed now to fade away. "I'll let you get back to your work," he said. "I'm satisfied with what I'm seeing here. Keep working as you have been, and I'll find some way to reward you for your efforts."

"Thank you," Joseph mumbled, unsure how he should react but filled with a great sense of relief. "I'll do my very best."

Potiphar turned now as if to leave, but he stopped himself before Joseph could reach for the shovel and start cleaning again.

"I'm making a trip to Thebes," he said, "and I'll need a personal valet to watch over and care for my horses while I'm there. If I bring you along, how quickly can you be ready to go?"

"I-I suppose I can be ready as quickly as you want me to be."

"Good. Go to the main house and ask for T'chet. Tell him to provide you with the things you'll need for the journey. And tell him to be quick about it. I'll expect you at my chariot immediately."

Joseph nodded and watched, bewildered, as his master strode away. He had just experienced his first close encounter with Potiphar. Little did he realize that it wouldn't be the last.

"Can you hand me a clove of garlic?"

Asenath looked where Ari was pointing then broke a clove from the bundle of garlic that dangled by a string from the edge of a nearby shelf. It was clear there was more to this than a simple lesson in food preparation. Ari had something on her mind and wanted to speak with Asenath alone. But, whatever this was all about, the charade of helping with dinner had to be played out first.

"Garlic and onions are good for the health," Ari explained, dicing the clove into a bowl of previously chopped onions. "I'm told that the great physician Imhotep often used them in his healing medicines. There's also nothing better for adding a quick dash of flavor to a dish. Will you hand me those greens? We'll mix them in next."

Asenath picked up the leafy vegetables Ari had indicated then waited while her foster mother chopped them and mixed them into the bowl. Several moments passed before Ari spoke to her again.

"It must seem strange to you that I prepare the meals for my family."

"Yes. A little," Asenath admitted.

"I wasn't born into the family of a priest or a royal advisor," Ari explained. "My father was a craftsman—a stonecutter. We didn't have servants to prepare our meals. I suppose I should appreciate the privilege of having servants to do my work for me, but I was taught the value of laboring with your own hands; and I've tried to pass that along to my own two children. The traditions of our families are important. So are the traditions of our people."

Asenath wasn't quite sure where this was all going; but, before she could attempt to figure it out, Ari finished with the salad and pointed again to the shelf.

"Do you see those two clay jars?"

"Yes."

"One is filled with oil and the other with vinegar. Will you get them carefully down and bring them to me?"

Asenath nodded, retrieved the red-hued jars, and stooped down to hand them to Ari. Now more nervous than before, she waited while Ari unstopped the jars and poured a little of each liquid over the simple salad she'd just created.

"Do you ever doubt our religious traditions?"

This question caught Asenath completely off guard, though she probably should have expected it after what Ari said previously.

"I do my religious duties without complaint," Asenath replied, her voice tense and toneless. "I give proper respect to the gods of Egypt."

"I'm sure you do," Ari replied with a calm smile on her lips. "But even the daughter of a high priest can doubt the gods if they seem to have abandoned her. If ever you need someone to talk to . . . if ever things seem too hard . . . always remember that we are here for you. I know our family must seem like a poor substitute for your own, but we've grown to care about you these past few months. And we love you as if you were our own daughter. I'm always here if you need to talk to someone about how you're feeling. Netchem and Setmosis are also here for you."

"Thank you," Asenath said. But she was struggling now to keep the sudden anger which had flared within her from coming through in her voice. Over the past few weeks, she'd started to care about the family of Setmosis, too. She'd disregarded the council of her father and begun to trust them. But she would trust them no more. Netchem had revealed her words from the temple. She'd told her parents what Asenath said about being a priestess and following the gods. Her father was right. She couldn't trust anyone in Avaris.

"I made some bread earlier," Ari said as if the last part of their conversation had never even occurred. "If you'll carry that, we can get all this food to the garden table in only one trip."

Asenath spotted a bronze plate with a triangular shaped loaf of bread on it. It rested near the clay oven, and she grasped the tray with both hands and followed Ari out of the courtyard.

She had a thing or two she wanted to say to Netchem now. But it would have to wait until neither Ari nor Setmosis were around. One thing was certain. She would never share her innermost feelings with another living being. Especially not with Netchem.

Chapter Notes

It is quite possible that stables such as those described in this chapter could have existed on the estate of a wealthy Egyptian like Potiphar. In Egypt, ownership of horses and chariots was an important symbol of both status and power, and the captain of Pharaoh's guard would have had both. The writings of one scribe report that a chariot was worth about 8 *deben* of silver—a small fortune that usually only a nobleman or some other personage of great importance could afford. An ancient stable at Pi-Ramesse which is thought to have belonged to Ramses provides an example of what an Egyptian stable may have looked like. Ramses' massive stables covered an area of nearly 17,000 square meters and contained rows of halls with stalls. The halls were connected to a vast courtyard, and the floors were sloped for collecting horse urine. The collected urine was most likely used for softening leather, dyeing cloth, or fertilizing vineyards. If Potiphar did own stables, Joseph could have been occupied in them with a large variety of tasks.

TEN

JOSEPH STOOD QUIETLY BESIDE THE CHARIOT and held the horses' reigns while Potiphar spoke with his wife at the threshold of the house. She was staring over his shoulder, a faint smile playing across her lips, and it made Joseph nervous the way she kept making eye contact with him. Perhaps he was the topic of their conversation, but he still didn't like the way she watched him.

He was puzzled and nervous about this unexpected assignment. He was nervous about being under close and careful scrutiny all the way to Thebes and back. There was also a fear within him that his father might somehow find out he was in Avaris, come searching for him, and not find him when he arrived. Common sense told Joseph that he was lost to his family forever, but his heart couldn't help but hope.

He wasn't the only one who had tense feelings about this, although Pekhti's worries were based on entirely different fears.

"The master is going to take you permanently away from the stables," Pekhti said, "and I'll lose the best worker that I have. I know it's about to happen. He's seen how hard you work, and now he's going to make you his personal manservant or give you some other important task."

"What task is more important than caring for his horses?" Joseph asked. "You know he loves them more than anything. He'll leave me here. He's already told me he's pleased with my work in the stables. I'm sure you have nothing to worry about."

"No," Pekhti insisted, shaking his head. "I don't know exactly what he's planning, but he has something else in mind for you or he wouldn't be taking you with him to Thebes. It's a test, Joseph. And if you pass his test, you'll be moved to a better job. Mark my words. Changes are about to happen. You won't be working in these stables much longer."

To Joseph this wasn't actually a comforting thought. He'd grown used to the stables. They were his refuge from this strange and frightening world, and a part of him hoped that Pekhti's predictions would not come to pass.

"I'm just a slave," he said, trying to convince himself as much as to convince Pekhti of it. "You're worrying over nothing. I'll be back shoveling in the stalls the moment I return."

Pekhti's only reply to this was a mournful shake of his head.

It was only natural to wonder what Potiphar's true intentions were. Even to one as new to Egypt as Joseph, it was obvious that these were unusual circumstances. The suspicious stares of the chief steward only served to confirm that observation. A responsibility like this should be reserved for a trusted servant like Pekhti or T'chet. This was still bothering Joseph when Potiphar gave his wife a quick, farewell kiss and strode swiftly back to the chariot.

"Have you ever traveled by chariot before?"

Joseph shook his head.

"Climb up next to me," Potiphar said, taking the reigns from Joseph's hands. "Hold onto something solid and hold onto it tight."

Joseph stepped onto the sycamore footboard, moved forward, and curled his fingers around the bronze, shield-like piece that curved around the front of the chariot. He realized a moment later why he'd been instructed to grasp something solid. Potiphar's whip cracked over the backs of the horses, the chariot lurched forward, and Joseph swayed and nearly lost his footing.

His first sensation was one of sickening dizziness. It started at the top of his head and quickly spread down into the pit of his stomach. But once he adjusted to the motion, something entirely unexpected happened. This was nothing like riding on a camel or a donkey. This was like riding the crest of a wave or sailing across the sky on a billowing gust of wind. There was something exciting about the feel of the air rushing past his face, about the spokes of the wheels spinning into a blur beside him, and about the thunder of the horses' hooves as their staccato beat echoed in his ears. He had never experienced anything quite as exhilarating as this, and he doubted that he ever would again.

Potiphar smiled when he noticed the grin on Joseph's face, and Joseph realized it was the first time he'd seen his stern master smile. But the smile soon faded, and Potiphar's voice sounded serious when he spoke.

"We will be accompanying Pharaoh to Thebes for an important official visit," he said. "My job is to serve as his bodyguard while he discusses taxation and tributes with the ruling family of the city. While I'm with him, I expect you to be busy watching over my horses. Protect them with your very life if necessary."

Joseph nodded, but he also wondered at these unusual instructions. Were Potiphar's horses so valuable that someone might try to steal them? Or was there something else about this journey that worried the master?

"These are dangerous times," Potiphar said as if he sensed Joseph's unspoken questions. "There are those who challenge the right of the Hyksos kings to rule over Egypt. The powerful families of Thebes are a particularly great threat to Pharaoh; and, because of this, Khyan will be visiting their city with a great show of force. Most of the royal bodyguard—which I just happen to command—will be present. There will also be over a hundred military chariots in our procession. If violence breaks out at Thebes, my chariot will be needed. I'll be depending on you to protect the horses and keep the chariot in good working order. Has Pekhti taught you the basics of caring for a chariot?"

Joseph nodded. It had been a quick lesson, but he felt confident that he could do everything required of him.

"I know you won't let me down," Potiphar said. "That's why I've brought you with me."

This sounded like a compliment. But another thought occurred to Joseph. He was a slave. He was expendable. If someone was to be lost in bloody conflict, it was better that a slave die than a free man perish. He immediately tried to fight off this negative feeling, and was grateful for the reassuring words Potiphar spoke next.

"I'm not expecting any real trouble," Potiphar said, "but I wouldn't be where I am today if I hadn't learned to be cautious. That's why I'm warning you about these things. It's better to be overly prepared than dead. I'm not yet ready to meet Osiris in the afterworld, and I'm sure you aren't either."

He paused for several long moments then looked Joseph over with a critical eye. It was the kind of look a general might give a soldier just before battle. It was as if he were making a quick calculation about the depth of Joseph's courage and character. Finally, he nodded his head, seeming to be satisfied with what he saw.

"Have you ever used a sword?" he asked.

"Yes," Joseph answered. "But never against another man."

"Could you if your life or the safety of my horses depended on it?"

"I was taught how to defend my father's flocks," Joseph said. "I had to know how to fight in case they were attacked by wild animals or were in danger of being stolen by thieves. I've fought against wild beasts, but usually with a bow and arrow. I've never had to use a sword against men."

"Take this," Potiphar said, drawing a short sword from a metal cylinder attached to the shield-like frame of the chariot. The sword had been nestled amidst a cluster of arrows, and Joseph hadn't noticed it until now. "Keep this sword with you at all times until we return to Avaris. And be constantly alert. From now on, *I* am your father and these horses are your flock."

Joseph nodded, surprised that he was being trusted with a sword. But nothing that had happened today was anything he would ever have expected.

"I wouldn't normally bring a mere slave with me on a matter of such importance," Potiphar said. "To be completely honest, I don't know what possessed me to do it. But something told me I should. Something inside. Perhaps it is the will of the gods. At any rate, I will have to teach you how to handle this chariot before we reach Thebes. What do you know about them other than the few things Pekhti instructed you in today?"

Joseph knew that chariots with four spokes on each wheel were used only as carriages. Those with six spokes were made for battle. Beyond that, he knew relatively little.

"Not much," he sheepishly admitted. If this was the test Pekhti had mentioned to him, he was failing it miserably. But Potiphar just smiled and patted the rim of his chariot with pride.

"The chariot is what made the Hyksos people great," Potiphar said. "When my ancestors first crossed into Egypt, it was their skill with horses and chariots that gave them the mastery over the land."

Joseph breathed a quiet sigh of relief. This wasn't a test. Potiphar just wanted to tell him about the two things he loved most—chariots and horses—and Joseph listened with interest as he spoke.

"In battle," Potiphar continued, "a chariot is manned by two soldiers—a driver and a bowman. Together, they make a formidable opponent. Naturally, they aren't invincible—a chariot can be overturned, leaving its occupants at the mercy of the enemy. But my ancestors even thought of that when they designed their war chariots. You notice that the back of the chariot is open . . . "

Joseph glanced behind himself and nodded.

"If the chariot begins to overturn, your best chance to survive the experience is to jump off the back before it rolls on top of you. In a battle, you'd do this first then cut the horses free from their harnesses and ride one of them away to safety."

"Have you ever used a chariot in battle?"

Potiphar's face grew momentarily grim. He eventually nodded and said, "As I've already told you, these are dangerous times. Khyan has put down several rebellions already. If all goes well on this journey, we'll avoid having to fight yet another."

They were approaching the palace of Pharaoh now, and Potiphar forgot conversation as he guided the chariot onto a broad, monument-lined boulevard that looked wide enough to accommodate at least fifteen chariots rolling side by side. The street cut a wide swath from the outer, defensive walls to the very heart of Avaris; and Joseph could see the royal palace, the administrative center of the Hyksos empire, waiting for them at the end of the boulevard. But it was another sight that filled him with sudden awe. Battle chariots! More than he would have even imagined existed! Even though Potiphar had mentioned the large number that would travel with them in Pharaoh's royal procession, the actual awesome sight of it still caught Joseph off guard.

The chariots were arranged in crisp, orderly formations, and they crouched eagerly before the palace walls. Their burnished bronze hulls were shining in the early morning sunlight. More than a hundred pairs of Pharaoh's finest royal stallions pawed impatiently at the earth—their brave, feathered headdresses fluttering softly in the breeze—and there were soldiers everywhere Joseph looked. They bristled with armor and weapons, and they moved to and fro among the waiting chariots like a swarm of angry ants. This looked more like a frantic preparation for war than the precursor of a peaceful royal visit to a vassal city.

"Impressive, isn't it?" Potiphar said with a grim smile on his face. "This should make the Thebans think carefully about where they will place their loyalty. Even those stubborn, leading families will think twice about opposing Pharaoh."

Joseph nodded. He was too stunned to actually speak.

"Stay with my chariot," Potiphar commanded as they came to the head of the chariot formations. "I must inform Pharaoh of my arrival." He wheeled the chariot quickly into place then dropped the reigns into Joseph's hands. Without even a parting glance, Potiphar disappeared into the milling crowd of charioteers and soldiers.

Joseph felt completely out of place—even more so than usual—and he felt more distanced from his family than he'd felt at any time since his unwilling departure from Canaan. He was being immersed into a totally alien world. He was being swallowed up by it.

Slowly, he stepped down from the footboard and walked to the team of horses at the head of the chariot. He patted each horse gently on the muzzle and paused to scratch one of them between its ears. The horse gratefully rolled its head toward him and whickered with pleasure.

"What do you think?" Joseph asked, whispering in the horse's ear. "Will I ever return to Hebron? Will I ever see my father and my family again?" The horse answered him with another soft whicker, and Joseph allowed a sad smile to cross his lips.

"You're right," he said as if the horse had answered his question. "I can't give up hope. God is merciful, and I have to trust in His wisdom. No matter how bad it seems, it would be much worse if He weren't here guiding and helping me." A warm, calm feeling came over him as he whispered these words. It only lasted a few moments, but it was enough to renew some of his faith. He would see his family again. Whether in this life or the next, he didn't know; but it was all in God's hands and it would work out for the best. He had to believe that. And he had to believe that he would be blessed if he patiently endured to the end. He would give the Lord the best effort he had. It was all he could really do.

From the temple gate, Asenath had a clear view of the procession that was gathering before Pharaoh's palace. She wasn't the only one watching. Many of Avaris' citizens had assembled in the shadows of the monuments to watch the official departure of Khyan. There were smiles on their faces, and their conversation was cheerful. She could see that they took pride in the power and glory of their pharaoh and their city. But Asenath didn't share any of these feelings. There were much darker emotions stirring within her breast.

At heart she was still a daughter of On, and this gathering of Pharaoh's forces brought back unpleasant memories of his fateful visit to her own city. It was a procession like this, albeit a much smaller one, which had come to take her away from her home and family. She furrowed her brows with angry indignation as she remembered Pharaoh's cunning use of his power.

Khyan was now approaching his chariot. His tall, white, helmet-like crown, the cobra uraeus on his forehead, and the false beard on his chin made him stand out from the crowd of soldiers. He was mounting the same chariot he had used for his visit to On. Even at this distance, Asenath recognized the large, blue scarab emblem that ornamented the gold-plated carriage of his chariot. The scarab was made from the coveted stone which Egyptians called *chesbet*—a deep-blue gemstone flecked with golden specks of pyrite. The entire emblem was framed by a Syrian motif of symmetrical date palm fronds. It was a visible symbol of the political, military, and economic power this Hyksos king now wielded.

Unconsciously, Asenath glanced down at the oval shaped amulet which she always wore around her neck. This, too, was carved from *chesbet*; but hers was etched with the cross-like shape of the *ankh*, the Egyptian symbol of life. Her father had purchased it for her when she was little because it reminded him of the penetrating color of her intense, blue eyes. But he might never look into her eyes again, and she might never again look into his. She felt a painful tremor in her heart as she thought of this.

The stone was supposed to be magical. It was supposed to protect its wearer from evil. But it hadn't protected Asenath from Khyan. And the god Ra and the goddess Isis whom she had both once worshiped hadn't protected her from Seth. Angrily, she turned away from the offending sight of Pharaoh and found herself standing suddenly face to face with Setmosis.

"It's an impressive sight, isn't it?" he said.

"Yes," Asenath replied, trying to force a pleasant smile to her lips. "Very."

"You're a part of this, you know. You are Hyksos. This is your heritage."

Asenath nodded, but she bit her tongue and held back her true feelings. Right now she didn't want to be Hyksos. Right now she would rather be anything but that.

"Are you enjoying your temple training?" Setmosis asked. He didn't usually engage her in conversation, and she got the sneaking suspicion that he was probing for a reaction. Maybe Netchem had told him as well as Ari about her dislike for her temple duties.

"It's nothing like I ever imagined it would be," Asenath evasively replied. *There! Try to decipher my thoughts and feelings from that.*

"Everyone has a place in Egyptian society," Setmosis said, staring up at the sky as if he could see something there that she couldn't. "Just like our pyramids, our society has structure and order. The slaves, farmers, and laborers form the base of that pyramid. The next level belongs to the craftsmen. Then there are the scribes, doctors, and so forth up to the very pinnacle of the pyramid—the pharaoh himself. We each have our place, Asenath. We must be content with who we are and where we are. The pyramids would crumble if the stones could remove themselves from their places . . . ."

She knew what he was getting at. She understood the not so subtle message he was sending her. But she kept her face emotionless and merely nodded her head. Setmosis, however, lowered his gaze from the sky and fixed his eyes upon her in a penetrating stare. He wanted more than a nod of the head, and she couldn't withstand the power of his authoritative gaze. In this respect, he was much like her father.

"I have no intention of removing myself from my place," she said, lifting her chin a little and willing herself to look him in the eye. "I am a priestess of Egypt. I will obey the gods, and I will do nothing to bring dishonor upon myself or my family."

Setmosis looked thoughtfully at her then nodded and smiled in a fatherly way. "Just remember to be content in this," he admonished. "One day your heart will be weighed against the feather of truth and justice. If you doubt the gods and their wisdom, your heart will be cast to Ammut to be devoured, and you will lose the great gift of eternal life."

Asenath nodded and held her tongue yet again. It was a struggle to bear chastisement in silence. She was the daughter of a high priest and not used to being disciplined by anyone other than her father. But she saw the necessity of humility in this particular instance, and she suffered it all with the dignity befitting the daughter of the high priest of On.

"You're a fine young woman," Setmosis said, "and you'll make a fine priestess. But you still need time to grow in self-discipline and knowledge. You've been forced to make great sacrifices for one so young, and I understand how difficult that must be. How you deal with what has been placed upon you will determine how high you rise. Seth has smiled upon you. Accept him and he will make you great."

"Thank you," Asenath said, the words leaving a sour taste on her tongue as she spoke them. "I'll do my best."

"That's all that can be expected of you."

He smiled once again, turned, and walked away; and Asenath choked on the anger she had been fighting so hard to hold back. Now she knew why Khyan had put her with the family of Setmosis. It was so that she could be chastised and humiliated. It was so that someone could always be nearby to watch her every move. And Netchem was just a spy of her parents, instructed to befriend Asenath so that she could reveal it to them anytime Asenath started to stray away from the path Pharaoh had set for her.

They could take her from her family. They could take her from her home. They could even force her to work in the despicable temple of Seth. But they could never force her to think or feel the way they wanted her to. She wouldn't allow it! She refused to be Pharaoh's slave.

Chapter Notes

1. *Chesbet* is the ancient Egyptian term for the stone we call "lapis lazuli" or "lazurite." Lapis is a semiprecious stone that is usually a deep, azure blue often flecked with golden particles of pyrite. In ancient times, especially in ancient Egypt and Babylon, it was a highly coveted gemstone. It was associated with deity and royalty because of its rich blue color and was purported to possess magical powers. In some ancient references, it is erroneously referred to as "sapphire." Besides being a favorite jewelry item of priests and royalty, lapis—in its crushed form—was the main ingredient in the ancient pigment "ultramarine." Some Christian traditions claim that this mineral was the fifth stone of Aaron's breastplate.

2. In the religion of ancient Egypt, the principle of *ma'at* was very important. It was believed by the Egyptians that a deceased person's heart would be placed on a scale in the afterlife and weighed against the "feather of *ma'at*" which represented both truth and justice. If the heart of the deceased came up short in the weighing, he or she would suffer a second death by being thrown to a beast called *Ammut*—a fearsome creature with the head of an alligator, mane of a lion, and mismatched body parts of other animals. One of the responsibilities of a priest or priestess was to know the proper spells that would help an Egyptian pass the tests of the afterlife and avoid this awful fate.

ELEVEN

PHARAOH'S RECEPTION IN THEBES was much different from the one Joseph had witnessed at Avaris. There were people lining the streets here, too; but this crowd wasn't nearly as enthusiastic as the one in the Hyksos capital or in the other cities they'd traveled through. It was subdued and unfriendly. Pharaoh didn't hold sway here the way he did in most parts of the Hyksos empire. Joseph had been told that Thebes had its own king, ruling by permission of Khyan so long as the king of Thebes remained allied with the Hyksos. But this alliance seemed tenuous at best.

"You see now why Pharaoh had to come here in such force," Potiphar said, his voice low as he surveyed the watching eyes of the crowd. "You can feel it, can't you? You can feel the resistance. The baronies of this region will revolt in an instant if they think they can overthrow the pharaoh."

Joseph glanced back at the seemingly endless line of chariots behind him. He didn't see any weakness there. It seemed impossible that anyone could overthrow a man who commanded such might as this, and Khyan seemed to feel the same sentiment. Unaffected by this cold reception, he stepped easily from his chariot and strode boldly to the group of Thebans who awaited him at the head of the street. He was a broad-shouldered, well-muscled man, and his presence was as imposing as any monarch's should be. The Thebans, who watched with disdainful eyes as he approached, still shifted nervously when he came near them.

"Khyan, I see you've made your arrival here in safety," the man at the head of the group said—a thin, bald man who Joseph guessed was the city's high priest.

If he noticed the familiar way the man addressed him or the lack of proper title, Pharaoh made no sign of it. Instead, he smiled. But the darkness in his eyes belied the good-natured smile on his lips.

"I hope our welcome in your city will be friendlier than the one we received outside of it," Pharaoh remarked.

"Oh? What happened?"

"You don't know, Menhotep? I thought you knew everything that goes on in this region. I was sure word of the attack on my procession would have reached your ears by now."

"Robbers," Menhotep said, nodding. "I'm sure it must have been robbers. The city has been plagued by them lately."

"Well . . . not to worry, my good friend. It's fortunate for Thebes that I brought so many men of my own with me. Your good city will no longer need to be worried about those *robbers*."

Menhotep's face suddenly became drawn and tense. He tried to hide this sudden change in emotion, but it didn't escape Joseph's notice. And it most certainly didn't escape Pharaoh's.

"You . . . you've captured them? You have them in your custody?" Menhotep asked.

"No."

Some of the arrogance returned to Menhotep's face, but his smugness was short-lived.

"I had the chief of my royal guard execute them," Khyan coldly announced. "Potiphar is remarkably good at such things."

Joseph noticed a nervous twitch start at the corner of Menhotep's mouth, and it took several moments before the high priest of Amun could find his voice to speak. "I see . . . ," he finally mumbled. "Then I suppose you have done our city a great service."

"Don't thank me now," said Khyan, grinning fiercely. "You'll have plenty of time to do that later."

This was a shrewd pharaoh. Joseph had heard as much, but he could see it now. And he could see that Menhotep as well as Pharaoh knew exactly where these "robbers" had come from. But this victory was Pharaoh's. The rebels of Thebes hadn't expected Khyan to arrive with such a large force. They hadn't expected to lose their "robbers" to the swords of his troops.

"Shall we proceed to the great hall?" Pharaoh asked. "I assume that Nebireyeraw is waiting for me there. What's wrong? Was he too busy with matters of state to take a few moments to greet me?"

"The pharaoh of Thebes has been busy preparing a feast in your honor," Menhotep said, adding slight emphasis to the word 'pharaoh.' "But, if you'll follow me, I'll take you right to him."

"My men and horses will first need a place to gather and rest."

"Of course," Menhotep replied. "There's a place by the river where the horses can graze and the men can rest. I'll have my servants lead them to it." Menhotep motioned to two of the men in his delegation, and Pharaoh motioned to Potiphar. Several members of the royal guard moved to Pharaoh's side, but Potiphar hesitated for a moment and turned quickly to Joseph.

"Follow the rest of the chariots to the river," he whispered, handing the reigns to Joseph. "When you're there, have Muteth and Neb watch my horses." He paused to point out the two soldiers he'd just mentioned. "I had plans to take care of some important business of my own today," he continued, "but, judging by everything else that's happened so far, I doubt I'll have time to do it myself." He stopped, paused again, and untied a small, leather pouch that was dangling from his belt. Joseph had a momentary, unpleasant memory of the pouch Judah had emptied into his hands the day Joseph was sold, but he quickly blinked that image away.

Potiphar surveyed him with a concerned frown on his face. "One of the finest goldsmiths in all Egypt lives here in Thebes," he said. "The last time I was here, I commissioned him to make a special piece of jewelry for my wife. These Thebans are slow to accept our leadership but quick to take our money . . . " He stopped and twisted his lips into a wry smile. "This is a bag of turquoise from Pharaoh's Sinai mines." He weighed it in his hand and glanced at Joseph, weighing *him* again as he had already done so many times before. "Take this bag to the market. Find the merchant named Patep and give it to him." He held out the bag, and Joseph hesitantly took it from his hand.

"What's in this bag is worth more than the life of a slave," Potiphar said. "The jewelry is worth even more than that. Do you understand what's expected of you?"

Joseph nodded and carefully tied the bag to his own belt.

"Don't let anyone know that you have that," Potiphar cautioned. "There are those—both with us and against us—who would think nothing of slitting your throat to get it. This is a very important errand. One I wouldn't normally entrust to anyone but myself."

"I understand," Joseph said. Personal integrity was important to him. Even more important than freedom. He would do whatever was required to prove his integrity to the man the Lord had chosen as his master. "I won't fail you," Joseph said. "The jewelry will be here for you when you come for it."

Potiphar didn't respond. There was a trace of doubt in his eyes, but he had no time to reconsider his decision. Pharaoh was casting impatient glances in his direction, and he had to go.

The chariots were now wheeling slowly around, following Menhotep's servants to the river; and Joseph quickly brought Potiphar's chariot into line behind them. He felt the eyes of Thebes weighing heavily upon him; but the calm, life-giving waters of the Nile were peacefully beckoning from the opposite direction.

The monuments and buildings of Thebes were an impressive sight, and the natural beauty which God had bestowed upon this place impressed Joseph even more. Lush, green date palms and bounteous fields of grain clothed the banks of the Nile in a soft, emerald robe. Above them, magnificent, pinkish-red cliffs looked down, crouching along the other side of the river, guarding that approach to the city like a massive, stone sentinel. Where the pink stone of the cliffs and the azure blue of the sky reflected off the water of the river, hippos lounged; and, when they yawned, their mouths gaped wide to reveal the large, tusk-like teeth that convinced the crocodiles to keep their distance. An ibis also waded between tall stalks of papyrus, and a flock of wild geese winged toward the sky. Joseph became so engrossed with the beautiful sight that he nearly rammed the chariot in front of him. Fortunately, he brought Potiphar's chariot to a halt before this happened.

They had arrived at a large, open area along the river. It was a grassy place where the horses could graze and the soldiers could rest. He waited until he saw where Neb and Muteth were going to leave their chariot and then found a place next to them. After he had checked to make sure the horses had plenty of grass for grazing, he left the chariot and horses in the custody of the two soldiers and made his way back into the city.

He didn't attract as much attention alone and on foot, but Joseph still felt an occasional pair of eyes watching him. He looked more like the Hyksos than the Thebans—he was of a similar racial background to Egypt's conquering rulers—but he was also dressed more like a farmer or a slave than a soldier, and this seemed to draw more curious than hostile glances.

He had no idea where the market was located, so Joseph chose to follow a broad, paved street that many people seemed to be traversing. The markets in most cities were located in approximately the same place, so he didn't bother asking directions. That would have just brought more attention to himself—which was the last thing he wanted. The weight of the bag hanging from his belt reminded him of this.

From almost his very infancy, Joseph had been taught not to worship false gods and stone idols, but he seemed constantly to be surrounded by them whenever he ventured out into an Egyptian city. In Avaris, his eyes had been assailed by graven images of Seth which seemed to lurk on every street corner. Here it was rams. Rams leaped on pillars, rams glared down from walls, and ram-headed sphinxes crouched along the street he followed. The ram was the sacred animal of Amun, patron god of Thebes; but it was also a reminder of a different life and a different land. Joseph felt a sudden, wistful yearning for the peaceful hills and valleys of Hebron where he had once cared for his father's flocks.

It wasn't much harder to find Patep than it was to find the market. The goldsmith's pavilion dazzled Joseph's eyes as the sun reflected off a hundred pieces of jewelry and an equal number of miniature figurines. Patep's table was bent under the weight of replicas of Egypt's many gods; and here, too, were more of Amun's sacred rams.

Joseph wondered suddenly why God would command his family not to worship idols yet thrust him into the midst of a nation of idol worshipers. It was hard sometimes to understand the will and purposes of God. It was difficult to accept that a life of slavery would ultimately be for his good. Had he somehow inadvertently sinned? Was he now being punished for it? Or was God just chastening him to make him strong? Whatever the Lord's intentions were, Joseph knew he must bear the trial with patience no matter how much he personally struggled with it. Joseph shrugged his shoulders now as if that might shrug off the unbearable emotional burden of his afflictions and moved carefully toward the treasure-laden table.

The merchant who watched over the golden wares was a bent, thin man with a sparse ring of hair around his bald head. His eyes were dark—almost black—and he stroked the stubble on his chin with greedy anticipation. Joseph saw two men with swords standing almost unnoticed in the shadows of the pavilion and realized that they were here to protect the merchandise. The penalty for theft was severe, but Patep's handiwork offered a tempting target that might be difficult for a would-be thief to resist. Joseph looked again at the table and understood why the merchant might hire guards.

Patep looked Joseph over and frowned. Then his greedy, darting eyes found the bulging pouch on Joseph's belt, and he smiled when he spoke.

"As you can see," Patep said, "I sell only the finest quality of merchandise. Is there something in particular I can interest you in?"

"Yes," Joseph said. He smiled back but watched the merchant guardedly. "I've come for a specific piece of jewelry. Are you the goldsmith named Patep?"

"I am. And I have jewelry. Any kind of jewelry you can think of. All crafted from the finest Nubian gold."

"This isn't for me," Joseph explained. "I was sent here by Potiphar."

"Ah! Potiphar! The famed captain of Khyan's royal guard. Do you have the turquoise?"

"Yes," Joseph said. "May I see the item?" He didn't know why, but he didn't trust this man. He felt like he shouldn't reveal the turquoise until the jewelry was safely in his hands.

"I have Potiphar's jewelry," Patep said. "The finest piece I've ever crafted. But everything I create is the finest ever made. Here. See for yourself." Patep reached behind the seated figurine of a lioness-headed goddess and brought out an object which he placed on the table before Joseph. Joseph picked it up and examined it, aware all the time that the two guards were scrutinizing him with cold eyes.

The small piece of jewelry in his hand was exquisite. Joseph would have recognized this as an object of great value even if he weren't the one carrying the small fortune that was meant to pay for it. It was a golden armband, artful in its simplicity—slender, graceful, feminine. And the glittering emeralds that graced its surface were so carefully placed that they remained almost unnoticed until a ray of sunshine caught on their facets and burst suddenly forth in a brilliant, scintillating display of light. Potiphar's wife must mean a great deal to him. His wife would surely be pleased to receive such a splendid gift.

"It's wonderful," Joseph said, his voice hushed. "I've never seen anything quite like it before."

"Of course you haven't! And you never will again," Patep said. "Everything crafted by my hand is unique. One of a kind." It was obvious that Joseph's compliment pleased the man. But it was also obvious that he was more interested in something besides compliments. His eyes kept drifting to the bag on Joseph's belt, and he began to cough impatiently.

"The payment," Joseph said, nodding. He quickly removed the bag from his belt and spread its contents across the table.

Patep scooped up a handful of the polished stones and allowed them to trickle slowly through his fingers. "Excellent!" he murmured. "Turquoise from Khyan's Sinai mines. It's all here. Just as Potiphar promised. Imagine what I can create with this!"

Joseph dropped the armband into the now empty bag and tied it quickly to his belt. He had the feeling that he should depart as quickly as possible, so he nodded at Patep and backed away from the table. But Patep seemed reluctant to let him leave.

"Be careful with that," Patep said. "There are all kinds of thieves out there who would like nothing better than to get their hands on such a valuable item. I would hate to hear that you were found in the desert with your throat slit open."

"I'll be careful," Joseph replied. "Thank you for your concern."

"You're not Hyksos, are you?" Patep's eyes were glowing with a strange light. It made Joseph feel even more nervous than before. "You're 'apiru," Patep continued. "You're a slave, aren't you?"

Joseph didn't know what 'apiru meant, but he did know that he needed to be on his way.

"I'm the humble servant of Potiphar," he replied, "and I must quickly return to my duties. Potiphar is waiting for this."

He didn't waste any extra time in idle chatter. The prompting that he should leave was growing stronger, and he hurried back across the open market, eager to put distance between himself and the odd goldsmith. He could feel eyes upon him again. Everywhere in this city there were eyes watching. This time, however, he knew exactly who they belonged to, and when he turned to shoot a cautious glance over one shoulder, he saw Patep speaking with the two armed men in the shadows, pointing in Joseph's direction.

Joseph gripped the hilt of Potiphar's sword. No would-be thief would dare approach him once he reached the river and the soldiers. It was time for this adventure to end. It was time to get back to the ordinary life of a slave. He would leave the dangers of this city to the soldiers. Thebes was like dry tinder, ready to ignite, and Joseph didn't want to be in the middle of it when the sparks burst into flames.

The daily routine of being a priestess was mundane and boring. But free time was even worse. Normally, Asenath would look for Netchem so she could have someone to talk to instead of being alone like this with her troubled thoughts. But today she was much too angry with Netchem to speak to her. She stayed in her room, hoping Netchem would be too afraid or too embarrassed to seek her out, and her anger festered more and more with each new minute she spent alone.

"Great goddess," Asenath murmured as she knelt before a miniature replica of Isis. "The pharaoh says that Seth chose me to serve him. But my father says you marked me at birth as a child of your own—that you gave me eyes as blue as yours to show all who look upon me that you are my friend and protectress." She paused for a moment, her chest tightening with emotion, and she struggled fiercely against the unwelcome emotions that gripped her soul. "If you hear my prayer," she finally continued, " . . . if you're really there listening to me, then allow me to leave this abominable city and return to my own home in On. I will serve you as a priestess any other place you ask. Just free me from Pharaoh and this awful place . . . "

Slowly, Asenath got to her feet, and she waited several moments for an answer. She wanted a sign. Anything that could tell her she wasn't alone in this unfriendly world. But both heaven and earth remained silent. Isis didn't answer. The goddess must be almost as deaf as the stone idols the priests and pharaohs erected in her honor.

Asenath realized now that she would never get help from any of the gods or goddesses of Egypt. If she wanted salvation from her sorrows, it was up to her to work it out on her own.

"I'll run away!" she said, hoping her fierce threat might provoke some response from the unseen world. "I'll escape at night and run back to On!"

It sounded good when the words first spilled from her mouth. But then she realized that On was the first place Pharaoh's men would go to find her. And when she was once more in their hands, they would bring her back to Avaris, watching her even more carefully than before.

"I'll go to Thebes then," she said, a hint of desperation in her voice. "The people of Thebes have no love for Pharaoh. And they have no love for his evil god Seth. I can find shelter among them. They'll hide me from Pharaoh, and I'll serve as a priestess in their city."

This seemed like a better idea than the first. But only if she ignored two glaring flaws in her plan. First of all, a young girl traveling alone through the desert would almost certainly meet her death there. The only other way home was by river, and travel on a Nile barge would most likely end in quick recapture followed by a humiliating return to Avaris.

No matter how much she thought about it—no matter how hard she tried—it was always the same. She was helpless. She lacked the wisdom, power, and resources to free herself from this never-ending nightmare.

"Asenath?"

The apprehensive voice came to her ears from the other side of the door, and Asenath tightly pressed her lips together when she heard it. Maybe if she didn't answer, Netchem would think she wasn't there and go away so that she could be left alone to wallow in her own misery. But her so-called friend was a persistent girl.

"Asenath, I know you're in there. If you don't want to talk to me, I understand. But I need a chance to speak to *you*. I hope you'll at least listen to what I have to say."

"Go away!" Asenath snapped, not even bothering to hide the anger in her voice. "Haven't you already said enough?"

"I-I've come to apologize. I didn't mean to hurt you or make you angry."

"You should have thought about that before you started telling my problems to your mother and your father! If you were a real friend, you never would have betrayed me that way!"

For several long moments the room was filled with silence. Finally, Netchem's voice—trembling and tearful this time—spoke once more through the door.

"I was afraid for you, Asenath," she said. "So I told my mother you were unhappy here. And when she started asking me what kinds of things you were saying, I didn't know how not to answer her. I was worried about what the gods might do to you if you kept talking like you were talking. And I was worried about what you might do."

"What I might do? What do you mean by that?"

"I . . . I was afraid you might do something dangerous like run away. Or maybe even do something worse."

Asenath winced. Had her dark inner turmoil been that transparent? Her anger faded a little, and she walked slowly to the door.

"Can I come in?" Netchem asked cautiously from the other side. "Can we talk?"

Asenath pulled the door open, and the two girls stared uncertainly at each other for several long moments. Netchem didn't enter until Asenath motioned that she could.

"What did you think I would do?" she asked as they both stood just inside the door, staring awkwardly at their feet. "What did you think I would do that was worse than running away?"

"You seemed so depressed. You seemed like you didn't even want to be alive. I didn't want you to . . . to . . . "

"I would never take my own life," Asenath said. "Whatever unknown life it is that waits beyond this world is more frightening to me than the problems I have to face here. But it means a great deal to me to know that you care. I guess I can see why you might have thought you should talk to someone."

"I didn't tell anything to my father," Netchem said quickly. "I know how he is. I know how he overreacts about things. I talked to my mother because I wanted advice about how to help you. I wouldn't have said anything to her if I thought you would be all right on your own. I'm sorry, Asenath. Will you ever forgive me?"

"I forgive you," Asenath replied, slowly nodding her head. "But you shouldn't waste your time worrying about me. Sometimes I feel depressed, but it's only because life is so different for me than it is for you. You have your father right there with you at the temple. Your mother is here in the house whenever you come home. I have no one. I'm all alone."

"You're not alone," Netchem said, taking one of Asenath's hands into her own. "You have my family. You're my best friend, Asenath. And as long as Pharaoh keeps you here in Avaris, you're my sister as well."

Asenath stared at Netchem in surprise. When she spoke this time, there was no trace of anger in her voice. "I'm sorry I was so rude, Netchem. I didn't mean to say such hurtful things to you."

"It's all right," her friend replied with a shrug. "I understand. Maybe I should have told you how much I was worried about you before I told everything to my mother."

"You did the right thing. I would have done the same for you if I thought you were going to . . . well, . . . do what you were thinking I might do."

They were silent again, then Netchem moved impulsively forward and gave Asenath a quick, short hug. When she was done, she took an awkward step backward and stared again at her feet.

"Sometimes I'm unhappy with my life, too," she said, surprising Asenath. "Sometimes I like to wander into the city and escape for a while."

"At least you can escape. I'm not allowed away from the house or the temple."

"You are if somebody else is with you."

"Your parents are too busy to escort me around the city every time I get tired of being trapped here."

"I never said they would be your escorts."

Asenath looked carefully at Netchem and scowled. "I don't want you getting into trouble on my account."

"I'll be with you the entire time," Netchem replied. "And my father never specified that it had to be him or my mother who went with you. They'll never even know that we were gone. We'll be back before evening prayers start at the temple."

"And where will we go."

"I don't know. Someplace close. Pharaoh's workers are putting up a new monument on the other side of his palace. We could go see that if you'd like."

"That would be more interesting than sitting around here all day," Asenath admitted. "I'd like that."

The two girls exchanged guilty, conspiratorial smiles, and soon they were on their way.

It was a brighter day than usual, and Asenath was immediately grateful for the black *kohl* she had used in the morning to line her eyes. Not only did *kohl* serve as a cosmetic, but it also protected one's eyes from the glare of the sun and the eye infections that were so common among those who dwelt in these harsh desert climes. But even the protection of the *kohl* wasn't enough to keep her from squinting each time their path took them from the shadows of walls and buildings into the full, undiluted strength of Egypt's sun. She had spent so much time in the house and temple that her eyes were no longer used to unfiltered daylight.

"Why don't you like Avaris?" Netchem asked after they had walked in silence for several long minutes. "Is it because of the people, or is it something else?"

"I don't know any of the people," Asenath replied. "I spend all my time in the temple, and the only person I really know there is you.

If everyone here is like you, it must be a very nice place. It's just . . . it's just that . . . "

"It's just what?"

"It's not the people," Asenath said. "And it's not the place. It's the situation that upsets me."

"You don't like that Pharaoh has trapped you here," Netchem said, nodding her head sympathetically.

Asenath nodded back. "I miss On, and the freedom I had there," she said. "I miss being with my family, and I miss every other part of my old life that I might never have again."

"When I asked my father why Pharaoh forces you to be here," Netchem said, "he told me that sometimes we have to give up part of our freedom to do the service the gods have called us to. It's all a part of *ma'at*—the natural order of the universe."

"And you believe that?"

"I-I don't know, but—"

"The natural order of the universe isn't fair," Asenath said, her voice bitter. "It hasn't been fair to me since the day Pharaoh arrived in On."

"But, even so, it does no good to fight against it," Netchem said. "Those who fight it only hurt themselves. You can't escape the station the gods have assigned you to."

"Is that also something your father told you?"

Netchem turned her eyes self-consciously to the ground, and that was all the answer Asenath needed.

"I wish I could believe and accept such words," Asenath said, letting out a slow, frustrated breath. "My father taught me the same things your father has taught you. But, for some reason, it doesn't feel right to me anymore. I don't feel that I should be destined to be a priestess. I don't feel that your father or my father or even Pharaoh has the right to decide the rest of my life for me. I'm a person. Not a piece of property."

She almost slipped up at this moment and told Netchem about

the puzzling dream about the oxen and the wheat, but she held back. Even though she now understood why Netchem had gone to her mother and even though she was now ready to forgive her for it, she wasn't quite ready to trust her friend with this.

"If the gods don't mean for you to be a priestess," Netchem said, interrupting Asenath's thoughts, "what is it that you think you're supposed to be?"

"I don't know," Asenath replied. "If my father ever gets his way, I'll be the wife of a Theban prince. But I don't know that I'd be any happier with that than I am with this. I know I'm just a girl and it's not my place to say such things, but I wish the gods would let me choose my own destiny in life."

"Maybe you'll become a *high* priestess instead of just an ordinary priestess," Netchem suggested, trying to sound helpful. "Maybe that's your true destiny. You'd have more control over your own life then."

"The gods would never allow that to happen. I question them too much."

"Then maybe you'll marry one of Pharaoh's sons and become queen of all Egypt."

Asenath wasn't sure if Netchem was teasing or serious. But a moment later a huge grin spread over Netchem's face, and Asenath laughed with her before she realized what she was doing.

It was the first time Asenath had laughed since arriving in Avaris, and she was surprised at the sudden feeling of warmth it created inside her. It felt nice to laugh along with her foster sister; but, at the same time, this momentary lapse in her diligently groomed misery seemed to her like a betrayal of herself and her family.

"What's wrong?" Netchem asked, noticing the quick change in Asenath's demeanor. "Did I say something wrong?"

"No," Asenath replied. "It's nothing. Where's the new monument you told me about? Is it far?"

"No. Not far. We're almost there."

"We should hurry. I don't want you getting in trouble if your parents figure out we've left the house and temple without telling them."

"It will be all right," Netchem assured her. "We're not too far from the house. It's not like we've left the city or run away from home."

Asenath nodded, but she wasn't quite as optimistic about how Netchem's parents would react to this unplanned outing. She'd been a prisoner here much too long. Even if Setmosis and Ari didn't mind, she was certain Pharaoh would never approve of his prisoner wandering off into the city with only a young girl her own age as an escort.

It took only a few minutes to reach the construction site of the new monument, and Asenath was amazed at the large number of laborers who had been gathered there to complete Pharaoh's project. Stone cutters and slaves swarmed around the building site like a colony of ants whose hill had been disturbed, and she and Netchem stood at a respectful distance and watched.

The monument here was to be a great, stone obelisk; and groups of sweating, grunting slaves strained at their tasks as they pushed massive stones up a ramp to create the next level of the obelisk. The temples of Ra in On had such spired, stone columns in their courtyards. It surprised Asenath to see firsthand what efforts it took to create such man-made wonders. Perhaps this was what it might have been like to watch the workers of an earlier era constructing the great, stone pyramids of Zoser and Khufu. She forgot for a moment that the blood running through her veins was Hyksos. At the moment she felt completely Egyptian, and a great pride in her people's adopted heritage swelled within her.

"Look how quickly their chisels become dull," Netchem said, pointing out a team of men who were standing nearby and handing out fresh copper chisels while they raced to sharpen previously dulled ones. "It must be a difficult life being a builder. It makes me glad to be a priestess."

"Yes," Asenath replied, nodding. "Me, too."

There was order and discipline here on a scale that filled her with awe. But there was also pain. She could see it in the faces of the stone cutters as they gritted their teeth and rubbed dusty hands over aching muscles. She wondered now if perhaps her life wasn't quite as bad as she had assumed it was. Despite everything else, the gods truly had blessed her with easier burdens than those heaped upon the backs of these poor souls. There were different kinds of bondage. Maybe she should be grateful she hadn't been assigned a worse one.

"What is the purpose of this monument?" Asenath quietly asked after staring for several quiet, long moments at the builders. "Is it a monument to one of the gods?"

"No," Netchem replied. "It's for Khyan. It's something to remind future generations of the power and greatness of our king."

Asenath had to struggle to keep an angry, unhappy scowl off her face. Khyan? A great king? A truly great king would be able to maintain order in his kingdom without kidnapping the daughters of Egypt's high priests. But though her lips yearned to say as much, she kept it to herself. She didn't want to offend Netchem, and put another strain on their still growing friendship.

"I think we should go back to the house," Asenath said. "I need to get out of the sun and lie down for a while."

Netchem examined Asenath with worried brown eyes. "I'm sorry. I didn't know you were getting tired. Are you not feeling well?"

"I'm all right. I just didn't sleep well last night. I need a little more rest before we have to go back to the temple today."

Netchem nodded, but it was obvious by the look on her face that she knew there was something besides fatigue behind this sudden desire to depart from the monument. At the moment, however, Asenath didn't feel like giving explanations; and, to Netchem's credit, she didn't press for any.

"Rest sounds good," Netchem said instead, in her usual cheerful manner. "I think I might take a short nap myself." She paused for a moment then added, "Did it help to get away from the house and the temple for a while?"

"Yes. It was just what I needed today."

This time her expression matched the cheerfulness in her voice.

"Good. I was hoping it would make you feel better."

"It did. You're a good friend, Netchem. Thank you for caring about me."

Netchem's smile grew a little wider. At least one person in Avaris cared how Asenath felt. She could always be grateful for that.

Chapter Notes

1. The term *'apiru* (sometimes written as *Habiru* or *Hapiru*) is a word that may have been used by the ancient Egyptians to refer to Hebrews or Hebrew slaves. Some scholars point out the similarity of this word to the Hebrew term *'ibri*, suggesting that the Hebrews' label for themselves was ultimately taken from this Egyptian term. Joseph is only referred to as a "Hebrew" once in the scriptural account of his life (Genesis 41:12). It's interesting to note that the word is immediately followed by a reference to his earlier servitude to Potiphar which could be reemphasizing the fact that he had once been this man's slave.

2. Although many obelisks existed throughout Egypt—some of them still standing today—the monument described in this chapter is a fictional one.

3. Asenath is only referred to twice in the Old Testament (Genesis 41:45, 50 and Genesis 46:20). Her story as told thus far is entirely fictional.

TWELVE

H E WAS ALMOST TO THE RIVER when Patep's two henchmen caught up with him. Joseph had moved swiftly, dodging through crowds while using buildings and objects to hide himself; but, somehow, they still managed to catch up with him. And now all avenues of possible escape were cut off. He was trapped on a small side street with tall, smooth walls to either side of him—the would-be thieves advancing from ahead and behind. Their superior knowledge of the city had given them the advantage over him. His options were limited. He could voluntarily hand over the bracelet, hoping they would spare his life. But even if they allowed him to live, he wasn't sure if Potiphar would be so kind. The only other action left open to him was to use the sword he'd been given to defend his master's property. It was no choice really. His master had committed an important task into his hands. What good was Joseph's life if he couldn't be trusted?

"You have something we want, *'Apiru*," the man in front of him said, turning his head to one side to spit on the ground before flashing Joseph a wicked grin. "If you hand it over now, we'll kill you quickly. Otherwise, it will be my great pleasure to make your death as long and painful as possible."

Joseph drew Potiphar's sword from his belt and warily studied his adversaries. One of them was a big, bare-chested brute with a bald head and a thick, scraggly beard. He didn't look Egyptian to Joseph.

He was probably an Ishmaelite. The other was big and powerful, too; but his face was clean shaven, and his head was covered by a *nemes*—a traditional, Egyptian head cloth.

"I can't give you what rightfully belongs to my master," Joseph quietly said. "And I'm not going to easily give up my life either."

Both men paused, stared at him for a moment, then broke into laughter. With malicious sneers on their faces, they continued to advance upon him.

Joseph had never used a sword in actual combat, but he had practiced with sticks against his brothers. At least *he* had been practicing. To his older brothers, it was always a miniature battle for supremacy. And the day he grew skilled enough to start beating them at it, he quickly learned how seriously they took their "practice." These men had the same thirst for blood in their eyes that Judah had shown whenever he crossed his stick with Joseph's. But these weren't sticks, and these men intended to do more than leave him with throbbing fingers or a bruised shoulder.

Joseph lowered himself into a defensive stance, and the first blade sliced toward him. A quick shift of his body moved him out of harm's way, and he struck the blade down with his own so that its tip hit the earth, sending a loose spray of dust and gravel into the air. Before the surprised swordsman could recover for a second attack, Joseph grasped him by the tunic and sent him sprawling to the ground. The second man now darted in, hoping to do better than his partner, but Joseph whirled around and drove the man back with several vicious swipes from his own blade.

"You fight better than a slave," the bald, bearded man muttered, rolling to his feet and casting Joseph a menacing glare. "But you're still going to die. There are two of us and only one of you. How long do you think you can hold us both off?"

Truthfully, Joseph realized it probably couldn't be long. As strong as he was, it would take strength beyond his own to come off the conqueror in this deadly situation. Even as he thought this, a quick, barely audible prayer rolled off his lips.

"God of my fathers," he whispered. "Thou hast saved me already from the hands of my brothers. Spare Thy humble servant from these men as well . . . "

Joseph didn't have time to finish his hastily uttered prayer. The first man motioned suddenly to the second, and they attacked this time together. One swung at Joseph's head; the other thrust at his back. Amazingly, Joseph managed to twist away from one blade and block the other. But he didn't escape completely unscathed. A sharp, burning sensation down one arm warned him that he had been struck, and he could feel his own warm blood trickling from his shoulder to his elbow. It was a superficial wound. One that would heal quickly. But a nasty looking scar would be left behind.

"That was only the beginning of your pain," the bearded man said, sneering like Zebulun did whenever he managed to best Joseph. "By the time we're done with you, you'll no longer have arms or legs."

They rushed at him again, this time coming from the same direction. A quick series of metallic clangs echoed down the street as Joseph deftly blocked their strikes. They backed quickly away from the fury of his counterattack, but they didn't move quickly enough. Both of them now had wounds of their own.

There was hesitancy in their eyes now, and they both paused to gasp for breath and reevaluate the situation. He wasn't nearly as easy to kill as they'd expected him to be, and Joseph could see a shadow of doubt covering their faces. But ultimately, it was something far greater than Joseph's own skill with a sword that saved him. Soldiers from the river—attracted by the metallic ring of clashing sword blades—began to gather at one end of the street; and, the moment they came, Joseph's attackers turned to slink angrily back into the city. God had saved him. If the help had come any later, there might have been nothing left of him to save.

"What's going on here," one of the soldiers—a captain—demanded, marching authoritatively up to Joseph.

"I was on my way back to the river," Joseph said, gasping for breath and placing a hand over his stinging wound, "when I was attacked by those men." He nodded his head in the direction his adversaries had gone then looked back at the captain.

"I know you," the captain said. "You're Potiphar's slave. What were you doing? Were you trying to steal something from those men?"

He thought about telling the captain about the bracelet. Then he thought about how Potiphar had warned him that even Pharaoh's own soldiers might attempt to rob him of it. Joseph closed his mouth and stared at his feet.

"You don't want to answer me? Well, we'll see what Potiphar says about that when he gets back. Go back to the river and stay there. You're lucky Potiphar gave you a sword. You'd probably be dead now if he hadn't."

Joseph did as he was commanded but waited until no one was watching to secretively pat the pouch at his side and make sure the armband was still there. Assured that it was, he hurried quickly to attend to his master's chariot.

God had saved him from death. But his servitude to the Egyptians would still go on.

"How did Pharaoh's discussions go today?" Mutekh asked as he accompanied Potiphar along the bank of the river.

"I think Pharaoh made it clear that the tributes are to be paid on time," Potiphar replied. "Our troubles with this city aren't at an end, but they should at least be somewhat more manageable for a while."

"And what about the rumors that Nebireyeraw intends to lead a revolt against Khyan? Do you think it's actually going to happen?"

"Our chariots showed Nebireyeraw exactly what Pharaoh intends to do if he suspects any kind of revolt. I don't think the Thebans will give us any serious troubles anytime in the near future."

"Speaking of troubles," Mutekh said. "Your slave got himself into a bit of trouble today."

Potiphar stopped dead in his tracks and reached out a hand to stop Mutekh, too. "What do you mean by that?" he demanded. "What kind of trouble did he get himself into?"

"He nearly got himself killed from what I've been hearing," Mutekh replied. "Apparently he made some enemies in the city, and Akhmim found him fighting them off in an alley."

"But he's still alive. Right? They didn't take anything from him did they?"

Mutekh stared at his captain curiously. "He's still alive. I don't know if they robbed him. But what could a slave possibly have that would be of worth to anyone else?"

Potiphar didn't answer that question. Instead, he asked one of his own.

"Where is he now?"

"With your horses the last time I saw him. Over by that cluster of palm trees."

Potiphar nodded and left his bewildered lieutenant standing alone behind him. He should have never trusted a mere slave with such an important task. He lowered his brows into an angry scowl. If that foolish slave had lost Neferset's new armband . . .

Joseph was kneeling next to one of the horses when Potiphar stalked silently up to him. The boy had just finished applying a poultice to one of the horse's legs and was now wrapping it in a clean bandage.

"What happened here?" Potiphar demanded, his anger growing even more upon seeing one of his prized horses injured.

"I was grooming them and noticed that this one was favoring his left foreleg," Joseph answered. "It must have gotten injured when our procession was attacked. The wound is a minor one. I think it will heal quickly."

Potiphar nodded but said nothing. The horses looked good. The dust of the long journey had been scrubbed from their coats. Their manes and tails were brushed free of snarls. But Potiphar now noticed an ugly streak of dried, crusted blood on Joseph's right arm and shoulder, and his anger immediately began to fade. Whatever else had happened today, the boy had obviously fought to protect Potiphar's property. The question was, had he been successful?

"You've been injured." Potiphar leaned forward to get a better look at the wound.

"Yes. But it's only a scratch. I'll take care of it as soon as I'm done with the horses." Joseph finished bandaging the injured leg of the animal then stood and faced his master. "I almost forgot," he said. "You probably want the piece of jewelry you sent me for." He untied the leather turquoise pouch from his belt and handed it over to Potiphar, seeming to be glad to be rid of it.

Potiphar stared at the bag for several long moments then fastened his gray eyes on Joseph. "Leave the horses and tend to your own wound now," he quietly said. "If you haven't eaten yet, I also want you to get yourself something to eat. That's an order."

Joseph looked down at his wounded arm and shoulder. Only now did he appear to realize how bad it looked. "Yes. I suppose I'd better do that," he said. "Thank you."

Potiphar shook his head in wonder as Joseph moved slowly to the riverbank to dress his wound. Pekhti had tried to explain how dedicated and self-motivated this slave was, but until now Potiphar had dismissed that glowing report as an overly enthusiastic exaggeration. It was clear to him now, however, that this slave . . . this Joseph . . . was no ordinary boy. Despite his normally cynical view of slaves and servants, Potiphar found that he was starting to like this boy. More importantly, he was beginning to trust him.

It was a pity Joseph was only an 'apiru slave rather than a free Egyptian. He might have made a good steward otherwise. Even a good *chief* steward. Potiphar thought about that for a moment then chuckled to himself. He imagined the look he would find on T'chet's face if the current chief steward ever found out what was going through Potiphar's head now.

Perhaps making Joseph into a chief steward was a little too much at this point in time, but there had to be some way to reward him for his remarkable loyalty and service. However he eventually decided to reward him, Potiphar was certain he could profitably put this boy's talents to use. It was just a matter of deciding how that should be. And there would be plenty of time to figure that out. The trip home was a long one.

THIRTEEN

"What do *you* want?"

Although he'd never met him before, Joseph knew without being told that this was Potiphar's chief steward. Pekhti had warned him about the man and, judging by the look of sheer contempt on T'chet's face, he was probably as foul tempered as Pekhti had described him to be.

"The master told me to meet him at the house today," Joseph said. He smiled and made his voice as pleasant as possible despite the fact that the chief steward was looking him up and down with disgust.

"I wasn't informed that anyone would be meeting with the master today," the steward said. "And Potiphar informs me about *everything*."

"On the trip home, Pharaoh's procession stayed at Memphis longer than was expected," Joseph said. "We arrived in Avaris late last night. The master told me to come to the house as soon as my duties at the stable were finished. He said he had something important to discuss with me. Perhaps he didn't want to wake you over such a small matter."

The steward opened his mouth, and Joseph could see by the look in the man's eyes that he was about to give a verbal lashing. But, before he could chastise Joseph, T'chet was interrupted by a soft voice coming from out of the house behind him.

"Who is that at the door, T'chet?"

"Only a slave, my lady. He claims to have been summoned here by the master."

T'chet moved respectfully to one side as a slender figure in a light, linen *kalasiris* slipped past him. She leaned lazily against the doorframe, waved a hand before her mouth as if to stifle a yawn, and stared at Joseph with her mesmerizing, brown eyes.

"I remember you," she said. "You're the slave who accompanied my husband to Thebes." She glided a little closer and looked up into Joseph's brown eyes.

"Yes. That was me," he said, taking an involuntary step backwards. "If the master is away now I—"

"T'chet," Potiphar's wife interrupted, turning toward the steward behind her. "Don't just stand there. Find one of my maidservants and have her bring breakfast to the great hall. Tell her to bring enough for two."

Before either T'chet or Joseph could protest, Potiphar's wife slipped her arm through Joseph's and led him into the cool interior of the house.

"I don't think I've learned your name yet," she said, looking into his eyes again. "Do you have one?" A smile wafted across her lips, and Joseph swallowed uneasily before he answered.

"My name is Joseph," he said.

"Joseph. What a fine, masculine-sounding name." She absentmindedly stroked his arm as she spoke, and his discomfort over this situation doubled. He pondered how he could dismiss himself without offending her, but she didn't give him opportunity to do anything but move along beside her to wherever it was she was taking him.

"I am Neferset," she said, "and I understand that I have you to thank for the safe arrival of my newest piece of jewelry." She glanced down at one of her slender, white arms, and Joseph followed her gaze.

She was wearing the sparkling, golden armband that had nearly cost him his life.

"Your husband went to a great deal of trouble to get it for you," Joseph said. "He must love you very much."

Neferset wrinkled her nose and frowned. "My husband loves his horses and his work. He thinks that small trinkets like this will make up for all the time he spends away from me."

He was uncertain about how he should respond to this, but several servants—all of them female—suddenly rushed in with two low, wicker chairs and a table. They seated Neferset on one side of the table, and when their mistress was comfortable, they guided Joseph to the opposite seat.

"You must tell me what happened when you went to get the armband," Neferset said, reaching across the table, clasping one of his hands in her own, and staring deeply into his eyes. "I want to hear every detail of it."

"There's really not much to tell," Joseph said, carefully drawing his hand free and pretending that he had to scratch his arm with it. "Some of Pharaoh's soldiers happened upon me and the thieves before the thieves could take it from me. Otherwise, it would have been lost."

"That's not how I heard it." She ran one finger gently down Joseph's injured arm, but her eyes were still fastened on his.

"This is a beautiful house," Joseph said, desperate now to turn her attention away from him. He tilted his head to look at the hieroglyphic murals that covered the walls of the room and acted as if he were fascinated by them. "It must have taken a very long time for the painter to finish all of this."

"Yes. I suppose."

"Is there a meaning to the hieroglyphs? Do they tell a story?"

"Something about the gods, I assume. Or about how to escape annihilation and make it to the afterlife. If they're not praising some king, then they usually preach some message about the gods." Neferset yawned, making it clear that she was bored with this topic, but Joseph pressed on with it anyway.

"I've always been fascinated by the Egyptian system of writing," he said. "My great-grandfather, Abraham, spent part of his life in Egypt, and some of his writings were done in Egyptian. My father taught me to read a little before . . . before I was brought to Avaris."

"That's very interesting," Neferset said, stifling yet another yawn. "Personally, I find reading and writing to be dull, tedious, and time-consuming. But I guess there would be no work for the scribes if we didn't have it." She laughed, and Joseph smiled politely. He wasn't sure if she was joking or serious. Fortunately, he was saved from the necessity of a response by the arrival of more maidservants carrying a large, silver platter.

"Help yourself," Neferset said, waving a hand toward the food. "I don't imagine you had time to eat before coming to the house. I apologize for my husband. He creates so much work for himself that he can't even keep track of his appointments."

Joseph nodded, but he was staring at the platter and only half hearing what she was saying. His mouth had begun to water the moment the food was placed on the table before him. Several pome-granates had been sliced into pieces, and drops of their pulpy, red juice glistened like tiny rubies against the mirrored surface of the serving platter. There were also fresh, plump dates; tender slices of melon; and sweet, honeyed cakes waiting to be savored. Since be-coming a slave, Joseph had eaten no meat and very little fresh fruit or vegetables. His diet consisted mostly of hard, dry bread and an oc-casional dried date. What to Neferset was probably a light breakfast looked to Joseph like a royal feast.

"What's wrong? Don't you like any of these fruits?"

"No. I mean, yes. Yes, I like all of them."

Neferset removed a melon slice from the tray, and Joseph took some of the juicy, red pomegranate seeds. He was painfully aware that she was watching his every move, but the food was so tempting that he couldn't resist it.

"How long have you been with us?" Neferset asked.

"What?"

"How long have you been here serving as our slave?"

"I-I don't know," Joseph stammered. He realized suddenly that he had lost track of the time. It seemed like an eternity since he was sold into slavery, but it might be only a few days, weeks, or months. His life was so unchanging that time seemed no longer to exist. "Less than a year, I think. More than a few months."

"Strange that I never saw you until my husband took you with him to Thebes," Neferset mused, picking a grape from its stem and twirling it thoughtfully between her fingers. "Where has my husband been hiding you all of this time?"

"I work in the stables," Joseph said. "I feed and care for the horses. That's where I spend most of my time."

"I guess I'll have to make more visits to the stable . . . , won't I," she said. She smiled, watching him carefully as she placed the grape to her lips. Joseph realized all too clearly that she was flirting with him, but he couldn't quite figure out why a woman who appeared to have everything would be interested in a mere slave such as himself.

As delicious as the food was, he wished now that he could disappear back into the stables and escape her unnerving, unwavering gaze. Where was Potiphar? And how was Joseph supposed to handle this painfully uncomfortable situation? He tried once again to think of an excuse to dismiss himself, but the situation was suddenly remedied for him.

"It's about time you got here," Neferset said, looking over Joseph's shoulder as Potiphar strode suddenly into the room. "I haven't the strength to entertain all the guests who show up for your missed appointments." She curled herself, cat-like, in her chair and cast her husband a languid smile.

Joseph immediately got to his feet, bowed to his master, and tried to muffle his quiet sigh of relief.

"My apologies," Potiphar said. "To both of you." He moved over to the table to give his wife a quick kiss of greeting. Then he turned to Joseph and nodded. "Important business at Pharaoh's prison called me temporarily away. The prison is one of my many official responsibilities, and I had to oversee an execution there this morning. I'm sorry to keep you waiting, Joseph."

He made this announcement as if he were discussing something as trivial as what he'd had for dinner the night before, and Joseph decided Potiphar must have witnessed countless such executions to speak so casually about one now.

"If my darling wife will excuse us," Potiphar said, "I'd like to walk to the stables with you and discuss an idea that kept pressing itself upon my mind on our return trip from Thebes. I think you'll like what I have to say."

Neferset picked another grape from the cluster on the silver tray and made a great show of being bored with what was going on around her. "Go about your uninteresting business," she said when Potiphar gave her another apologetic smile. "I'll stay right here and finish my breakfast. Don't worry about me. I'll be fine here all by myself."

"I won't be long," Potiphar reassured her. "This will only take a few minutes. I'll be right back, and then we'll enjoy breakfast and some conversation together."

Joseph cast a nervous glance at Neferset and followed his master out of the room. Her eyes no longer lingered on his. In fact, they studiously avoided him as if he'd suddenly ceased to exist. He couldn't quite figure this woman out, but there was one thing he knew for sure. It would be best if he avoided ever crossing her path again.

"I hope my wife didn't bore you with her idle chatter," Potiphar said as they walked past the servants' quarters and moved toward the stables. "She'll talk your ears off if she has the chance to make you her captive audience."

Joseph searched for an appropriate response, but Potiphar didn't wait to hear one. Instead, he got right to the point of why he'd asked Joseph to meet him at the house today.

"I've decided that I'm not tapping into your full potential if I leave you to work in the stables," he said. "Because of this, I've devised a plan to show us both where your talents can best be put to use. I'm pleased with the work you're doing in the stables. Don't get me wrong about that. But I feel my estate will benefit if you are trained to do more than just care for the horses."

Joseph felt a nervous prickle of excitement move up and down his spine. This was going to be important for him. He could sense it even before Potiphar revealed it all.

"Pekhti is going to be upset about this," Potiphar went on, shaking his head, "but I want you to rotate duties. Three days in the stables, three days in the house, and three days with the chief of my flocks. Then back to the first duty again and so forth. I want you to learn how to manage the responsibilities of each of these jobs. I'll have you work side by side with my stewards until you know your duties well enough to do them on your own."

"When would you like me to begin?" Joseph asked. Even though he knew Pekhti was going to feel slighted, he felt a thrill of excitement at this unprecedented opportunity. If nothing else, this change was certainly going to break up the current monotony of his humdrum existence.

"The new arrangement will begin today," Potiphar replied. "Your first three days will be with Pekhti. He'll complain less if I leave you with him at the start. And it will also give me time to make the other stewards aware of what I expect from them. Is all of this agreeable to you?"

Joseph vigorously nodded his head. It was more than agreeable. The Lord truly was watching over him, and he felt a warm flood of gratitude beginning to encompass his heart.

"Good. Let's find Pekhti and tell him. The sooner he finds out, the sooner he can get used to the idea. Things are going to change, Joseph. I'm certain you'll find that life in my service is about to become much, much better for you."

PART TWO

And his master saw that the Lord was with him,
and that the Lord made all
that he did to prosper in his hand.
And Joseph found grace in his sight,
and he served him:
and he made him overseer over his house . . .

Genesis 39:3-4

FOURTEEN

MORE THAN FIVE YEARS HAD PASSED since she was brought to Avaris. Her father had attempted six times to convince Pharaoh to return her to On, but nothing he said could change Khyan's mind. And nothing, therefore, had changed for Asenath.

No. That wasn't true. Some things *had* changed. But none of the changes were anything Khyan had anticipated. He expected to indoctrinate her in the worship of Seth. As she grew from a girl to a woman, he expected her to forget her old family and her old ways and become a loyal Hyksos priestess. None of that had happened. Instead, Asenath doubted the gods more than ever before. She hated Seth, she hated Khyan, and all of this hatred was now a black stain upon her soul. Her disdain for Seth and all things Hyksos had hardened into cement. But Asenath had learned the necessity of hiding these feelings from those around her, and she was much better at it now than she had been five years before. Even Netchem, who was so good at discerning the thoughts and moods of those around her, rarely suspected just how deep Asenath's feelings ran. But those feelings were close enough to the surface today that Netchem did sense that something was wrong, and she immediately began to probe Asenath about it.

"What's wrong?" Netchem asked. Her voice and the sound of gravel crunching under her sandaled feet reminded Asenath that Netchem was walking beside her, and she quickly looked away from the statue of Seth where she had been staring with spite-filled eyes.

"I was thinking that I'm old enough to marry now," Asenath said, finding a topic that would safely explain her gloomy mood. It wasn't much safer than what she was really thinking about, but at least these were feelings Netchem was already aware of.

Netchem nodded sympathetically. "And you're worried because Pharaoh has reserved the right to select your husband for you."

"That's part of it."

"There's more that bothers you?"

"Yes. Much more."

"Like what?"

"Like what if he chooses a man I can never love? What if I'm not ready to be married yet? He can marry me off on a sudden whim, and I have absolutely no say in it."

"I wouldn't worry too much about it yet. Pharaoh hasn't mentioned anything to Father, and he consults regularly with Father about you."

"Somehow that fails to comfort me."

"Whoever Pharaoh eventually does choose for you, he will undoubtedly be a very powerful and influential man. You should feel fortunate."

"Fortunate?" Asenath stared at Netchem until her foster sister looked away. "I should feel fortunate that my entire destiny rests in the hands of the pharaoh?"

"All right," Netchem replied. "Maybe 'fortunate' isn't the best word for it. But you can't know whether or not it will be bad until it actually happens. Father can always go before Pharaoh to plead your case if a man you don't want is chosen. That should bring you some comfort."

"My own father has gone before Pharaoh six times in my behalf," Asenath said, "and that hasn't softened the king's heart. His wish is law, and he changes his decrees for no one."

"Maybe it will be all right," Netchem said weakly. "Maybe you'll be happy with his choice. Like I've already said, you can't know until the choice has been made."

Asenath didn't give a reply to that. She just stared at her feet and shook her head. She should have run away all those years ago when the thought first entered her head. Even if she had died in the attempt, it would have been better than this. She still wasn't sure what had convinced her to do otherwise.

"No matter what happens," Netchem said, still trying to be comforting, "I'll always be here for you. You can come to me for comfort if Pharaoh marries you to one of his old, boring advisors."

"Thank you for that most reassuring thought," Asenath said with a scowl.

"You know I'm just teasing you," Netchem said, laughing. "I'm sure it will be better than that. Your fame is spreading all over Egypt, and there are plenty of eligible young men hoping that Pharaoh will choose them to be your husband."

Asenath grimly shook her head. "I never sought fame," she said. "I'd gladly give away the fame of being Pharaoh's prisoner just to have the freedom to choose my own path through life. The only reason any of those men are interested in me is because it is the king who will determine my future. Somehow that makes me seem more valuable and desirable than what I really am."

"No. It's not just that," Netchem disagreed. "You're also the most beautiful and intelligent woman in Avaris. You seem more meant to be a queen than to be a priestess."

Asenath blushed. But only for a moment. "Not everyone thinks that," she said. "I know someone who thinks *you're* the most beautiful woman in Avaris."

Now it was Netchem's turn to blush, and Asenath gave her foster sister a conspiratorial nudge on the shoulder.

"How long do you think it will be before Ptakh asks you to marry him?"

"I-I don't know. Ptakh is afraid of my father. He's afraid to ask."

"Who wouldn't be afraid of your father? But your father likes Ptakh. He wouldn't be training him to be the next chief priest if he didn't. I think you should encourage Ptakh to try."

"Maybe in a few years from now," Netchem said, becoming suddenly coy. "Maybe when he and I are both a little older."

"At least you have some say in who you marry," Asenath went on, becoming gloomy once more. "I would trade places with you in an instant except that I wouldn't wish my own circumstances upon even the worst of enemies. Becoming a part of your family is the only good thing that has come out of this captivity for me."

"Perhaps Seth will soften Pharaoh's heart," Netchem said, placing a comforting hand on Asenath's shoulder. "You've served Seth loyally for all these years now. He surely knows your heart, and he will certainly reward you for it."

That comforted Asenath less than anything Netchem had said up to this point.

"Come on," Asenath said. "It's time to replenish the incense." She inclined her head toward the temple. "Seth is waiting right now for me to happily fulfill my duties."

Over the past five years, almost nothing had changed. Nothing that would help Asenath at least.

"I've come to seek the aid of the temple," Potiphar said.

Setmosis nodded his head. "Of course," he replied. "Any favor I have power to give is yours for the asking. You've always been generous in your donations to the temple treasury. How is it that I can help you, Captain of Pharaoh's Guard?"

Potiphar stepped into Setmosis' home and glanced uncertainly around himself. Then he took a deep breath and looked the chief priest nervously in the eye. Nervousness was not one of Potiphar's usual traits. Setmosis was immediately intrigued.

"I have need of a new chief steward," the captain said. "I'm sure the embarrassing rumors about my old chief steward have already reached your ears."

Setmosis nodded. He was aware of the situation with T'chet. Who wasn't? By now the entire city must have heard the rumors of T'chet's indiscretions with Potiphar's wife. But T'chet had now been executed, and only a fool would do more than nod when Potiphar brought it up again. Setmosis, of course, was no fool.

"I can recommend several scribes who would make excellent chief stewards," he quickly offered. "All of them are honest men, and all of them have been trained in the temple school."

"Actually, I've already selected a man for the job," Potiphar said. "It's a different kind of favor I'm about to ask."

"Oh?" Setmosis raised his eyebrows then motioned with one hand for Potiphar to follow him into the great hall. Potiphar, however, declined. He remained where he was and said, "The man I've chosen already serves in my house. Every task I give him prospers in his hand. More importantly, he is a man of complete and total integrity. I would trust him with my very life. The only skill he currently lacks is the ability to properly keep official records in the Egyptian manner. He may be just a slave, but his mind is keen, and I have no doubts about his abilities to handle the job once he's received added training in writing and weights and measures. If it would be possible, I'd like someone from the temple to teach him."

Setmosis was intrigued. He knew of a few other men who had put particularly loyal slaves in charge of their other servants. There were even some who had placed a slave in charge of their entire household. But there was no slave in all Avaris who had stewardship over the kind of wealth Potiphar possessed. This was interesting. Very interesting.

"I'm certain I can find someone who will be willing to take on this task," Setmosis said, trying not to seem too astonished by what Potiphar had just told him. "How often can you spare your steward to come to the temple and study?"

"These aren't the usual circumstances," Potiphar said. "I was hoping for a different kind of arrangement. I'm wondering if it would be possible for someone to come to my home a few times each week and train him there."

Setmosis rubbed his chin thoughtfully. "I suppose that could be done," he said. "But I'll need a little time to find someone who can be temporarily spared from his duties on those days. I—"

"I'm willing to pay an appropriate fee for this service," Potiphar interrupted. "Joseph doesn't need the full training of a scribe. I only need him to learn enough to keep the records of my estate in order. The sooner he can begin this training, the better it will be for me and my properties. At the moment, I'm doing all the record keeping of my properties *and* serving Pharaoh at the same time. As I've said, Joseph is a fast learner. I don't anticipate it will take long before he learns enough to entirely take over the record keeping by himself."

"I'll need a day to consider this," Setmosis replied. "Give me until tomorrow. I'll have a teacher ready for you by then."

"Thank you," Potiphar said. "I knew I could depend on you for help."

"We are both humble servants of Pharaoh and the gods. It's in our best interests to help each other."

Potiphar gave Setmosis a grateful nod of his head then made his departure. When he was gone, Setmosis walked back through the house, searching for Ari. It was always good to get her input when unexpected things happened. She quite often recognized things in a situation that he missed entirely.

"I've just spoken with Potiphar," he announced, when he found her in the hall. "He had a strange request to ask of me."

"Potiphar? What brings him to our house? Not another execution I hope."

"No. It was nothing like that. He's looking for someone to teach writing to his new steward. He's chosen an untrained slave to fill the vacancy left by T'chet."

He was pleased to see that his wife was as startled by this news as he had been, but it took her only a moment to recover. Then she nodded her head in understanding.

"It's because of Neferset," Ari said. "Perhaps Potiphar believes she will be less tempted to seduce a lowly slave than to shame herself and her household in the arms of a freeman like T'chet. For the sake of this new steward, I hope Potiphar is right."

Setmosis smiled. Ari had a way of seeing right to the core of a matter. If she were a man she would have made an excellent chief priest. A better one than himself, in fact.

"You seem to understand Potiphar quite well," he said. "So tell me what you think about this. What would he want in the way of a scribe to train this slave? Who of my priests would he choose if he were me?"

"What about Asenath?"

Setmosis blinked several times then gaped at his wife, surprised. "Asenath?" he asked. "What makes you suggest her?"

"You yourself have said many times that she's more skilled at reading and writing the hieroglyphics than any man or woman you've ever known. Potiphar is an important man. Wouldn't he want the best the temple has to offer?"

"Yes. But she's . . . well, she's not a man."

"Why does a teacher have to be a man? Couldn't she teach this new steward just as well as any of the priests?"

"Of course she could. But would it be appropriate?"

"If anyone needs time away from the temple," Ari softly replied, "it's Asenath. She rarely spends time anywhere but here in our home and across the street at the temple. It might help her to feel less like a prisoner and more like a human being if you give her an assignment away from the temple complex."

"What do you mean by that? She spends time other places. She goes with you to the market. She goes places with Netchem. She—"

"She's never allowed to go anywhere unless she's accompanied by one of us," Ari interrupted. "If she was going to run away from

Avaris, don't you think she would have already tried it long ago? It's time for both you and Pharaoh to begin to trust her more. She needs you to place your faith in her. She needs a chance to prove to herself and to everyone else around her that she's an intelligent worthwhile person."

"And you believe something like this would do that for her?"

"I know it would."

Setmosis paused, stared at the ground, and shook his head. Ari was right. He knew she was. But whether she was right or not, that didn't change the fact that Asenath was a girl and that Pharaoh would probably disapprove of anything that would take her beyond Setmosis' immediate supervision.

"I'd have to secure the approval of Pharaoh," he said with another slow shake of his head. "I don't know that he would approve of a young priestess being alone with one of Potiphar's male slaves. Even if Pharaoh does agree to this, she will have to teach the slave in a public place where other slaves and servants are coming and going."

"Of course. And if anyone can arrange it, I'm certain you can."

Setmosis smiled and shook his head. "There are some men who would think it a scandal for a wife to speak her mind so boldly to her husband."

"Yes," Ari replied, smiling sweetly back at him, "but you're not one of them. Asenath is restless. She's practically a woman now, and she yearns to be treated like an adult. Even Netchem is entrusted with more personal liberty than she is. I think this will be the best thing that's happened to Asenath since her arrival in Avaris."

"I still don't know. I should bring this idea before Pharaoh."

"Why? So that he can tell you no and take away a perfect opportunity for Asenath to grow and become the person she has the capability of becoming? It's time for Pharaoh to let us make some decisions of our own about what's best for Asenath and her life."

"So be it," Setmosis replied. "You've convinced me. But if Pharaoh ever finds out that we've let her out of our sight . . ."

"He won't find out. We'll just have to make sure he never knows."

Setmosis nodded. He hoped he wouldn't live to regret this decision later.

FIFTEEN

ASENATH STOOD ALONE in Potiphar's garden, examined her surroundings, and inhaled the redolent fragrance of flowering plants. This was the first time she had been away from the watchful eyes of Setmosis or one of his priests or a member of her foster family since coming to Avaris, and the unexpected freedom filled her with a warm euphoria that was hard to describe. But she knew this feeling couldn't last. This brief moment away from her political bondage was nothing more than that—a brief moment—and it wasn't the real freedom she craved. Long ago she had hoped and believed that some merciful being would provide her an unexpected avenue of escape. That hope had eventually died, and her enjoyment of this solitary moment faded as the hopelessness of her situation confronted her once again. Annoyance was quick to fill the void left behind by the dying feeling of euphoria.

Potiphar's slave was already supposed to have been waiting here for her. It wasn't supposed to be *her* waiting for *him*. She had paced this garden for at least half an hour now, and her face darkened with a scowl as she stared toward the garden gate. A solitary sentry leaned there against the wall. He yawned, smiled, and nodded when he saw her looking his way. But there was no sign that the chief steward would be arriving anytime soon. Being away from Setmosis and the temple gave Asenath too much time to dwell on her own personal problems. She resolved that she would give this impudent slave a severe tongue lashing when he finally arrived.

"Where is he?" she muttered, glaring at the garden pool and watching her reflection glare back at her. "I didn't come here to stand around all day and smell flowers! Since when does a slave have the right to make a priestess wait?"

She toyed for a moment with the lapis amulet that hung around her neck, considering whether she should go back to the temple or continue to wait here. It wasn't really a hard decision. She'd rather be anywhere but at Set's temple. But she also didn't like being forgotten as if her presence here didn't matter.

She'd never before taught anyone how to read or write, and she wasn't exactly sure how she would do it when the slave actually showed up. This tempered her impatience just a little, but it didn't keep her from considering again all the different ways she could chastise him when she had the chance. She had been trained in the hieroglyphic writing system in the temple school at On, and the priestess who trained her there would have never tolerated such willful disrespect for a teacher. It was a great privilege to learn to read and write—a privilege most *Egyptians* never received. It was almost unheard of for a slave to receive this kind of training. She would have to remind him how lucky he was. She would have to warn him of just how easily the opportunity could be taken away. If he proved to be as unmotivated and incompetent as she was expecting him to be, her tenure here as his teacher would be a very short one indeed.

"I apologize for keeping you waiting."

Asenath jumped, spun around, and then she narrowed her eyes when she realized who it was that had just startled her.

"One of the master's horses was very ill, and I had to prepare a medicine for him. Otherwise, I would have been here much sooner. Please forgive me for arriving so late."

Asenath's blue eyes flashed dangerously, and she tried to remember the verbal reprimand she had prepared for her new student, but she became unexpectedly tongue-tied as her eyes met his.

"My name is Joseph," the tall, young man said, his face lighting with a smile. "You must be Asenath."

"Yes . . . that's my name. Asenath." Her face flushed. This was nothing at all how she had intended to introduce herself. She felt like a fool. But several things about this new student caught her off guard. This man wasn't what she had expected. She wasn't exactly sure what she had anticipated, but he definitely wasn't it. He looked too young to be a chief steward, and he carried himself with too much quiet self-assurance to be a slave. A slave wouldn't walk so tall and so straight. His face was honest and intelligent, and he moved with quiet dignity. She wasn't sure whether she was facing a peasant or a prince.

"I'm not too late for us to begin a lesson, am I?" Joseph asked, glancing over at the small stack of materials she had placed on a table a servant had set up for her by the pool. "I'm really sorry you had to wait so long. I would never make a teacher wait if it wasn't an absolute emergency like the one we had here today."

Asenath pulled her eyes away from his to break the momentary trance that had taken her. She did her best to appear dignified and unruffled, but she was sure she must be failing. That alone fueled enough of her dying anger to help her get her wits about herself.

"Sit over there near the pool," she said, trying to make her voice sound cool and commanding. "We need to get started. Now."

She feared that this strong, handsome, dark-haired man must think by now that she was the world's greatest idiot, but she intended to make it clear who actually was in charge here. This in mind, she did her best to make a great show of annoyance as she gathered up the writing materials she had brought for the first lesson.

"The study and memorization of the hieroglyphic texts takes considerable self-discipline and concentration," she said, fixing his eyes with an icy stare. "Part of self-discipline is showing up on time. Since this is your first lesson, I will accept your apology. But I expect that it will never happen again." She paused for a moment, trying to think of what to say next, then rushed on as she saw his mouth move to speak. "We will begin your training by studying the cursive hieroglyphic script," she briskly said. "You'll learn by copying passages from a temple scroll like the scribes do." She paused again to hand Joseph the bundle of materials she had brought from the "House of Life"—the scriptorium-school that was a part of the temple complex of Seth—and she watched him as he curiously examined its contents. "That is a temple scroll," she said. "It is used to train all the new scribes, and you will be spending many long hours copying from its text. The small container there with the reed pen and the red and black ink cakes is a scribe's palette. The blank roll of papyrus is for you to write on. Do you have any questions?"

Joseph meekly shook his head.

"This is the traditional posture for writing," she explained, motioning for Joseph to sit cross-legged on the ground as she now did. She took the temple scroll from him, unrolled a little of it, and draped it across her legs. "Unroll the blank papyrus between your knees as I have done and hold the pen like this." She paused to place the pen in his hand then took his hand in hers to position it over the papyrus in the proper way. But the pleasant sensation she felt when her hand touched his startled her, and she quickly pulled away. "Make sure you keep your hand from touching the papyrus," she said, being careful to avoid his eyes. "If you touch it before the ink dries, you'll smudge the characters."

She watched to make sure he had the right idea about how to sit and how to hold his writing instruments then took the scribe's palette from him, moved closer to the garden pool, and added a few drops of water to the dry ink cakes in the palette. Carefully, she stirred the water into the cakes until an inky paste was formed, and then she placed it back on the ground next to him.

"You have papyrus and ink," she said. "Now all you need is a text to copy. That's what I brought this for." She pointed to the scroll in her lap and repositioned herself where Joseph could clearly see the text. "Try to copy this first line of characters," she said. "It won't take long for me to see if you even have the slightest chance of getting this."

Joseph smiled as if what she had just said amused rather than annoyed him, and he studiously began to copy the characters she had just pointed to. For some reason, that calm smile irritated her, and Asenath watched the smooth, bold strokes of his pen, determined to find a flaw in what he was doing. But there were no flaws in his writing, and she soon found herself looking more at the movements of his hands than the new line of characters he was reproducing on his own blank scroll. It wasn't until she allowed her eyes to wander to his face that she realized what was happening to her, and she quickly looked back down at the papyrus, desperate to find something wrong with either this man or his writing.

"What is going on here?" Asenath suddenly demanded after she had studied his hieroglyphic characters for several long moments. "This isn't the first time you've written Egyptian characters. Who are you? Who are you really?"

Joseph looked up at her and wrinkled his brow in confusion.

"You're not a slave," Asenath accused. "A slave couldn't write so perfectly the first time he set eyes on a scroll. What is this all about? Is this some kind of joke at my expense?" She looked around the garden, half-expecting to see either Setmosis or Potiphar standing there, laughing at her; but, other than the guard at the wall who had turned to curiously stare at her when he heard her voice raise, there was nobody around but her and Joseph.

"I'm not sure what you're talking about," Joseph said. "I'm a simple slave—a servant of Potiphar."

"Then how do you write so well? How do you write as if you've done this before?"

"I was trained in the writing of my own people," Joseph said. "My father told me that God has blessed me to be a quick learner. I suppose the God whom I worship must have given me a gift for languages and writing." He paused, shrugged his shoulders, and waited quietly while she continued to stare at him with unconvinced eyes.

He seemed sincere enough, but Asenath was embarrassed now and wasn't quite sure what she should say next. When she looked away and didn't speak, Joseph asked, "Are you going to teach me the meaning of what I've written? Or is that to be saved for another lesson?" There was a hint of humor in his voice, and Asenath found herself more flustered than ever before.

"I'll show you the meaning right now," she said, grateful for something that would momentarily draw attention away from herself. "We'll start here with the first set of characters."

Quickly, she explained to him how hieroglyphics were learned. They were to be taken in as short sets of characters rather than individual symbols, and she had him point to each one, repeating it aloud after her, to familiarize him with the process. When this short exercise was complete, she randomly pointed to words to see what he remembered. To her amazement he remembered them all. He had a mind as keen as any priest or educated official she had ever met. He wasn't anything at all what she expected of a mere slave.

Perhaps there was a lesson to be learned from this. Maybe it was wrong to judge a man by his place in life or his outward appearance. The feelings of superiority she'd felt when she first arrived here today, quickly changed to shame.

"There's something not right about all of this," Asenath said. She shook her head and gave Joseph a deep, probing look. "You're not a slave. You can't be."

"I wish I weren't," he replied with a wan smile, "but I assure you that I am. I am a humble servant of Potiphar, purchased by him at the slave market."

"Then how did you get there? How did you end up in that market as a slave? Were you accused of some crime and sold to Potiphar as your punishment? Or were you brought here as a prisoner of war from another land?"

Joseph looked cautiously into her eyes. She could tell he wasn't sure how much he actually wanted to say to her. But finally he lowered his eyes, dropped his shoulders, and said, "My brothers sold me."

"What?"

"My brothers sold me to a traveling band of Midianites."

The pleasant look that seemed to be the usual expression of his face was gone now, and there was pain etched there instead.

"I don't understand," Asenath said, her voice dropping to a whisper. "Why would your own brothers sell you into slavery? Why didn't your parents stop them?"

"My father was far away in Hebron when my brothers did what they did to me," Joseph said. "He didn't know it was happening. But I should have been more cautious. All of my brothers but Benjamin have hated me for as long as I can remember. That hatred is what brought them to do this. And I suppose the dreams I had didn't help the situation."

"Dreams?"

"It's . . . it's a long story," Joseph hesitantly answered her. "I don't want to interrupt the lesson . . . "

"Our lesson is finished. I don't mind hearing about your dreams. I mean . . . if you don't mind telling me."

Joseph shrugged. He took a deep, trembling breath before giving a brief account of his two dreams—one in which sheaves of wheat representing his brothers bowed to his own sheaf and another where the sun, the moon, and eleven stars bowed down in submission before him.

"If your dreams mean what you told your family they meant," Asenath said after he had finished, "I can see why your brothers would be angry. But that gave them no cause to make a slave of you, and perhaps the dreams don't even mean what they seem to mean. In the temple, priests and priestesses are taught about dreams and their meanings, but they don't always come to pass."

Joseph shook his head. "The dreams mean what I said they mean. The God of my fathers gives dreams, and He also gives the interpretation of dreams. The meanings of both were made clear to me, and they were made clear to my brothers as well. They mean what they mean."

"Then your God has abandoned you," Asenath declared. "He allowed your brothers to thwart His plans."

"Men can't thwart God," Joseph replied. His voice was filled with surprising conviction. "And God doesn't forsake His children. His children often abandon Him, but He never abandons them. God is still with me. Look how greatly He has blessed me. I was the lowest of slaves, and now I am chief steward over all my master's possessions. Even in captivity my God is blessing my life."

Asenath wasn't convinced—but she was curious—so she decided to probe this slave further. "And who is this God that you believe so strongly in?" she asked. "Why do you still have faith in Him?"

"The God I serve is the only true and living God," Joseph replied. "He is the God of Abraham, Isaac, and Jacob. The Creator of this world. The Father of our spirits. There is a wise purpose for everything the Lord has allowed to happen to me, and I must hold fast to faith and place my trust in Him. Eventually He will show me the purpose for all that I've suffered at the hands of my brothers. Eventually He will make all things right."

Asenath shook her head. Her faith in the gods of Egypt had done her no good. How could it be any different with the foreign God of Joseph? Anyone could have a dream and say it came from a god, but how could they know he was speaking to them if there was no more evidence than the dream itself? She suddenly remembered the strange, repeating dream she'd once had and decided to test Joseph's ability to interpret it.

"This God of yours . . . does He ever speak to you? Does He speak to you in ways besides dreams? In ways that can't be mistaken?"

"He speaks to my heart," Joseph replied. "He speaks peace to my mind and gives me comfort when all seems lost. And as a boy, when I studied the writings of prophets in the tent of my father, God opened up my mind to understand the mysteries of His kingdom."

"Will He speak to you right now? Could He give you the interpretation of a dream if I told it to you?"

Joseph looked carefully into Asenath's eyes, studying her for several long moments before answering. "God doesn't provide signs to the curious," he said. "But He will reveal Himself to the honest in heart who humbly seek after truth. Tell me your dream. If the Lord chooses to give an interpretation, I will tell you the meaning of it."

Now it was Asenath who took a deep breath. Suddenly she felt very nervous. Egypt's gods had failed her at every turn, and she didn't know why this foreign God of Joseph would be any more willing to help her than they had been. But . . .

"This dream came to me for several nights in a row," she plunged in, afraid she would become too embarrassed to speak if she waited too long to begin. "It happened some time ago. But, even now, it weighs upon my mind as if it has great significance to my life. The dream was the same each time it came to me, and it happened something like this. I dreamed that Pharaoh came to me and led me to a field by the Nile. The field was empty except for a great ox that plowed without the guidance of a farmer's hand. Then the time of inundation came, and the waters of the Nile covered the land. When the waters receded, I saw two stalks of grain growing side by side in the field. The waters came a second time, they receded again, and the two stalks of grain had multiplied. There was grain as far as the eye could see. More stalks than I could possibly number. Does this dream make any sense to you?"

Joseph was silent for a very long time. He stared at the ground and his mind seemed to withdraw into some deep, inner recess of his soul. When he finally looked up at her, there was a strange calmness on his face and a light in his eyes.

"The ox represents a man," Joseph said, staring through her as if he were seeing into her dream rather than looking into her eyes. "He is a powerful man in Egypt. A man that Pharaoh will choose to be your husband."

Asenath felt a strange, frightening sensation pass through her. How did this slave know this? How did he know of Pharaoh's decree that he would choose her husband? Had Potiphar told it to him? For a moment she began to believe that Joseph's God really was talking to him, but then she realized that it was common knowledge among many in the city that Pharaoh held this part of her destiny in his hands. A clever man could make that fit into her dream. Or could he?

"Who is this man?" she asked, curious despite herself. "Who will my husband be?"

"I don't know. That remains for God to reveal in His own time. I can only tell you what has been revealed to me at this time."

"All right. What about the grain then? What did the two stalks of grain mean?"

"The first two stalks represent your children. You will have two sons, and they will be multiplied upon the earth like the grain was multiplied in the field. You will be the mother of a great posterity— the mother of great nations."

Asenath stared at Joseph, dumbstruck. She had pondered the dream for years with no success, yet he had come up with a logical interpretation in only a few short moments. And somehow it all made sense to her. Somehow—and she couldn't explain how it was done—the truth of his interpretation actually seemed to be speaking to her heart—to the very core of her soul.

"How do you know all of this? How is it so clear to you when it was such a mystery to me?"

"It can't be done by the wisdom or power of man," Joseph replied. "The interpretation of dreams has to be given by God. My father told me that I have the gift of dreams and interpretation of dreams. God speaks the meaning to my heart, and I listen."

This slave was more than a slave. There was something different about him from any man Asenath had ever met, and it frightened her. Even her father, with all his knowledge of Egyptian magic and the clever artifices of persuasion, didn't possess the power she sensed in Joseph. Yet he made no outward display of it like the priests in the temples. This was something she couldn't completely fathom.

She wanted to learn more about this strange, young Hebrew. She wanted to find out all she could about him. But Asenath sensed she would have to proceed with caution. There would be other opportunities to question this slave. There would be time to learn the nuances of his personality and depth of his character.

"I need to get back to my duties at the temple," Asenath said, abruptly ending the conversation about her dream. "Keep the scrolls and the palette I brought to you and practice whenever you have the time. Try to remember the meanings of the words you've copied today."

Joseph nodded and carefully gathered the supplies into one arm. When he had finished, he got to his feet and extended one hand to Asenath. Hesitantly, she accepted the proffered hand and allowed him to help her to her feet. His hand was warm and strong, and she allowed hers to linger in his for a few moments longer than necessary. Then she pulled her hand self-consciously back and turned her eyes away from his.

"When can I see you again?" Joseph asked. "I mean . . . when will you return for the next writing lesson?"

"In two days," Asenath replied. "We'll work on hieratic and on numbers. Those two things will be most useful to you as chief steward. Remember to practice your writing. Goodbye."

She didn't want to leave. She wanted to stay in the garden with him, discussing his strange foreign God and basking in the warmth of Joseph's presence. But another part of her wanted to run from the strange sensations that had begun to wildly churn inside of her. She couldn't understand her own emotions, and she felt feelings that shouldn't be awakened by a mere slave. She was confused. She anticipated being with Joseph again, and yet she dreaded it at the same time. None of this made any sense to her. None of it at all.

His eyes were watching her as she hurried out of the garden, but she pretended not to notice. Her life was about to be drastically altered again. She sensed this. She just didn't know why or how.

For several long minutes, Joseph stood alone, watching the place where Asenath had left the garden. He couldn't seem to rid his mind of her image. The memory of her lovely face kept floating before his mind, etching itself deeper and deeper into his memory. And his heart was swelling with a conflicting whirlwind of emotions.

Never in his life had he seen such eyes. He kept losing himself in the memory of those mesmerizing, shockingly blue eyes. And, when he managed to clear that image from his mind, he would see again the soft lines of Asenath's face and the long, dark hair that framed it.

"She has a face as lovely as a goddess," Potiphar had warned him a day in advance. "But don't let that fool you. The girl has an angry spark that's going to ignite one day. You don't want to be the one who provokes it."

Joseph had seen some of that anger today, but mostly he'd seen the fiery determination that lurked just beneath it. While giving Asenath the interpretation of her dream, he had been impressed to believe that her anger was a product, in part, of a bravely honest heart—a heart that would embrace truth once she found it. He pondered that for a moment and allowed himself once more to become immersed in the memory of her lovely, blue eyes. But he didn't indulge himself for long. Vigorously he shook his head, chastising himself for allowing the girl's beauty and the force of her determined personality to charm him.

"Don't be a fool, Joseph," he said. "She's an Egyptian priestess. You're a slave. If you're going to dream, dream of things that are possible."

He had precious little time for daydreaming anyway. The brief interlude in the garden had been a pleasant one; but there was still a great deal of work awaiting him today, and it was time he got back to it.

The first order of business was to ride down to the river and check on Potiphar's fields. Potiphar had already expressed a concern about those fields and the harvest he was expecting them to bring in, and Joseph realized he needed to make an official appearance there. Since T'chet's termination, no one had really checked on the activities of the farmers. Obviously this was weighing heavily upon Potiphar's mind, and it would be good if Joseph could ease some of that concern the next time he met with his master.

He shuddered a little as he thought about T'chet. He shuddered again as he thought of the transgression that had angered Potiphar to the point of sentencing the man to death. The lure of Neferset's beauty had been too much for the former chief steward, and he had paid the ultimate price for his indiscretions. But Joseph had the feeling that Neferset was as much to blame as T'chet. That woman frightened him. He didn't like the way she watched him every time he came near the house, and he didn't like the way she suddenly appeared at his side at the most unexpected moments. It was as if she were lying in wait, searching for opportunities to be near him.

"I give you charge of everything in my house," Potiphar had told him on the day he was appointed to take T'chet's place. "Everything I have is yours to do with as you please. Everything but my wife."

Joseph didn't miss the subtle, implied threat. And perhaps after the incident with T'chet his master felt the threat was necessary. But he needn't have worried about Joseph. With or without a warning, Joseph would definitely keep his distance from Neferset. He had no intention of repeating any of T'chet's mistakes.

This thought was fresh in his mind as Joseph made his way to the stables; and, because of it, he took the course that would least likely lead him past the watchful eyes of his master's wife. Pekhti was waiting for him when he arrived, and a pair of horses was already harnessed to a chariot for his use.

"Thank you, Pekhti," Joseph said as he took the horses' reins from the chief groom.

"How did you know I was ready to leave for the fields?"

"I saw the young priestess departing for the temple. I assumed you would come here next."

They were both silent for a moment, and Joseph patted the muzzle of one of the two horses, thinking about Asenath again. It was several moments before he realized that Pekhti, with an amused smile on his face, was scrutinizing him.

"What?" Joseph asked. He raised one eyebrow questioningly.

"I was thinking that it must be distracting for you," Pekhti said in Joseph's own native tongue.

"I'm not quite sure what you're talking about. Distracting? What must be distracting?"

"*Ta sherau nefer er aa-ur*," Pekhti replied switching back to Egyptian. "The girl is very pretty. A young, unmarried man such as yourself would have to possess great discipline to keep his eyes on his writing."

"I'm a slave. She's a priestess. I try to keep that in mind, and that keeps everything else in perspective."

"Then the master has found the right man. If you can keep your eyes off the priestess, you can surely withstand any of his wife's advances."

This conversation had turned into something that Joseph didn't want to pursue, so he quickly changed the subject.

"This is my first time visiting the master's fields," he said. "What advice would you give me? How should I approach the farmers?"

Pekhti's face lit up. Things had been a little awkward between them since Joseph's sudden rise to power, but the look on the face of Joseph's old mentor showed he was pleased that Joseph would still turn to him for advice.

"The farmers are a difficult lot to figure," Pekhti said. "They're not much more than slaves themselves, but they can be much more stubborn and unyielding. Potiphar commands their respect by the mere fact that he owns and controls the land they depend upon for their survival. But you . . . well, you're a slave, and a slave is the only thing in Egypt lower than a farmer. I imagine that they will be slow to accept your leadership. T'chet never earned their respect and the

harvests suffered as a result. It will be critical for you to earn that respect as quickly as possible. I wish I could tell you how to do it, but I
have no worthwhile advice to offer."

Joseph pondered for a moment, then soberly nodded his head.
The farmers weren't the only ones who were slow to accept him. It
was still a struggle to command the respect of any of Potiphar's servants—even the other slaves. He would need God's blessings and help
if he ever hoped to succeed.

"Whatever happens," Pekhti said, "pay especially close attention
to the barley fields this year. As long as the master's horses are fed, he
will be happy with you. And if that fails to please him, a strong batch
of the beer that barley will make will cause him to forget why he's
angry." He chuckled at his own joke, trying to put Joseph at ease, and
Joseph allowed a tense smile to creep across his face.

"Well, I guess I'd better be about the master's business," Joseph
said, stepping into the chariot and taking the reins from Pekhti's
hand. "There's no use putting this off any longer."

"You'll be fine," Pekhti said, grinning again. "Your foreign God
watches over you. I've never met a man more favored by his God than
you are. He has put you over all Potiphar's other servants. The way
your God favors you, you may someday end up ruling Egypt."

"I'll just be happy if He keeps my neck off the chopping block,"
Joseph replied, shaking his head. "I can't help but feel pity for T'chet
and his family every time I think of the circumstances that took him
from this position and put me into it."

"T'chet deserved everything that happened to him," Pekhti said,
spitting on the ground to emphasize his disgust. "He deserved to
be executed. He was arrogant, greedy, and cruel. And he stole from
the master. *In more ways than one.*" He paused to glance meaningfully in the direction of the house, and Joseph knew he was referring
to Neferset. "When T'chet goes before Osiris to be judged," Pekhti
said, "Anubis will throw his heart to Ammut, the Eater. But you have
nothing to worry about. Your heart is in the right place. You won't
suffer the same end as T'chet."

"Thank you," Joseph said, smiling a little. "I only wish the rest of Potiphar's household felt the same."

"Give them time. They'll eventually see that, slave or not, you're the best man for the job. And, even if they don't, you'll be so much better than T'chet that they'll be forced to give you at least some grudging respect."

Joseph nodded in appreciation then flicked the reins over the heads of the horses. He waved a nervous farewell, and moved the chariot toward the outer wall that separated Potiphar's property from the rest of the city. It took him only a few minutes to reach the outskirts of Avaris; and, from there, it was only a few minutes more until the river and the fields that lined its banks. He stopped at the edge of the nearest field and surveyed it quietly.

Tall stalks of barley and wheat greeted him as they waved in a hot, dry breeze; but the team of farmers working not far away hadn't noticed him yet. They were using a *shaduf,* a long, wooden lever with a bucket at the end, to lift water from the river to the fields, and their bodies were glistening with perspiration from the effort. Joseph, looking around, noticed a sturdy wooden post at the edge of the field, and he took the chariot there to tether the horses. Once he was certain they were secure, he moved over to examine the ripening harvest.

Each spikelet of wheat held two full, red kernels; and even one who had not been trained in the techniques of farming could see that the time of harvest was near at hand. It made an uneasy knot form in the pit of Joseph's stomach to think about the monumental task that was surely looming just ahead of him. His father had taught him the mathematics for estimating the size of a piece of property, and he felt fairly confident that he could estimate the amount of harvest that should be brought in from these fields. But he still had only a vague knowledge of the Egyptian system of measurement that would make his calculations understandable to his master. Potiphar was expecting him to keep very precise records of grain production, and that meant that Joseph needed Asenath to teach him measurements as soon as possible. More importantly, he needed the Lord's help to learn it quickly enough so that it would be of use to him when the harvest came.

There was nothing he could do about the grain at the moment—nothing but allow it to ripen in the sun—so Joseph turned his eyes back in the direction of the farmers and trudged slowly in their direction. A sacred ibis, on its way to the delta marshlands, flew over his head, and the cry of another bird rang out across the field as he startled it from its hiding place. The wheat was almost as tall as Joseph's shoulders and could nearly hide him from sight, but the farmers soon spotted him, and their curious whispers and glances turned hostile when they realized who he was.

"Greetings!" he called out as he drew near to them. "The harvest is looking good." He waited for a response, but none of the men answered him. They just stared. Stared and drummed their fingers threateningly against the hard, wooden handle of the *shaduf*.

"I'm Joseph, the new chief steward," he tried again. "The master has sent me to inspect the fields."

"We know who you are," one of the men said as Joseph came clear of the tall wheat. There was no warmth in the man's voice, and his eyes were cold and menacing. Joseph's arrival brought no joy to this group of men. But he kept his voice calm and even, despite the tense knot in his stomach that grew harder with each new, passing moment.

"If you know who I am," Joseph said, "then you know that I have power over all Potiphar's properties . . . *and servants.*" He allowed a moment for the last two words to sink in.

Then he tapped one of the gold bracelets that extended from his wrist half-way up his forearm.

Each bracelet was emblazoned with the hieroglyphic insignia of Potiphar—a visible symbol of Joseph's authority. But he quickly saw that even this wouldn't be enough to gain the cooperation of these men.

"Who is the steward over Potiphar's fields?" Joseph finally demanded.

"I thought you were." The man who spoke was the one who had given Joseph the unspoken challenge, and he took one bold step forward to stand in front of the others.

"That's not what I meant," Joseph said, trying not to become flustered. "What I want to know is who is the chief farmer among you?"

"I am."

"Then you must be Uhen." Joseph matched the gaze of the scowling man with an unwavering gaze of his own. "I trust the master has informed you what will be expected of you?"

Uhen didn't answer, but Joseph could tell by the displeased look on the man's face that he knew exactly what Potiphar expected of him.

"Come with me," Joseph commanded. "I want to see where the master's fields begin and where they end. I want you to show me."

"Won't it be easier for you just to look over the written records?" Uhen asked. There was a malicious gleam in his eyes, and his fellow farmers snickered; but Joseph didn't back down. He understood the not so subtle hint. They viewed him as a slave who wasn't intelligent enough to decipher written records let alone rule over Potiphar's vast properties. But Joseph answered the challenge with a deceptively pleasant smile. Uhen would have to do better than this. Joseph had grown used to taunts and threats long ago in the household of his own father. These farmers had much to learn before their skill matched that of the sons of Jacob.

"Yes, it would be easier to check the records," Joseph calmly replied. "But it wouldn't be very accurate, would it? We all know that, among other things, the master caught T'chet tampering with those records. And we also know that I can't trust records kept by a dishonest man. That leaves me with two options. Either we can walk these fields together so that I can accurately estimate what the harvest should be, or I can make an estimate using my own imagination. I have a large imagination. I imagine a huge harvest. I imagine you filling all the master's granaries with it."

Uhen gave a soft snort of disgust, but he finally lowered his eyes in submission. The rewards of resisting this new, young chief steward were not worth the extra work he would bring down upon his own head and the heads of his fellow servants if he didn't do as Joseph wanted.

Reluctantly, he shuffled forward. "Follow me," he grunted. "I'll show you the markers Pharaoh has set at the edges of the fields."

"Thank you," Joseph said. He smiled again, but the smile wasn't reflected in his eyes. He paused to fix each of the remaining farmers with a firm, meaningful stare before he and Uhen moved away together across the field.

The fields were quite large; but he was still surprised at just how large they really were. Potiphar must be even wealthier than he had at first thought. There were three sections to Potiphar's fields. One area—the largest—was filled with barley. The next area was a vast field of red wheat, and the third and smallest area was a garden of fresh vegetables. Joseph could see rows of the strong-tasting onions and garlic which Egyptians were so fond of and other rows of lettuce, peas, beans, cucumbers, and leeks. Egypt lived secure in the knowledge of the Nile's annual inundation and the renewal of life its waters brought to the earth. Some lands were not fortunate to be blessed with such an abundance of water. Egyptians could usually feel confident that their fields would produce more than enough to meet their needs. Only an unimaginable catastrophe could change that.

When his short inspection of the fields was complete, Joseph dismissed Uhen and returned to the chariot. He now had a slightly better understanding of the scope of his responsibility here, but he still had no idea about how he was going to manage it. His next task, however, was more suited to his past experience. Across the delta where the marshlands began were the rich pastures where Amakh, the keeper of Potiphar's herds, watched over the cows, sheep, and goats; and Joseph felt as if he were being transported back to his old life in Hebron as he arrived here with the chariot. He paused for a long while to gaze across the rich, green grasses, and he wondered suddenly if the drought in Hebron had ever ended. Was his family managing to find grazing lands for their flocks and herds? Had the Lord continued to prosper His faithful servant Jacob?

Thoughts of home were always painful, so Joseph quickly fought to turn his mind to other things. Work—an endless supply of mind-numbing work—was his usual cure for the sorrow of separation from home and family. And now that he was chief steward, he would have a broad variety of work to keep his mind occupied. Work was an unexpected blessing from God. He supposed he could be grateful for that. He would gladly accept any blessing he could get.

Chapter Notes

1. The writing system of ancient Egypt consisted of several different scripts, each with its own unique purpose. A highly literate Egyptian would have been proficient in both the printed and cursive forms of the written language, and a scribe's knowledge of the language often determined how high he could rise in the hierarchy of Egyptian society. The most difficult of all the scripts was the hieroglyphics which were used on monuments and for other public inscriptions. But, at the time of Joseph, a beginning writer would have first learned the flowing, cursive script called *hieratic*. Archeological evidence suggests that this was learned by copying passages from temple texts. Hieratic was the common script in use for day-to-day writing such as making household lists, personal letters, notes, etc. and it evolved at a later date into an even more flowing script known as *demotic*. It's likely that, at some point in time, Joseph would have become literate enough to use the hieroglyphic and hieratic scripts which were in current use during his tenure as royal vizier.

2. Asenath's dream is not historical or scriptural. It is a fictional part of this story. Joseph's ability to interpret dreams, however, is clearly recorded in the scriptures. (See Genesis 40 and 41.)

3. The type of wheat Westerners are currently most familiar with was not known in Egypt at the time of Joseph. The wheat grown in the fields of Egypt was a red wheat known as *emmer (Triticum dicoccum)*. "White" versions of wheat (such as *Triticum aestivum*), seem not to have been introduced into Egypt until the much later arrival of the Greeks.

SIXTEEN

ASENATH AROSE EARLY on the morning of her second lesson at Potiphar's property. It wasn't difficult to do. For the past two days, she hadn't felt much like eating or sleeping. All she could seem to do was think about seeing Joseph again, and it angered her that she couldn't fight that feeling off.

"Is something wrong?" Netchem had asked after dinner the night before. "You haven't seemed like yourself these past few days."

"What do you mean?" Asenath answered, shifting her eyes evasively to one side.

"I don't know. It's like your mind is somewhere else. You're not worrying again about who Pharoah's going to marry you to, are you?"

"No, I'm not thinking about that," Asenath said. She relaxed a little now, glad that she could give a truthful yet safe reply.

"All right. If it's not that, what is it then?"

"I have a lot on my mind," Asenath said. "Teaching the hieroglyphics isn't as easy as I thought it would be." She wasn't going to tell Netchem what was really wrong. How would she explain that she couldn't stop thinking about Potiphar's slave or that she kept reliving the brief moment when the tall, dark-eyed steward had innocently touched her hand? If word of such feelings got back to Setmosis, she'd never be allowed away from the temple again.

"I think it's odd that Potiphar is having you go directly to his home to teach," Netchem said. "Why doesn't he just send her to the temple school to be trained? Wouldn't it be easier for everyone that way?"

"The slave I'm teaching is Potiphar's new chief steward," Asenath replied, realizing now that there would be no easy way out of this conversation. "His duties prevent him from straying far from Potiphar's properties."

"You're teaching a man?" Netchem's eyes opened wide with surprise. "Why didn't Father ask one of the priests to do it?"

"Perhaps he thought the priests would be too busy with their temple duties," Asenath quickly answered. "I don't know. All I know is that Potiphar wanted someone who would be willing and able to come to his estate. It must be that my duties at the temple aren't as vital as everyone else's. Whatever the case, I'm not going to question the choice. I'm just grateful for the opportunity to go someplace other than this house or the temple."

Netchem nodded. "It's wonderful that father and Pharaoh are finally starting to trust you. It's taken them far too long to do so."

"You haven't told me how things are going between you and Ptakh," Asenath said, seizing on a topic that might distract Netchem from this one. "Have you had a chance to talk with him lately?"

"Yes." A dreamy look entered Netchem's eyes, and Asenath fought to hold back a triumphant smile. "We ran into each other outside the temple gates this afternoon."

"You two are 'running into each other' quite often these days," Asenath teased. "Do you think your father has figured out yet that you like Ptakh?"

Netchem blushed. "I don't know. But I'm not going to tell him. And you already promised not to tell anyone either!"

"I give you my solemn word. I won't tell another living soul."

Netchem visibly relaxed. Then she returned to the very subject Asenath most wanted to avoid. "But my life's not as interesting as yours. Tell me more about this chief steward. Why did Potiphar choose a slave to replace his last steward?"

"I don't know," Asenath said. "Maybe he chose a slave because he doesn't want to draw any more attention to the problems in his household. Maybe he wants a man of low enough status that his wife won't be interested in that man."

Netchem nodded. "That makes sense, I guess. So, tell me. Is this new steward ugly as well?"

"I-I wouldn't say that," Asenath cautiously replied.

"Then you're saying he's young? Handsome?"

"He's a slave. My job is to teach him. Not to judge whether or not he's attractive." She said this a little too abruptly, and Netchem stared at her for a few moments. Then the light of understanding flickered to life in her eyes.

"You *do* find him attractive, don't you."

Asenath didn't answer. She squirmed uncomfortably and tried to find a way to answer Netchem's teasing accusation without really answering it. But Netchem spoke again before she could.

"You don't have to worry. I won't tell Father. He'd just worry about it and not let you go back there to teach again. Besides, I know you would never do anything inappropriate."

Asenath smiled, but she continued to squirm. She was glad when Netchem finally turned her attention from the subject.

Netchem was right about one thing. Asenath would never let anything inappropriate happen between herself and a mere slave. She was determined to find a way to dislike her handsome, good-natured student. And yet, for one who was so determined to quench the emotional flames that had been ignited inside her, she was doing the oddest things. This morning, for instance, she'd gotten up early so that she could bathe and carefully brush out her long, black hair. She tried to tell herself she was just doing this to present the proper image of authority when she appeared before Joseph again. But she knew it wasn't true. Authority had nothing at all to do with her desire to look good. If she were to be honest with herself, she'd have to admit that she was hopelessly infatuated with Joseph.

This realization now dawning upon her, Asenath angrily pulled the brush through her hair and grimaced as it caught itself in a snarl. It would be much easier to groom herself if she did as the other priest-esses did and shaved her head, but she grimaced even more at the thought of that. To shave one's head was an act of religious purifica-tion. The temple workers, both male and female, did this and then the women donned carefully styled wigs to cover their baldness. Asenath knew it annoyed Setmosis that she still hadn't submitted herself to the ritual, but it was one of the many things she still stubbornly resisted. To do it would be to admit that she was now and would always be a priestess of Seth. There was a part of her that gained defiant satisfac-tion, therefore, from this quiet act of resistance.

Asenath set the brush down, took a moment to ornament her raven hair with a simple, golden headband, then turned her attention to the final details of her appearance. From the wooden box contain-ing her personal possessions, she removed several important items: henna, to redden her lips and nails; pumice, to soften her skin and rub away unwanted hair; myrrh, to perfume her skin with its fragrant oil; and kohl, to outline and heighten her eyes. When all was done, she put on her best linen *kalasiris* and examined her reflection in a polished, bronze mirror.

It was silly really. It was silly to worry so much about her appear-ance when nothing could ever happen between herself and Joseph. He was a slave. She was a priestess. Any romantic feelings between them would be forbidden. But she took the mirror again and made sure she hadn't missed anything. Maybe this, too, was a quiet act of defiance. Maybe this was her way of fighting against Pharaoh and the powers of Seth. Whatever her reasons might be, she finished off her preparations by fastening her lapis amulet about her neck then rushed out of her room into the hall. She was in such a hurry and her mind was so distracted that she nearly collided with Netchem as she came into the corridor.

"Oh! Excuse me!" she exclaimed. "I'm sorry. I wasn't paying attention where I was going."

"Wherever it is, it must be important," Netchem answered her with a laugh.

"What? Why do you say that?"

"Because you look so nice today, I'd swear you were about to present yourself before Pharaoh."

Asenath blushed. Then she frantically searched for an explanation for her appearance. When she could think of none, she opted instead for acting like she was in too big of a hurry to give an answer.

"I'm sorry," she said. "I don't have time to talk. If I don't leave right now, I'll never get there on time."

"Get there? Get where?"

"I'll talk with you later. Goodbye, Netchem."

"You're on your way to Potiphar's estate. Aren't you."

Asenath stopped in mid-stride. When she turned to risk a glance over her shoulder at her foster sister, she saw an amused, knowing smile on Netchem's lips.

"It's nothing like what you think," Asenath said.

"Oh? Tell me. What is it that you think I'm thinking?"

"I don't know. But I'm sure it's nothing like what you think."

Netchem looked Asenath up and down, tapped an index finger against her lower lip, and allowed her smile to grow even larger. "Let's see," she began. "You're wearing your best *kalasiris*. Your hair and your makeup are more perfectly done than they've ever been since you arrived here. All of that points to the fact that you're interested in someone."

"I'm not interested in anyone. I just want to make the proper impression on my student."

Netchem nodded her head. "You'll make an impression. I'm certain of that. The real question is what kind of impression are you trying to make?"

Asenath blushed. Then she suddenly became angry. But she fought to hide that anger.

"Your father always says that the outer appearance of a priest or priestess should command the respect of her subordinates," she said. "I've just decided to follow his advice."

Netchem continued for several long moments to smile. But finally that smile faded, and a look of concern replaced it.

"Be careful," Netchem said. "You've already had enough sorrow in your life. Don't allow your heart to lead you into more of it."

"I don't know what you're talking about," Asenath stiffly answered. "But I do have to be on my way. I'll see you at the temple when I get back. Goodbye, Netchem."

Quickly, she exited the house and did her best to convince herself that Netchem would forget her suspicions and everything could go back to normal. But she knew that wouldn't happen. She also knew her friend was right. She had to bring an end to the silly fantasies and the unwelcome feelings that were swirling around in her heart. The only problem was that this was going to be harder than it sounded.

For some mysterious reason, the walk to Potiphar's estate seemed to take twice as long as the last time. Asenath felt her pulse racing, and her palms began to sweat. She hoped Joseph would already be waiting for her at the garden when she got there, but she also hoped he wouldn't be. If he were late again, it would give her a reason to scold him, and she hoped that would break the spell she was under. But she had no such luck. He was dutifully waiting beside the table when she arrived, and the scrolls and scribe's palette she'd left with him had been carefully set out on the tabletop. She didn't quite know what to say when he stood up with a smile and greeted her.

"Good morning."

She stood for several long moments in awkward silence. She'd forgotten how tall he was. She'd also forgotten how broad his shoulders were. But his eyes were still the same. They were the deep, warm, friendly eyes which had been haunting her mind ever since she'd met him. Her heart began suddenly to beat faster, and her legs grew weak.

"G-good morning," she mumbled, realizing that he was waiting for a response. "How did your practice with the hieroglyphics go?"

"I think it went well," he said. "Would you like to look over my writing? Hopefully it will meet with your approval."

Asenath nodded, moved to the table, and quickly unrolled Joseph's practice scroll. She was grateful for something "teacher-like" to do and scanned his work with a critical eye. Unfortunately, there was nothing on the scroll to criticize. Her eyes widened as she unrolled and unrolled until she came to the end of the scroll to find it entirely filled with bold, cursive hieroglyphs.

"You've filled it," she said, stating the obvious. "You've filled the entire scroll."

"Yes," Joseph said. And then his countenance dropped. "Was I not supposed to do that?"

"No . . . I mean, yes . . . I mean . . . how did you do it in so few days?"

"I stayed up late every night," Joseph said. "I copied from the other scroll like you told me to until I ran out of room."

"You've done very well," Asenath said, trying to hide her amazement. "And do you remember the lines I taught you?"

"Yes. I've been memorizing those words in my mind ever since you left. Do you want to see how much I remember?"

Asenath nodded and turned her eyes back to his work. Anyone could copy incomprehensible symbols from a scroll, but understanding those symbols was something altogether different. She picked one of the most difficult words and asked Joseph to identify it. One by one after that she pointed out every word they had discussed. He knew them all.

This was no ordinary man—of that Asenath was certain. But she wasn't sure what it was that made him so different. She stared at him for a moment, and a sudden, unmistakable impression came into her heart. Her destiny and his were somehow inextricably intertwined. The revelation made a chill go up and down her spine.

"How did you remember it all?" she cautiously asked, coming back to her senses again. "How did you remember all those words after such a short lesson?"

"I noticed when you were having me copy them that certain symbols were repeated in certain words. I realized that some of the symbols stand for sounds, and I used those sounds as clues to remind me what word I was looking at. I think I figured out what some of the rest of this text means as well. Do you want me to tell you?"

Asenath was unsure what to do. She again allowed her eyes to scan the entirely filled scroll. "I-I didn't bring another scroll with me," she said. "I wasn't expecting you to fill this one so quickly. But, yes, you can go through and show me what you've deciphered. After that we'll look at the meanings of the words you don't yet know."

"Do you think we could take a few minutes at the end of our lesson time to cover something else as well?" Joseph asked.

"Perhaps. What is it that you want to learn?"

"I need to know numbers and measurements. I need to know the Egyptian way of measuring volumes of grain, sizes of fields, and distances. Will you teach me?"

"Today would be as good a day as any," Asenath said, shrugging her shoulders. "Perhaps it would be good to start with that first. How did you measure things in your homeland? Did you have a certain method of determining length?"

"Our unit of measure was the length of the area between the elbow and the tip of the middle finger," Joseph replied.

Asenath nodded. "It's the same in Egypt. In fact, I believe the people of many other lands have adopted their system of measurement from the royal Egyptian cubit. All you'll need is the proper vocabulary and the rest should be easy for you."

She paused, motioned for Joseph to extend his arm, and waved her hand along the area he had just described. "We call this length a *meh*," she said. "It is subdivided into seven *shep*—the width of a human palm—and the smallest unit is a *zebo*—the width of a finger. If you want to measure something very long, the unit of measurement would be a *khet* or an *ater*. Do you have something for us to measure? That would be the best way to help you remember."

A broad grin spread across Joseph's face. "As a matter of fact, there is something I would like to measure," he said. "But do you have time for a short chariot ride somewhere?"

Asenath stared at him and frowned.

"Don't worry," he reassured. "I promise it won't take long. And you did ask if there was something in particular I wanted to measure."

It wasn't the length of time that worried Asenath. It was the chance that someone from the temple might see them together. One glance at this tall, strong man and Netchem would no longer be the only one who suspected Asenath might be attracted to Joseph. She pondered the risks for several long moments but finally nodded her head. It would be nice to spend time with Joseph in a place other than the garden. It would give her a chance to observe him in a different environment. Maybe that was all it would take to release her heart from the perplexing whirlwind of emotions that now grasped it.

"I'll take the shortcut," Joseph promised, seeing that she still looked hesitant. "No one will even notice that we're gone from the garden."

She frowned again, wondering if he could read thoughts as well as interpret dreams. But he eagerly hurried from the garden, motioning for her to follow, before she could change her mind. Teaching this man looked as if it was going to be a small adventure as well as a part-time occupation. That was fine with her. She needed more adventure in her life.

Chapter Notes

Egyptians are believed to have standardized a unit of length sometime around 3000 B.C. The royal Egyptian cubit (called *meh* in Egyptian) was the basic unit of measurement and was borrowed, with slight variations, by many surrounding countries. To account for the obvious difference of body proportion from one person to the next, cubit sticks or rods of uniform length were cut from stone or wood. Modern measurements have confirmed that the Egyptian system was surprisingly accurate.

SEVENTEEN

H E COULDN'T HELP BUT NOTICE how beautiful Asenath looked today, and Joseph savored the scent of her hair as she rode in the chariot beside him. The social barriers separating them were insurmountable. But here—in a chariot, with the wind rushing past their faces—class differences didn't seem to matter so much.

"Have you ever driven a chariot?" Joseph asked.

"No. I don't think I'm brave enough to try that," Asenath replied, smiling shyly and quickly shaking her head.

"Why not? You don't know until you try."

"And what happens if I lose control of the horses and crash the chariot? How is Potiphar going to feel about that?"

"You won't lose control. I'm here to help you."

"I thought I was supposed to be the teacher and you were supposed to be the student." She cast him a stern glance, but her shimmering blue eyes were laughing.

"Here. Take the reigns," Joseph urged.

Asenath looked uncertain, but she cautiously accepted the reins and allowed Joseph to move behind her to guide her in what she should do. With his arms around her and his hands lightly touching her wrists, Joseph showed Asenath how to guide the chariot where she wanted it to go and how to increase or decrease the speed of the horses. For a few moments, he forgot that he was a slave, and she seemed to forget that she was a priestess. But he remembered his reason for bringing her to the fields the moment they came in sight of them, and the reality of his existence came rushing back at him.

"Guide the horses toward that wooden pole," he said, "and pull back on the reins a little. We'll tether the horses to the pole, and you can show me how to measure the fields."

"The fields?"

"Yes. You didn't say the object had to be small."

Asenath laughed and Joseph felt an odd warmth flood through him as he listened to the sound of her soft, feminine voice. It was a voice he would like to get used to—a voice he would like to wake up to every day. But the impossibility of that took some of the happy exhilaration out of this time alone with her.

"All right. We'll measure your field," Asenath said, shaking her head at him. "But, from now on, I'm going to ask a few more questions before I allow you to decide the direction our studies will take. Let's get started. I wish we'd brought a roll of papyrus with us, but you seem to have a good enough memory. We'll write down the measurements when we get back to the garden."

"I'm glad you're so agreeable about this," Joseph said, "because I need to know the sizes of these fields before harvest begins. If you show me how to measure the first section, I'll come back later and practice on the others."

"Show me the markers," Asenath replied. "We'll measure the length first, and then we'll measure the width. I'll show you how to determine the number of *setjats* in this field. A *setjat* would be about one hundred cubits squared. We'll need a large measurement like that to do this."

"Good. And after that, you can show me how to measure volume. I'll need to know how much grain this field produces."

"Let's just worry about length and area today, shall we?" Asenath said. Her face was stern, but her eyes were still sparkling. "I think the basic measurements of length will sufficiently fill our time today."

Joseph nodded, enjoying this. It was harder for his teacher to act like a teacher when they were away from the scrolls and the ink. Today the two of them were beginning to know each other as people rather than just a teacher and a student. He knew he was on emotionally dangerous ground, but it was a danger he couldn't help but face.

"Let's start here," Asenath said, breaking off a stalk of wheat and holding it up alongside Joseph's forearm. She broke a little more off so that it was a cubit in length and then instructed him to measure the field with it. It went faster than he had thought—faster than he had hoped—and when they were done, he realized that the fields were even bigger than he had first estimated them to be.

"You're a good teacher," he said as they followed the edge of the field back to the chariot. "I think I've got at least this part of Egyptian measurements figured out."

"I think you got it before we even started measuring," Asenath said, lightly touching her chin with one forefinger and watching him again with her deep, blue eyes. "If everything comes this easily to you, our lessons will be over much sooner than I expected."

"I'm not as fast a learner as you seem to think I am," Joseph said. "I'm sure it's going to take a very long time before I learn everything Potiphar wants you to teach me."

"We shall see," Asenath said. A faint smile crossed her lips, and then she jerked her head around as a shriek rang out across the field. It was a sound of both pain and horror, and Joseph spun around with her, dropping his makeshift cubit rod to the ground.

"What was that?" Asenath whispered, her face suddenly going white.

"I don't know," Joseph answered. He craned his neck so that he could see across the top of the wheat and a frantic flurry of motion at the opposite end of the field caught his attention. Something had happened—something terrible had happened—and the farmers were gathering at the scene. "Come with me!" Joseph commanded. He grabbed Asenath's hand and led her across the field behind him. It was a good thing he held onto her. If he hadn't, he would have lost her in the wheat. It was taller than she was. But they burst out of the field together at the opposite end of the field, and they both gasped for breath as they approached a ring of panic stricken farmers.

Joseph released Asenath's hand, pushed his way into the circle, and found the motionless form of a man lying there.

"What's going on here?" he demanded. "What has happened?"

"It was an asp!" one of the servants hissed. His eyes flickered nervously toward the tall grain through which Joseph and Asenath had just passed.

"It sank its fangs into Uhen," another servant said, pointing to the motionless form on the ground, "and then it disappeared into the field over there."

Joseph felt the blood drain from his face. The farmer was pointing to the bent stalks of wheat where Joseph and Asenath had just emerged, and he realized suddenly just what kind of danger he'd just exposed the young priestess to. He could have never forgiven himself if harm came to her. He would never bring her away from the safety of Potiphar's garden again.

"Stay close to me," Joseph whispered to Asenath in a low, hoarse voice. Then he knelt down beside Uhen to carefully examine him. The man wasn't dead, but his breathing was shallow and his skin was clammy to the touch. Although Joseph didn't know much about venomous snakes, it didn't take an expert to realize there wasn't a lot of time for asking questions.

"You two," he commanded, picking out two of the farmers at random. "Take your sickles and search the edge of the field. Kill the snake if you find it. And you two . . . " He pointed at two others. "Carry Uhen to my chariot." He paused for a moment, trying to think of what he should do next, and then he turned to Asenath. "Do you know of any good physicians in the city. Do you know of anyone who might be able to save this man?"

Asenath looked pale, but she nodded her head, and Joseph took her hand reassuringly in his own.

"Stay close to me," he whispered again as they hurried with the servants to the chariot. "If someone else gets bitten, I don't want it to be you."

He didn't pause to await her reaction to this statement; but if he had looked carefully, he would have seen surprise followed quickly by a warm glow in her eyes. Something was happening between him and his beautiful teacher. And it was too late to turn time back.

Since the days of Imhotep, the revered physician and famed architect of Zoser's step pyramid, Egypt had boasted some of the finest physicians in the world. But even the skilled doctors of Avaris were unable to save Uhen from the toxic venom of the asp. Not wanting anyone else to suffer the same fate, Joseph left Asenath in the safety of the temple and returned alone to the field. He carefully sought out the snake, determined to destroy it himself; and all the while he was completely unaware how his actions were affecting his fellow servants. But it did affect them. In a way he would have never imagined.

"The servants are talking about you," Pekhti informed him the next day. "They saw how Uhen stood against you, and yet you tried to save his life. They say that a mysterious God watches over you. They believe it was your God who sent the asp to strike down Uhen, and they fear he will strike down anyone else who opposes you."

"I don't believe the God I worship would strike down Uhen just because he tried to defy my authority," Joseph said. "The God of my fathers is a merciful God. He gives life, and He takes it away. But He is longsuffering with His children. Perhaps Uhen's death served a useful purpose, but his life wouldn't be taken just to make mine easier."

"Perhaps you underestimate your own God," Pekhti said. "But

whether or not your God struck Uhen down, the servants have more respect for you today than they did yesterday."

"I don't want to rule by fear," Joseph said. The very thought of it distressed him. "That wouldn't be pleasing to God."

"You needn't worry about that," Pekhti said, clapping a supportive hand on Joseph's shoulder. "You won't need the power of fear to control Potiphar's household. The farmers and servants were impressed by your compassion and your concern for the safety of others. Long after their fear of your God wears off, their respect for your example will remain. Today you have actually become Potiphar's chief steward. You've become it in more than just name."

"Nothing about me has changed," Joseph said. "I'm the same person I've always been. You know that, Pekhti."

"Yes," Pekhti agreed. "You've always been a man of character. But now everyone else sees it as well. The farmers watched as you tried to save a man who treated you as his enemy. They watched you return to the field and risk your own safety to preserve theirs. Now they've told others so that all Potiphar's household knows what you've done. The servants will now follow you more willingly than they would ever have followed you before. Your leadership has been established."

Joseph hoped Pekhti was right. And he had to admit that there was a big difference in the way Potiphar's servants now treated him. Where there had earlier been hostile glares and thinly veiled animosity and contempt, there were now friendly greetings and polite nods. It appeared that his job would be infinitely easier than it had appeared it would be only a few days earlier. But there was much more to be grateful for than just that.

A strange and miraculous thing had happened in the past few days. Joseph still longed to see his family—especially Benjamin—but he was thinking less often of them now and more often of Asenath. It was a bittersweet situation to find himself in. He enjoyed every last moment he spent with her, but he knew those moments would eventually come to an end. One day the lessons would be over, and the emptiness inside him would be twice as painful as it had been before.

It was unavoidable. Someday all contact with the beautiful priestess had to be cut off, and then he would have nothing to look forward to but a long life of servitude.

Pekhti had informed him once that some masters rewarded their slaves, after a long life of faithful service, with their freedom. He clung to the hope that this would happen for him; but, even if it did, it probably wouldn't happen until he was an old man. Not that he couldn't still marry and be blessed with posterity. Abraham had been blessed with Isaac in his old age. But Asenath wasn't going to be around that long. Besides that, the Lord had someone in mind for her—a great and powerful man in Egypt. Not a mere slave like Joseph. He already knew all of this from her dream. So why was he allowing himself to fall in love?

Joseph shook his head with discouragement. In some ways it seemed so unfair. He wasn't perfect, but he'd done everything in his power to keep God's commandments and faithfully serve Him. Being sold into slavery was a terrible blow. Falling in love with a woman who could never be his was even worse. He'd never fallen in love before. Why did it have to happen now? And why did it have to happen in such hopeless circumstances? The moment he met Asenath he had felt an unmistakable connection to her. It was as if he knew her from a time long before . . . As if his heart recognized her from the life before this. Wasn't his bondage bitter enough? How could God give him such joy only to send it with the knowledge that it must soon be taken away?

Joseph shook his head again, but this time with determination. He wasn't going to allow thoughts like this to dwell in his mind. He knew better than that. He knew such thoughts weren't coming to him from God, and he knew they could only bring him greater sorrow than he was suffering now. God had blessed him, and God would continue to bless him. Just because he didn't understand what was happening didn't mean the Lord had abandoned him. It was times like this when greater faith was required, and God wouldn't leave him without the capacity to exercise that faith. He didn't have time for self-pity, anyway. There was yet another concern that called for his attention. Some might have dismissed this concern and gone about their normal life as usual. But Joseph had experienced too many prophetic dreams to ignore this one.

He had awakened the night after Uhen's death in a cold sweat, his heart hammering against his rib cage as if it were trying to escape. The dream had seemed so real that it took him several moments before he realized he was safe in his own bed instead of standing in Potiphar's field where the dream had taken place. Joseph thought back now and tried to remember everything that had happened. The dream seemed vitally important though he still didn't understand it.

It had started out pleasant enough. Joseph remembered dreaming that he was walking alone through Potiphar's wheat field, examining the stalks, and feeling that this would be a bounteous harvest. He was about to leave the field to go back to the house, but an odd noise from the east caught his attention. He paused, turned, and noticed a strange, whirling cloud heading his direction. His instincts told him to run, but his feet seemed cemented to the earth, and he could only stand and stare. The cloud came closer and closer until, finally, it engulfed the field. It drowned everything in a thick, choking blackness, and Joseph woke from his dream gasping to draw in air.

His dreams had never been like this before. They had never left such an ominous shadow hanging over his soul. So he decided that when it was light enough, he would visit the fields and find Khep. Khep was Uhen's son, and Joseph had chosen him, after Uhen's death, to be the new overseer of Potiphar's fields. If anyone could predict a possible threat to the crops, Khep would be the one.

It was shortly after the crack of dawn when Joseph found the young farmer in the vegetable gardens. They greeted each other with polite nods, and Joseph lowered himself to his knees to weed a row of onions alongside Khep.

"I need to ask you something," Joseph said after they had weeded in silence, side by side, for several long moments. "I believe you're the most knowledgeable man on matters concerning the master's fields, and I need your opinion."

"I'll tell you anything I know," Khep said, obviously pleased that Joseph would seek his advice. "What would you ask of me?"

"Is there anything," Joseph said, "anything at all, that could endanger this crop before the time of harvest?"

"The season of *shemu* is already upon us," Khep said. "We have plans to begin the harvest in only six days. I see nothing that could harm the crops between now and then."

"Nothing?" Joseph pressed.

"No one can predict every disaster that could possibly happen," Khep answered. "But I see no sign of any problem."

Joseph nodded. It sounded like a reasonable assessment. But something still felt wrong.

"What if I decide that we should start harvesting the crop today?" Joseph said. "Is it ripe enough to be stored in the granaries?"

"There's no reason for that," Khep answered, and there was a hint of annoyance touching his voice. "We've already made our plans for when the harvest will begin. Not even Pharaoh's fields will be harvested before ours."

"Is it ripe enough?" Joseph repeated, his voice firm.

"Yes, but—"

"I feel the strong impression that we should begin the harvest early," Joseph said. "I want you to gather the farmers and begin today."

Khep's face turned red, and Joseph saw the same belligerence in his eyes that had been in Uhen's eyes on the day he confronted Joseph. But the dark feeling of warning was hanging too heavily over Joseph's heart for him to back down.

"If you and the other farmers begin the harvest today, I'll make sure that you're adequately compensated for the inconvenience," Joseph promised. "Your wages will be doubled during the harvest, and I will hire extra men to help you when it comes time to dredge the canals. As the representative of the other farmers, does that seem fair to you?"

Khep stopped weeding and stared at Joseph to see if he was serious. When Joseph met his gaze with unwavering eyes, Khep nodded his head.

"We'll start the harvest before midday," he said. "But what about the master? What will he say when he finds out what you've promised us?"

"Potiphar has placed stewardship over all his lands and monies in my hands," Joseph calmly replied. "I am fully ready to take responsibility for my actions. All I expect of you in return is to make a swift and thorough harvest."

Khep stood up, dusted his hands on his *shenti*, and gave Joseph a solemn nod. "It will be done as you have asked," he said. "I'll gather the others immediately."

The harvest had been going on for two days now. Joseph had completed a third lesson with Asenath, and the business of Potiphar's estates was going along as usual. It appeared that his nightmare had been nothing more than that—a nightmare. He was even beginning to question the wisdom of his bold promises to Khep. Would Potiphar also be questioning Joseph's decisions? This uncertainty nagged at him all throughout the day; but the self-doubt vanished entirely the moment a terrified servant came running into sight.

"Joseph! Joseph!" the servant called out. He was running as fast as his legs would carry him, and his face was drawn and pale.

"What is it?" Joseph asked, a concerned frown on his lips.

"*Senekhemu* . . . ," the servant gasped. "*Locusts* . . . coming out of the desert . . . so many you can't even see the ground . . . They're going to destroy what's left of the harvest!"

"Gather all the servants," Joseph commanded. "Every one of

them. Send them to the fields. I'll tell them what to do when I get there." He didn't wait for a reply. Instead, he spun on his heels and dashed toward the stables. He had never dealt with a swarm of locusts before, but he knew it couldn't be good. He prayed for guidance as he grasped the shaft of the swiftest chariot and pulled it to a place where he could hitch up the horses.

Joseph's heart was pounding in his throat by the time he got his chariot out into the open expanse of the delta. First there had been the asp and Uhen's death. Now there was this. His beginning term as chief steward was turning out to be anything but a golden era. But the purpose of his dream was now clear, and he was grateful to the Lord for watching over him. Because of that nighttime warning, the greater portion of the harvest would be saved, and Potiphar would fare much better than the other landowners of the delta.

His first intention was to head for the fields, but Joseph decided instead to go out into the desert and get a good look at the mindless foe he would soon be fighting. It wasn't difficult to find that enemy. He remembered from his dream that the danger had come from the east, and he quickly spotted a menacing shadow looming there. It was gathering itself at the edge of the desert, ready to hurl itself against the defenseless outskirts of the fields—and it was a horrifying thing to behold. It looked as if the desert sands had vomited up a thick, black cloud that roiled and churned as it stretched itself like a diseased hand toward the tender stalks of the fields. Something inside of Joseph revolted at the thought of going closer to that living, black mass—even the horses resisted his efforts to guide them in that direction—but he decided he could better prepare the defense of the fields if he got a good look at what was attacking them. Determined, he forced himself and the horses to go nearer.

Farmers from the fields of other landowners were side by side with Potiphar's farmers at the front edge of the swarm. They were hacking and smashing, stomping with unshod feet, pounding with frantic fists. It was a futile gesture. It was clear to Joseph that there were far too many insects to kill this way. Even if every man, woman, and child in Avaris came out to join the attack, the locusts would eventually overwhelm them. The war had to begin at the fields themselves. Every last grain that could be saved had to be saved. There would be plenty of time to smash locusts later.

"Go back to the fields!" Joseph called out to his own people as he came close enough to see the glistening, pinkish-yellow bodies and the long, barbed legs of the locusts. "We might still have time to save what's left of the crop if you go back to the fields now!"

He didn't wait for them to follow his orders. He rushed back to begin the work himself, and could only hope they would see the wisdom of this action. There was much of the harvest still left to be done. He would save what he had the ability to save.

Chapter Notes

1. The term *asp* is used interchangeably to describe both a small species of Egyptian cobra and the *cerastes*, also known as the horned viper. The Egyptians symbolically associated asps with gods and kings, and the image of the asp was used to decorate crowns of pharaohs. Popular legend has it that Cleopatra committed suicide by allowing an asp to bite her—evidence of just how lethal the ancients considered its strike to be. The King James Version of the Bible makes mention of the asp twice, once in Deuteronomy 32:33 and again in Isaiah 11:8.

2. In the Bible, the term *locust* is used to refer to several different crop-destroying insects. The most dangerous type of locust is the desert locust, a short-horned grasshopper which forms migrating swarms that destroy all vegetation in their path. During cooler parts of the morning and at midday when temperatures are high, a swarm will settle on the ground; but, when temperatures are right, swarms can fly for ten to twenty hours, covering great distances and wreaking havoc wherever they go. Middle Eastern countries currently take steps to prevent outbreaks of locusts, but such plagues were disastrous in ancient times and could last from one to over twenty years.

3. The two most important seasons affecting Egypt's crops were *akhet*, the season of inundation, and *shemu*, the season of the harvest. *Akhet* began with the rising of the Nile's waters in July which led to an inundation of the fields

sometime around August. Main crops were later sown in the months of October and November after the water levels dropped. The resulting crops ripened from January to April and were harvested during the season of *shemu*.

EIGHTEEN

ETMOSIS WALKED SLOWLY toward the altar, carrying the
ceremonial dagger that would be used to make the special sacrifice to
Seth, and Asenath and Netchem walked with him, one on each side.
The sacrificial bull shuddered at their approach as if it knew what was
about to happen, but any struggle on its part was futile. The ropes
that bound it to the stone altar held too firmly against the pressure of
its straining muscles, and the whites of its eyes went wide with fear
as it realized its helplessness. There was no escape. The bull had been
raised to this purpose, and its fate was sealed. At Pharaoh's command,
it was to become an offering to Seth.

Asenath looked away as her feet brought her closer to the altar.
She didn't particularly enjoy this part of her duties, and she never
watched when a priest plunged the dagger into the heart of a frightened beast. She always focused her eyes instead on the smoldering
incense it was her duty to carry. She did that today as she set it in
its place on a bronze stand beside the altar steps. This done, she and
Netchem remained at the bottom of the steps, dropping respectfully
to their knees while Setmosis climbed to the top to stand majestically
over the trembling bull.

"Great Seth," he chanted, tilting his head upward so that his face
was pointed towards the sky. "Lord of the storms and the desert winds.
We offer to you this sacred bull, that your wrath may be appeased,

and that you may look down upon this people and smile . . . "

Asenath braved a glance at the jackal-like head of Seth's stone image, and she tried to imagine those canine lips curled back into a pleased smile. The image that entered her mind made her shudder.

"Call back the plague that has been sent forth to destroy our crops," Setmosis continued. "Calm the east winds and turn them against this pestilence."

Asenath joined the priests and priestesses behind her as their voices rose suddenly in a droning, rhythmic chant; and Setmosis lifted the ceremonial dagger high above his head, this simple action causing the chant to increase in pitch and intensity.

Though her voice was lifted up with the voices of the others, Asenath's heart was elsewhere right now. Instead of Seth, she was thinking of another God and a faithful 'apiru slave who served Him. Once again she questioned the gods of her own people.

To Asenath, a god was harsh. A god was distant, cold, and apathetic. That's what puzzled her about Joseph and his God. He seemed to know his God on a personal level, trusting Him when things went wrong and believing that all things would work together for his good. How could one have such trust in a being he had never seen? What were mortals to a god other than insignificant pieces in a great, eternal puzzle? Asenath realized that she would give anything to know a god that could inspire that kind of love and trust. She would like to have the faith and calm self-assurance Joseph seemed to have. But she wasn't Hebrew. She was Egyptian, and she had her own gods to serve.

The ceremony ended, and Asenath dutifully followed the priestesses out of the room. The priests remained behind to prepare the meat of the sacrificial bull. When she and Netchem were far enough away that it was no longer necessary to maintain a humble silence, Netchem approached her.

She'd been expecting this. Ever since Joseph showed up with her at the temple with the dying Uhen in his chariot, she had been expecting Netchem to question her. And Netchem's eyes were glowing with a thousand unanswered questions.

"I've been waiting to talk to you since yesterday," she said. "That man you came here with. Was that Potiphar's slave? The one he's making into a chief steward? The one you've been teaching?"

"Yes. His name is Joseph." The direct approach seemed best. Maybe if she openly answered all of Netchem's questions, she wouldn't arouse any more suspicion than she already had.

"He didn't look like a chief steward to me," Netchem said.

"Oh? What did he look like then?"

"More like a prince." Netchem smiled and Asenath felt her cheeks go warm. "It's too bad he's only a slave," Netchem went on, "because he looks like the men you only find in dreams. There has to be something wrong with him. He can't look that perfect and not have some glaring flaw. What is it, Asenath? You're his teacher. If there's anything wrong with him, you must have seen it. What is it that's wrong with him that the gods would make him a slave?"

He had no flaws. At least none that Asenath could detect. He was as perfect a man as she could imagine. And there was no reason why a god—his God or any other—should make him into a slave.

"He's dutiful," Asenath replied, squirming uncomfortably beneath Netchem's stare.

"Honorable. And I've never met anyone who learns so quickly. If there's anything wrong with him, I'm yet to find that flaw."

Netchem nodded, but she continued to look carefully at Asenath.

"You don't have feelings for him, do you?"

"What kind of a silly question is that?"

"I don't know. I just don't want you to get hurt. It would be easy to fall in love with a man like him—even if he is a slave."

"That could be true," Asenath said. She realized all too well how true it was. "But as you've said, he's only a slave. Do I seem foolish enough to allow myself to fall in love with a slave?"

"No. I guess not. I just wanted to make sure. Because I've noticed a change in you—in your eyes and in your voice—and I had to be sure it had nothing to do with him."

"The only relationship between Joseph and me is the relationship of a teacher to a student," Asenath lied. "That's all it's ever going to be."

Netchem looked again at Asenath, her eyes doubtful. But finally she nodded her head and allowed the subject to drop.

"Do you think the sacrifice will work?" she asked. "Do you think Seth will drive the locusts away?"

"I don't know. I think Seth will do whatever Seth wants to do."

"Father told me the order to make this sacrifice came directly from Pharaoh. He commanded that these special prayers and sacrifices be carried out until the locusts are driven away. None of us are to leave our duties at the temple until the plague is over. We'll all be required to stay here to assist with the prayers and sacrifices."

Asenath felt her countenance drop and hoped that Netchem didn't notice. She had been entertaining the slim hope that, despite the locusts, Joseph would still find time for the next lesson. Now the hope of seeing him was crushed. She hadn't realized until now just how much happier she had become since meeting Joseph. She'd hardly even thought about home since becoming his teacher.

"I'm sorry," Netchem said, her quick eyes not missing the change in Asenath's mood. "I know how you like to escape from the temple. I just thought I'd warn you in advance. Before Father says something."

"Duty before all else," Asenath replied with a sigh. "At least that's what my father always used to tell me. 'Priests and priestesses have to subordinate their own desires to the will of Pharaoh and the gods.' Those were always his exact words."

"I'm sure it won't last long," Netchem said, trying to sound as reassuring as possible. "The locusts will surely leave as quickly as they've come."

Yes. They would leave. But the fields would be barren, and

educating a slave might no longer seem important to Potiphar. These locusts were going to ruin everything.

Life wasn't fair—she already knew that—but sometimes it was more unfair than usual. Today was one of those days.

"What can you tell me about locusts?" Joseph asked. "How soon would you guess that they'll reach these fields? And how fast will they consume the crops once they get here?"

"They'll start flying in the afternoon," Khep replied. "They don't like to fly when it's too hot, and now is the hottest time of the day. But when it cools, it won't be long after that. The wind is blowing this direction, and large swarms always seem to travel downwind. We have a few hours at most. Once they take to the air, they'll be here in a matter of minutes. And then . . . " He let his voice trail off. Joseph understood what he meant.

Again, Joseph looked out across the large expanse of grain and barley that still remained to be harvested. He realized it would take a miracle to harvest even a small portion of what was left. But he believed in miracles. There was always hope where God was involved.

"We'll do whatever we can," he said. "With God's help, it will be enough. Are you with me in this? Are you willing to fight the locusts and save what we can?"

Khep and the other farmers looked less than hopeful, but they nodded their heads.

"Good. Khep, I need you to organize a last minute harvesting effort. More servants will soon be arriving from the manor, and we'll collect as much of the grain as we can get. We'll deal with the locusts when they get here."

Khep directed the other farmers to gather the harvesting tools then turned to speak to Joseph in private.

"Forgive me for doubting you," he said, bowing his head and

staring at his toes. He struggled for several moments as if searching for what to say but finally continued. "If not for you, we would have lost everything. You must be more than a man. You must be a god to predict the future as you do." He began to drop to his knees, but Joseph stopped him before he could.

"I'm not a god," Joseph said. "I'm a man. But a God has saved the greater portion of these fields. It was the God of my fathers who revealed this destruction to me. If you would worship a God, give thanks to Him." Joseph clapped Khep warmly on the shoulder and then walked with him toward the other farmers. "Come," he said. "There's much to be done. Show me how to help with the harvest. We'll need every pair of available hands."

The harvesting effort was organized quickly. The male servants attacked the grain with their sickles and the female servants followed along, gathering the grain into large, shallow baskets. The filled baskets were then dumped into small carts which were pulled by donkeys to the threshing floors in front of Potiphar's granaries. It was a monumental task. They were attempting to do in a few hours what would normally take many days, and it was obvious to Joseph that any grain they gathered wouldn't amount to much. But they had to try. He couldn't expect God to help them if they didn't do everything that He had already given them power to do. And, for once in his life, Joseph found himself grateful for the hot, Egyptian sun. If Khep was right, the heat would buy them a few more hours of precious time. They needed every hour they could get.

Joseph left it to Khep to set the other servants to work as they arrived in small, nervous groups from Potiphar's manor, and he labored alongside all of them, asking no more of them than he asked of himself. He only stopped occasionally to mop the perspiration from his brow, and it was at one of these moments that he heard the low ominous, droning. He'd heard it once before. He'd heard it in his dream. It was an unnatural roar, the sound of untold millions of vibrating insect wings, and it sent an involuntary chill up and down his spine. Those around him, noticing how he tilted his head to one side to listen, stopped what they were doing, and they listened, too. A murmur of fear swept like a wave across the field.

"Pekhti!" Joseph called out, seeing his old mentor among the servants. "Take my chariot back to the stables." He looked around and saw several women, their faces pale, beginning to weep and realized he needed to do something about them, too. "Take the women with you," he added. "They shouldn't have to be here when the swarm arrives. What's left to be done will be done by the men."

Pekhti nodded and Joseph turned to search for Khep. He waved his arms above his head until he got the young farmer's attention.

"Khep! Take this one last load to the threshing floor. See that the servants there get all of the threshed grain into the granaries. You should also take the donkeys somewhere where they won't be stressed by the swarm. We've saved as much of the crop as we've had time to save. Now we fight the locusts for what's left."

A quick glance at the horizon showed him that the fight would be quick in coming. There was a cloud approaching from the desert. He might have mistaken it for a sandstorm if he hadn't known what it really was. It was a pinkish-brown, oddly swirling cloud; and, just as in his dream, Joseph had the urge to turn and run. But he fought his fears and did what he could to give courage to those around him. Courage might be all they had to carry them through this. Courage and the power of God.

NINETEEN

THEY DESCENDED ON THE FIELD in a thick cloud of destruction. Joseph felt them tangling in his hair, felt their wings beating against his face, and thought for a moment that he would drown in them. But, finally, the last of the locusts settled to the ground, and Joseph went after them, swinging and pounding with the shovel he had snatched up from the ground.

The battle was waged only in one part of the fields—the section that hadn't yet been harvested—but even that seemed too large an area to defend. For every one locust that was killed, ten more marched relentlessly forward to take its place. There were just too many of them. The wheat and barley were being systematically destroyed by this nightmare army of insects.

If Joseph thought this was as bad as it could get, he was wrong. He heard a series of soft, plopping sounds that he at first thought was the sound of locusts tumbling to the earth as they crowded each other on the stalks. But then he realized the sound was made by the wheat itself. The locusts were busily stripping the leaves from the stalks, and when the leaves were consumed, the mandibles of the pestilent insects started on the stalk itself. Joseph watched helplessly as ripe heads of wheat were severed from their stems and sent tumbling to the ground. The locusts below, which were eating any edible plant matter that came beneath their mandibles, were quick to start on the severed heads of grain. It seemed that this was a battle Joseph must certainly lose.

Fortunately, much of Potiphar's grain was already safely stored in the granaries. Potiphar would have bread for his household and barley for his animals when the neighbors around him had none. But what good was a chief steward who wouldn't fight for his master's property to the very end? If even one single head of grain could be spared, Joseph felt it was his job to rescue it, and he searched desperately for a plan. Only one thing came into his mind, and he shouted it out to Khep.

"Burn the fields!" he shouted. "Burn the areas that have already been harvested! If we can stop the locusts there from coming here, we might be able to manage what's left."

Khep nodded and motioned for several of the farmers to follow him while Joseph directed the continuing efforts of those who remained. Soon the battle was being waged on two fronts. Khep and his crew lit and managed small fires to clear the harvested areas, and Joseph and his crew fought locusts, smoke, and fatigue. The battle went on until the sun disappeared behind the horizon. And then the entire party of servants, too tired to go home, fell to the earth where they had fought their hopeless battle and quickly succumbed to exhaustion.

It wasn't until the sun rose again the next morning that Joseph got a chance to really see the effects of a locust invasion. It was a depressing sight. Vast patches of earth were scarred and blackened. Where there was vegetation, it had been trampled by men and shredded by locusts. Most of the grain that had fallen to the ground was befouled, and the few stalks of grain left standing were a pitiful sight. Here and there Joseph could still see a locust moving, and his skin crawled in memory of the countless insects he had brushed from his arms and neck during the previous day's work. But most of the swarm were either dead or had moved on to search for new fodder now, and what little good grain Joseph could still find could safely be harvested. The odds, however, of finding salvageable grain seemed slim.

Potiphar's fields were a disaster. The other fields of Avaris were a total loss. And Joseph would soon find out that the other cities of the delta had fared no better. There would be much distress in Egypt this harvest season.

It appeared that God intended to test Joseph's new stewardship to its very limit.

The last few days had been the most miserable of Asenath's life. Not because of the increased workload at the temple, but because of her separation from Joseph.

"He's only a slave," she kept telling herself as if she were chanting the repeating lines of a temple prayer. "It will only bring misery to fall in love with him." But the most logical arguments of her mind couldn't turn her heart from its intended course. During the day, Joseph was always on her mind. In the night he was in all of her dreams. She was on a collision course with disaster, and she couldn't seem to turn herself away from it. She was thinking of him again right now, wondering where he was and when their lessons would resume when she nearly collided with a man in the street before the temple gate.

"Oh! Excuse me!" she exclaimed.

The man put a hand on her arm to steady her, and she discovered with surprise that it was Potiphar.

"Good afternoon, young priestess," he said. "I didn't hurt you did I?"

"No. It was all my fault. It was very clumsy of me. I should pay better attention to where I'm going."

She nervously smoothed the wrinkles from her *kalasiris* and tried to think of something appropriate to say, but only one thing came to mind.

"I haven't been able to meet with Joseph for several days now," she said. "Will you be ready for him to continue with his writing lessons soon?"

"I think things are back under control at the estate," Potiphar said, nodding. "You can resume where you left off as soon as you'd like. How is he coming along? Does he have the aptitude for reading and writing?"

Asenath opened her mouth to speak, ready to pour out praises for Joseph's incredible progress. But then she stopped herself and rephrased what she had been about to say.

"Joseph is eager to learn," she said, staring absently at the temple wall as if Joseph and his studies meant nothing to her at all, "but it will be at least two to three years before he becomes competent with the written language." It was a blatant lie. She was certain he would master the basic writing skills of a chief steward in less than a year. But she had already secretly determined that she would drag these lessons out as long as she possibly could.

"I'll have to leave that judgment to you," Potiphar said. "I'm no expert on writing. But I am an expert on chief stewards, and I know that Joseph is the best chief steward I've ever had. He harvested most of my crops before the locusts even came, and he fought to protect what remained after they arrived. There's no telling how many *khars* of grain I might have lost if not for his extraordinary foresight. The crops of my neighbors were virtually annihilated while most of mine were safely stored in my granaries. It's curious how he was able to anticipate this plague, isn't it."

"Yes. It's amazing."

"Keep training Joseph for as long as you are both willing to continue," he said. "Since he came to my estate, everything placed in his charge has prospered. The more knowledgeable he becomes, the better he'll be able to manage my affairs."

Asenath nodded and looked for an excuse to be on her way, but Potiphar spoke again before she could go.

"Speaking of managing affairs," he said, "I've come to bring offerings of thanks to the storm god in appreciation for the protection of my crops." He turned now and gestured toward two of his servants who were patiently watching over a small group of goats. Asenath noticed with disappointment that neither of them was Joseph, but she tried not to let it show on her face. A chief steward couldn't be expected to be pulled aside for such a trivial task. He was probably at the estate right now, supervising whatever recovery effort was needed in the aftermath of the recent disaster.

"Is Setmosis at the temple today?" Potiphar asked. "I would like to present these goats to him to be sacrificed to Seth."

Asenath groaned inwardly. The last thing she wanted was to be called back into the temple to carry more incense for more sacrifices. But she put a pleasant smile on her face when she answered him.

"Let me find him for you. If you'll wait outside the gate, I'll announce your arrival."

Potiphar nodded and Asenath hurried back through the temple gate. It took only a few moments to find Setmosis who was instructing several new priests in the scriptorium, and she waited patiently in the corner of the room until he had time to step aside to speak to her.

"I thought you had gone home for the day," he said, smiling. "Ari is going to accuse me of making a temple slave out of you if you don't show up at the house soon."

"I was on my way there," Asenath explained, "but I ran into Potiphar in the street. He's waiting outside the main gates to speak with you."

"The captain of the guard is here? To see me?" He looked at her with concern, and then shook his head. "I wasn't aware that he would be coming today."

"He's arrived with offerings for the temple," Asenath quickly said. "Four goats."

"Times have been bad for Avaris," Setmosis said, seeming relieved at her explanation. "But Seth still seems to be providing for his temple. Good. We will gladly accept Potiphar's offering. Do you have time to help me accept his offering?"

She forced a strained smile to her lips again. All she wanted was to leave the temple and seek out Joseph, but every event seemed to conspire against her.

"If you need me, I will help."

Setmosis studied her for a moment, but then shook his head and smiled in a fatherly way.

"Actually, I can take care of this on my own. You've spent many hours here these past few days, and you've earned some time away. Take the rest of the afternoon for yourself. There will be plenty of time for new sacrifices in the morning."

Gratefully, Asenath nodded her head, and then she cautiously brought up the thing that was plaguing her mind. "I was thinking I might stop by Potiphar's estate to set up a time to restart Joseph's lessons," she said. "Would that be all right?"

"Joseph? Oh, you mean the slave. Yes, of course. But stop at the house first to let Ari know where you're going. She'll worry if she doesn't know where you're off to."

She imagined that Setmosis would worry, too. Worry about Pharaoh's wrath if she disappeared and couldn't be accounted for. Worry that she might do something he disapproved of. But she was so glad for the opportunity to see Joseph again that she forced that angry thought from her mind.

Ari was busy in the kitchen when Asenath arrived at the house. Once Ari had been made aware of where she would be, Asenath straightened her hair and fairly raced to Potiphar's house. Her heart was floating on a cloud of happiness, and a smile was tugging at the corners of her mouth, but the estate seemed oddly deserted when she got there. With disappointment she realized that Joseph and the rest of the servants were probably away at the fields, working to clean up the mess the locusts had left behind.

She considered the prospect of walking to the fields to find him but quickly rejected that idea. It was much too far, and it would also make her eagerness to be with Joseph much too obvious. Bitterly disappointed, she lowered her head and turned to walk back the way she had come. A friendly voice stopped her before she got far.

"Can I help you with something? Are you looking for somebody?"

Asenath turned and saw a man with a pair of horses leading a chariot her way. Hesitantly, she said, "I . . . I was looking for Joseph. But it appears he isn't here today. I'll come back and talk with him another time."

"He's directing the clean-up of the master's fields," the man said. "But I'm on my way there right now. Is there a message I can take to him?"

"No," Asenath said. "No, thank you. Perhaps I'll return tomorrow and see if I can catch him here then."

The man looked at her more closely and a light of recognition flickered suddenly through his eyes. She didn't know him, but he obviously recognized who she was.

"You're Joseph's teacher from the temple, aren't you," he said.

Asenath nodded.

"Joseph has told me all about you," the man said. He bowed low and then looked Asenath over with interest. "I never really realized . . . " He stopped, reconsidered what he was about to say, and favored her with a broad grin. "Joseph will be disappointed if he finds out that he missed you. Do you have time to meet with him at the fields? If you don't mind sharing the chariot with me, I would be pleased to take you there."

"No," Asenath said. "Thank you, but—"

"It's a short journey by chariot," the man interrupted, motioning toward the chariot's empty platform, "and I'll be happy to bring you back to the city after you've spoken with him. My name is Pekhti, chief groom of Potiphar's stables. I'm at your service, young priestess."

Asenath hesitated. But when Pekhti motioned again to the chariot, she went against her better judgment and allowed him to help her in. If ever there was a time to run from her rapidly growing feelings for Joseph, now was that time. Instead, she was running headlong into it.

"Joseph is a fine man," Pekhti said as he climbed up beside her and started the chariot into motion. "I've never met a better man— slave or free."

She nervously wondered why he was making her the recipient of this glowing report; but, whatever his reasons, this was an unparalleled opportunity to ask all of the questions about Joseph she'd never had the chance to ask. She had several of them on her mind and decided to start with the safest of the questions.

"Potiphar mentioned to me that Joseph decided to harvest the fields early," she said. "Do you have any idea what prompted him to do that?"

Pekhti grew unexpectedly silent and seemed unsure about whether or not he should answer that. But after looking carefully into her eyes, he began to speak. "Did Joseph ever tell you how he became a slave?" he asked.

"He told me about his dream," Asenath replied. "And he told me how his brothers sold him into slavery because of it."

Pekhti nodded. "Joseph says his dreams come from his God. He believes his dreams can bring him warnings and even reveal future events. You're a priestess. I'm sure you understand such things better than I do."

Asenath nodded. But she didn't truly understand. Egypt's gods had never revealed anything to her—by dreams or any other means. Although Egyptians had developed standard interpretations for specific types of dreams, the direct and clear communication Joseph seemed to have with his God was peculiar. Asenath still struggled to comprehend what it might mean.

"He wouldn't say much about it," Pekhti continued, not noticing her short pause for reflection, "but Joseph did mention to me that some kind of disturbing dream convinced him to do this. His God seems to watch over him. Most of the time that is."

Asenath said nothing, but she thought she knew what Pekhti was thinking. Joseph's God watched over him, and yet He had allowed Joseph to be sold into slavery. It was a puzzling, paradoxical situation.

"Perhaps his God intends eventually to give him his freedom," Asenath suggested after several long moments of silence. "He must be a powerful god if he can know the future and show it to Joseph. Maybe He'll use that power to set Joseph free."

"Maybe," Pekhti said. "But I don't see Potiphar releasing Joseph while he's bringing such profit to the estate. If Joseph is ever given his freedom, it will only happen after many long years of service have passed by him."

Unfortunately, this was probably true. Asenath understood this at least.

The chariot was now racing from the city toward the fields, and Pekhti entertained Asenath with anecdotes of Joseph's life since Joseph's arrival in Egypt. By the time she spotted the granaries at the far edge of the fields, Asenath felt she knew Joseph far better than she had before. The stories Pekhti told to her were candid descriptions of a noble man—an honest, faithful man of character. It was clear to her now why she felt so attracted to him, and she couldn't keep a smile from springing to her lips when she finally caught sight of Joseph in the fields.

He was standing tall and straight in the midst of Potiphar's servants, directing their activities, and he didn't at first notice the chariot's approach. A *nemes* protected his head, and a white *shenti* was held around his waist by a broad, leather belt. Asenath couldn't help but marvel at how much more he resembled a pharaoh than a slave. When he did hear the chariot and turned to face it, she was pleased to note that a smile lit up his face. She hoped the smile was meant for her.

"This is a pleasant surprise," Joseph said as Pekhti brought the chariot up next to him. She could tell that he was trying to restrain his true emotions, but that couldn't stop a broad grin on his face from showing how happy he was to see her.

For her part, Asenath wished she could throw her arms around his neck and tell him how miserable she had been without him for the past several days. But she was uncomfortably aware of how closely Pekhti was watching the two of them, and she remembered that any show of emotion between a priestess and a slave would arouse immediate suspicion. Joseph was also aware of Pekhti's probing eyes, and he quickly attempted to take the focus of attention away from himself and Asenath.

"Pekhti," he said, clapping the man warmly on one shoulder. "Were you able to find the master?"

"Yes. I talked to him before he left for the temple. He seems to agree with your assessment of the situation and wants to double the guard at the granaries. He also agrees that we should remove as much grain as possible to a safer place at the estate. Grain has suddenly become a very valuable commodity. Until Pharaoh gathers the tributes from the cities to the south, things will be a little tense in Avaris."

"And when will the extra guards be arriving?"

"This afternoon. Until then, we'll have to keep a close eye on things."

Joseph nodded, and stared thoughtfully at the granary until Pekhti finally decided it was time to politely dismiss himself. "I'll just go along and see how the work is progressing," he said. "You and the priestess probably have things to discuss." There was no missing the unmistakable twinkle in his eye; but if he suspected their feelings for each other, Asenath somehow knew he would never reveal it to anybody else.

"I was hoping you'd come and find me," Joseph said, more relaxed once Pekhti was gone. He lightly touched her arm and led her to the back of the granary where they could be away from probing ears and eyes. "I would have found you first, but my duties kept me here. I haven't left the fields since the plague began."

"I assumed that would be the case," Asenath said, nodding. She felt suddenly, inexplicably, shy; but she also felt warm and safe in Joseph's presence. "My duties kept me away from you as well," she continued. "The temple has been such a busy place since the locusts arrived. There have been sacrifices and more sacrifices. I thought I would never get away from that place."

"This plague has been a hardship on everyone," Joseph said. "It will continue to be difficult for quite some time."

Asenath nodded and both of them fell silent for a few moments. Finally she said, "I've come to schedule the day for our next lesson. I . . . " She stopped speaking again, unsure of what to say next, and Joseph's eyes locked with hers. It was so quiet this time that she could hear the sound of her own beating heart. Her lower lip trembled a little as Joseph leaned closer to her, and she started to close her eyes, half-expecting him to kiss her. But she should have known him better than that. As his lips came frighteningly close to hers, a startled look suddenly came into his eyes. She realized that he was remembering what she remembered—that he was a slave and she was a priestess—and what he was about to do was forbidden. He quickly pulled himself away.

Disappointment and embarrassment flooded over Asenath. She wanted to cry out and run. But she saw that he was almost as embarrassed as she was, and all she could think to do was stare at her feet. Of course he wouldn't kiss her! He was too honorable to cross a line that shouldn't be crossed. Her heart felt as if it would tear itself into pieces as she once again came to understand the depth of the social gulf that separated them.

How unfair were the gods and the unwritten rules of Egyptian society! She'd suffer any amount of pain in exchange for a moment in Joseph's arms. But he knew the rules as well as she did, and he would never allow either of them to break them.

"I should be able to meet with you tomorrow," Joseph said, taking a step back, and speaking to her in a strained voice. She risked a quick glance at his face and saw reflected in his eyes a pain that matched her own. But he quickly turned his head to one side to hide it.

"Shall we meet at the garden?" he asked.

"Yes. I'll meet you there. In the morning?"

"That would be good."

"I should let you get back to your work," Asenath said. She took two steps backward and turned her body toward the city, but he stopped her before she could go.

"You're not walking back to Avaris are you?"

"Setmosis and Ari will worry if I'm away too long. I have to go."

"I don't want you to leave."

Asenath stared at Joseph, and her eyes widened with surprise.

"I-I mean I don't want you to leave alone," he stammered, his face flushing. "If you give me a few minutes to put things in order here, I'll take you back in one of the chariots. Pekhti and Khep should be able to take care of things here while I'm gone."

Asenath nodded, and Joseph moved reluctantly away from her. While he spoke with Khep and Pekhti she had time to ponder what had almost happened, and she silently chastised herself for wanting it. She should have listened to Netchem's warnings. She should have never allowed herself to fall in love with a slave. But it was too late now. It was everlastingly too late. And her heart would never feel the same again.

TWENTY

JOSEPH SAT CROSS-LEGGED beside the garden pool, a papyrus scroll spread across his lap. The scribe's palette was in its usual place beside him. But there was nothing usual about today's lesson. It was tense. Strained. Asenath wouldn't look him in the eye, and conversation was sparse. Once Joseph finally did catch a glimpse of Asenath's blue eyes, he saw pain and embarrassment there—pain and embarrassment he knew *he* had caused her. But what was he to do? If he confessed that he had fallen in love with her, it would only bring greater pain to both of them. His heart was already twisted with agony. Would it be right to give her hope in something that could never end in happiness?

"How does this look?" he asked, finishing the last character he'd been asked to copy and showing it to Asenath.

"It looks fine," she said. But she wasn't even looking at the papyrus. Instead she was staring into the pool with a sad, distant look in her eyes.

He wanted to tell her. His tongue ached to be loose to speak. But he still held back. He was a slave. It wasn't his place to speak the words he wanted to say to this beautiful Egyptian priestess.

"Joseph?" Asenath quietly said after staring for several more long moments at the pool.

"Yes?"

"There's something I have to know. I don't believe you'll lie to me, because you're the most completely honest man I've ever met . . . " She paused. She seemed afraid to go on. But Joseph already knew what she wanted.

"Asenath," he said, gently touching her face and turning it so that she would be forced to look into his eyes. "What you want me to say . . . I . . . I just don't know if . . . " He stopped, shook his head in frustration, but then forced himself to go on. It had to be said. He could see that now. "Asenath," he finally blurted out, "I love you. I think I've loved you since the first day we were together. But I'm only a slave, and—"

He didn't get to finish the last sentence. Asenath collapsed suddenly against him, wrapping her slender arms tightly about his neck. His lips met hers before he realized what was happening, then he pulled away and desperately grasped her small hands in his own.

"I love you," he repeated. "But I'm a slave. And you're a priestess. I'm also Hebrew, and I serve another God. We can't let this happen. We—"

"I will serve *your* God," she quickly interjected. There was determination in her voice, but there were also tears in her eyes. "I will forsake the gods of Egypt for you. I will find some way to set you free. We . . . we could run away together. We could return to your land and—"

Joseph shook his head and stopped her. "I am bound by an oath to serve Potiphar and never to leave this land. It would also be wrong of me to ask you to serve a God you still don't know. Someday the feelings you have for me will fade. Someday—"

"My love will never fade! And I wish to know your God. Teach me of Him." Her voice was pleading now—desperate. "Allow me to decide for myself if your God is real. And if He is, perhaps He will help us. Perhaps He will make a way for this to work."

Joseph hesitated. None of this could lead to anything but more sorrow for both of them.

Even if the bonds of his slavery could be removed and even if Asenath worshiped the God of Israel, there was still her dream to consider. Maybe she had forgotten her dream, but he hadn't. And he couldn't forget the interpretation he had given her. But he looked once more into her deep, blue eyes and couldn't bear to add more pain to the pain he already saw there. Slowly, he nodded his head.

"I will teach you of my God—of His character and attributes," he said. "But until I am free, we must obey the laws and codes of Egypt. Your society has clearly set the lines that a slave cannot cross. I won't cross over them. We both have to agree to that."

Asenath vigorously nodded her head, and some of the pain seemed to melt from her eyes. A hopeful smile crossed her lips, and Joseph prayed that he had just done the right thing.

"What is your God like?" she asked. "Does He take the form of a man or a beast?"

"We are created in His image," Joseph replied. "And we—all mankind—are His children."

"His children? Does He know us and love us as a mortal man would know and love his own children?"

"Even more."

"Then why does He allow disaster to befall us?"

This question caught Joseph entirely off guard. He hadn't seen it coming.

"I've always thought the gods of Egypt were cold, distant, and uncaring," Asenath said. "But if your God is our Father, why would He allow you to become a slave or allow hordes of locusts to devour the crops of Avaris? I don't understand this. What kind of a god would allow such misery, injustice, and chaos to reign upon the earth?"

Joseph was silent for several moments. He could see that Asenath truly did desire to understand—not just to accuse—so he chose his words carefully before he opened his mouth to speak. "The gods of Egypt seem uncaring because they are nothing more than graven images fashioned from stone and precious metals," Joseph began. "Egypt's gods exist only in the minds of their worshipers. But the God of my fathers lives. I don't always understand His ways, but I have faith that He loves us and that all things are done with our ultimate good in mind. There is another life beyond this one, and all that we suffer here—if we suffer it well—will serve to make our next life more glorious and happy. God expects us to endure our trials well. After we do all that we can, He will provide the necessary blessings."

Asenath stared at her reflection in the pool and pondered that for a moment. Joseph could tell by the look on her face that she wasn't perfectly satisfied with his answer, but at least she was considering it.

"You say that your God lives." She looked up again and stared deeply into his eyes. "You claim that Egypt's gods are false. Do the gods of other people and of other lands exist, or does your God alone rule the universe?"

"There is only one true and living God," Joseph replied, "and He is the God of my fathers. If you will pray to Him with true intent, He will speak to your heart and let you know that the things I tell you are true. You are His daughter. He loves you, and He wants you to know Him."

"Perhaps there is a purpose to all we suffer," Asenath said, staring at her hands which were folded now in her lap. "Perhaps this is why He sent you to Egypt. Perhaps this is why I too was brought to Avaris. Maybe He brought us together so that we won't have to bear our suffering alone. But it still seems like a cruel and unkind way to accomplish those purposes. If your God is all-powerful, it seems He could find better ways to accomplish His will."

Joseph stared thoughtfully at the blue sky above them. Somehow the thought that all of this loneliness and bitter anguish of soul was probably the only path he could cross over to know Asenath made all his afflictions seem a little easier to bear. But how could he impart to her the same knowledge that gave him his faith? He would have to pray long and hard about this.

"We should continue with our writing lesson," Asenath suddenly said, casting a nervous glance at one of the house guards who had wandered through the garden entrance. "But I truly do want to learn more about your God. Will you keep teaching me? Will you teach me more the next time we meet?"

"Nothing could make me happier," Joseph said and smiled.

"Good. Now let's try something new. We'll work with numbers. You're going to need them to make the records. I hope we'll be recording more of what was saved than what was lost. Either way, it sounds like Potiphar's will be the brightest record in Avaris."

"God has blessed Potiphar," Joseph said. "And He has blessed me as chief steward. He does look over us and watch out for our interests."

"I hope so," Asenath said. "I hope *our* best interests will be looked to as mercifully as Potiphar's were."

Joseph felt a sudden inner pain, but he was careful to hide it from her eyes. God's blessings weren't always what one expected or hoped for. Sometimes the exact opposite of what was hoped for was what was given. Even so, it always worked out to glorify God and bring blessings to the righteous. But it was rarely an easy path to follow. Joseph could only hope that he and Asenath would have the strength, courage, and faith to walk this path to its end. At the moment it was all he could do.

"Joseph! Can you come to the house for a moment?"

He had been lost in thought, thinking about Asenath and the heartfelt feelings they had revealed to each other today. Now Joseph turned to see Neferset, beckoning to him from the front entrance of Potiphar's house. He didn't like entering the house when the master was away. It made him uncomfortable to be there even with several other servants nearby. He had heard rumors about Neferset. Persistent rumors about her and the former chief steward. And something had been warning him from the first moment he met her that it was best to keep his distance. So it was with great caution that he approached her now.

"Yes? Do you need me for something?" he asked.

"You're always so busy," Neferset said, pulling with an index finger at her bottom lip.

"You really should stop by the house more often for some casual conversation and a rest from your labors."

"The master gives me enough time to rest," Joseph said. "But there's much to tend to on this estate. I hope I haven't been forsaking the needs of the house. I've tried to give you the most reliable servants. Are any of them not working as they should?"

"They're all working just fine," Neferset replied. "But there are some things in the house that only a strong man like yourself can do."

"I can send over two extra male servants if you need some heavy work done today," Joseph quickly offered. "Most of the work in the fields and vineyards has been completed. I'm sure a few of the male servants can be spared."

"Actually, I think I'll only need one man. Just you, Joseph."

He wasn't sure what to do, and she seemed to notice his discomfort. She took pleasure in it he decided. But he was determined to avoid the appearance of all evil. Whatever her intentions might be, he wasn't going to be caught alone with her in the house.

"The master has asked me to go into the city to purchase some new slaves before the market closes," he said. "I have to leave now if I want to purchase the best ones. Can I stop by the house when I return?"

"Of course. But don't take too long. I'll be expecting you."

She could expect him all she wanted. She could expect him to show up as late in the day as possible when he knew Potiphar was scheduled to return. He would be sure to find ways to delay his own return to the estate until he was certain that Potiphar was back.

Neferset cast him an inviting glance as she moved back into the house, but Joseph pretended not to notice it. He could avoid her today, but he couldn't avoid the unpleasant task Potiphar had charged him with. Despite the plague of locusts and the destruction that had come with it, Potiphar's household was prospering greatly. With increased prosperity came an increased need for labor, and Joseph was charged with the distasteful task of purchasing more slaves to provide that labor. He hated the thought of binding another soul to the same fate that had taken him. The only bright spot in it all was that he might be saving these slaves from a much worse master. If only he could save them all.

Joseph checked to make sure the bag of gold Potiphar had given him was tied securely to his belt, and then he nodded to the guards as he passed beyond the vast wall that encircled the house and its outbuildings. Besides his abhorrence of slavery, there was another reason why he didn't relish the thought of going back to the slave market. Already it was bringing back painful memories of his own moment on the auction block. It was one thing to buy a goat or a pig or a horse, but it was a degrading thing for a human to be bought and sold. He was lost in the memory of his own moment there when a hand grasped him from behind and pulled him several steps backward.

At first he was startled. Then he was confused. But then he felt the blood drain from his face as a chariot thundered over the spot where he would have been standing had the hand not pulled him back. Several more chariots followed after the first, and the breeze from the spokes of their spinning wheels blew across his face.

"You nearly took a trip to the world of the dead," a voice behind him said. "You need to watch better where you're going."

"Yes. You're right. I didn't even see them coming. Thank you."

"The procession from On," the stranger said, nodding his head in the direction of the departing chariots. "Potipherah, the high priest of On, has come to visit his daughter."

Potipherah? That was Asenath's father. Joseph was immediately interested. And curious. But he'd have to wait until his next meeting with Asenath before he could find out what had prompted her father's unexpected visit.

"My name is Ta."

"What?" Joseph turned away from the swirling dust which had been left behind by the chariots and stared with confused eyes at his rescuer.

"Ta. That's my name. I'm the chief baker at Pharaoh's palace. At least for the time being."

"I'm pleased to make your acquaintance, Ta. Very grateful, in fact. You just saved my life."

"Someone's life ought to be saved," Ta said, his voice mournful and his head shaking sadly from side to side.

"I don't understand. What do you mean by that?"

"Nothing. Nothing at all. My problems don't matter to anyone."

"My name is Joseph. And, again, I thank you for saving my life."

"Joseph? An odd name. You're not Egyptian, are you?"

"No. I'm Hebrew," Joseph replied. "I'm one of Potiphar's slaves."

"You belong to the captain of Pharaoh's guard? The chief executioner?" Ta shuddered.

"He's always treated me fairly," Joseph said. "He's not a cruel master."

Ta laughed a humorless laugh and shook his head. "Tell that to his victims at the execution block," he said. "I'm sure that will bring them great comfort."

Joseph shifted his feet uncomfortably, unsure of how he should react or what he should say. Finally he said the only thing that came to his mind. "As far as I know, only criminals and enemies of Pharaoh have need to fear Potiphar."

"All you have to do is displease Pharaoh and you have cause enough to fear Potiphar," Ta replied. The corner of his eye twitched a little, and he shook his head again. "The Master of Largesse displeased Pharaoh, and he paid for it with his life. Anyone who works for Pharaoh has cause to fear Potiphar."

"Even his baker?"

"Especially his baker! Every time I walk into the palace kitchen my life is on the line. What if I bake something and Pharaoh doesn't like it? Or what if something I cook for him makes him sick! I'm a dead man! I'm as good as dead!" Ta moaned and wildly shook his head.

"Has something happened at the palace?" Joseph carefully asked, sensing something more behind all of this. "Is Pharaoh displeased with you right now?"

"I allowed the kitchen grain bins to go empty," Ta said. "I was going to refill them as soon as the harvest began, but now there will be no harvest and there will be no grain. The locusts have ruined the crops, and they've ruined me as well!"

"Surely Pharaoh won't blame you for that. He must be a reasonable man. You had no control over the locusts."

"No. But I did have control over the grain bins. When there's no bread left for Pharaoh's table, I'll be cast into prison, and your master will execute me. I've been wandering the city, seeking to purchase grain, but there's none to be found. I'm a dead man. I'm as good as dead!"

"Are you telling me that Pharaoh has no more grain? None at all?"

"He has grain. There is grain left in his storage granaries from the last harvest. But I dare not ask for it. He already promised me the most severe of punishments if I allowed something like this to happen again." He buried his face in his hands and shook his head.

"What if I had grain to trade?" Joseph asked. "Would you have something of value to give in return?"

"You have grain?" Ta's countenance suddenly brightened and hope added color to his cheeks.

"I do, but I will need something in return."

"Anything! Name your price! I'll give you anything you ask for!" He grasped Joseph by both arms and stared at him with pleading eyes.

"It will have to be something my master needs but doesn't already have," Joseph replied as he gently freed his arms from Ta's desperate grip. "It has to be something equally as valuable as the grain I give."

"I only have access to food," Ta said. "Pharaoh has a surplus of dried dates. Would that work?"

Joseph shook his head.

"Fresh meat? Pomegranates? Onions?" Ta's voice was becoming desperate again.

"Don't you have anything else?" Joseph asked.

"Wine! I have wine! The finest wine in Avaris!"

Joseph thought about that for a moment. "I was unable to save very much from the vineyards," he said, "and Potiphar was looking forward to this year's new batch of wine. I think we can make a trade if this wine is as fine as you claim it to be."

"You've saved my life," Ta said, dropping to his knees and placing numerous kisses on Joseph's hand. "How can I ever thank you?"

"You saved my life. Now I'm helping you. I think we can safely say we're even now."

Ta got back to his feet, and Joseph feared that the man was about to embrace him. But then a new look entered Ta's eyes, and he took a suspicious step backward.

"You told me you were Potiphar's slave."

"That's correct."

"Then what kind of a trick is this?"

"I don't understand. This is no trick. What are you talking about?"

"You're a slave," Ta said. He pointed his finger dramatically into the air as if that one phrase answered every question. "What kind of man would allow a slave to sell his grain? Are you a thief as well as a slave?"

"I'm not a normal slave," Joseph replied. "I'm Potiphar's chief steward."

"Chief steward? Ha! You expect me to believe that?"

"I will be back at Potiphar's house this evening. If you are interested in trading wine for grain, bring the wine to the front gate and ask for Joseph. It's up to you whether you decide to come or not."

He could see no use in arguing with the man. If Ta was desperate enough—and Joseph was certain he was—he would show up at the house, and he would bring the wine. The choice was Ta's to make.

Joseph turned away and strode purposefully into the city—this time a little more watchful for chariots. He could feel Ta's eyes following him, but he didn't turn to look back. Perhaps he, too, would be a little skeptical if a slave suddenly announced that he had authority to dispense of his master's property. Joseph himself would hardly have believed it just a few short weeks ago. But he would hardly have believed that his own brothers would sell him into slavery.

The events life dealt out were not always what was logical or expected. Thus far, they hadn't been for him.

TWENTY-ONE

"A<small>SENATH?</small>"

"Yes?"

It was Ari. She had opened the door to Asenath's room and was cautiously peeking in.

"May I speak with you for a moment?"

"Yes. Come in."

There was a strange look on Ari's face—one that Asenath couldn't decipher—and she immediately became worried. "Is something wrong?" she asked.

"No, nothing is wrong."

If nothing was wrong, then why was that look on Ari's face?

"You have a visitor," Ari said. "He's waiting for you in the main hall."

Asenath groaned inwardly. The fact that she was a political prisoner was bad enough. But lately it had been made even worse by the plague of suitors Pharaoh had more and more frequently been sending to the house of Setmosis to meet her. Pharaoh could decree that he would choose her a husband, but he had never made a decree that she must be polite to the candidates he sent, so she prepared herself to rebuff yet another would-be suitor.

"I'll be there in a moment," Asenath said, rolling her eyeballs and not even trying to disguise the annoyance in her voice. "Tell him . . . whoever it is . . . that I need a few moments before I can see him."

"This isn't what you're thinking it is," Ari warned, her voice emotionless.

Asenath looked up, expecting an explanation, but Ari had already walked back into the hall and shut the door quietly behind her. For some reason, Asenath felt a cold chill pass through her.

As she made her way to the great hall, she tried to keep a calm, disinterested look on her face, but her heart was pounding wildly against her ribs. The thought came to her to run and hide from whatever it was that was waiting for her out there; but, instead, she lifted her chin and made her entrance with the dignity befitting the daughter of a high priest. She was shocked into stunned silence when she saw who was waiting for her.

"What's wrong? Don't you recognize me? Don't I even get a hug?"

"Father?" She stared in disbelief for several moments. But then the surprise of the moment melted away, and she rushed forward to fling herself into his arms. Tears of joy were streaking down her cheeks even before he had the chance to return her warm embrace.

"I thought for an instant that you had forgotten me," Potipherah said, laughing, as he took Asenath's face in both of his hands and tilted it back to carefully study her. "Can this be my little Asenath? Can this be the small wisp of a thing that left my home a seeming eternity ago? You've grown so much I hardly even recognize you."

"I-I can't believe you're really here," Asenath said, laughing and sobbing all at once. "I've missed you so much. You can't possibly know how much I've missed you."

"No more than your mother and I have missed you. You can be sure of that."

"Where is mother? Is she here? Has she come with you?"

"No. I thought it was best that she remain in On. But you'll be seeing her soon enough." He held Asenath out at arms length again and carefully looked her over. "It's amazing how you've grown," he said, shaking his head and clucking with his tongue. "And, if anything, you've grown twice as beautiful as you were before. The young men of On will be pounding at my door the moment I get you back."

"Back? Back to On?" She stared at him, dumbfounded.

"Yes. After all this time, I've finally managed to convince Pharaoh to let you return. You will spend the next two years in On before being called back to Avaris to be married." He stopped at that part and angrily shook his head, but the huge grin on his face couldn't be entirely erased. "But don't worry about that. I have plans of my own for you. We'll deal with Khyan when the time is right."

"What . . . what are you talking about?" Asenath stammered. "What's going on?" A moment before, her heart had been full with joy, but that was all draining away as his words began to register in her mind. "Pharaoh is sending me home? I won't stay in Avaris any longer?"

"I thought you would be as thrilled about this as I am." Potipherah frowned and looked at her carefully, but Asenath quickly forced a smile to her lips.

"I'm thrilled," she said. "Of course I'm thrilled. I just don't want to get my hopes up and have them dashed." This was a lie. There was only one emotion in her heart right now, and that was fear. Fear that she would soon be far from Joseph. Fear that she might never see him again.

"Don't worry about that," her father replied. "You *will* be returning to On. You leave with me tomorrow after my business with Pharaoh is completed. Your ultimate freedom from Pharaoh won't be long in coming after that. The priesthood of On is still powerful. More powerful than Pharaoh realizes."

Something about his last few words made a cold chill pass through Asenath's heart, and the smile she continued to give him was half-hearted. But he was already thinking about the return trip home and didn't seem to notice. "I have my barge waiting for us up the river," he said. "First thing in the morning we'll start our voyage back home. But Pharaoh wishes to meet with me first. I wish I could spend the rest of the day and evening with you. I'm sorry that I have to leave you alone again so soon after my arrival."

"It's all right," Asenath replied. She stopped to kiss her father on the cheek though not with as much enthusiasm as she had shown before. "While you take care of your business with Pharaoh, I have business of my own to attend to. What's important is that you're here and that . . . that things will soon be as they should be . . . "

"Yes. Things *will* be as they should," Potipherah assured. He drew her close again and gently stroked her hair. "Things will very shortly be as they should."

Joseph greeted Ta at the main gate of Potiphar's house and carefully looked over the flasks of wine which Ta had placed in a small, mule drawn cart.

"This wine is of the finest quality," Ta assured him as Joseph opened one of the flasks to sniff its contents. "But in these times, grain is a far more valuable commodity. I'll be happy to part with this for the grain."

"And my master will be happy about the exchange. Bring your cart through the gate and follow me."

Ta looked nervously at the burly guards who were sullenly watching him from their places on either side of the gate, but he did as told and followed Joseph to Potiphar's corn bins. Several servants were already waiting there, and they quickly unloaded the cart. Just as quickly, they filled several large baskets with grain and placed them in the straw Ta had used to cushion the precious flasks of wine.

"These servants are going to accompany you back to the palace," Joseph said. "And, if I were you, I would use some of that straw to cover the grain. Until the tributes come in from the less affected areas, people will do desperate things to get their hands on a cargo like this."

Ta nodded, quickly covered the baskets, then moved forward and extended a hand. "Thank you," he said, pumping Joseph's hand up and down. "From the bottom of my heart, I thank you. You've saved me from Pharaoh's wrath. It is a kindness I will never forget."

"Just don't forget to avoid Pharaoh's wrath in the future," Joseph cautioned. "Next time it might not be so easy to save yourself."

"You can be sure I won't allow the grain bins to go empty again," Ta assured him. "I won't make that mistake twice. Again I thank you. May the gods shower you with their favors."

"I serve one God," Joseph replied, "and He blesses me daily. But thank you."

Ta and the servants moved slowly toward the front gate, and Joseph turned his eyes toward the setting sun. He shaded his eyes, checked the position of the sun in the sky, and made a quick mental calculation about how many more minutes of daylight remained. He had brought the slaves back to the estate and gotten them settled in the slaves' quarters, but he would be hard pressed to finish the remaining tasks he had set for himself today. He also remembered, groaning as he thought about it, that he still hadn't gone to the main house as Neferset had asked him to do. Hopefully, Potiphar would be back from Pharaoh's palace by now. He would feel much safer if Potiphar were here.

Tiredly, Joseph set his steps in the direction of the house but stopped as a vision of beauty caught his eyes. A smile jumped immediately to his lips.

"Asenath!" he exclaimed. "What are you doing here? I wasn't expecting you until tomorrow."

"I'm leaving," she said. Her eyes flitted between his eyes and the ground. "I'm leaving for On in the morning. My father has come to take me."

"What?" It took a moment for this information to register in his brain. It took another moment for him to realize how upset she was. "You're leaving? You're leaving Avaris? How long will you be gone?"

"For at least two years." She paused, shook her head, and then looked imploringly into his eyes. "What are we to do, Joseph? I can't bear to be away from you. And my father has secret ambitions for me. I'm certain of it. He might try to choose a husband of his own for me while I'm out of Pharaoh's grasp."

"Pharaoh is powerful," Joseph said, feeling his heart begin to sink. "Your father is a wise man. I'm sure he wouldn't do anything to raise Pharaoh's wrath."

"He believes the future of Egypt lies in Thebes," Asenath said, shaking her head in a sorrowful fashion. "Believe me, I understand my father and how he thinks. He has always been determined to marry me to a prince of Thebes, and I fear that he'll try it now. I . . . I don't want to leave you, Joseph. If I do, I'm afraid I may never see you again."

Joseph stared at her, his arms hanging limply at his sides. But he wasn't quite sure what to say. And the dream she had earlier related to him swept yet again through his mind.

"What would your God have us do? What does He speak to your heart?" she asked.

He didn't know what God would have him do. His heart felt empty, and his mind was numb. But he didn't have time to answer. Asenath suddenly threw herself into his arms, and he held her close against him, not caring for once whether it was proper or not. Her tears wetted his tunic, and he gently stroked her long, dark hair.

"Run away with me, Joseph!" she pleaded. "Take me with you to your own land and your own people. I don't want to leave you. I don't want to leave!"

"I-I've made a covenant," he stammered. "I am bound by my conscience and my honor to stay. If not for that covenant, I would take you anywhere you asked. Even to the ends of the earth."

"Then what are we to do?" she sobbed. "Will your God not help us? Will no one help us?"

"It will be all right," Joseph assured her. But even his own faith was beginning to waver. "Trust in the Lord. Pray to Him, and He will protect you."

"But I am the priestess of an Egyptian god," she said. A hint of fear came into her voice as these words escaped her lips. "Why would your God listen to my prayers?"

"Because He's not just my God. He's your God, too. You are His daughter. He loves you, and He will listen to your prayers. He will do what is best for you."

"And what if my father's desires are what is best? What if your God allows him to choose my husband for me?" She closed her eyes and turned her head away, unable to face her worst fears. "Or what if Pharaoh's plans seem best to your God? Your God seemed to think that it was best for you to be a slave. Am I to fare any better? What is marriage to a man I don't love but another form of slavery?"

"Whatever God desires is right," Joseph said his conviction returning despite the circumstances. "If this is His will for you, He will provide a way for you to find happiness in the midst of your afflictions."

"And what about *you*?" she demanded. "Has He done that for you?"

Joseph tilted her face towards his and tenderly placed a hand against her cheek. "Yes," he whispered, his eyes glowing with all the love he felt for her. "Yes, He has."

"You deserve better than this!" Tears welled up again in her eyes, and Asenath leaned more heavily against him. "You deserve better than a life of slavery in Egypt. You deserve better than me."

"No, Asenath. No man could possibly deserve better than you. Least of all me. You have to be brave. You have to have faith. Pray to God with all the intensity of your heart. He will hear and answer your prayers. I promise you He will."

"You're so brave," she whispered. "I wish I had the courage you have. But I'm so afraid. What if I truly never see you again?"

"You'll see me again," Joseph said. "I can feel that much in my heart. Maybe it will be in a month. Maybe it will be in a year. But my days will be much longer and harder when I no longer have our lessons to look forward to."

"Don't forget to work on your hieroglyphics," Asenath said, trying to sound brave as she sniffled and dried her eyes with the palms of her hands. "Be sure to practice every night."

"I will."

Asenath attempted another smile, but it wouldn't come, and she threw her arms around him in a hopeless way. A moment later, Joseph felt the warmth of her lips against his.

"Don't fall in love with another woman while I'm gone," she said, pulling back and giving him a stern look. "Wait for me. If we both have to wait for eternity to come, wait for me."

"I'll wait," he promised.

They stood in silence again. Not knowing what to do. Not knowing what to say. The sun was setting, and the horizon was a flaming sea of red and orange and yellow. Finally, Asenath stretched up on her toes and kissed Joseph once more—this time on the cheek. Then she turned and ran toward the city. The slender silhouette of her body against the bright palette of the horizon was the last thing Joseph saw of her.

TWENTY-TWO

THE CHARIOT RIDE TO THE RIVER was nothing like the one she'd taken with Joseph. That ride was exciting. Exhilarating. This ride, however, carried Asenath through a dark cloud of despair. It was difficult to act cheerful when Pharaoh's charioteers deposited her and the rest of Potipherah's entourage on the river bank, but she did her best to feign happiness for her father's sake. Fortunately, she had plenty of time to collect her emotions and her thoughts before she had to speak with him again. Pharaoh had accompanied their procession to the barge, and he pulled Potipherah off to one side before anyone could board. While the two men spoke, Asenath wandered away from the restless group of priests and servants and found herself a place under a palm tree where she could rest and be alone.

She had prayed the entire night previous to this departure. She had prayed the way Joseph taught her to pray, and she had done it to his God. Strangely enough there had even been moments when she thought his God might actually be listening to her. But this morning it didn't seem like it. She was leaving. She was leaving Avaris and leaving Joseph. And Joseph's God had done nothing to prevent it.

Her father's conversation with Pharaoh ended all too soon, and Potipherah motioned for her to join him. Together they watched Pharaoh's company gallop slowly out of sight, then walked together toward the barge.

"Remember how you used to travel with me when I went on official business to Thebes?" he asked as he guided her toward the boarding plank.

"Yes, I remember."

"You used to love this barge. You were always exploring every last cubit of it. Every cabin, every plank. It drove your mother mad with worry. She followed you everywhere because she was afraid you would fall overboard and drown."

Asenath nodded. That fate didn't seem so bad right now. But she glanced around and smiled a little as old memories returned to her.

Potipherah's barge was a monument to his power. It was long enough to seat thirty rowers and was constructed from the finest imported cedar. There were three decks, a lounge, a dining room, and a kitchen. There were also separate cabins for the high priest, his family, and his servants and guests. Asenath could see that a fresh coat of white paint had been applied to the thick cedar planks and that colorful banners on long poles had been unfurled in her honor. But she felt too numb inside to enjoy the gesture. She kept turning her eyes back to Avaris, wondering if she would ever see Joseph again.

"The cook has prepared breakfast for us," Potipherah said. "Come. It's waiting for us on the upper deck's dining area."

She followed him in silence. She didn't feel much like eating, but she didn't want to ruin his good mood. This was supposed to be a time of celebration. She was going home after a long absence, and she needed to act the part of a dutiful, happy daughter.

Once they reached the gold and ivory table on the upper deck, they seated themselves, and her father offered her some fruit from a copper tray. She took a thin slice of melon and some pomegranate and shifted nervously as he stared at her and smiled.

"It's so good to have you coming home," he said. "The house hasn't been the same without you."

"I'm happy to be coming home," she lied. "There will be a lot of catching up to do."

Potipherah nodded. Then his face took on a serious look. He stared silently at his hands for several long moments then glanced absently toward the stern, listening for a moment as the helmsman barked out orders to the oarsmen and got the barge moving slowly toward the middle of the river.

"Now that we're alone, away from the prying ears and eyes of Avaris," he said, "I need to speak candidly with you."

She didn't look up. She pretended to be greatly interested in the pomegranate seed she was holding between the tips of her index finger and thumb. He went on speaking anyway.

"It's time for us to start thinking about your future, Asenath. Your *real* future. It's not here in Avaris. It's not even among the Hyksos. The gods want greater things for you. Khyan will eventually be trampled beneath the feet of the true kings of Egypt. Your future is in Thebes, my daughter, and it is time for us to do something about it."

"Pharaoh will never allow it. He'll never allow me to marry one of Nebireyeraw's sons." She continued to study the pomegranate seed as if it held the key her destiny. But her father seemed unconcerned about her apparent lack of attentiveness. He also didn't seem worried about anything Pharaoh might do if he were ever to learn that they had been having this conversation.

"Pharaoh will have no say in anything that happens after today," Potipherah boldly declared. "The locust plague has weakened him, and the people of true Egyptian blood will soon turn against him. It's time for us to ally ourselves with Thebes. When the king of Thebes decides to make his play for power, we need to be on his side. And that's where you come in."

Asenath stared at him with dull eyes, no longer able to maintain her charade of being happy. "What exactly do you mean by that?" she asked in a lifeless voice.

"Thebes and On are the two greatest centers of religious authority in all Egypt," he said. "A union between our two cities could prove powerful enough to topple Khyan's government. Khyan has finally made the mistake I've been waiting for. Now that you've been allowed to come home, we will have plenty of time to forge a bond between you and the eldest son of Nebireyeraw. With you married to Sebeka-mzaf, our two cities will be ready to challenge Khyan."

"And what if I don't cooperate?"

Potipherah stared at his daughter, dumbfounded. But his surprise only lasted a moment. He shook his head at her and laughed.

"What has Khyan done to you?" he asked. "Has he somehow managed to turn my very own daughter against me?"

"He hasn't turned me against you. I've learned to think for myself. And I'll keep my own counsel as to whom I will marry." It was a bold thing to say to her father. More bold than anything she'd ever said to him before. But he didn't back down.

"You have no say in whom you will marry," he replied. "If you don't choose Sebekamzaf, Khyan will choose someone for you. The choice I'm offering is the only real choice you have."

In a way, he was right. But the choice he offered wasn't any more pleasing than any choice Khyan had to offer. Stubbornly, she shook her head.

"It won't work. Even if I go against Pharaoh's decree and marry this son of Nebireyeraw, my misery will still be assured. Pharaoh is too powerful. Your plan will fail and we and the people of our city will be doomed."

"It won't fail," Potipherah replied, a touch of anger now rumbling in his voice. "The people are suffering from the loss of our grain, and Khyan still demands his tribute. It will be easy to turn the masses against him."

"Do they love you more than him?" Asenath asked. "Has the temple of Ra released the people from its tribute? Khyan has cut his tribute by three-fourths. How much has the priesthood of Ra cut its tribute?"

Potipherah leaned back and shook his head. He looked at Asenath for a few more moments then turned his eyes away in disgust.

She would have never challenged her father like this in the past.

Her time in Avaris had changed her. But the change wasn't due to Khyan or to her training in the temple of Seth. In part her change was a spiritual one. She was beginning to believe the things Joseph had taught her. He'd told her that the sons and daughters of men were first created spiritually by a wise, eternal God who was their Father. If she were truly a daughter of Joseph's God, didn't that give her greater worth than this? Wasn't she something more than a mere tool to be wielded in the battle between her father and Pharaoh?

Even as she thought this, Potipherah abruptly raised himself from the table, looming over her. His face was dark and his eyes were flashing like two hot, angry coals. He could force her to marry whomever he pleased. She didn't have the physical strength to stop him from doing it. But she was still determined to resist. If she were to be married to a Theban prince, it would happen against her will. She wouldn't go happily or easily into this misguided union.

"You and I will discuss this matter later," Potipherah said, struggling to calm himself even as his face flushed a brighter color of red. He shook his head at her like he would do at a child throwing a tantrum; and, for some reason, this angered her. But she wasn't about to be outdone, and she gave no sign that his actions were affecting her. "After you've had time to be away from Avaris and the false ideas they've been putting into your head," he said, "we'll talk about this like two rational adults. Until then enjoy your breakfast." He stomped from the dining cabin and Asenath felt hot tears gather in her eyes. Luckily he didn't turn back to see how his angry words had affected her.

She didn't want to anger or displease her father, but this was something she just couldn't do. If not for meeting Joseph, she might have passively gone along with her father's wishes. Fortunately for her, she *had* met Joseph, and it gave her the strength to stand up for what she believed was right.

Asenath pushed herself away from the table and wiped the tears from her eyes. Black *kohl* smeared across her face and across the backs of her hands, but she gave it no notice. There wasn't anyone here to impress with her appearance. The only man she cared to impress could do nothing to halt her departure. There was nothing for her to do but go someplace where she could be alone and cry without being seen.

She found the solace she craved in the private cabin that had always been hers. Someone had already put her small box of possessions there, and a bed with a wooden headrest had been brought in. She ignored all of this and cast herself to her knees in the middle of the floor.

"God of Joseph," she prayed, clasping her hands together while she raised her eyes in desperation toward the heavens, "I will give up the gods of my own people to know You. I will do anything You ask of me. All that I ask in return is for You to save me from the plotting of my father and make a way for Joseph and me to be together. Allow me to choose my own destiny. Allow your faithful servant, Joseph, to be a part of it . . ." In all her time praying to all the different gods of Egypt, she had never heard or felt any response. But today—praying to Joseph's God—something happened. Today she felt a strange, warm sensation burning in her heart. An unexpected peace washed gently over her.

Joseph was right. His God did speak to the hearts of men. He was speaking to hers right now, only she wasn't quite sure what was being said. She wished Joseph were here. He could help her. He could help her understand. She needed his strength, faith, and wisdom to get through this. She felt so helpless and incomplete without him.

Joseph felt numb inside. Asenath should have been meeting with him in the garden today. She should have been working with him on the hieroglyphics like she had so often done before. But she was far away by now, and the day seemed longer knowing that he might never see her again. Though he was trying to keep himself occupied with hard work, Joseph couldn't seem to keep thoughts of Asenath from intruding upon his mind. He kept reliving details of the much too brief moments he had spent with her. He recalled the way she would scowl and twist her mouth to one side when she was pondering a problem, the way a warm tingle traveled up his arm whenever their hands touched, and he thought about the times he had caught the scent of her hair when she leaned over his shoulder to examine his writing. Thoughts of her had been tormenting him all day long, and he didn't know how much more of it he could take.

"You're looking rather gloomy today."

Joseph jumped, startled, and turned to see Neferset watching him. She had been watching him a lot lately, and it never failed to make him nervous. Now was no exception.

"I'm sorry. I didn't mean to startle you."

"It's all right," he said, not quite sure how to respond. "I was thinking about something and not paying attention where I was going."

"Where *are* you going? To the stables?"

Joseph nodded. "One of the master's horses has been sick," he explained, "and it needs a little extra attention. I've been helping Pekhti with the extra burden each morning."

"Is that how it works?" There was a strange glint in Neferset's eyes. "Does one have to be sick to get attention around here? Perhaps if I were a horse, I would be receiving more attention and care."

She was walking along beside him now, and Joseph glanced nervously at her, coughing into his hand. "The master surely loves you more than his horses," he said. "I'm certain he would give his entire fortune if that's what it took to keep you safe from sickness and harm."

"I wasn't talking about getting attention from my husband."

He felt her eyes piercing through him, and he had a good idea what she was getting at. But Joseph kept his face expressionless, acting as if he had no idea what she was talking about. When he didn't respond to her statement, she forged ahead on her own.

"I'm attracted to you," she said. "I hope that doesn't surprise you."

He felt panic tighten the muscles in his stomach, and his brain whirled with fear. He tried to think of something to say to ease the discomfort of this situation, but nothing suitable came to mind.

"You've been busy with that young priestess and her lessons," Neferset went on, "but she's gone now. It's time for you to start paying attention to what you can and should have rather than what you'll never get. *Maai ari-n en-n unnut setcheru,*" she whispered seductively into his ear. "Come, let us make for ourselves an hour reclining together. Lie with me, Joseph."

Joseph's eyes opened wide in shock, the color drained from his face, and he took a quick step backwards.

"Behold!" he exclaimed. "My master knows not what happens with me in the house, and he has committed all that he has into my hand. There is none greater in this house than I; neither has he kept back any thing from me but you, because you are his wife. How then can I do this great wickedness and sin against God?"

"Consider my offer," Neferset said, seeming amused rather than offended by his words. "My husband will be gone this evening, and I'll be alone at the house. All the servants will be dismissed. There will be no one there to see you. No one will ever have to know."

"I-I have to be getting to the stables," Joseph stammered. "Pekhti will be wondering where I am."

"Go then," she said, smiling and waving the backs of her fingers in the direction of the stables. "But don't keep me waiting tonight. I'll be expecting you."

He didn't wait to see what would happen next. His heart told him to flee, and he listened to it. Quickly, he moved across the yard into the cool, musty interior of the stables. Only then did he stop to breath and to allow his mind to ponder what had just happened.

This was not good. This was not good at all.

Joseph felt his legs shaking uncontrollably beneath him, and he involuntarily jumped when Pekhti's voice rang out across the stables to him in greeting.

"Good morning, Joseph. You're as good as your word. You came exactly when you told me you would."

Joseph nodded his head, still struggling to regain his composure, and Pekhti immediately sensed that something was not in order.

"What is it?" he asked. "You look like you've had a near brush with death. Is something wrong?"

"Something wrong? Yes. Something is wrong. Something is terribly wrong."

"What's going on? How can I help you?"

Joseph looked at his friend, unsure about just how much he should say. But there might be a measure of security in having a witness—even if only a secondhand one—to what had just transpired.

"The master's wife wants me to come to her tonight while he's away."

Pekhti vigorously shook his head, and his eyes widened with alarm. "Don't do it!" he said. "Whatever else you do, don't go near the house tonight!"

"I don't intend to. But I'm worried. I have a bad feeling about this. A very bad feeling."

"Of course you do. We all know what happened to T'chet when he got involved with the master's wife. Your best defense against Neferset is to keep your distance. She's not going to say anything to her husband as long as you don't. Just keep your distance. Trust me in this. You'll be fine as long as you stay away from her."

Joseph nodded. Pekhti was right, of course. But following his advice would be easier said than done. The inescapable duties of a chief steward often brought Joseph into the house, and Neferset seemed to know his routine well. There would be ample opportunity for her to catch him alone in the room of records, or the great hall, or any of the other places where his duties took him. He would have to not only be cautious, but he would have to seek the Lord's protection as well.

"Once she sees that you won't betray your master or your standards," Pekhti said, seeing that Joseph was still uneasy, "she'll move on to easier targets. One of the lesser servants will fall prey to her charms, and she'll forget about you."

Joseph nodded again. But he wasn't entirely convinced that it would be as easy as that.

"How are the new slaves working out?" he asked after a moment of silence, eager to change the subject. "I tried to pick two for you who looked like hard-working, trustworthy men."

"They're doing an adequate job," Pekhti replied, nodding. "Nothing like what you used to accomplish, but they're getting the job done."

Joseph took a wooden shovel that was leaning against a pillar and listened to it scrape against the ground as he shoveled manure away from the walkway. He hadn't heard that sound for some time now. In a way, he almost missed the anonymity of his former job.

"How long is she going to be gone?" Pekhti asked.

"Who?"

"The young priestess."

"I don't know. At least two years." He could feel Pekhti watching him—probing his every movement and expression—and he realized they were now going to enter into a new and, if it were possible, even more uncomfortable conversation.

"I think your God is the one who sent her to be your teacher."

The same thought had many times before crossed Joseph's mind, but he didn't let on that it had. "Why do you say that?" he asked instead.

"Because your God watches out for you. He has ever since you've arrived here. And you've been happiest since she became a part of your life. I don't think any of this happened by accident."

"She's a wonderful teacher," Joseph said, forgetting momentarily about Neferset as the pleasant memories of his times with Asenath came rushing back at him. "I've learned a great deal from her."

"Yes, I'm sure you have. It's a shame she has to be a priestess and you have to be a slave."

Joseph looked up from his shovel and eyed Pekhti with a concerned scowl on his face.

"The two of you would make a good pair," Pekhti said, smiling and not turning away from his gaze. "You seem like a perfect match for each other."

"You know something like that isn't possible," Joseph said. "It would take an act of Pharaoh to make it possible for Asenath and me to marry. And besides that—" He cut himself short and shook his head.

"What? Are you afraid she doesn't love you in return? I've seen young people in love before. Asenath cares deeply for you."

"Thank you," Joseph said. "But it's not that." He stared intently at the tiled walkway beneath his feet and scuffed at it with the toe of his sandal. "It's not that at all."

"Then what is it? You don't think she's coming back from On?"

Joseph looked at Pekhti again. Hearing someone else voice his own concerns brought back all the persistent impressions that had been nagging at his soul. But he didn't know what to say, so he went back to shoveling.

"She'll be back," Pekhti reassured him. "Her father won't dare defy Pharaoh. She'll return soon enough."

"I hope so."

"But you still don't believe it. I can see that. What is it that you think is going to go wrong?"

"I don't know," Joseph replied. "I just know what my heart tells me, and it's telling me I won't see her again anytime soon."

"Your God wouldn't do that to you. It wouldn't be fair. To you or to her."

"Whatever the will of the Lord is," Joseph said, "is what is fair and right. I don't understand why He wouldn't allow her to come back, but there's a righteous purpose in everything He does."

"How can you have faith in a God like that?" Pekhti demanded, shaking his head. "How can you have faith in a God who requires you to accept all things that happen to you without ever complaining? How can you accept a God who lets you suffer when you've done everything He could possibly ask of you?"

"Faith takes self-discipline," Joseph replied. "This life is a test, and it was never meant to be easy. But my God is also a loving God, and He will never leave me alone in a time of despair. He has promised to bless those who love Him and serve Him. In the end, I've always received the blessings He's promised."

"Except the promise that you would rule over your brothers. That one hasn't happened, has it."

"This life isn't over," Joseph said. "Someday I'll understand. Someday all God's promises will be fulfilled."

Pekhti shook his head and rolled his eyes. "I'm beginning to think that nothing can dampen your faith in your God."

"I'm not as spiritually strong as you think I am," Joseph said. "But I'll endure whatever God sees fit to inflict upon me for as long as I can. His wisdom is greater than my own. And so are His purposes."

They were both silent for a moment—Joseph staring at the shovel and Pekhti staring at him—then Joseph hesitantly asked, "Pekhti, how did you figure out that I'm in love with Asenath? Is it that obvious?"

Pekhti laughed. "It's so obvious that even Potiphar knows it. You and she seem to be the only ones who don't see the love struck shine in the other's eyes."

The color drained from Joseph's face, and he had to struggle to maintain his composure.

"I love her," he said. "But nothing that would offend either the laws of Egypt or the laws of my God has ever happened between us. I promise you that."

"No one is suggesting that it has," Pekhti replied. "Why do you think Potiphar trusts you so completely? He knows you would never do anything dishonorable. I know it, too."

"Thank you. I appreciate the trust you have in me."

"Your God has blessed you before," Pekhti said, clasping a hand on Joseph's shoulder in an encouraging way. "Perhaps He'll do it again. We never know what a new morning will bring us. Perhaps it will bring you the blessings you desire."

"I hope you're right," Joseph said.

But one thing bothered him and made it difficult to believe the Lord would ever give him the blessing he most wanted. He kept remembering the dream that had come to Asenath. And he envied the man it had promised her to.

"Come on," Joseph said, eager to clear such depressing thoughts away. "Let's see to that horse. I have an herbal remedy that used to work on sick sheep. I think it will help our sick horse as well."

If only all his problems could be as easily solved as the healing of an ill horse. But what herb was there that could cure the turmoil in his heart. And how was he to protect himself against Neferset. He would have to put his trust in God. That was all he'd ever really had power to do.

TWENTY-THREE

ASENATH FELT LOST and completely out of her element. In Avaris, she had usually detested her temple duties. But now—now that she was free of them—she didn't know what to do with herself. At first it had been wonderful to be free of at least a part of her political captivity. She was with her father and mother again. She was reacquainting herself with old friends and familiar sights. The only thing that really detracted from her happiness was the longing she felt to be with Joseph. But the novelty of being home didn't last long, and boredom was quick to set in.

Back in Avaris, if the temple wasn't keeping her busy Ari was. But Asenath's mother had a different idea about how a young woman of the upper class should spend her time, and as she paced along the flat rooftop of her parents' home, Asenath reflected on the most recent discussion they'd had about that.

"It's not the place of the daughter of a high priest to work in the kitchen or clean the house," her mother, Seshep, told her. "We have servants to do that. One day you will be the wife of an important man and hold the title 'Mistress of the House.' At that time, you will direct the activities of the servants. But you must never do menial labor like cleaning or cooking. That would be lowering yourself to the level of a servant. You would never be able to command their respect that way."

Ari had seemed to command the respect of her servants. They adored her in fact. But Asenath knew it would be futile to argue that point with her mother.

"Then what am I to do with all this spare time?" Asenath had finally asked. "Am I expected to just sit around the house and be idle all day?"

"Your job right now is to do your best to find a husband," Seshep said. "And I would suggest that you strongly consider your father's wishes. If you allow him to pursue a union with Nebireyeraw's son, you'll have a part in the choosing of your husband. If not, there's nothing for you to do but wait for Pharaoh to drag you back to Avaris and marry you to some man three times your age. You seem not to understand that even in Egypt it is not the place of a woman to defy a man."

Almost instantly, Asenath felt a spark of anger ignite within her. She was tired of being pressured about this. Not a day had gone by without either her mother or father pushing her to marry Sebeka-mzaf, the eldest son of the king of Thebes. But she fought down the anger and managed to keep her voice steady when she replied.

"You know how I feel about that," she said. "And you know what kind of danger we will be in if Pharaoh ever finds out what father has been planning."

"You would be safe in Thebes. Khyan will think twice about attacking such a powerful city. And even if he does decide to take action, by the time he finds out, it will be much too late. Your father and Nebireyeraw have already discussed their strategy for dealing with Khyan."

Asenath angrily shook her head and walked over to the low, stone wall that formed a protective railing around the roof of her family's house. She slumped against it and stared over the rooftops toward Avaris. More and more of her time each day was being spent up here, alone, on the roof. Neither of her parents ever bothered to look for her here, and it gave her some peace from their constant talk of marriage and political ambitions. But time to herself also brought its share of problems. When she was alone her mind dwelt more and more on Joseph, and that made her so miserable she could hardly stand it.

"One would think you left something very important in Avaris the way you come up here and stare in that direction every day."

Asenath spun around, surprised and—for some strange reason—embarrassed as well.

"You scared me, Nesmut. How did you know I was here?"

"You used to come here all the time when you were a little girl. When something was troubling you this was where I would find you."

"You always have known me well, haven't you," Asenath said, smiling sadly. "Sometimes I think you know me better than my own mother. Maybe that's because you spent more time with me than either of my parents ever did."

"Your father is a busy man. And your mother runs a large house. Now what is it that bothers you. You can tell me, young mistress."

"I could always tell you almost anything, Nesmut. But not this. This secret can't even be shared with you. Not yet at least."

Nesmut nodded, but Asenath knew she wouldn't give up so easily. And Asenath wasn't so sure herself that she could keep this painful secret bottled up inside for long. She had never been able to tell Netchem. But Netchem, like Asenath, was a member of an important Egyptian family. With Nesmut it might be different. She was a servant and might not be shocked to hear from Asenath's own mouth that she had entirely lost her heart to a slave.

"The evening meal will be ready soon," Nesmut said. "I just came to warn you that your mother will be calling for you."

"Thank you," Asenath said. "I'll be right down."

Nesmut disappeared down the stairs, and Asenath turned to cast one last, yearning glance in the direction of Avaris. Her return home was nothing like she had for so many years imagined it would be. Nothing at all like she had thought. She only hoped her life would soon get better.

Jacob removed the torn fragments of the coat from the special box where he preserved them and held a piece in his hands, staring at it with dull, pain-filled eyes. Even after all these long years the colors of Joseph's coat remained bright and unfaded. So did the memory of his loss.

He had never recovered from the death of his firstborn child by Rachel. All his daughters and all his sons—even Benjamin—couldn't fill the void that had been left in his heart. God didn't seem to have any comfort to give him either. He hung his head and shook it as his heart overflowed once again with grief. But there wasn't nearly enough time to indulge himself in it. A noise outside the tent alerted him that someone was coming, and he quickly dropped what he was holding back into the box and hastily pushed the lid back in place. He turned just as a hesitant hand parted the flap of the door.

"Father? Are you in here?"

"Yes, my son. You may come in."

Benjamin, the youngest of Jacob's eleven remaining sons, stepped hesitantly into the tent. His intelligent, brown eyes—eyes that had always reminded Jacob of Rachel and Joseph—glanced for a moment at the only half-closed lid of the wooden box, then he looked quickly and respectfully away.

"Does it upset you that I still grieve over Joseph?" Jacob asked, nodding meaningfully at the box.

"It upsets all of us that you grieve," Benjamin quietly answered. "We wish we could bring you more joy."

"My family does bring me joy," Jacob said. "You most of all. But there will always be an emptiness inside me that none of you can fill."

"Why won't you let us comfort you, Father?" Jacob could see that his son was struggling to understand, and he wished that he, too, could understand so that he could properly explain it. But words failed to express the loss he constantly carried within him.

"There is a part of a man's heart that dies each time he loses a wife or a child," Jacob said. "I know I should allow my heart to heal. It's just . . . just . . . " He stopped speaking and shook his head. "Maybe if your brothers had been able to find a body . . . Maybe if someone had witnessed it happen . . . Maybe then I could say goodbye and go on with my life. Sometimes a part of me wants to believe that—"

"That he's still alive?"

Benjamin immediately lowered his eyes, embarrassed that he had interrupted his father, but Jacob gave him a tired smile and nodded his head.

"But the coat," Benjamin whispered. "The blood."

"I know," Jacob said, lowering his eyes now and shaking his head. "I know how foolish it must seem. But, other than the coat, I have nothing tangible to show that Joseph is dead. Your mother has a grave and a pillar in the way to Ephrath. Joseph has only a torn coat in a small, wooden box. I had no body to lay down in a grave. I had no chance to bid him one final farewell."

"It wasn't your fault, Father. You and Mother both blame yourselves for what happened, but it wasn't your fault. You taught me that if a person lives righteously, God will not allow his life to be taken before his time. Wasn't Joseph righteous?"

"Yes. He was a very righteous young man. Just like you."

"Then God would have spared Joseph and brought him safely home if it wasn't his time to die."

"You're right," Jacob answered. "Of course, you're right." But that didn't make the burden any easier to bear. And there was no way to adequately explain that to Benjamin. "Come," he said, standing up and clapping a hand warmly on his son's shoulder. "Your brothers will be returning from the pastures soon, and your mother will be setting out dinner. You and I still have the pack animals to look after."

Benjamin nodded and obediently followed his father from the tent. He was a fine boy and the only comfort Jacob had left to his soul. Whatever else happened to this family, he was determined not to let any harm befall this son. After everything else he had lost, surely the Lord wouldn't require Rachel's only remaining child to be taken from him. Surely God would pity an old man in this.

TWENTY-FOUR

O VER A YEAR HAD PASSED since Asenath's departure for On, but Joseph hadn't forgotten her. If anything, his feelings for her had grown stronger. But how bitter it was to know that she could never be his and to realize that slavery had begun all over for him the moment his heart became attached to her.

Joseph frowned and pounded his mallet a little harder against the wooden pole of the broken *shaduf*. Most Egyptian girls were married before they turned fifteen. Asenath was already older than that. Pharaoh would certainly give her to one of his trusted nomarchs or advisors the moment she was brought back to Avaris.

"Careful," Khep said. "If you pound any harder you're going to break it even worse than it's already broken."

Joseph looked up, suddenly aware where he was, and his face flushed with embarrassment. "Sorry," he said. "I got lost in thought and forgot about what I was doing."

"It looks like everything is fastened in place again," Khep said. "Should we try it with a bucket now?"

Joseph nodded, and Khep fastened a bucket to the far end of the pole. Together, they swung it out over the river bank, dipped the bucket into the water then brought it back up to the top of the bank beside them again. Khep nodded his head in satisfaction.

"This is one of the best things we Egyptians ever invented," he said. "A thousand years from now I predict that farmers will still be using it. We once had to depend entirely upon the inundation of the Nile, but now we can bring the water to us when the river runs low. Only a drought like Egypt has never before seen could keep us from growing our crops."

"The man who built the first *shaduf* was inspired of God," Joseph agreed. "It is an important and remarkable invention."

"You always speak of this God of yours," Khep said, leaning against the *shaduf* and glancing at Joseph with a look of interest on his face. "Who is this foreign God that you worship? By what name is He known?"

"My God is Jehovah," Joseph said. "And I am His humble servant."

"Do you mean to tell me that you were a priest in a temple of this God before you were sold into slavery?"

"No," Joseph replied, shaking his head. "I serve Him by covenant. He made sacred promises to my great-grandfather, Abraham, and Abraham's posterity now bears the right and responsibility of serving Him."

"I never much understood religion," Khep said. "Its mysteries and secrets have always seemed to be reserved for the priests. But maybe you can teach me about your God one of these days. I'd like to learn."

Joseph eagerly opened his mouth to respond, but then he remembered the business that was waiting for him back at the house.

"I would be more than happy to teach you about my God," Joseph said, "but the master is waiting to meet with me this afternoon to go over the records of his properties. Perhaps we can finish our discussion when I come back to the fields later today."

"Of course. I'll look forward to it. And thank you for the help with the *shaduf*," Khep said. "You saved me half a day's work already."

Joseph clapped Khep on the arm then turned and jogged toward his waiting chariot. He'd nearly forgotten about the meeting with Potiphar, and the last thing he wanted was to anger the master. The chariot bore him quickly across the stretch of land separating the fields from the edge of the city. When he reached the house, he left the horses and chariot in the able hands of Pekhti and raced toward the house. He was panting with exertion when he came through the front door.

"I was wondering when you would finally get here."

The voice startled him, and Joseph spun around to see Neferset, her eyelids half-lowered, watching him from across the great hall.

"I'm sorry if I'm a little late," Joseph said. "I was helping Khep in the fields and lost track of the time." He paused and looked around, seeing no sign of Potiphar. "Is the master waiting for me?" he finally asked.

"A messenger came from the palace just a few minutes before you arrived," Neferset said, and she moved closer—uncomfortably closer—to Joseph. "He came to inform me that my husband won't be able to keep his appointment with you today."

"I understand," Joseph said, turning his shoulder toward the door and taking a few sideways steps in that direction. "Did he say when the master would like to reschedule our review of the records?"

"You've been avoiding me," Neferset said, ignoring his question. She moved steadily toward him until he was backed up against one of the many supporting pillars that lined the hall. "Why do you avoid me, Joseph? Don't you realize what I can do for you? Don't you realize what we can do for each other?"

"I-I should leave," Joseph said. "The master—"

"The master is away," Neferset interrupted. "For the time being, you and I are entirely alone. It's just you and me in the house, Joseph. All the other servants are away. Stay here with me. My husband will never know what passes between us. Lie with me, and I will give you everything you desire." She wrapped her slender arms around his neck, and Joseph tried to slip free. But Neferset tangled her fingers in the fabric of his tunic and pulled herself against him.

"Will you reject me again?" she demanded. "Am I not beautiful enough for a Hebrew slave?"

Frantically, Joseph pulled back and felt his tunic rip. But the least of his concerns at this moment was a ripped tunic.

"I won't let you leave," Neferset said, holding more tightly to his garment. "You're not going to escape me so easily this time. You've ignored my offers for more than a year now. But I won't allow you to turn me down today."

He pulled away again, and this time the tunic came off in her hands. Before she could stop him a second time, he darted away and fled from the house.

He thought he heard her calling for the guards even as he ran to escape her, and a dark feeling of doom wrapped itself around him.

He had a great deal of faith in God. No matter how bad things had gotten in the past, the Lord had always been there to help him. But he couldn't see any way to survive this. Despair momentarily overwhelmed him. All the blessings he'd obtained in Egypt were about to be savagely ripped away.

The unexpected visit of the delegation from Thebes had surprised her. The announcement that Nebireyeraw himself had come, too, put her into temporary shock. He was here to arrange a marriage—a marriage between herself and his son, Sebekamzaf—and Asenath felt as if she were spinning through a murky cloud of confusion and despair. It was all she could do to keep a forced, empty smile on her lips as she muddled her way through an awkward conversation with the man her father had chosen as her future husband.

"Your father was telling me today how Khyan kept you locked up in Avaris like a bird in a cage," Sebekamszaf said. "How did you tolerate such indignities?"

"I had a measure of freedom," Asenath replied, thinking that this indignation was worse than any Khyan had ever heaped upon her. "There are those who have much less than I did."

"Still," he insisted, "you must have yearned to be free. You were little more than a hostage to keep your father in line. What Khyan has done is an insult to you and to your family, not to mention a mockery of the order of Egypt. It's an outrage that should be avenged."

"Is vengeance so easily achieved?" Asenath asked, watching the prince carefully. "Khyan is powerful. Even the kings of Thebes rule by his permission only." Her last remark was a carefully calculated one, and she watched to see how Sebekamzaf would react to it. He reacted exactly as she'd expected he would.

"Khyan has as much power over Thebes as a fly has over a lion," Sebekamzaf said, his voice rumbling with undisguised contempt. "He thinks his evil storm god will protect him, but soon the fame of Amun will spread throughout Egypt. With Amun watching over us, the armies of Thebes will sweep the Hyksos out of Egypt. Egyptian land will never again be occupied by foreign kings!"

His face was red, and his eyes were flashing. He would make a hot-headed monarch when he took the throne of Thebes. Asenath could easily envision a man like this rushing headlong into war, but she didn't want to imagine the bloody consequences that would follow.

"Someday I will be Pharaoh of all Egypt," he continued, oblivious to the expression of horror that had unconsciously crept over her face, "and I will need a queen to rule at my side. The future of Egypt rests in the hands of my family. Now is the time for your family and the city of On to join with us."

"Join you? In what way?" Asenath felt her stomach knot up with apprehension. She already knew what type of "joining" he was referring to, and this conversation had now reached the point she'd been dreading all throughout the evening.

"Your father and my father have made arrangements for us to wed," Sebekamzaf said, folding his arms smugly across his broad, bare chest. "When that union is complete, our two cities will be unified as well. We will make our move against Khyan and reclaim Egypt's lost glory. All is arranged. I have come to formally announce that I will take you as my bride."

She felt her heart sink into the pit of her stomach. It was happening. Everything she had dreaded was coming to pass. Her father had made his final move for power, and he would sacrifice the happiness of his own daughter to get it. Cold fear spread from her heart into her limbs, and then another emotion ignited. It was a return of her earlier feelings of anger, and that anger quickly fanned itself into leaping flames.

"I won't marry you," she said, a belligerent edge to her voice.

Sebekamzaf looked at her, bewildered. He moved his mouth, but no words came out. He was a prince and unaccustomed to being refused, but he quickly regained his composure.

"You won't marry me?" He said the words slowly. Then he shook his head and laughed. "But the arrangements have already been made. You have no choice in the matter."

"I am a slave to no man," Asenath said, her voice cold as ice, "and I assure you, I do have a choice in the matter."

"You're a woman," Sebekamzaf said, dismissing her comment with a wave of one hand. "It's not the place of a woman to make such decisions. Decisions like this are best left in the hands of men."

"Maybe if men would pay more attention to the counsel of women, Egypt wouldn't be in such a state of unrest." She said it boldly, and she began to gain courage from her own boldness. "You and my father and your father can make all the plans you want, but I won't be forced into a marriage that will bring me nothing but unhappiness. I'd rather die than marry you or any other arrogant prince of Thebes."

"I don't think I've made myself clear," Sebekamzaf said.

"No. I don't think I've made *myself* clear," Asenath interrupted. "I am Hyksos, and I would rather marry the lowliest of slaves than spend one day as your wife. If the Hyksos are such lowly dogs as you seem to think we are, then how did we conquer Egypt and build such an empire? Go back to Thebes, Prince Sebekamzaf. Go back and let your people know that a Hyksos woman would rather marry a jackal than be the queen of a Theban pig!"

These were uncharacteristically harsh words for her; but she had caught a glimpse into the soul of this man, and she didn't like what she saw. He was a conceited, self-important pig. He wasn't worthy even to cross through the shadow of the man she loved. She would never marry Sebekamzaf. Never!

"If the life of a slave is what you desire," Sebekamzaf hissed, an angry sneer on his face, "then I'm certain that the life of a slave can be arranged. I could make it so that your children and your children's children were forced to break their backs under the burdens of my people. But a contract between my father and your father has already been made. You are to become my wife, and there's no way for either of us to avoid it. I think I'm going to enjoy the challenge of breaking your stubborn spirit. Sooner rather than later you'll learn the proper place of a woman."

Asenath stared at him in disbelief. Did such vanity and arrogance actually exist in this world? Did he really believe that he or any man had the power to force her to marry against her will?

"Get away from me," she commanded, pointing to the stairs that led from the rooftop patio to the house below. She turned her back on him and stared with blurred vision across the city landscape. "Get away from me now!"

Strangely, Sebekamzaf didn't seem angered by this final outburst. "You'll change your mind about me later," he said. "When you see that the future of Egypt lies in Thebes rather than Avaris, you'll see me in a different light."

She heard him turn, and she heard him move slowly down the stairs; but she continued to stare in the opposite direction, refusing to dignify his departure with even a sidelong glance. When she was certain he was finally gone, she crumpled against the stone wall at the roof's edge. Tears began to flood her eyes.

"God of Joseph!" she whispered, lifting her imploring, tear-filled eyes toward the heavens. "Help me . . . please help me . . . " She tried to listen in her heart for an answer. She tried to listen the way Joseph had told her to. But she wasn't even certain she expected an answer. She had spent nearly her entire life worshiping the myriad gods of Egypt and didn't have much faith that Joseph's God would honor her with an answer now.

More words began to form on her lips, but the soft tread of sandals on stone steps warned her of another person's approach. Quickly, she got to her feet, and she dried her eyes with a corner of her *kalasiris*, wiping away all traces of emotion with it. No matter the intensity of her distress, she refused to allow Sebekamzaf to see her in a moment of weakness. To her relief, she found herself confronted instead by her father.

"That seems to have gone well," Potipherah said. "I don't know what you told the young prince, but he seems very impressed with you and wants to move immediately forward with a marriage."

Asenath's mouth fell open in disbelief, but she was only stunned for a moment. "I told him that he was a pig and that I would never marry him," she whispered icily. "And I'm telling you the same thing now."

Potipherah stared at her. He seemed, for a moment, to think that she was joking. But the coldness in her blue eyes was enough to prove that she wasn't.

"How could you?" she demanded when he remained thoughtfully silent for several long moments. "How could you do this to your own daughter? Do you truly think you own me? Like you own this house? Or . . . or . . . like one of the horses from your stables?"

"There are times when we have to sacrifice our own desires to accomplish the greater will of the gods," Potipherah said.

"Spare me your priestly rhetoric!" Asenath retorted. She spun away from him and steadied herself by placing both hands against the lip of the stone wall. "This has nothing to do with the will of the gods," she said. "This has everything to do with you. Do you intend to make me a slave to Sebekamzaf just like your ambitions made me a slave to Khyan? Would you do this to satisfy your own lust for power?"

"It is fortunate for both of us that Sebekamzaf was impressed enough by your beauty to overlook your sharp tongue," Potipherah said, his voice low and angry. "One day you will learn that power is everything. In Egypt, if you have no power, you have nothing."

"Power?" Asenath scoffed. "What do you know of power? There are slaves who understand more about true power than you ever will."

"That's enough!" Potipherah snapped. "No matter what it is that they taught you in Avaris, I am still your father. Tomorrow we depart for Thebes. You will marry the son of Nebireyeraw, and our two cities will march together against Khyan. Avaris will be destroyed before the people there even realize what is happening to them."

Asenath stared at her father in disbelief. He was a madman! Did he really think he could bring down the earthen fortifications and the stone towers of Avaris? He was going to destroy both his family and his city, and there was nothing she could do to make him see the foolishness of his actions.

But even if she had thought to try, there was no time to reason with him. Potipherah clapped his hands sharply, and two male servants appeared at the top of the steps behind him. "Take my daughter to her room," he commanded. "See to it that she remains there until we depart tomorrow for Thebes."

Her mouth dropped open again, and she stared at him in disbelief. But she didn't resist when the servants approached her, one on each side, and nervously grasped her arms. They feared her. She could sense that they feared her because she herself was a priestess. But they feared her father even more.

"I thought you loved me," she said in a hoarse, dry whisper as they led her past him. "I thought you wanted me to be happy."

"I do love you. And that's why I must do this."

She was escorted swiftly to her room, and the guards took up positions outside her door. Once again she was alone. Once again she was a prisoner. But this time she was the prisoner of her own father. Escape was impossible. The high window in her room had bars to keep intruders out, but now the bars would hold her in. Only a God could save her from this.

TWENTY-FIVE

A SENATH LOOKED FOR THE THOUSANDTH TIME at the barred window of her room, and a deep cough outside her door reminded her that she was still her father's captive. She scowled, but it was only an attempt to fight back the tears of frustration that were threatening to break free. This was an impossible situation. She was powerless to escape. If she could claw her way with bare fingers through cold, hard stone, she would do it. But it was useless to even attempt an escape. The sun had gone down long ago, and it would come back up much too soon. Once the new day arrived, she would be carried off to Thebes where—for the rest of her days—she would truly be a captive.

There was nothing left to do now but hang her head in defeat and cast herself upon her bed for a restless night's sleep; but something at the far end of the room caught her eyes before she could do this. It was a harp. Long unused, it had been collecting dust in the corner since the day she was taken away to Avaris. She had been tutored in its use as a young girl, and it had often soothed her soul in the past. Now she took a few moments to brush away the dust and tighten the loosened strings. When she absently plucked one of those strings, a sweet, reverberating tone echoed off the stone walls of her room.

Many years ago, Nesmut had tutored her in the playing of the harp, and Asenath reclined on her bed and picked out the notes and chords of a soft, sad tune she'd been taught. It surprised her how easily it all came back to her despite the many years separating her from her lessons. She thought of all that had befallen her since that last lesson, and a single, warm tear trickled down the side of her face.

Asenath often wondered where Joseph was and what had befallen him in her absence. She wondered now if she would see him again in either this life or the next. It seemed a cruel trick of fate that she and Joseph had been brought together only to be separated by the impassable gulf of their differing places in society. It also seemed ironic that she would gladly sell herself into slavery to be with him but was soon to end up a slave of a much different sort. Where was Joseph's God? Why didn't He answer her pleas for help? She had offered to forsake all her own religious upbringing to worship Him. She was willing to turn against her own gods if only she could know that everything Joseph had taught her about his God was true. It would help if she could at least receive an understandable response to her many prayers.

"You play as beautifully as I last remember. Your time away from On doesn't seem to have diminished your talent."

Asenath's hand fell away from the strings of the harp, and she looked up in surprise. Nesmut had slipped quietly through the door and was standing just inside the room.

"Please don't stop on my account," Nesmut said. "I just came to check on you. Your father wants to know if you're still awake and if there's anything you need."

"Anything I need?" Asenath demanded. "Since when has he begun to care about what *I* need or desire?" She spoke the words venomously but immediately wished she hadn't. This wasn't Nesmut's fault. She shouldn't take her anger out on the messenger when it was her father who had placed her in this miserable, hopeless situation.

"It's an awful thing your father is doing," Nesmut said, her voice sympathetic. "I can't imagine how you must be feeling right now. If there were any way I could help, believe me, I would."

"There's nothing you or anyone can do for me," Asenath said, her voice lifeless. "Not unless you can open solid stone walls or work even greater miracles like changing my father's heart."

"I can't do any of those things," Nesmut answered. "But I can listen. I can always do that."

Asenath nodded. "Yes. I could always count on you to listen. I remember how you used to check on me at night right before I went to sleep. You used to listen to my concerns then. If I was afraid of the dark, or sad, or worried, you were always there to listen."

"I'm afraid those problems were much simpler than this one," Nesmut said. "But I'll do anything for you that your father will allow me to do."

Asenath shook her head and began once again to strum the harp. "This problem is even larger than you realize," she said. "It's not just about being married to Sebekamzaf. There's more to it than that. Much, much more."

Nesmut raised an eyebrow, and Asenath unconsciously continued.

"I'm in love, Nesmut," she said. "I've met a man in Avaris—the most remarkable man I've ever known—and I can't imagine living my life without him. When I'm with him, I feel like I'm the center of his world. He seems to see me as I can become and not as I am. Sebekamzaf isn't half the man that Joseph is."

"Joseph?"

"Yes. His name is Joseph."

"That's not an Egyptian name."

"You're right. It's not. He's *'apiru*—a Hebrew slave."

"It would be best not to make mention of *that* to your father," Nesmut cautioned. "He's upset enough about the things you said to Sebekamzaf. He'll take you to Thebes in chains if he finds out you've fallen in love with a slave."

"I don't care what he thinks," Asenath said, strumming the next chord a little harder than the preceding ones. "He may be able to make me a slave to a husband of his choice, but he can never make a slave of my heart."

"I'm not saying that what your father is doing is right," Nesmut said, "but maybe it's best that you will no longer be able to see this slave in Avaris. A love like that is doomed to end in sorrow. There's no way around it."

"Better a sorrow of my own choosing," Asenath said, her voice crisp with anger, "than a life of misery imposed on me by someone else."

Nesmut was silent for a few moments, and Asenath detected a barely perceptible shake of the woman's head. The faithful servant turned to leave, but paused at the door to say one last thing. "Your music is very soothing," she said. "It even soothes the guards outside your door. I noticed one of them beginning to nod off when I came to the room to check on you." She slipped silently out the door, but not before giving Asenath one last, meaningful glance.

Asenath puzzled over that parting remark and then her fingers trembled as she realized what Nesmut had really meant. It was late. The guards at her door were getting tired. Is that what Nesmut was hinting at? Asenath remembered how Nesmut had gotten her, as a child, to drift off into sleep by playing soft, calming tunes on the harp. Hope—something that had abandoned her for several long hours now—flickered in Asenath's heart, and she suddenly recognized a possible answer to one of her prayers.

Perhaps there was still some slim hope of escaping an unhappy, ill-fated marriage to Sebekamzaf. If she could lull the guards into sleep before a fresh pair came to take their places, it might be possible to slip out of this room without being detected. She didn't have much time, and she couldn't make any mistakes. But at least she had the seeds of a plan, and that was more than she'd had before.

She played the harp now like she had never played before. Softly, lightly. Every note and chord was a beckoning call to sleep. She played until her own eyes began to droop with exhaustion so that she was forced to pause every now and then to violently shake her head to keep herself awake. Then, when she could stand the wait no longer, she placed the harp carefully on her bed, straightened her shoulders with determination, and snuffed out the flame of her small oil lamp. After a few moments of groping her way through the darkness, her searching fingers felt the coarse grain of the wooden door, and, ever so gently, she eased it open. She opened it just a crack. One eye carefully scanned the hallway beyond her room, and she saw that one of the guards was slumped to the floor against a pillar. By the rhythmic rise and fall of his chest and the low, muffled snore that escaped his lips, she knew he was asleep. She couldn't see or hear the other guard, and this worried her a little. He was either at the other side of the door, blocked from view, or else he had left his post for a few moments and might be back at any moment. Whatever the case may be, she couldn't afford to wait any longer. She had to take the risk and make a dash for freedom.

Cautiously, she placed one foot outside the door, simultaneously drawing in a slow, trembling breath. Tense with both hope and nervous fear, she peeked around to the side of the door which had been hidden from her view, and then she let out a barely audible sigh of relief. The other guard had left his post. If she was going to escape, now was the time to do it.

Asenath slid the rest of her body into the hall and quietly closed the door behind her. As it creaked on its hinges, the guard at the pillar stirred and shifted his shoulder to a new position. She froze in place, certain the wild rhythm of her hammering heart would wake him if the unoiled hinge didn't; but, mercifully, his eyes remained closed and he slumbered on.

Asenath darted on the tips of her toes to the end of the hall, then slipped around the corner and flattened herself against the wall. She only gave herself a few moments to collect herself and catch her breath before making one last, mad dash to the front of the house. Once there she hid herself in the shadows near the front door.

She wasn't free yet. The regular guards would be watching the front entrance, and another set would be watching the back entrance at the garden wall. She hadn't thought of that when she was escaping her room, and despair hit her again as she realized that she was no freer here than she had been back in her room.

What was she thinking? How could she escape a man as powerful as her father? And, even if she did, how could she ever hope to make it back to Avaris alone? She was desperately attempting to sweep these crippling thoughts from her mind when the slapping echo of footfalls came her way. Quickly she pressed herself into the shadows, trying to make herself as much a part of them as she could, and she sucked in a quick breath of air as her father came into view.

At first she was certain that her attempt at escape had been discovered and that her father was coming to take her back to her room. But his eyes didn't see her in the corner. In fact, he seemed to be moving with unconcerned ease. He casually unbarred the main door, stepped out into the cool darkness, and left the door ajar behind him.

"The servants guarding my daughter's room are growing weary," he said, his muffled voice echoing back to her ears. "Come with me. I'll find two of the house servants to take your posts. My greatest concern is that her room be properly guarded tonight, and I trust the two of you to do that."

Potipherah reentered the house, the guards close behind him, and Asenath slipped quickly down into a sitting position on the floor. She wrapped both arms tightly around her body and tried once again to stifle the sound of her breathing which seemed like nothing less than a fierce roar. But neither Potipherah nor the guards noticed her. Her father calmly barred the door behind them and then they disappeared down a hall.

This time she didn't dare wait until her nerves were settled or until her pounding heart could calm. She darted to the door like a silent wraith and cautiously lifted the wooden bar. She could hear her own blood rushing like a sandstorm in her ears and her muscles were tight with fear; but, like a frightened animal, she flung aside this last obstacle to her freedom, ready to bolt away into the darkness. And then a more calm, rational thought entered her heart. Instead of running, she took the time to carefully and deliberately close the door behind her. Perhaps her father wouldn't notice that the bar had been removed. Or perhaps he would believe he had forgotten to bar it before he left. Everything she did now had its share of risks, but she would buy extra time wherever she could find it.

She was free. Free for the moment at least. And every step she took away from this house brought her one step closer to Joseph. Just the thought of once again hearing his gentle, strong voice filled her with warmth and added courage. She wasn't quite sure how she was going to get back to him, but she would. She could feel it in her heart. Somehow she and Joseph would be together again. Somehow his God would make it happen.

Potiphar stared in disbelief at the torn, linen garment in his hands. He turned it over and over again then looked up at Neferset with vacant eyes.

"It's his," she said, her eyes burning bright with anger. "It belongs to your chief steward, Joseph. This Hebrew servant which you brought into our house came to mock me. But I called for the guards, and he left this garment in my hands and fled."

It was difficult to believe. It was difficult to believe that out of all Potiphar's servants Joseph would be the one to do this to his wife. But the evidence was here in his hands. And the guards had already confirmed that Neferset called for their help and that Joseph was seen fleeing from the house. Potiphar clenched the garment, balled his hands into fists, and ripped the tunic apart in his hands.

"Where is he?" he asked, his voice surprisingly calm despite the sense of betrayal and rage he was feeling inside. "Where is this Hebrew dog who would attack my wife and mock my name?"

"The guards are holding him in his quarters. They kept him there until you could decide what to do with him."

Potiphar dropped the torn garment to the tiled floor and stepped over it as he moved with determined steps across the house. Of all the things he disliked most, the greatest of them was to be made to look like a fool. This Hebrew slave had done just that to him.

How could he have trusted a slave? How could he have made the same mistake with Joseph that he had earlier made with T'chet? He had exalted Joseph above all the servants in his house, had given him charge of everything—everything except his wife—and was this how he was repaid?

The punishment for such a crime was clear. It was death. And Potiphar, chief of the executioners, was no stranger to the delivery of that sentence. The consequences for this betrayal would be swift and immediate. But even as he withdrew his sword from its scabbard, unexpected doubts began to intrude upon his mind. Unwillingly, he slowed himself and thought.

There was something strange in Neferset's behavior tonight. From the moment she delivered her accusations to him, there had been an odd, veiled look in her eyes. It was almost as if she were hiding something from him. The longer he thought about it, the more he realized that she didn't act like a woman who had been abused and nearly raped as she claimed to have been. There was more of vengeance in her eyes than distress or fear or humiliation—all the emotions he would expect to see. This put Potiphar in an uncomfortable position. How was he, with a clear conscience, to carry through the death sentence on a man whose words he would trust more than the words of his own wife?

There was no doubt that Joseph had been in the house with Neferset. The guards were trustworthy, and they wouldn't lie about seeing him run. His garment was also in Neferset's possession. But there were still all these confusing doubts!

Potiphar gave his head an angry shake. Whatever it was that had happened here today, the 'apiru should have never approached his wife—even if she encouraged it. Some kind of harsh penalty had to be imposed. Something that would satisfy Neferset and leave Potiphar's authority undiminished. The problem was that she'd probably settle for nothing less than Joseph's death.

The course of his footsteps changed, and he placed his sword back in its scabbard as his now deeply troubled mind struggled to discover what the gods would have him do. He didn't want the blood of an innocent man crying out against him, but he also didn't want to lose the love of his wife and the respect of his servants. He found himself suddenly entering his garden—a place he didn't often visit—and he looked around himself at trees and bushes which had been manicured to perfection.

 For the first time in his memory, every part of his property was in perfect order. It surprised him to realize that he no longer even knew the value of his possessions or the amount of income going in and out. He had trusted Joseph that completely. He had placed all the affairs of his estate in Joseph's able hands and had prospered because of it.

An anguished expression spread covered his face. The fact that he was about to lose the best chief steward he had ever seen bothered him almost as much as the accusations Neferset had leveled against Joseph. Every man had a flaw. But did Joseph have the terrible one Neferset accused him of? If only the young Hebrew were being charged with a minor offense. If only it had been stealing or shirking a few unimportant duties. Potiphar could give a small, meaningless punishment for a minor transgression, but he couldn't ignore this. As the commander of Pharaoh's most trusted and elite soldiers, he knew what could happen if an offense of this nature weren't severely punished. If he did nothing, he would instantly lose the respect and obedience of his servants. Soon every servant would be doing whatever he or she pleased. What was he to do? How could he possibly do anything less than take Joseph's life?

"He's still in there," one of the two guards said when Potiphar finally arrived at Joseph's door. "He hasn't given us any trouble."

Potiphar nodded and struggled to control his emotions. "Bring the slave before me," he said, his voice a low rumble. "It's time to deal with his crime."

PART THREE

And Joseph's master took him,
and put him into the prison,
a place where the king's prisoners were bound:
and he was there in the prison.

Genesis 39:20

TWENTY-SIX

J OSEPH LOOKED DOWN AT THE CHAINS that bound his wrists and ankles and felt momentarily lost in despair. He had done nothing to offend the laws of God. He had done nothing to betray his master. Yet here he stood—about to be locked away in prison—and God showed no sign of preventing this terrible injustice. It would be very easy right now to turn away from the Lord. Joseph had suffered every affliction the Lord had seen fit to send upon him and hadn't once murmured or complained. The temptation to start now was strong, but he held his tongue, shook his head, and listened sorrowfully to the rattle of his chains.

The thoughts that pressed in upon him now didn't come from God. He recognized the author of these thoughts, and he wasn't about to listen to the enemy of all righteousness. But the knowledge of where such temptations came from gave him no solace. He needed the comfort of God, and God seemed to be nowhere near in this dark moment of anguish.

An image of Asenath's face wafted momentarily through his mind, and Joseph felt an even heavier weight of despair fall upon him. What would she think when she heard that he had been cast into prison? How would she feel when she learned what crime he was accused of? Would she, too, doubt his moral integrity? His eyes burned from the effort of holding back tears, and he thought he might choke on the hard, painful lump that had formed in his throat.

It took a supreme effort of will-power to hide this overwhelming despair from the prison keeper.

The keeper at this moment was removing a large, iron ring from his belt, and he inserted a huge key into the heavy, wooden beam of the door they had come to. The keeper lifted the key, engaged the hidden brass pins that held the beam immovably in place, and grunted as he slowly slid the beam to one side. That done, he pulled on an iron ring that was the handle, and the door groaned open on its massive hinges.

Joseph stared into the dark cell and got the uncomfortable feeling that he was about to be swallowed by the very jaws of hell. But he didn't have long to ponder it. The keeper took his arm and violently forced him in.

"This will be your lodgings," the keeper said, glaring at Joseph with contempt. It was the same look Potiphar's guards had given him after Neferset accused him of assaulting her, and it pierced him to the soul to see it. "But don't get too comfortable," the keeper warned. "I'm sure you'll be executed by morning. I'm surprised it hasn't happened already."

"I haven't committed any crime," Joseph said. "I was falsely accused." He looked the man straight in the eye, just as he had looked Potiphar in the eye when he was confronted about what happened. But the prison keeper just laughed.

"Of course you were," he said. "Pharaoh's prison is filled with innocent men. No one here has done anything wrong. At least that's what they all tell me."

It did no good to argue. No one believed him. It was the word of a slave against the words of a master's wife, and no judge in Egypt would ever acquit him.

"It was a foolish thing to try to rape the chief executioner's wife," the keeper said. "Don't think me foolish enough to believe you didn't try it. I've seen Potiphar's wife. Greater men than you have risked more for lesser women than her. Even so, only the lowest of dogs would attempt to violate the wife of his own master in his master's very own house. The next time you see me, I'm sure I'll be leading you to the *nemmet.*"

Joseph involuntarily shuddered at mention of the "block of slaughter," and the keeper, noticing his discomfort, smiled.

"That's right," he said. "Now it's all starting to become crystal clear to you, isn't it? You should have thought about the possible consequences before you tried what you tried."

"I've already told you," Joseph replied. "I've done nothing. If Potiphar kills me, he'll be killing an innocent man. I'll stand clean before the judgment bar of God."

"God? It will take a god to save you now. If you manage to escape Potiphar's wrath, I'll know you're an innocent man. Only the innocent could enlist the aid of a god to save him from this." The keeper moved back into the outer corridor and pushed the door shut behind him. The thud of its closing echoed off the thick stone walls, and Joseph listened as the beam on the other side was moved back into its place. The clicks of the locking pins dropping back into their slots had a sound of dreadful finality.

Slowly, Joseph dragged himself and his chains into a corner of the cell where he slumped down to the floor and covered his face with his hands. He sat this way for several long minutes, the balance of faith and despair teetering precariously within him. It seemed like the harder he tried to be righteous, the worse things got. But he knew there was a God in the heavens, and he cried out one more time with what little hope he had remaining.

"God of my fathers," he whispered, lifting his eyes imploringly towards the heavens. All he saw above him was solid, impenetrable stone, but he tried anyway. "Give me strength to endure," he pleaded. "Give me strength to bear these afflictions and to not turn my heart against Thee . . . I know it's impossible for me of my own strength and power to escape this situation. But unto Thee, nothing is impossible."

Joseph paused for a moment as something attracted his eye. It was a glimmer of light, and it came from a narrow slit in the stone at the far end of his cell. There was an opening in the stone there—not even wide enough for a man to fit his hand through it, but big enough to allow a faint illumination of the prison cell. It must have been that the sun, as it dropped lower on the horizon, lined itself up perfectly with the opening, allowing a brilliant stream of light to shine suddenly through and fall at his shackled feet. It was a small thing. Some would have dismissed it as mere coincidence. But Joseph saw it as an answer to his prayer. If light could somehow penetrate the gloomy depths of this prison, the power of God could reach him here as well. The Lord was aware of his distress and would help him through this abysmal time of darkness. Joseph felt a sudden, unexpected warmth in his heart, and a tear traced a salty path down his face.

Day always followed night. *This* long, dark night would eventually end, and God would help him see the light of day once again. He would make it through this. Somehow, the Lord would provide a way for him to make it through.

She was dirty, she was tired, and her body ached from the long ordeal she had just been through; but joy flooded Asenath's soul as she stepped once again into the streets of Avaris.

Once she had despised this city. Now she thought she might cry with joy to see it again. And she made her feet move a little faster as she climbed the slope to Potiphar's house.

Joseph was still a slave of Potiphar, and she was once again a political hostage of Pharaoh; but none of that seemed to matter as long as she could be near the man she loved. Just the thought of seeing him again sent a warm tingle rushing through her. It seemed like an eternity since she felt his hand holding hers. It seemed like forever since their eyes had last met.

Anticipation fueled her feet, and she moved even faster than it was probably appropriate for a priestess to be seen moving. But she couldn't stay her feet. She would try the house first, and if he wasn't there, she would go to the stables and find Pekhti. Pekhti always knew where Joseph was. Even if Joseph were in the fields, she would force her aching legs to carry her there so that she could be with him once more.

It had taken one miracle after another to get back to Avaris. First there was the miraculous escape from her father's house. Then an equally remarkable turn of events had helped her to stay hidden while her father's friends and servants combed the entire city for her. Eventually she had managed to find a barge that was bound for Avaris, and the captain of that ship didn't care who she was as long as she paid her way.

Asenath put her hand to the bare spot just below her neck. Usually her lapis pendant hung there, but she would never wear it again. She had been forced to part with it as the price for her boat fare. It was her most cherished possession in the world, but it meant nothing to her if she lost Joseph. She smiled a little as she spotted the wall surrounding Potiphar's estate, and her heart swelled with warm anticipation. Soon she would be in Joseph's arms, and she didn't care if the entire world knew she was in love with him.

She knocked with barely restrained urgency at the front door of Potiphar's house, and a smile of anticipation was still on her lips when one of the maidservants answered. They all recognized her by now and knew that her business was with Joseph, but this maidservant—an Ammorite named Ketra—stared at her with uneasy eyes.

"May I help you?" Ketra asked after she had looked nervously at Asenath for several long, awkward moments.

"Yes. Can you tell me where Joseph is? He's not expecting me, but I must speak with him right away." Maybe it was that no one was expecting her to be back from On so soon. Or maybe word of her father's treachery had reached Avaris before she did. Whatever it was, Ketra began to shift nervously on her feet and would no longer look Asenath in the eye. "Can you tell me where he is?" Asenath tried again. "I'll go to him on my own if you'll just tell me where to find him."

"He . . . he is not here . . . Joseph is no longer chief steward here . . ."

"What? What do you mean he's no longer chief steward?"

"He . . . he has been thrown into Pharaoh's prison."

Asenath looked at the girl and prepared to laugh, but the fear in Ketra's eyes made it clear that this was no joke. "In prison? But he . . . he is Potiphar's most trusted servant. What could he have possibly done to be imprisoned?"

"Please," Ketra said, beginning to shut the door. "I must get back to my work. I—"

"No! Wait!" Asenath placed her hand against the door, refusing to let it be shut until she had answers to her questions. "Tell me what kind of treachery is going on here! Tell me what it is that's happened!"

"He tried to force himself on the master's wife," Ketra said, her face pale. "I'm sorry. I have to go now."

The door slammed shut in Asenath's face, and she stood, cemented to the spot, staring at the closed door. She was sure she must have heard wrong. She must have misunderstood what was being said. Joseph? In prison? She shook her head to clear her mind then frantically headed toward the stables. This was insane! Joseph would never do anything so awful. If anyone knew what was really going on here, it would be Pekhti, the chief groom, and she had to talk to him immediately.

The joy and warmth she had been feeling only moments before was now being replaced by a cold dread that twisted her stomach into knots. How could anyone even begin to believe that Joseph would commit such a heinous crime? He had always treated Asenath with the utmost honor and respect. Why would he treat any other woman differently?

She didn't know why, but a memory came quietly to her mind.

She remembered a time when she had observed Neferset watching Joseph as he studied in the garden. She remembered the wanton look in Neferset's eyes and the anger that seemed to be there when she saw Asenath with Joseph. Could he have fallen to Neferset's seductions only to be accused of rape so that Neferset could cover up her infidelity? It seemed possible, but Asenath still didn't want to believe it. She wanted to continue believing there was at least one man in this world who was everything he seemed to be and who would never let her down. Her own father had betrayed her. She wouldn't be able to stand it if Joseph disappointed her, too.

The warm, musky odor of horses assailed her nostrils as she burst uninvited into Potiphar's stables. Wildly, she cast her eyes about for any trace of Pekhti, then followed her ears to the sound of footsteps in one of the far stalls. Pekhti was there, walking with a brush in his hand around a horse, and he stared at her with the same surprise she had seen in the eyes of the Ammorite servant. But she didn't give him time to hide behind a closed door.

"Where is he?" she demanded. "Where is Joseph? I was just at the house, and a servant there told me he had been cast into prison. Is this true? Has he actually committed some crime?"

Pekhti's eyes filled with sadness, and he glanced away, unable to look at her. "It's true," he finally said. "He tried to rape the master's wife, and the master threw him into prison."

Asenath stared at him—too shocked to speak—and then she shook her head. "Do you really believe these accusations?" she demanded. "Do you really believe that *Joseph* would do such a thing?"

"I don't want to believe it," Pekhti said. "But the evidence . . . it was right there . . . He left his garment in Neferset's hands. I warned him to stay away from her. But maybe he didn't listen. Maybe . . . " Pekhti shrugged his shoulders then looked helplessly at her while she restrained an urge to scream at him in frustration.

"Joseph couldn't do such a thing!" she whispered instead. "He loves his God too much. He would never do anything to displease his God."

"Even the best of men sometimes slip. Even—"

"Not Joseph!" she snapped. "Never Joseph! Potiphar's wife must have lied. That's the only explanation for all of this."

Pekhti stared at her again, and this time his eyes filled with tears. "Don't you realize?" he asked. "Joseph was taken away two days ago. Even if he was innocent, it wouldn't matter. Do you know what the penalty is for a slave who attempts to rape his master's wife?"

Asenath felt the blood drain from her face, and her body went suddenly cold. Under Hyksos law the penalty for rape was death, and a slave received little or no opportunity to plead his case.

"Surely Potiphar knows Joseph better than that," she weakly murmured. "He wouldn't execute Joseph. Would he?"

Pekhti didn't answer. He just stared at her in silence. What could he say? They both knew the probable answer to her question.

But somehow she couldn't accept the inevitable. She had to find Potiphar. She had to find Potiphar and save Joseph before it was too late.

The sound of the key being inserted into the lock woke Joseph from his fitful sleep, and he rolled slowly to his side, all his muscles aching from another long night on the hard, stone floor. There was no bed in this dungeon—not even a little straw to make sleep a bit more comfortable. The whole purpose of this place, he decided, was to make its occupants suffer the worst kind of misery. Even the food he received here was barely enough to sustain life. It did manage to keep him alive, but it left his stomach mostly empty and his body weak from hunger. He truly had descended as low as it seemed one could get. He almost hoped this was the executioner coming to the door—coming to end his misery at the block of slaughter.

The sound of wood grating against wood, which always preceded the opening of the door, echoed abrasively in his ears, and he got slowly to his feet. Let them lead him to his death, he decided. But when they did, he would be standing tall. He was innocent, and he would not go to his death like a mongrel dog with its tail between its legs.

He had to squint the moment the door was opened—the light from the prison keeper's torch stung his eyes—and it was several moments more before he could see well enough to make out the stocky form of the keeper. It would be several hours yet before enough light came from the slot in the wall for him to see his own cell. But it was almost better that way. When he could see, the sight around him wasn't a pleasant one.

"I have good news for you," the keeper said, placing a wooden cup and a metal plate on the floor near the door. "It appears that Potiphar has decided to let you live."

Joseph felt a brief instance of hope, but the hope was quickly crushed.

"You won't be executed," the keeper continued, "but you will spend the rest of your life in this prison. The prison records will show that you were executed. So, as far as the rest of the world is concerned, you'd might as well be dead."

If he'd thought his heart experienced blackness when he was first brought down into this dungeon, it was nothing compared to what he was feeling now. The Lord had decided to give him a living death, and this cell was to be his tomb.

"If you ask me," the keeper said, "it would be better to be executed. I'm not sure if Potiphar is trying to show you mercy or punish you even worse. He either has great respect for you or despises you completely. Only Potiphar and the gods could answer that."

The cell door swung shut behind the keeper, and Joseph was thrust once again into stygian darkness. He heard the rustle of small creatures moving toward his food, and he almost decided to let them have it. Whether he ate or not, he was certain he would eventually die a slow, lingering death in this dungeon. But the gnaw of hunger in the pit of his stomach took charge, and he felt his way across the floor to rescue the food—if it could be called that—from the foraging of the beetles, scorpions, and other vermin that inhabited this place of darkness.

Joseph hungrily devoured the stale crust of bread that his search-ing fingers found on the plate and then probed through the darkness until he found the wooden cup. He gulped down the warm water that was in it, wiped his mouth with his bare arm, and dragged himself to the corner nearest the narrow slit in the wall. That thin opening in the stone was his only link to the outside world. Through it he received a little light in the daytime and faintly heard the sounds of the city. It was his link to sanity in this morbidly depressing place.

His family, except for his brothers, thought him to be dead. Now Asenath, if she ever returned to Avaris, would also think him dead. For all practical purposes, he'd might as well be. But, for some reason he couldn't explain, the Lord wanted him to go on living.

"God of my fathers," Joseph whispered through chapped, cracked lips, "give me strength. Please give me the strength to go on. I don't have enough to endure this on my own . . . "

He wrapped his arms around both knees—the best he could with both wrists shackled together—and he sank his head into them. He had always tried to do what was right. How could a life of righteous-ness lead to a place like this?

"Do you remember how I taught you to hold the bow?"

"Yes, Father."

The memory came rushing back at him like a gentle wave, and he closed his eyes, trying to visualize the face of his father, Jacob.

"When you're older," Jacob said, "one of your responsibilities will be to watch over the flocks. Sometimes wild beasts try to steal away with one of the sheep. You'll have to be constantly watchful, and you'll need to know how to protect the flocks. Pretend that clump of grass is a wolf. I want you to shoot an arrow at it to stop it before it reaches our sheep."

Joseph nodded and withdrew an arrow from the quiver. He was only six years old, but Jacob trained his sons for their work at a very young age. Joseph already knew how to milk the goats and care for sick or injured animals, and he was eager to prove to his father that he was ready for the next level of responsibility. But Jacob's hand closed gently around his and stopped him before he could attempt to nock an arrow to the string.

"Not that arrow," Jacob said, shaking his head from side to side. "Pick a different one, my son."

Joseph did as he was told, but he gave his father a questioning look.

"You're wondering why I don't want you to use that one?"

Joseph nodded, and Jacob knelt down on the ground beside him. "Let's look at this arrow," he said, holding it out across the palms of both hands so that Joseph could examine it. "Tell me what you see."

Joseph stared at the arrow for a long time and thoughtfully scratched his head. He didn't see anything. It looked just like all the other arrows. But then his eyes narrowed a little as he noticed something that he hadn't really seen before.

"This arrow is crooked," he said. It was only a little crooked, but it was enough so that even his inexperienced eyes could detect it.

"That's right. And do you know what happens when you try to shoot a crooked arrow?"

Joseph shook his head.

"I want you to try it. Then I want you to explain to me what happened."

Joseph once more put the arrow to the string and pulled back with all the might of his six year-old arm. There was a sharp twang as he released the arrow, and it sped away from the bow in a silvery blur. He expected it to hit the clump of grass or strike someplace near it; but, instead, it veered far to the left in a wobbling, unsteady course.

"What is it that just happened?" Jacob asked.

At first, Joseph stared in confusion; but it took only a few moments for his mind to work out an answer. "Crooked arrows don't fly straight," he said.

"That's right," Jacob replied, nodding his head in approval. "If you are ever in danger and one shot has to count, you don't want to trust in a crooked arrow. You can't depend on it to strike its target. It will stray far from its course and end up nowhere near where it was supposed to go."

Joseph nodded, his face a study of seriousness, and Jacob tussled his hair.

"You and I . . . we . . . are like arrows, my son. We are as arrows in the Lord's quiver, and we must keep ourselves straight so that He can depend upon us. We keep ourselves straight by living righteously and holding steadfastly to all the commandments the Lord gives us. Always be a straight arrow. Always be true to the Lord. If you are true to Him, He will be true to you, and wherever His course leads you, it will be for your good."

Joseph opened his eyes again and found himself once more in the thick darkness of the prison. He had attempted his entire life to follow the wise counsel of his father. Even in bondage as a slave, he had remembered that counsel and never failed to neglect God's commandments. The course God set for him had led him here. He didn't understand, and yet he had to accept it.

Perhaps he didn't understand because the Lord didn't mean for him to. Maybe he was meant to puzzle over this and learn in the same way he had learned from puzzling over the arrow. That which God required was always right. Joseph had faith in that principle. It was just so hard. Now, when he was lost in the darkness with a broken heart and a broken soul, it was so difficult to believe that all things would work out for his good. But he would keep trying. He wouldn't murmur. He would hold fast to faith. And he would wait for God to show him the light.

Asenath sat on her bed, mechanically stroking the grizzled back of the temple cat which had wandered into the house of Setmosis. She should be feeling sorrow right now. Grief. Something. But what she actually felt was much worse. She felt numb. Empty. Void of all light and hope.

The words from the prison list still floated tauntingly before her eyes, and she found it difficult to believe that the last she would ever see of Joseph was his name, in hieroglyphs, penned on the list of the executed. She thought she couldn't feel anything, but she was wrong. She *was* beginning to feel something now. It started out small, in the deepest recesses of her heart, but it soon spread and grew until it seemed it must entirely consume her. Rage filled her heart and soul. Joseph was dead now, but she was no less dead. What was life if Joseph wasn't here to share it with her? What was it but another, even worse kind of death?

She was angry at Potiphar's wife and at Potiphar, but she was also angry at Joseph's God. In all things, Joseph had trusted in his God and even believed that all his sufferings were for his ultimate good. His faith was so convincing that Asenath had turned from her gods and begun to look to his. She laughed bitterly to herself as she remembered how she believed Joseph's God was actually helping her during the hours of her escape from On. Considering the most recent turn of events, it may have been better to be Sebekamzaf's bride than to return to Avaris where the memory of a dead Hebrew slave would haunt her for the rest of her days.

What God was this that would betray a man who had been faithful in all things? What God was this that Asenath should honor and serve Him? Her anger fed upon itself and grew, but was suddenly interrupted when Netchem stepped tentatively into her room.

Asenath looked up, but she said nothing. She knew she would be unable to keep her voice from trembling.

"There's a man here to see you," Netchem said. "He's waiting for you on the temple steps."

Asenath nodded and got wearily to her feet. Some of her father's servants had probably been sent to find her here at the house of Setmosis. She doubted that they would dare to abduct her in broad daylight before the eyes of Netchem and the house servants, but she wasn't sure anymore whether or not that mattered. She had no fight left in her. The gods—even Joseph's God—did with her as they pleased.

She had no say in that matter. She had no control over anything in her life. Why fight that battle any longer?

Slowly she placed the cat on the floor and followed Netchem numbly across the house. Her eyes, usually sparkling and full of energy, were dull and lifeless when she reached the steps. But that didn't stop her from being surprised by who it was that had come to see her.

"I hope I'm not disturbing you," Pekhti said, giving a low, respectful bow.

"No. You're not disturbing me."

"I . . . I heard you paid a visit to Potiphar. And then you made another visit to Pharaoh's prison."

Asenath glanced over at Netchem who was waiting uncertainly behind her. She nodded that it was all right to leave her alone with this man, then she turned back to Pekhti as Netchem departed.

"Yes. I did both of those things," she said.

"I visited the prison, too." Pekhti looked at his feet and shifted them nervously. "I suppose they told you what they told me."

"They told me that Joseph is dead."

"He was a good man," Pekhti said after a moment of respectful silence. "And a good friend." Pekhti stared at his sandaled feet, then looked up at Asenath again, extending both hands toward her with a papyrus scroll held across his palms. "I brought this for you. I found it in Joseph's quarters."

Asenath stared at the scroll for several long moments before finally reaching out to take it from him.

"I have to get back to the master's stables now," Pekhti said, averting his eyes yet again. His voice was thick with emotion, and Asenath could tell this entire episode had been difficult for him. "If you ever need anything . . . even if you just need someone to talk to . . . let me know."

"Thank you," Asenath said, her voice no more than a hoarse whisper. "I appreciate your offer."

Pekhti nodded, turned, and walked slowly away, leaving her to stare with tear-blurred eyes at the scroll she was now clutching in her hands. She remained motionless, at the door, for several minutes, emotions churning wildly within her. When she could contain them no longer, she turned and bolted back to her room where she slammed the door, locked it, and collapsed to the smooth, tiled floor in a bitterly sobbing heap. Her body shook, and tears ran freely down her face. She had no more desire to live. She just wanted to die. But death was not an option for her. She had to go on living. Living and suffering.

She didn't know how long she remained there, sobbing on the floor; but, finally, she stemmed the tide of tears enough to notice the scroll that she had dropped to the floor beside her. Taking a corner of her *kalasiris* in one hand, she dried away the tears that had splattered onto the papyrus, and she moved to a sitting position where she could unroll it across her lap. She expected to see some of the many verses she had instructed Joseph to copy from the temple scrolls. She expected to see the beautiful, bold strokes of his handwriting and to remember the moments they had spent together in Potiphar's garden. Instead, she found something quite unexpected.

What she found was Joseph's own story, written in his hand and with his words. Some of it she had already learned in their conversations together, but much of it was new. He had written an account of his lineage, of his father and family, and of the treachery of his own older brothers. There was an account of his time in Potiphar's service and even a passage about Asenath herself. She traced the characters with her finger and felt fresh tears begin to come to her eyes. Above all else, there was one common thread that seemed to run through every line and every character that Joseph had written. Despite all the troubles that had come to him—despite the loss of his very freedom—Joseph's faith in his God still remained undimmed. There was hope in his words. He had faith that his God would eventually deliver him from sorrow and that all that befell him was for a higher, divine purpose. He had said it many times in person himself, and now it was as if he were speaking from the grave, saying it to her again. To the bitter end he wanted all mankind to know that he trusted in his God.

Asenath furrowed her brow and shook her head. "Oh, Joseph!" she whispered through her tears. "Your God has forsaken you, and I am left alone as well. What is to become of me now? What is to become of me without you?"

She was certain there was nothing that could ever console her. The light of joy had gone out of her world and would never shine on her again. But she had to somehow keep going. To do otherwise would be to dishonor the name of the man she so passionately loved. No matter what, she never wanted Joseph—in life or in death—to have any cause to be disappointed in her.

Chapter Notes

The simple tumbler lock which—in a much improved form—is still used today, was probably invented in Egypt sometime between 1000 and 2000 B.C. In ancient times it was constructed of a wood beam with drilled holes and with brass pins that fell into the holes to lock the beam in place. The keys for these locks were much larger than modern keys because the shank of the key was actually used as a lever to draw back the bolt. This is the type of locking system Joseph would have most likely encountered when Potiphar "put him into the prison, a place where the king's prisoners were bound" (Genesis 39:20).

TWENTY-SEVEN

THE WORLD COULD PASS AWAY, and he would never know it. Buried here in this dungeon, Joseph had lost all track of time. He could only guess at how long he had actually been here because every second felt like an hour and every hour felt like an eternity. But finally there was a break in the monotony of his existence. Today there were noises reaching down from the distant world above, penetrating into the depths of this world of blackness and despair. They were happy sounds. The noises of celebration. And now Joseph knew exactly how long he had been alone in this dank, lonely cell. This was the time of the festival of Seth. Joseph had seen many of them during his years of bondage. He had spent ten and one-half years in the service of Potiphar and now these six months in prison.

He could scarcely believe so much time had passed since his brothers sold him to the Ishmaelites. But, even more depressing, was the thought of how long it had been since he looked upon the lovely face of Asenath. The faces of his family were now only dim, fuzzy images in the distant recesses of his mind, but he could still remember every contour and every feature of Asenath's beautiful face. Even the ugliness of the prison couldn't dim that image. He liked to close his eyes and remember the precious time he'd spent with her, but the knowledge that he would never—in this life, at least—see her again was torture.

Tears traced a dirty path down Joseph's cheeks, and he turned his eyes—as he had already done so many times before—toward the heavens.

"Lord?" he asked. "How much longer will it be? How much more must I suffer before I find favor in Thine eyes? I haven't got the strength to last much longer. My faith is almost gone . . . " As had seemed to be the case for the last six months now, the heavens remained silent. But the silence was soon broken from other quarters. Joseph heard the familiar grate of the door bolt being withdrawn, and he heard the creak of the hinges as his heavy cell door swung open. This door was never opened at night. It only opened once each day, and that was early in the morning before the sun even rose. His only visitor each day was the surly prison keeper, coming to drop each prisoner's one meager meal unceremoniously on the floor. That visit lasted no longer than a few brief seconds, and it never came at night. Something, therefore, was not quite right about this visit.

Uncertainly, Joseph got to his feet. His chains rattled, and he squinted his eyes in an attempt to peer past the flickering glare of the torch's flame. Perhaps Potiphar had finally decided to follow through with an execution. The constant threat of this had hung over Joseph's head like an invisible executioner's ax. But tonight at least he no longer feared it. There were some afflictions even worse than death, and death seemed more merciful than a lifetime rotting away in the depths of this prison.

"You've come for me?" Joseph asked.

There was no answer. The keeper merely swayed unsteadily before him. And then Joseph noticed how dull and bleary the man's eyes were. The keeper took a step forward, staggered, and fell face down to the floor. He remained there, motionless, for several long moments— the torch sputtering and sparking at his side—before Joseph could work up enough courage to approach the burly, slumped form.

As Joseph got closer, he wrinkled his nose and turned his face away in disgust. The pungent stench of strong wine hung thickly in the air around the keeper. It was a simple thing to decipher what was going on here. The man was drunk. While the city drank to its storm god, the keeper had been hosting a one-man celebration of his own. Now it left him lying helpless, at Joseph's feet, with the prison keys dangling unprotected from his belt. Joseph tried to decide how best to handle this situation, and then his heart skipped a beat.

"Is this the answer to my prayers?" he wondered aloud as he suddenly realized the possibilities. "Are these keys now placed before me that I might free myself from this living death?"

He could do it. He could remove these shackles from his wrists and ankles and flee into the silent wastes of the desert. The keys were right here, and there was no one around to stop him. But a troubled thought entered his heart even as he stooped to reach for the instruments of his physical salvation.

He could take these keys and escape. But, if he did, this prison keeper was sure to pay for Joseph's freedom with his life. Somehow Potiphar or Pharaoh would eventually find out what had happened here tonight. When that happened, the prison keeper's punishment would be severe.

Still, Joseph had to do something. He couldn't just leave the man lying here on the floor. Somehow he would end up being blamed for it when the keeper woke up.

Cautiously, Joseph took the keys from the belt, found the smallest one, and removed the shackles from his body. He flung the offensive chains roughly away from him then knelt at the prison keeper's side.

"Let's take a look at you," he said with a grunt as he rolled the keeper to his back. "That fall couldn't have been good on your face." And it hadn't been. There was blood trickling from the prison keeper's nose, and there was also blood at the corner of his mouth. His entire face was puffy and swollen as if someone had pummeled him with a blunt object. Joseph really would get blamed for this if the keeper woke up in this cell. Yet again he would be blamed for something he hadn't done. The only option that left him with was to get the keeper some place else to clean, and if necessary, bandage him up. But Joseph couldn't just carry him away from here. Six months of inactivity and poor diet had left him so weak that even now he wobbled as he tried to stand. Gingerly, he grasped the man by both shoulders and shook him, hoping to rouse the man enough to get him to his own two feet.

"Wake up," Joseph said. "You don't want to stay here. Nobody in his right mind would want to stay down here."

"It's not fair," the keeper mumbled, his words thick and slurred as they fought their way through a drunken haze. "The entire city gets a holiday. But not me! No, Anebni! You get to watch the prison! You get to watch the prison all by yourself!"

"Let me help you to your feet," Joseph said. "You're not feeling well. Let's get you someplace where you can lie down and sleep this off."

"I . . . I know you," Anebni said, a broad grin spreading across his face. "You're . . . you're that slave of Potiphar's. Aren't you!"

"That's right," Joseph said, grimacing as Anebni staggered to both feet and leaned heavily against him. "Do you have a guard post or someplace where you go to rest? I think you should let me take you there."

"Follow me!" Anebni said, punctuating his words with a drunken belch. "It's this way!"

Joseph turned his head and wrinkled his nose. It was nice to know that his time in prison hadn't dulled all his senses. But he wished right now that his ability to smell weren't quite so keen. And he wished he had more power in his unsteady legs. He barely had the strength to keep Anebni from staggering into walls and dropping to the floor. And it got even worse when the inebriated prison keeper stopped to vomit. By the time Joseph finally got the man to his quarters, the job of getting the cow out of the mire so many years before seemed like a simple thing in comparison to this task.

Anebni was asleep the moment his head touched the wooden headrest on his bed, and Joseph placed the torch in a wall bracket so that he could look around and see if there was anything he could use to clean Anebni up. There was a rag on a wooden shelf on the wall, but the clay pitcher on the shelf below it didn't contain any water. Outside, however, just inside the main gate, he had seen a water clock that was used to mark the hours of the nighttime watches, and he quickly made his way there. He soaked the rag in the clock's container and stared up at the high prison walls as he rung out the excess water. There were two guards on the prison wall above him, but they didn't notice Joseph in the darkness. Involuntarily, Joseph's eyes turned toward the massive prison gate, and he thought again about how easy it would be to escape. But he only allowed the thought to linger a moment. Stubbornly he pushed it aside and went back to Anebni to clean the man's wounded face.

He realized as he reentered the prison keeper's quarters that he was still clutching the heavy ring of keys in his free hand. Again the temptation to escape struck him. But something inside told him that wasn't the right course of action. It was painful to ignore his own desire to flee when faced with a prompting that seemed to come from God. But he had never ignored the Lord's will before, and he wouldn't ignore it now. No matter what it seemed to be costing him in the short term, he would do as he felt directed to do.

"I don't envy you the headache you're going to have in the morning," Joseph said, addressing the unconscious prison keeper as he finished the job and tossed the blood-smeared rag into a corner. "But no one would envy me my situation either." Slowly he walked to a wall and slumped down into a sitting position against it. He was exhausted. If he had worked all day in one of Potiphar's fields, he wouldn't have been as tired as he was now. He didn't even have the strength to make it back to his cell. But at least tonight he would spend a few hours in partial freedom. It was almost a certainty that he would be locked up when morning came, but that didn't stop him from being grateful to the Lord for at least this one night out of his cell. He even started to mumble a prayer of gratitude, and that was the last thing he remembered before he opened his eyes to stare up the blade of a long, sharpened sword that was pointed at his neck.

"I don't know how you got out of your cell," Anebni said, "or how you got my keys . . . " He paused to nod at the iron key ring that was still clutched in Joseph's hand. "But if you make any sudden moves, this blade is going right down your throat."

Joseph didn't move. He remained perfectly still and watched calmly as Anebni, through bloodshot eyes, glared at him. They cautiously eyed each other for several moments until Anebni groaned, rubbed his temples with the thumb and middle finger of one hand, and motioned for Joseph to get to his feet. Joseph did as directed and waited to see what would happen next.

"I want you to stand right where you are and tell me exactly how you got out of your cell and into my quarters," Anebni said. "And I'd better like what I hear."

"You came to my cell last night," Joseph said. "You were drunk, and you passed out on the floor. I helped you here, cleaned you off, then fell asleep on your floor. I would have gone back to my cell, but I was too weak and tired to make it there."

Anebni stared at him and shook his head as he tried to think back to see if Joseph really was telling the truth. By the look on Anebni's face, Joseph could see that the previous night was still a thick, hazy blur to the man.

"There's one thing I don't understand," Anebni said, waving his sword beneath Joseph's nose. "You have my keys. Why didn't you open the prison doors and escape?"

"Potiphar would have killed you when he found out I was gone." It was a simple answer, but it left Anebni to grasp for an appropriate response. Finally, he just shook his head and motioned for Joseph to move toward the door.

"Until I can sort this all out, you're going back to your cell," Anebni said. "Start moving. You obviously know the way."

Joseph didn't argue, but he felt despair descend once more upon him. Anebni marched him back into his dark, depressing prison, and he hung his head in defeat. He could have had freedom. He could have ignored what his heart told him to do. But he'd done what he thought was right and would remain a prisoner because of it. If he'd thought his bondage was bitter before, it was nothing compared to what he was feeling now.

Potiphar looked across the table at his wife and felt the familiar nagging feeling that had been plaguing him ever since he put Joseph away in Pharaoh's prison. Neferset was a beautiful woman. He could see how a young, male slave, denied the opportunity to marry, might make unwelcome advances against her. Even Joseph, as dutiful as he was, had the normal desires of a man. Perhaps the frequent proximity to Neferset had been more than he could resist. Perhaps he had lost track of his senses for a brief few moments in time. But, as Potiphar watched Neferset daintily pick at the seeds of a pomegranate, doubts wracked his soul.

What if Joseph had been telling the truth? What if it was Neferset who had made the unwelcome advances and Joseph had been falsely accused to hide what she had done? Potiphar had his suspicions about his wife, but there were other things that worried his soul as well.

"One of the granaries has become infested with rodents," he said, eliciting only a casual disinterested look from his wife. "We've lost a large portion of our food stores."

"Don't you have cats around the granaries to keep something like that from happening?"

"Yes. But they all left. No one knows where they've gone."

"That's odd," Neferset said, looking down at her food again.

"Yes. Very odd." He paused to take a bite of his own breakfast then looked again at his wife. "Four of my best horses have also gone lame. And my best mare died last night. My flocks have also ceased to multiply. Our fortune is taking a turn for the worse."

"You can regain what we've lost. You're still one of the wealthiest men in Avaris."

Potiphar stared at her in silence. He didn't want to say what was actually on his mind, but the thought wouldn't seem to leave him. "I think Joseph's God is cursing us," he finally said. "His favor has been taken away from our household. In the six months since Joseph was taken away, my possessions have decreased by half."

"Make another offering to Seth," Neferset said. "Surely he is more powerful than Joseph's foreign God."

"Even the great god Seth can't help us if Joseph has been falsely accused." That got her attention, and he watched as her face filled with anger.

"Do you still want to believe *him*?" she demanded, her voice dripping with venom. "Do you still trust the word of a slave over the words of your own wife?"

"No, of course not," Potiphar lied.

"Then why did you say what you just said?"

"I don't know," he replied. "I suppose I regret losing him. He was the best chief steward we've ever had. For some reason I feel guilty about what happened. Like it was my fault, not his."

"He was just a slave," Neferset said. Her eyes were flashing wickedly now. "He was nothing. You've overseen the executions of mightier men than he. What is the life of a single slave that it should bother you?"

"You're right," he said. "I shouldn't be bothered by it. I apologize for offending you."

Neferset reached across the table and walked her fingertips seductively up his arm. "You haven't offended me," she said. "It was Joseph who offended me. And I'm glad you killed him. It's better that he's gone."

Potiphar winced. He hadn't bothered to tell her that he had only imprisoned Joseph, *not* executed him. But he was certain now—more than ever before—that keeping Joseph alive and withholding that important bit of information from her was the best decision he had made in quite some time.

"I know just what it is that you need," Neferset went on. "You need to appoint a new chief steward. Have you thought over the suggestions I gave you?"

"No. I've been too busy."

Actually he had thought about her suggestions. He'd thought a great deal about them. About how all the men she suggested were young and handsome. About how odd it was that a woman who had supposedly been assaulted by the last chief steward was in such an unusual hurry to get a new man into the house.

"I've had too many problems with young, inexperienced stewards," Potiphar said. "I've been thinking about appointing an older, more seasoned servant to do the job. Someone like Pekhti." Her look of dismay didn't escape him, and that look told him more than a thousand words ever could. What had he done? Had he really sentenced an innocent man to a life of imprisonment? If he could, he would let Joseph out. But to do so now would be a sign of weakness, and the captain of Pharaoh's guard could never afford to show weakness.

"I have to go to the palace," he said, pushing himself abruptly away from the table. "Don't expect me back until late tonight."

Neferset said nothing, but her dark eyes grew even darker. She refused to look at him as he walked out of the room.

He could effectively coordinate the troops of Pharaoh's royal guard. He could usually correctly gauge the loyalty and ability of a man. But he couldn't solve even the simplest problems of his own troubled marriage. He couldn't understand women, and he especially couldn't understand Neferset. It was easier just to leave when things became tense.

And maybe that's where all his troubles had begun.

"It's foolish of you to be angry with me. I was only trying to provide what was best for you. If you come with me now, it might not be

too late to salvage your future."

Asenath glared at her father, but he only smiled in return. If only he knew how angry she *really* was with him. She blamed him in part for Joseph's death. If she had been here six months ago instead of in On, she might have been able to stop the execution before it happened. Instead she'd been locked in her own room, seeking a means of escape and not finding it until it was too late. Everlastingly too late.

"I won't go back with you," she said. "I'm staying here."

"Why do you have to be so difficult?" Potipherah demanded. "You weren't this difficult before. What is it that has changed you so much?"

"I'm the same person I've always been. The only change is that I'm an adult now and no longer willing to let you determine who and what I will be."

"Don't fool yourself," Potipherah said, laughing. "You've already allowed someone to shape who and what you are. Khyan has turned you into the perfect Hyksos priestess. You've forgotten where your true loyalties ought to be."

"No," Asenath said, her eyebrows lowered and her voice icy. "It is you who have forgotten. You've forgotten that you, too, are Hyksos, and you're ready to betray your own people for a little personal gain."

Potipherah turned away from her and clasped his hands behind his back. It was what he did when he was dismissing the words of a subordinate, and it infuriated Asenath that he was doing it now to her.

"My loyalty is to Egypt," he said. "I am Egyptian, and I intend for my ancestors to be in power in Egypt long after Khyan and his Hyksos hordes have been driven from the land. The Hyksos dream will never come to pass. We will never be seen as true Egyptians unless we unite ourselves with the rightful rulers of Egypt—the kings and princes of Thebes. You and I are in the position to do that, Asenath. Now is the time to act."

"You act as if I'm a piece of property to be bartered and traded," Asenath answered him. "I'm not. And I won't allow myself to be. This isn't about my future. It's about yours. It's all about power and how you can get more for yourself."

"Yes, my willful daughter. This is about power. Those who have it are happy, and those who don't are not. You have power, Asenath. You have beauty, and you should use it to your advantage. Beauty, unfortunately, fades with age, and your power will fade with it if you don't use it while you have it."

"And you would have me use it to win the hand of that pig, Sebekamzaf. Is that it?"

"It's time now that you should be married. You should have been long ago and would have been if Khyan hadn't taken you from your home. Sebekamzaf is the best and only option you have. It's not like some other man has already won your heart."

Asenath turned her face quickly away, hoping to hide the sudden rush of emotion that filled her eyes; but she wasn't quick enough. Her father's sharp gaze discerned it all.

"You *have* fallen in love!" His expression suddenly softened, and Asenath looked momentarily back to catch a glimpse of the old father she remembered—the one who had once treated her as the most precious treasure in his house. "Who is he? Is he here? In Avaris?"

"There's no one," Asenath said, trying not to choke on the words. "You're mistaken. I'm not in love." Her father moved forward, grasped both of her arms, and turned her slowly around so that she was facing him. He searched her eyes carefully, even though she tried to veil the pain she knew was there.

"Don't think me to be an unfeeling man," he said. "I'm your father, and I care about you deeply. I just want what's best for you. Not just what's best now, but in the future as well. Perhaps I *have* been thinking more of my own success than of your feelings. Maybe I'm still thinking of you as the little girl who once brought warmth and joy to my house, rather than the woman you've become. I thought you didn't know what was best for you. I thought you were avoiding marriage until it was too late. But if you've actually found someone you love . . . " He stopped and shook his head. "I've been a fool that I couldn't see this earlier. Who is this man? Is he a priest? A government official?"

"I've already told you," Asenath said. "There's no one."

"I have to make one last official visit to Pharaoh's palace before I return to On," Potipherah said. "He summoned me here to discuss your future. There's no way I could ever convince him to marry you to a man I've chosen, but if there is a man here in Avaris of your own choosing—"

"No," Asenath said, cutting him off. "Let Pharaoh choose whatever man he's going to choose. It doesn't matter anymore. It just doesn't matter."

Potipherah studied her carefully—confused—and then took a step toward the door. "I can understand why you wouldn't be interested in talking to me," he said. "I can understand that you might still be hurt by what happened in On. Just realize that I did it all out of love. I never intended to hurt you." He took another step toward the door then paused and faced her once more. "And about what happened in On. You didn't—"

"No," Asenath interrupted. "I've said nothing to Pharaoh. I've said nothing to anyone. I made excuses to explain my early return to Avaris. You have nothing to worry about."

The look of relief that swept across his face was unmistakable. "Good. Then we'll talk later. I'll visit you one last time before my duties take me back home to On. I'd still like to know what kind of man could win the heart of my daughter so that she would prefer him over a prince."

Asenath didn't answer. There was no safe response that she could give. She stood as rigid as a statue as he came forward to kiss her on one cheek then watched in silence as he walked away. When he was gone, Netchem stepped cautiously into the open and came to her side. She had been waiting in the shadows at the other end of the hall where Asenath had placed her before her father entered the house. It was a security measure in case he decided to abduct her and take her against her will back to On.

"You've fallen in love?" Netchem asked. "You never told me you had fallen in love. That's wonderful! Father can speak to Pharaoh in your behalf. You and I can both be married at the same time. Who is he? And why didn't you tell me about it?"

"I'm not in love," Asenath replied, angrily shaking her head. "I wish people would stop saying that!"

"It would explain everything," Netchem said, not seeming to hear her. "Everything except how sad you've been since you got back from On all those months ago. It would—" She stopped and then looked at Asenath with dismay in her eyes. "Joseph!" she said in a shocked whisper. "You fell in love with Joseph!"

Asenath looked away. How often had she wished for someone to confide in—to cry with—as she expressed the deep aching in her heart? But not even Netchem had been allowed to hear this tragic secret. Now it seemed that the whole world would soon know, and the pain welled up with fresh new intensity at the thought of it.

"I-I'm sorry, Asenath . . . I'm so sorry . . . "

"I'm going back to my room," Asenath said, fighting back the flood of tears that was threatening to break loose. "Please make some excuse for me so that I won't be disturbed."

"Of course," Netchem said. She lowered her eyes and gave a sympathetic nod of her head, but she could never remain silent when she saw that a friend was hurting. "If you want someone to talk to," she called out after Asenath, "I'm always here for you."

"I know you are," Asenath said, not slowing her steps. "Thank you."

She'd planned on going straight to her room, but instead she found herself walking right out the back of the house. And, for some reason, her feet took her to the ugly, brick walls of Pharaoh's prison. There was a large area of raised earth before the prison—the place of public executions. There was a stone block where the heads or limbs of the accused were chopped off, and it was stained dark with the blood of many victims. It pained her to think that Joseph had died here in such an ignominious way. He deserved better than that. He deserved to live a long and a free life. And when he did eventually die, it should have been with honor.

She wasn't sure why she had come here. Maybe to say goodbye. Maybe to bring closure to this chapter of her life. But if that was it, it wasn't working. If anything, seeing the place where Joseph had died made her angrier and filled her with more bitterness than she had ever felt before.

"Where were You, God of Joseph?" she asked, turning her eyes toward the heavens.

"Where were You when Joseph needed You? Where were You when *I* needed You?"

She lowered her head and allowed herself to be enveloped by despair. She didn't know where to turn. She didn't know what god to worship. Her destiny seemed more uncertain than it ever had before. And it was just going to get more complicated. From what her father had just told her, it sounded as if Pharaoh was about to pick her husband. The thought of it filled her with a sudden, cold dread.

Chapter Notes

Ancient Egyptians had a variety of ways to measure time. Shadow clocks were used during the day, and the rising of certain stars was used to count the hours at night. A more reliable means of telling time was the water clock. In this simple device, a hole in one container would allow water to drip slowly into a second container. Marks on the water clock were used to calculate the passing of the hours.

TWENTY-EIGHT

"I s something wrong, Captain?"

"What? No. Nothing is wrong, my pharaoh."

Khyan watched Potiphar with a skeptical eye, but Potiphar avoided the pharaoh's gaze. There *was* something wrong. He just didn't know how to explain it without appearing weak. The problem was guilt. He was plagued by it. It gnawed at his soul day and night and wouldn't give him a moment's peace. One of the gods was tormenting him for Joseph's sake—he was certain of that—and he was also certain that he wouldn't find rest from it until he found some way to resolve all that had happened. He pondered this for several moments, but then he became aware that Khyan was still watching him, and he forced it all from his mind.

"What have you found out about the thefts from my household grain bins?" Khyan asked, watching him carefully.

"We still haven't caught the culprit," Potiphar said. "But we will. It's only a matter of time before he strikes again, and when he does, we'll catch him."

"Such breaches in the security of the palace make me wonder about my own safety," Khyan said, moving to his gold and ivory throne. "My confidence in the royal guard is wavering, Captain. In times like this, when Thebes is breathing threats of war, we can't afford any mistakes. Wouldn't you agree?"

"You are absolutely correct, my pharaoh. And I assure you that no harm will come to you or any of your family. The most loyal men in Egypt serve on your royal guard. Whoever steals from your grain bins is a petty thief and poses no threat to your life. But he will be apprehended and punished. I give you my word."

"Fine. See that it is done. But I also have another matter to discuss with you today."

"Another matter?"

"Yes. A matter that directly involves you. Especially since my prison is your personal ward and you should be aware of everything that is happening in it."

Potiphar shifted his feet nervously. He had been neglecting the prison lately. It reminded him of the troubles with Joseph and with Neferset, and that was enough in and of itself to keep him away. But he was also overwhelmed by more pressing matters. Ever since Joseph was removed from his place and thrust into the prison everything had gone to pieces. The tenant farmers were unhappy, Neferset was unhappy, the servants had become slothful. Only Pekhti seemed to remain loyal and productive.

"I-I'm sorry," Potiphar stammered. "I've been distracted lately. I lost a chief steward, and—"

"Anebni is bothering me about getting an overseer to help him in the prison," Khyan said, not even seeming to hear Potiphar's pitiful attempt at an explanation. "He claims that he's brought this matter to your attention, and nothing has been done about it. Is that true?"

"I already have an overseer in mind," Potiphar lied, hoping to buy himself some time to deal with this unexpected new problem. "I'll have it taken care of by tomorrow."

"Excellent! Who is it?"

"You . . . you want his name?"

"Yes. It would be nice to know it if Anebni sends another complaint to me before you have time to appoint this new overseer.

What is his name?"

"His name," Potiphar said, grasping desperately for ideas, "is . . . is . . . Joseph."

"Joseph? I've never heard of him. That name doesn't even sound Egyptian."

"He's not Egyptian. He's Hebrew. But he's the most qualified overseer I can think of. He was once my chief steward, and my estate prospered more under his hand than it ever has before or probably ever will again."

"I'm surprised you let him get away from you," Khyan chuckled. "But if he left a position as your chief steward for something else, how do you plan on convincing him to take a menial appointment as overseer in my prison? It's not the most pleasant of jobs."

"I . . . I think I can convince him," Potiphar said. "The question will be whether or not I can convince Anebni."

"Tell Anebni that this Joseph has the approval of the pharaoh himself," Khyan said. He sat down on his throne and leaned back into it. "Tell him if he complains to me again, I'll bring an end to his ability to complain. Permanently."

Potiphar smiled. Khyan had just solved two problems for him, and he felt as if a huge burden were being lifted from his shoulders.

"It will be done," Potiphar said. "I'll see that it is done immediately."

"Come with me. Come with me now."

Joseph blinked his eyes against the light and shook his head in confusion.

"Hurry up," Anebni said. "Unless you *enjoy* being locked up down here."

Joseph moved slowly out of his cell and was surprised when Anebni took a small key on his key ring and undid the padlocks that secured Joseph's chains. Unceremoniously, Anebni tossed the chains next to the wall and motioned for Joseph to follow him.

There was no sword pointed at his throat this time. No spear prodding against the small of his back. Anebni didn't even watch over his shoulder to see what Joseph was doing. It was strangely curious considering how cautious he had been when he brought Joseph back to his cell earlier in the day.

"I've been thinking about something," Anebni said as they stepped from the gloom of the dungeon into the bright warmth of the courtyard. "I've been thinking about how easily you could have escaped but didn't. I want to know why you decided not to kill me and leave when you had the chance."

"Because it would have displeased my God," Joseph replied.

"And it pleases your God for you to be locked up in a prison?"

"No. I don't think so. But I know it would displease Him even more for me to take the life of an innocent man—whether I did it with my own hand or allowed it to happen by the hand of another."

"Do you always do everything based on whether or not you think it will please your God?"

"Yes."

Anebni stopped walking, turned around, and stared at Joseph. Then he nodded his head as if he had come to some sudden decision. "As much as it defies logic, I think Potiphar is right. I think you will make a good *imy-ra*."

"What?" Joseph was sure his eyes were so wide that they looked like they would pop out, but he had to have heard wrong.

"With the approval of none less than Pharaoh himself, Potiphar has commanded me to appoint you as *imy-ra*—overseer—of this prison," Anebni said. "But there are conditions."

"Of . . . of course," Joseph stammered. "I would expect there to be."

"You will be required to swear an oath to me," Anebni said. "You are to swear an oath that you won't attempt to escape once I've given you the keys to the prison. Will you swear it?"

He was still so stunned by this sudden announcement that he almost couldn't find his voice to speak, but Joseph forced a response from his lips.

"As the Lord liveth," he said, "I will give you no cause to fear. I give you my word that I will not escape." There it was. He had once again made of himself a prisoner of his word. But his heart was filled with gratitude to God. The Lord had begun to bless him to make this captivity more bearable.

"Now it is settled," Anebni said. "You will be my new overseer, and you will receive special privileges in return. You will be allowed to come and go from your cell as you please. You will receive extra food so that you will have strength to do your duties, and you will have other privileges that normal prisoners don't have. It won't all be pleasant, but it will certainly be better than what you've experienced thus far."

"Th-thank you," Joseph whispered, trying to control the tears of gratitude that threatened to spill from his eyes. "Whatever tasks you see fit to give me, I will do them. I'll do all in my power to win your trust and approval."

"And I'll be happy for the help," Anebni said. "I've been asking Potiphar to get me a new overseer for more than a year now. I'm tired of doing the job of keeper and overseer both at the same time. You're not exactly what I had in mind; but, if what I've already been told is true, you'll do better than any other overseer. Follow me. I have something to show you, and I think you're going to like it. It's a gift. A gift for not fleeing last night."

Curious, Joseph followed Anebni across the courtyard until they came to a narrow set of steps that ascended to the top of one of the prison's towering, brick walls. Anebni took the steps two at a time in long, easy strides, but Joseph found himself easily winded as he struggled to keep up. His legs weren't used to such strenuous activity, and they burned from fatigue by the time he and Anebni reached their destination. But the sight which now greeted his eyes was well worth the effort. He found himself the sudden master of a commanding view of Avaris that stretched even beyond its walls to the Nile Delta beyond.

Joseph's eyes immediately fell upon familiar sights. A stone's throw in one direction was the estate of Potiphar. Not far in the other was Pharaoh's palace, gleaming like a polished, desert jewel in the mid-morning sun. Joseph could see members of the royal guard marching in rigid formations, like fierce lines of ants, and he could see officials of Pharaoh's court wandering in and out of the royal buildings. The fields he had once fought so hard to save also glimmered before him. From here they looked very much like a green, velvet carpet that someone had unfurled across the sands. There were also innumerable statues of Seth and Khyan, standing watch over the network of streets beneath him, and their sightless eyes seemed to lead his own eyes to the temple of Seth. The euphoria he had momentarily experienced ended, and his heart filled suddenly with pain.

Joseph wondered how long it would be before Asenath returned to that temple. And, when she did, how much longer would it be after that before she was forced to marry a man of Pharaoh's choosing? He lowered his eyes, silently bewailing his unjust fate; and, as he did so, his eyes fell upon the small form of a woman, standing beside the raised execution area where the condemned inmates of the prison met their ultimate end. Her head was lowered too, as if in mourning, and he wondered if she had lost a loved one to the executioner's blade. Would Asenath mourn him when she was told the tale of all that had befallen him? It hurt to think that his suffering might bring suffering upon her as well. Fortunately, he didn't have long to dwell on these thoughts. Anebni motioned to him, and they began their long descent back down the stairs again.

"It's quite a view, isn't it?"

"Yes, it is."

"I can't allow you beyond the front gates of this prison. Even though you're now an overseer, you're also still a prisoner. But if you ever need a breath of freedom, you can climb the wall and look into the world beyond. I'll inform the guards not to stop you if you desire to come up here and sit for awhile. It's not much, but it's my way of thanking you for sparing my life."

Joseph nodded, and Anebni smiled.

"This used to be a fortress," Anebni said. "Khyan's ancestors built their capital city around it after they defeated the old Egyptians. The old rulers of this place couldn't withstand our chariots and our bows. Our bows were much better than theirs. Have you ever used a Hyksos bow?"

"No, but my father taught me how to use an ordinary one when I was a little boy."

"Khyan loves to hunt with the bow. He goes into the marshes to hunt geese and other birds. I used to accompany him on his hunting trips. I was part of his closest personal guard. I served him for many years. Until I fell out of favor."

They had reached the bottom of the steps now, and Joseph saw a dark look of anger on Anebni's face. He sensed a story behind all of this, but he was unsure how he should respond to Anebni's sudden change in mood. Fortunately, he didn't have to. With a quick shake of his head—as if he were shaking off a bad memory—Anebni cleared away whatever gloomy thoughts he was thinking, and he forced a smile to his lips. "There's much for you to learn and little time left in the day," he said. "I can tell you my stories some other time. I'll show you where the food is kept and instruct you in how to ration it out to the prisoners. Tomorrow, before the sun is up, I'll go the rounds with you to teach you the morning routine. There will also be waste buckets to empty and prison records to update. I take it you know how to write?"

Joseph nodded.

"Good. Then this is going to work out even better than I hoped. Come with me. It's time for you to get started."

"Setma, have you seen that good-for-nothing baker, Ta?"

The female servant Thet had just stopped shook her head. "No. I haven't seen him. But he left his assistant in charge of the kitchen. You might want to ask him where Ta went."

Thet nodded and waved Setma on her way. She disappeared with her tray into Pharaoh's banquet room, and Thet marched angrily into the kitchen.

Ta had a habit of disappearing anytime he thought he wouldn't be missed. With all the commotion of servants coming and going during Pharaoh's banquet, tonight would be a perfect time to slip away unnoticed. But the lazy baker wouldn't have gone far. And his assistant would know where he was in case Pharaoh called for him to come to the dining hall.

The kitchen was a frantic flurry of activity. Cooks, servers, and helpers jostled each other as they fretted over dishes and dashed into the banquet room to worry over Pharaoh and his guests. It was the worst possible time to leave an assistant in charge, and Thet would let Ta know about it when he finally found him. But, at the moment, Thet was more concerned about the money Ta owed him than his incompetence as a chief baker. He clenched his teeth and balled up his fists as he thought about it. Thet's miserable excuse for a brother-in-law had been promising to pay him back for over a month now but always managed to avoid him when it came time to collect the payment. It was a wonder the man was still alive. He owed so much money to so many people, someone should have slipped a dagger between his ribs by now. He probably owed his life to the fact that Thet was Pharaoh's cup bearer—one of his chief advisors—and Ta's enemies feared the retribution Thet could bring upon them.

"Where is Ta?" Thet demanded when he spotted Ta's assistant at the far end of the kitchen. "I want to speak with him. Now."

"I-I don't know," the assistant stammered. "I'm sure he's around here somewhere. He—"

"Don't lie to me," Thet interrupted. "I know he's left you in charge while he's gone off somewhere that he shouldn't be. Where is he? Tell me now."

"He said he had a bad headache," the assistant said. "He said he would be out by the grain bins and that I should only disturb him if Pharaoh calls for him."

Thet wasted no more time on the assistant. Angrily, he pushed his way through the milling crowd of servants and went out the door leading to the courtyard where the grain bins were located. Brother-in-law or not, Ta was going to give an accounting tonight for all the money he owed.

"Ta!" Thet called out into the darkness. "Where are you? I know you're out here."

A quick movement by one of the grain bins caught his attention, and he lunged toward the shadowy figure who knelt there. Ta tried to escape his assailant's grasp, but Thet's strong hands held him by the collar of his linen tunic so that he couldn't escape.

"Are you trying to hide from me again?" Thet demanded. "Well, it's not going to work this time! I want my money back. I want it now!"

"I was just on my way to the kitchen with your payment," Ta said, groveling before his brother-in-law. "See? It's here. In the basket."

Thet peered through the darkness at the whicker basket Ta had dropped when he was discovered. It was tipped on its side now, and grain had spilled out across the flagstones of the courtyard.

"Grain? What kind of trick is this, Ta?"

"No trick," Ta said, putting his arms before his face as if Thet might strike him. "It's your payment. It's all I have to repay you with, but it troubled me to make you wait any longer than you'd already waited. You can sell it in the market for the price I owe you. My family will go hungry for a week, but we will suffer that so that you will be paid back quickly."

"I give you silver, and you give me grain that you've stolen from

Pharoah's grain bins?" Thet demanded. "What kind of a fool do you take me for?" He would have said more, but the shadows around him came suddenly to life. He was so startled by the sudden appearance of ten of Pharaoh's most trusted royal guard, that he let go of Ta and took a few steps backward. The darkened courtyard now bristled with spears and swords, and he realized something wasn't right.

"By order of the pharaoh, you are both under arrest," one of the ten—an officer—said.

"Arrest?" Thet stared at the officer in astonishment. "I am Pharaoh's chief cup bearer. For what, may I ask, am I under arrest?"

"The meal of Pharaoh has been poisoned," the officer replied. "You are both to be detained and questioned."

Thet looked at Ta—first with rage then with fear. But he had no time to protest or plead. He was dragged unceremoniously to Pharaoh's prison, caught up in the middle of a crime he had absolutely nothing to do with.

TWENTY-NINE

LIFE AS THE OVERSEER OF PHARAOH'S PRISON was not an easy one. It was a life of hard, manual labor and long, grinding hours. But it was better than being bound in chains, locked away in the darkest depths of the prison. Although he yearned constantly for his liberty, Joseph was grateful for the limited freedom he had. It was infinitely more than he had started with here.

Several weeks had passed for Joseph in his new calling of overseer, and, in that time, he had managed to make some significant changes. He had improved the diet and living conditions of the prisoners. He had organized the records. And, although Anebni resisted at first, he had finally managed to convince the keeper that prisoners—at least those accused of lesser crimes—should get a few minutes of fresh air and sunlight every now and then. Most of his work was tedious and uneventful, but the monotony on this evening was broken by the arrival of two new prisoners.

"These men won't be here long," the guard who had been sent to fetch him whispered as they walked together.

"Why do you say that?"

"Because they tried to poison Pharaoh, and Potiphar himself has come to lock them away. Whenever Potiphar is sent, an execution is sure to follow. You're the only man he's ever brought who escaped that fate."

Potiphar was waiting for them at the gate, and Joseph approached him nervously. Even though he was innocent of the crime of which he had been accused, it was still awkward to once again face his old master.

"These two men are to be locked up immediately," Potiphar said, seeming as uncomfortable about this unexpected meeting as Joseph was. "When you see Anebni, tell him that the criminals caught in Pharaoh's house are here."

Joseph nodded then motioned for the two bound prisoners to follow him. He made a low bow to Potiphar as he turned to leave, but Potiphar stopped him before he could go.

"Wait a moment. Don't leave just yet."

Joseph turned back and stood at attention. He wasn't sure what Potiphar would say to him, and Potiphar didn't seem sure either. It took several long moments before Potiphar opened his mouth to speak.

"I'm charging you with the care of these prisoners," he said. "Pharaoh wants them alive and healthy until he decides what their final punishment will be. See that his commands are followed."

Joseph nodded and waited for Potiphar to dismiss him. Finally Potiphar nodded for him to go. But before he left, Joseph couldn't help but notice the strange look in Potiphar's eyes. It was a probing look. An uncertain one. And Joseph thought he could even sense guilt. Perhaps now—now that so many months had gone by—Potiphar's anger had faded enough for him to begin questioning the truthfulness of Neferset's accusations. But Joseph had little time to ponder this. Potiphar was waiting for Pharaoh's instructions to be carried out, and Joseph hastily motioned to the prisoners to follow him. They moved behind him, with lowered heads, to the entrance of the long, dark dungeon corridor, and the guard followed closely behind them, watching carefully in case the frightened prisoners attempted to fight their way free. But neither of the condemned men seemed to be in any state of mind to try such a thing. They followed Joseph as meekly to the dungeons as his father's sheep had once followed him to pasture, and he turned to the guard before they'd taken more than a few steps down the dark corridor.

"I'll take the prisoners from here," he said. "You can return to your post if you want."

The guard didn't argue. No one liked to go down where the prisoners were kept. It was dark, it stunk, and it reeked of sweat, disease and urine. Joseph was more than accustomed to descending alone into its depths.

"I'll wait here at the top of the ramp," the guard said, a note of gratitude in his voice. "If they cause you any trouble, just shout. I'll come down and bring a quick end to it."

"Thank you," Joseph replied. He paused just long enough to remove a torch from a bracket on the wall then continued down toward the prisoners' new quarters. They followed close on his heels as if the darkness might consume them if they strayed too far from the light.

"This is all your fault," one whispered to the other after they'd walked in silence for several long moments. His voice was trembling, but there was also anger in it. "You got us here, Ta. You and your thieving ways!"

Joseph glanced over his shoulder. The prisoner who had spoken was a tall, distinguished man. The other was a shorter, nervous-looking person, and he didn't open his mouth to argue.

He stared intently at his shuffling feet, and Joseph thought he recognized something vaguely familiar about the man. He rarely forgot a face, and he was certain he had seen this man somewhere before. Perhaps it would come back to him after awhile. He would have to think about where their paths might have crossed.

"You'll be staying here," Joseph said, stopping now before one of the large, wooden doors. "You only receive food once a day—in the morning—but I'll make sure you receive a large portion. Apparently, Pharaoh wants you well taken care of."

"Only so we'll look good for our execution," the taller man said.

He glared accusingly at the shorter man, and that man shrank beneath his gaze.

He didn't usually ask the prisoners what real or imagined crime had brought them here. Most didn't want to talk about it. And when they did, they offered the information on their own. But Joseph's curiosity got the most of him this time.

"I was told you are both servants of Pharaoh," he said as he unlocked the door. The guard had already told him they were here for attempting to poison the pharaoh, but he wanted to hear their side of the story. Somehow they didn't look like murderers. "Why did Pharaoh accuse you and send you here?"

"I was in the wrong place at the wrong time," the taller man said, glaring at his companion yet again. "This fool of a brother-in-law is a thief. And not even a good one at that! I had the great misfortune of showing up when he was out of the kitchen in the process of robbing Pharaoh's grain bin. In the meanwhile, someone was poisoning Pharaoh's food and now he thinks this fool and I were behind it. My life is ruined because of this man's thievery and incompetence!"

"It's true," the shorter man admitted, moaning. "It's all true. This is my fault. But I needed the grain. And I swear I had nothing to do with any attempt to kill Pharaoh. I swear upon my life I didn't!"

"Your life is what it's going to cost you!" the taller man growled with an angry shake of his head. "Yours and mine! I'd strangle you myself, Ta, if I didn't know Pharaoh was going to do it for me."

Ta! Now Joseph knew where he had seen this man before. It was Pharaoh's chief baker. The one who had traded wine for grain.

"You're the chief baker in Pharaoh's palace, aren't you?" Joseph said.

Ta looked at him, fearfully, as if perhaps this, too, was a man he owed money to; but a light of recognition slowly filled his eyes, and he squinted through the darkness to better study Joseph's pale, bearded face. "I know you," Ta said. "You're Potiphar's chief steward. You . . . oh, no! Potiphar's sent you here to torture me, hasn't he?"

"No," Joseph reassured him. "I'm not here to torture you. I'm a prisoner in this place just as you are."

"A prisoner?" The tall man arched one eyebrow. "If you're a prisoner, what are you doing with the prison keys? Potiphar wouldn't let a prisoner oversee Pharaoh's prison. You're another one of Pharaoh's spies, aren't you? He's sent you here to trick us both into giving a confession. Well, I won't do it. You now know who of the two of us is at fault. I demand to be set free!"

"I don't have the power to set you free," Joseph said. "I admit it must seem strange to see a prisoner overseeing the activities of this prison, but I am a prisoner just as I say I am. I empathize with your plight. I know what it's like to be falsely accused. But only Pharaoh himself can release either of you from this prison." Joseph pulled the heavy cell door open and nodded toward it. "I'll have to ask the two of you to go in there now. I would stay and talk, but I have to go put your names on the prison register. You are Ta . . . " He nodded toward the baker. "But I don't know your name yet."

"Thet," the taller man said. "I am . . . I was . . . Pharaoh's cup bearer . . . his chief butler."

"You're not really going to leave us in *there*, are you?" Ta asked, peering apprehensively into the dark, musty chamber. "There's no light. Don't we get a torch? Something? Something to give illumination?"

"There's a small opening in the wall," Joseph said. "It will let a little light in, and your eyes will soon grow accustomed to it."

"What about these chains?" Thet asked, holding up his shackled wrists. "Aren't you going to at least remove these?"

"I can only remove your shackles when Anebni gives me the order to do it," Joseph said. "I'm sorry. I wish I could do more."

Thet shook his head, still distrustful of Joseph, and Ta stared at him with mournful eyes; but they both entered the cell, and Joseph shut the door slowly behind them. Now two more men would suffer the fate he suffered. The thought didn't bring him any comfort.

THIRTY

PHARAOH'S BUTLER AND BAKER REMAINED in ward at the prison for several months. And, true to his word, Joseph took extra care in providing for their physical needs. Providing for their psychological needs, however, was another matter altogether, and the best he could do was listen to their complaints and give them his sympathy. Usually when Joseph showed up at their cell, they were bickering with each other or standing, with arms crossed, with their backs to each other. But this morning it was different.

"Good morning," Joseph said, trying to sound cheerful. "I've brought your breakfast, lunch, and dinner." He waited for a response. His attempts at lighthearted humor normally brought a chuckle or at least a reluctant smile. But Ta and Thet didn't seem to hear him today. Their faces barely even registered that they recognized he was here.

"Why are you both so sad today?" he tried again.

Still no response. He was about to set their bowls on the floor and leave when Thet looked up at him and spoke in a lifeless voice.

"We both had dreams last night," Thet said. "We think the gods have sent us each a message, but we have no interpreter to give an explanation."

"Do not interpretations belong to God?" Joseph said. "Tell me what you've dreamed, and I will ask my God for the interpretation of it."

Thet looked skeptical, but Joseph put the food bowls on the floor, placed the torch in a wall bracket, and moved over to sit beside him. "My God has given me the meanings of dreams before," he said. "He can give me the meaning of yours as well."

"All right," Thet replied, shrugging his shoulders. "I guess it can't hurt to let you try." He fell silent for a few more moments and stared at his feet, but finally he began. "I dreamed that a vine was before me," he said, "and in the vine were three branches. It was as though it budded, and its blossoms shot forth." He made an exploding motion with his hands to illustrate and then continued. "And the clusters brought forth ripe grapes. Pharaoh's cup was in my hand, and I took the grapes and pressed them into the cup. Then I put it in Pharaoh's hand. Can you give me an explanation of that?"

Joseph closed his eyes and sat in silence for several long moments. Thet watched him, nodding as if he'd known all along that this dream would be too difficult for a mere prison overseer to unravel. But Joseph's silence wasn't brought on by an inability to understand. He was listening. He was listening in his heart for the interpretation. In this prison he had learned well how to listen for the voice of God, and he didn't speak until that whispering came.

"This is the interpretation of it," he said. "The three branches are three days. Within three days Pharaoh will lift your head up and restore you to your place. You will deliver Pharaoh's cup into his hand the way you did when you were his butler." He paused for another moment then added something of his own. "Remember me when things are well with you, and make mention of me to Pharaoh to bring me out of this prison. I was stolen away out of the land of the Hebrews, and I've done nothing here to be put into this dungeon. I'm innocent of the crimes I've been accused of just as you are innocent of the charges made against you."

"If what you say is true," Thet said, still looking doubtful, " . . . if your interpretation is right and I'm restored as chief butler, I will mention your plight to Pharaoh. I give you my word on that."

"Thank you," Joseph quietly replied.

"Your interpretation of Thet's dream seems good." It was Ta's voice, coming hopefully from the other side of the cell. "But what about mine? Can you interpret mine as well?"

"Tell me your dream," Joseph said. "It is not by my power that the interpretation comes but by the power of God. If my God gives me the interpretation, I in turn will give it to you."

"I was also in my dream," Ta said, his voice eager now, "and I had three white baskets on my head. In the uppermost basket, there were all kinds of foods baked for the pharaoh, and the birds ate them out of the basket. Will I be released from the prison as well? Does this mean that I, too, will be replaced to my position?"

Joseph was silent again. But this time it wasn't because he was waiting for an interpretation. He knew the interpretation of this dream. It came to him the moment he heard it, and he didn't know how to mercifully give such information.

"Don't you have an interpretation for me?" Ta asked after Joseph had remained silent for a very long time. Ta's voice was edged with fear now, and Joseph opened and closed his mouth—several times—before he finally mustered the courage to speak.

"Yes," he said slowly. "Yes . . . there is an interpretation for you."

"Then what is it? Tell me?"

"This is the interpretation," Joseph said. "The three baskets are three days—"

"So I will be released!" Ta triumphantly interrupted. "Pharaoh will lift me up out of the prison as well!"

"In three days," Joseph continued, "Pharaoh will lift your head off from you and will hang you on a tree. The birds will eat the flesh off your body—"

"No!" Ta interrupted again—this time with terror in his voice. "It can't be! You said good things to Thet. Why won't you say good things to me also? There has to be another interpretation. There has to be another way to look at it!"

Joseph shook his head. There was no other message for Ta. His crime would cost him his life. And it would cost him in a terrible way. To an Egyptian, the desecration of one's body by birds or beasts was tantamount to dying a second death. Great pains were taken to preserve the body in order to ensure a blissful afterlife. Pharaoh's punishment was not only meant to deprive Ta of his mortal life but of his afterlife as well.

"I will pay Pharaoh back for all the grain I took," Ta mumbled, speaking more to himself than to either Joseph or Thet. "I'll throw myself at his feet and beg for mercy. Surely he'll show mercy to me if I do that."

"I have to go," Joseph quietly said, getting back to his feet and dusting himself off. "I have to take food to the other prisoners. I'll be back later today. Just in case either of you need anything."

His words had brought hope to one man and devastated another. But they were not his own interpretations. They were God's, and he had to give what God inspired him to give. That's what he'd had to do when the Lord gave him the interpretation of Asenath's dream—despite the great personal pain such an interpretation caused him—and that is what he'd been compelled to do now.

Joseph shook his head, and wondered why he'd ever been born. Was his only purpose in life to suffer? Or was there some grander purpose behind all this that he wasn't yet allowed to know?

Whatever God desired of him, he hoped it would soon be made manifest to him. At the moment he wasn't sure how much longer he could go on.

Shortly after the visit of Asenath's father to Avaris, even more men than usual began to make official appearances at the house of Setmosis. All of them were powerful men of influence and wealth. They all brought gifts, and they all came to court Asenath. At first it amused her. Then it annoyed her. Finally, it became an outright nuisance. But Netchem was thoroughly enjoying every moment of it. She delighted in keeping track of Asenath's many would-be suitors almost as much as she delighted in her own upcoming marriage. One of the men in particular was more persistent in his visits than the others, and this one seemed to be Netchem's personal favorite. She was almost as vocal about who she thought Asenath should marry as Asenath's father had been about Sebekamzaf.

Asenath shuddered every time she thought about that close call. One false move during her attempted escape and she could have very well ended up in Thebes married to the city's haughty prince. But she was no happier about the men Khyan now sent to court her than she had been about Sebekamzaf.

"Senmut is here to see you again," Netchem said, smiling broadly as she greeted Asenath in the courtyard. "He's waiting for you in the garden."

Asenath rolled her eyes. "Tell him I'm too busy to see him," she said. "Or tell him I'm not here. I don't care what you say. Just get rid of him."

"Are you going to remain an unmarried woman forever?" Netchem asked. "Are you going to turn away every man who shows even the slightest interest in you?"

"I prefer to choose my own husband," Asenath said, a little more tersely than she had intended. "I didn't need my father to make the selection for me, and I don't need you to do it either."

Hurt flashed through Netchem's eyes. But even this harsh remark didn't deter her from her intended purpose.

"Joseph is dead," Netchem said. "You have to come to terms with that. You have to go on with your life. And, even if he were still alive, it would make no difference. A priestess cannot marry a slave. I'm sorry if it hurts you to hear this, but his death was probably the most merciful thing that could have happened to either of you."

Asenath choked on the hurt and anger that boiled up inside of her. The muscles in her neck and shoulders tightened, and she fought the tears that wanted to well up in her eyes. She was about to say more hurtful words to Netchem, but all she could choke out was, "You don't understand. You'll never be able to understand."

"All I understand is that you're lonely," Netchem said, taking one of Asenath's hands into her own to pat it in a gentle, concerned manner. "I see that all the light has left your eyes. All the joy has left your life. I want you to be happy again. But you won't ever be happy if you continue to lock yourself away in your room and refuse to enjoy the human companionship that can still be yours."

"And what would you have me do? Run off and marry the next man my father or Pharaoh sends to me with gifts and flattering words? Marry a man I don't even love?"

"No. I never said that. But you can at least give some of these men a chance. Senmut is a handsome and compassionate man. I know because I've talked with him while you've hidden from him in the temple or in your room. He could take care of you. He's a no-march, Asenath—a governor—and he lost his first wife in childbirth only a few years ago. He understands what it's like to lose someone you love. You might find you have more in common with him than you think. Maybe that's why my father convinced Pharaoh to send him your way."

"Your father? How would your father know what I had in common with Senmut?" Asenath stared accusingly at Netchem, and her friend looked hastily—guiltily—away. "You told him. Didn't you? You told him about Joseph!"

"I had no choice," Netchem said. "You wouldn't tell him, and he knew something was wrong. He wouldn't leave me alone until I told him all that I knew. What else could I have done?"

"You could have told him it was none of his business," Asenath hissed, her blue eyes flashing with anger. "You could have told him he would have to talk to me if he wanted information about my private, personal life. Did you tell him that Joseph was a slave? Did you tell him that, too?"

"No. He only knows that you were in love and that the man you fell in love with died. I knew if I told him more than that he would be angry, and it would cause you trouble you didn't need. He thinks the man was someone in On and that his death is why you returned so unexpectedly."

"You shouldn't have done it," Asenath angrily murmured. "You shouldn't have told him anything."

"I'm sorry," Netchem whispered, her voice contrite. "You know my father. You know how powerful he is. I couldn't defy his wishes. Even for you . . . "

Asenath sighed loudly and forced some of her anger to dissipate. She did know Setmosis. She knew how hard it was to stand up to him, and she knew Netchem, of all people, would be unable to do that. At least Netchem had the presence of mind to hold back the more dangerous details. Asenath could be grateful for that. And perhaps it wouldn't hurt to humor both Setmosis and Netchem by at least talking to Senmut. She'd already rebuffed the man several times, and a simple conversation wasn't exactly the same thing as a commitment to marriage. If for no other reason than to make Netchem happy, she would do this.

"All right," she finally said. "I'll talk to Senmut. But from now on, I want you to stop meddling in my affairs. Do you agree to that?"

"I'll cover for you at the temple this evening," Netchem said, grinning. "Hurry! I told him you would be right there."

Asenath cast Netchem a withering glance, but Netchem just laughed and skipped away. It annoyed Asenath just how well Netchem could predict her actions and reactions. This time, however, she was predicting wrong if she believed for even one moment that anything would come of this brief conversation with Senmut. Asenath had made up her mind that she would never marry. A conversation with a man—even one who had experienced the same kind of loss as she had—wouldn't change that.

Her footsteps were quick as she crossed through the house. She just wanted to get this over with and get back to the numbing monotony of her temple duties. But her pace slowed as soon as she reached the edge of the garden, and she felt sudden, unexpected anxiety.

It had been so many months since she talked to a man in anything other than a perfunctory manner. She felt unsure of herself and almost turned back to tell Netchem she had changed her mind. But that wouldn't solve her problems. Senmut, or some other man, would just come back again, and Netchem would pester her even more than she had before. Asenath took a deep breath and forced her feet to carry her into the garden.

Senmut heard her approach and turned, with a low bow, to greet her. She responded with a brief nod of her head then stared uncomfortably at her toes. She'd never actually seen Senmut until today, but she was forced to grudgingly admit that he was not an unattractive man. He was almost as tall as Joseph, although lacking Joseph's strong, muscular physique. A broad, golden collar covered his upper chest and shoulders, and a ring of office weighed down one of his fingers. He was exactly the type of man Asenath's father would approve of and exactly the type of man she had sworn she would never marry. A sudden memory of her dream of the field and the ox came back to her, and she vowed again not to let Joseph's interpretation of it come true. She wouldn't allow an unsolicited dream to determine her future. She wouldn't let Joseph's God be right.

"I hope I'm not taking you away from any important duties," Senmut said, nervously twisting the large ring around his finger.

"Netchem is going to cover for me at the temple," Asenath replied. "What is it that I can do for you today, Governor?"

"This isn't actually an official visit," Senmut said, smiling. "I only heard that the daughter of Potipherah serves at the temple of Seth, and I came by to pay my respects."

Asenath nodded then motioned to one of the stone benches that faced the garden pool. They both seated themselves, and she folded her hands nervously in her lap.

"Setmosis has a beautiful home," Senmut said, crooking his neck to stare around himself.

"Yes," Asenath answered. "Yes, he does." She noticed that Senmut's eyes were focused on her again, and she looked quickly away.

"It's true," he said after a few moments of silence. "It's true what I was told about you."

"What you were told about me? And what is that?"

"They say you are as beautiful as the goddess Isis. It isn't a lie."

Asenath felt her cheeks grow warm, and the blush that started there spread quickly across her face.

"I had to turn to Isis for comfort and strength," he said, his voice suddenly becoming hollow. "She is the protectress of women, and I once begged her for the life of my wife. But the will of gods and goddesses is greater than the desires of men . . . "

"Yes. I suppose it is," Asenath said when he fell silent again.

This was possibly the most awkward conversation Asenath had ever been in, and she prayed that it would soon end.

"It's hard to understand why the gods allow such things to happen," Senmut said. "I still don't understand their ways. Perhaps if I were a priestess like you, I would understand. But I'm merely a normal man with no understanding of religious things."

Despite herself, Asenath felt sudden compassion towards this man who—like herself—had lost so much. But she wasn't quite sure how she should comfort him. She was a priestess, it was true, but she found no more solace in the beliefs she had been raised with than this man seemed to have. She had no words of comfort to give.

"I'm sure you're not interested in hearing about my problems," Senmut said, shaking off the momentary melancholy that had overcome him. "And I'm sure I'm keeping you from more important things. If you need to get back to the temple—"

"I won't be missed," Asenath interrupted. "I can stay and talk for a while."

Senmut's face lit up, and Asenath smiled—really smiled—back at him. Maybe she could never love again, but at least she had met someone who could understand the kind of loss she had experienced.

She enjoyed this momentary connection. It was a pity that a moment was all she could allow it to last.

Chapter Notes

From the time of the Early Dynastic Period, Egypt was divided into administrative districts called *nomes*. The governors of these districts are referred to as *nomarchs*, and their duties included such tasks as administering justice, supervising public works, and collecting taxes. Many of these local governors wielded great power and prestige.

THIRTY-ONE

DISCOURAGED DIDN'T EVEN BEGIN TO DESCRIBE how Joseph felt about his life. His interpretations of the butler's and baker's dreams had come to pass. Pharaoh had restored Thet to his place and Ta was hanged from a tree. But two full years had passed since then, and Thet had failed to keep his promise. Pharaoh had not been told about Joseph's plight, and Joseph was still a captive in prison. It seemed likely that he would remain a captive for the rest of his days.

The sun was descending in a glowing sea of red light, soon to disappear beneath the horizon, and Joseph sat at the top of the prison wall, watching it go down. He could see the farmers leaving their fields and the city dwellers returning to their mud brick huts. But one person, at least, seemed to be unaware that the day was about to end. A lone chariot wound its way through the streets of Avaris, and Joseph wasn't alone in noticing it.

"It looks like Senmut is making another unofficial visit," one of the prison guards said to another as he pointed toward the chariot.

"Senmut? Who is he?"

"The nomarch of Khmun. But he spends so much time here, Pharaoh ought to make him the nomarch of Avaris."

"Khmun is a nice place. What does he find so fascinating about

Avaris that he doesn't stay in his own city and enjoy being a nomarch there?"

"A woman."

"It's always a woman, isn't it?" the second guard said, laughing. "Who is she? A princess? The daughter of one of Pharaoh's advisors?"

"No, she's a priestess."

"A priestess?"

Joseph felt his heart begin to beat faster. But it was an uncomfortable beat. A painful rhythm. Although he'd only been half listening before, he now hung onto each and every word that fell from the two guards' lips.

"I hear she's a very beautiful woman," the first guard said, "and the daughter of the high priest of On. Many powerful men have been seeking her hand in marriage. They've been flocking to the temple to court her, and they've been petitioning Pharaoh for her hand."

"And Senmut stands the best chance?"

"My sister is married to one of the temple priests. She says Senmut has almost won over the heart of Potipherah's daughter."

It felt as if his heart were being ripped in half, and Joseph stumbled blindly down the steps that led to the courtyard below. He'd known it would happen. It had to happen. The interpretations he received from the Lord always came to pass. The only ones which didn't seem to happen were the ones that involved him. But nothing could have adequately prepared him for this moment or for the wrenching pain he felt inside.

He knew the guards were watching him—probably with bewilderment on their faces—but he was too overcome with despair to care. He staggered across the courtyard, ran through the dungeons, and plunged himself into the darkness of his own cell. The blackness there matched the black anguish in his soul, and he buried himself in it. He had tried to be faithful and trust in the Lord. He had refused for all these years to murmur against his God and had endured unimaginable trials and tribulations despite his righteousness. But now he fell to the cold floor of his cell—tears flowing unchecked from his eyes—and he didn't believe he could endure another moment of it.

"God of my fathers," he whispered. "I have endured every burden Thou hast called upon me to bear. I have done it all without complaint, and I have trusted that it would be for my good. But I have no more strength to endure. Please . . . bring this to an end. Take away my despair!"

It was silent in the dungeons tonight. Dark and silent. It seemed that the light would never come. But somewhere deep within Joseph's soul a faint spark of hope still lingered. It was a tiny, flickering light which stubbornly refused to be extinguished. Strange considering that his greatest wish now was to die.

"Aten! Where are you? Come to my room! Immediately!"

Khyan was pacing around in a state of great agitation when Aten entered his bedchamber. It was unusual to see the king like this—he was usually boisterously joking with his personal servants or casually looking over the latest royal decree when Aten entered in the morning. But something serious seemed to be disturbing him today. Whatever it was, its effect on Khyan even made Aten feel uneasy.

"I am here, my king," he said when Khyan continued to pace as if not even seeing him in the room. "What is your bidding?"

"Gather all the magicians and wise men of Egypt. Bring them to my throne room at once. I'm badly in need of their skills this day."

"Perhaps *I* can be of assistance to you," Aten said. "If you will just explain to me what it is that ails you I—"

"Can you interpret dreams?"

"No, I—"

"Then do what I've told you and summon those who can!"

"Yes, my Pharaoh. I will send messengers out at once."

Pharaoh's brusque dismissal made Aten simmer inside with resentment, but he was careful to hide his feelings. He was good at hiding his anger and fear. That was probably the only thing which had saved him after his failed attempt to poison Khyan—that and the fact that suspicion had quickly fallen upon the two fools, Thet and Ta. But they weren't the only fools in this court. Khyan was the biggest one of all. Even now, after pardoning Thet, he still believed it was that idiot baker, Ta, who had tried to kill him. For the time being, Aten would have to encourage that belief. Then, when the time was right, he would find another way to rid Egypt of its insufferable king so that he could place himself on the throne in the deceased monarch's stead.

Outside Pharaoh's quarters now, Aten clapped his hands and a servant immediately appeared. "Pharaoh desires to have the wise men and magicians of the kingdom appear before him," Aten said. "Call in the royal messengers and notify the keeper of the pigeons. I will also need scribes to prepare official notices. Can you remember all that?"

The servant nodded.

"Then go. The last time I saw Pharaoh this upset, someone got hanged because of it."

The servant dashed from the room, and Aten rubbed his temples with both hands. It was going to be a very long day. He could sense it already.

"What's going on?" Asenath asked, watching with Netchem as Setmosis and a small contingent of lesser priests departed hastily from the temple. "Where are they all going?"

"It's Pharaoh," Netchem whispered. "He's called for the priests to come to the great house. Something important is going on there, but I'm not sure exactly what it is."

"Has anything like this ever happened before?"

"Only once. Remember? He called all the priests in when the

locusts destroyed the fields. But this must be even more serious. He's sent messengers all across the land. I even saw the carrier pigeons released from their cages. You don't think another disaster like the locusts is about to befall us, do you?"

Asenath felt a cold chill run up and down her spine. She still remembered the locusts, and how Joseph had sent her with Pekhti to get back to the city before they descended. But even the city hadn't been free of them. Her skin crawled as she thought about it. There was only one thing she could think of that would be worse than that. War with Thebes.

"Is it true what I've heard?" Netchem asked, changing the topic although her face still showed her worry. "Is it true that you now favor a marriage with Senmut?"

"He's discussed it with me again," Asenath admitted. "But neither he nor I have power over that. The choice is Pharaoh's, and I fear that he will make that choice soon."

"I'm sure my father can influence that decision," Netchem said, placing a reassuring hand on Asenath's arm. "If Senmut is the man you favor, he will bring it to Pharaoh's attention."

Asenath smiled weakly. It was true that Senmut was the best of all those who had courted her, but she was still in love with Joseph. For some reason, her heart continued to reject the realness of his death despite all the proof to the contrary.

"It will be all right," Netchem said, misinterpreting the look on Asenath's face. "I know you're frightened, but I'm certain that Pharaoh will consider the wishes of your heart. Senmut is loyal to Pharaoh. I can't imagine Pharaoh choosing another man after discovering that you have fallen in love with one of his most loyal nomarchs." She smiled again, patted one of Asenath's hands, then hurried off to attend to her own temple duties. Asenath waited until she was gone before allowing the half-smile to fade from her lips.

For two years now, Senmut had courted her. He was a wonderful man, and he could probably make her happy. But it felt like she was betraying Joseph to even think about marrying another man. At the moment, she was beginning to wish that she hadn't promised Senmut she would marry him if Pharaoh approved of it.

She had tried to convince herself that he would help her forget Joseph. She had tried to convince herself that she could happily go on with her life again. But she couldn't seem to persuade herself of this any more than Netchem had been able to convince her that it was best that Joseph had died. It wasn't for the best. It wasn't right. And she didn't know how she could ever be at peace. If only she could have died the same day Joseph did.

Thet had never seen anything quite like this before. Pharaoh's throne room had been crowded all day with priests, sorcerers, governors, physicians, and advisors. All of them had listened to his dream, but none of them had managed to supply an interpretation that pleased him. Pharaoh was so disturbed by this dream that he wouldn't eat and he wouldn't drink. He was becoming more and more irritable as the day wore on, and his patience was all but gone.

"Is this all that any of you have to offer me!" he roared, glaring at the large assemblage of men who nervously stood before him. "Where has the wisdom of my wise men gone? Where is the power of my priests and magicians? I've brought you here for counsel and answers, but your feeble interpretations trouble my heart even more than it was troubled before!"

Thet, who had been lingering in the room for several hours now, once again felt the persistent prompting that had been coming to him all day. With it he felt an overwhelming sense of guilt. Guilt had been gnawing at his soul ever since he heard about Pharaoh's dream, and it plagued him even more now that the wisdom of Pharaoh's advisors had failed. All of this was reminding him of a promise not kept. He was reminded of the personal cowardice that had prevented him from fulfilling his vow to Joseph, and he felt like the lowliest creature on earth.

Perhaps none of these men could properly interpret Pharaoh's dream, but a prisoner who was the overseer of Pharaoh's prison could. Somehow Thet had to build up the courage to finally make amends for his unforgivable ingratitude.

When Pharaoh threw the great banquet and restored Thet to his place, he had feared to make mention of Joseph. It was fear of Potiphar, the chief executioner, that had stayed his tongue. He had escaped death once, and he didn't want Potiphar searching for a reason to put him in that situation again. He had no doubt that Joseph was an innocent man. No man could receive such marvelous power to interpret dreams unless he stood guiltless before his God. But Thet feared retribution from Potiphar more than he feared Joseph's God. At least he *had* feared Potiphar more. Until today.

The power of Joseph's God was hanging over the chief butler. He could feel Joseph's God watching him as surely as if the God were right here in Pharaoh's throne room. And there was no doubt in his heart as to what this strange, foreign God wanted him to do. He wanted Thet to speak to Pharaoh. He wanted Thet to tell Pharaoh about Joseph's power of interpretation so that Joseph could finally be released from the prison. Thet trembled when he looked across the room at Potiphar, but he trembled even more when he sensed the growing impatience of Joseph's God.

"Is there no one in all Egypt who can explain this dream to me?" Pharaoh demanded, getting up from his throne and pacing angrily before the assemblage. "Is there no one who can interpret this message from the gods and bring peace to my soul?"

Thet took a hesitant step forward. Then another. He nervously raised one hand, and all eyes turned toward him. A murmur swept across the room. The great ones of Egypt were watching him, and Pharaoh's cold eyes seemed to pierce right through him.

"What do you want, Thet?"

"I-I know of a man who can interpret your dream," Thet stammered. "I know a man who has successfully interpreted dreams before." He glanced over at Potiphar and struggled to hold back an involuntary shudder. Then he looked back at Pharaoh.

"Go on," Pharaoh said, his interest piqued. "Tell me, Thet. Who is this man?"

"I remember my faults this day," Thet said, lowering his eyes in sudden shame. "Pharaoh was wroth with his servants, and put me in ward in the captain of the guard's house—in Pharaoh's prison—both me and the chief baker. We both dreamed a dream in one night, I and he, and we were troubled in the morning when we awoke . . . " Pharaoh was watching him intently now, and he realized the entire room was tense with anticipation.

"There was a young man there with us," Thet continued, "a Hebrew, servant to the captain of the guard . . . " He stopped this time to cast another nervous glance at Potiphar. But it was too late now. He had already risked the wrath of the chief executioner, if he stopped now he would be angering a much more dangerous man. Not to mention a God. " . . . and . . . and we told him our dreams, and he interpreted them," he said. "As he interpreted, so it was. Me he restored to my office, and the baker he hanged. It all came to pass on the day Pharaoh released us from his prison."

Pharaoh looked greatly pleased, but Thet was still trembling.

"Tell me the name of this man," Pharaoh said. "Tell me so that I may bring him here to interpret my dream."

"His name is Joseph," Thet replied. Potiphar was deathly quiet, but Thet could discern no emotion—either anger or displeasure—on his face. "He is both a prisoner and overseer of Pharaoh's prison," Thet finished.

"Bring this Joseph to me," Pharaoh said, turning to Aten who stood close to his throne. "Bring him here at once. Today we shall see if the wisdom of a Hebrew servant is greater than that of Egypt's supposed wise ones."

Thet shrank back into the corner of the room, but not before Potiphar cast him an unmistakably threatening glance.

Pharaoh was pleased. For the sake of his life, Thet hoped he'd made the right decision.

Chapter Notes

The word *pharaoh* is derived from the two Egyptian words *per* and *aa* which are translated as meaning "great house." In early times, as in this chapter, these words referred to the residence or palace of the king. Eventually, the term came not only to refer to the king's house but became a title for the king himself. The term *pharaoh* didn't actually come to refer to the king himself until *after* Joseph's time, but because it is the term used in the King James Version of the Bible and the term that is familiar to most readers, this title has been used in this novel.

THIRTY-TWO

"Joseph! Come now! You need to come to the gates immediately!"

Joseph set a pair of buckets on the stone slabs at his feet, then he looked up at the guard who was frantically motioning for him to come out of the dungeon.

"Don't just stand there," the guard said. "One of Pharaoh's own chief advisors is here to find you. He's been sent to bring you to the great house. Pharaoh himself desires to speak with you."

"Me? Why would Pharaoh want to see me?"

"You'll have to ask him that question yourself. Come on. Aten is an important man, and he doesn't like to be kept waiting."

Joseph nodded and followed, but he was sure he must have heard incorrectly. Pharaoh wanted to speak with him? He shook his head and stared in surprise at the small procession of important-looking men who waited for him across the courtyard. Anebni was speaking to one of them. The man was thin, probably in his early fifties, and his head was shaved in the fashion of priests and royal advisors. His linen robes of government office confirmed that he was, indeed, an official of Pharaoh's court. Joseph felt his heart begin to hammer uncomfortably against his ribs.

"Is this the man? Is this the one you call Joseph?"

"Yes." Anebni nodded his head nervously. "This is my overseer."

Aten looked Joseph up and down and shook his head with disgust. "We can't take him before the king of Egypt looking like this," he said. "This man needs to be shaved, and his clothes—if you can call such rags clothing—aren't fit to touch human skin." Aten sniffed now and wrinkled his nose. "A bath wouldn't hurt either," he said, turning his head away.

Joseph didn't care for the superior attitude of this royal advisor. He didn't like being examined like a horse or a dog, and he didn't like being talked about as if he wasn't even there. Admittedly, he was an unsavory sight to any who had never set foot inside a prison, but that was no fault of his own. He wanted to say as much, but held his tongue and suffered these indignities in silence.

"We don't have proper facilities for the prisoners to bathe or shave," Anebni apologetically explained. "And the only clothing they have is what they come into the prison wearing."

"This won't do," Aten insisted, shaking his head. "If we can't clean him up here, we'll have to do it outside of the prison. Bring him to my house. We'll take care of it there. Hurry. We don't have all day."

Anebni looked uncertainly at Joseph then shrugged his shoulders. Together they followed Aten out the prison gates, Anebni barely having enough time to take the prison keys from Joseph and hand them to one of the guards.

Joseph felt as if he were in a waking dream. This was all so sudden, and it all seemed so unreal. But it was happening nonetheless. Aten and his entourage now led Joseph through the city streets, and they didn't stop until they reached a house that was even larger than Potiphar's. It was the first time Joseph had been beyond the prison walls in nearly three years, and he was dizzy from the suddenness of this freedom. He wasn't given much time, however, to savor the feeling. Aten commanded the rest of the procession to wait outside, and he rushed Joseph into the house. Here Joseph was instructed to quickly bathe and shave himself. A fresh, white *shenti* and a clean, white tunic were ready when that was done; and Aten's servants gave him a hasty haircut. This finished, he was once again brought before Aten.

Aten walked around him several times. He looked Joseph over with a critical eye, turned Joseph's face from side to side, then nodded his own head with approval. "You look presentable," he said. "Come. We mustn't keep Pharaoh waiting."

As they walked toward Pharaoh's palace, Joseph tried once more to decide whether or not this was real. The idea that Pharaoh was sending for him was too fantastic for his brain to accept it. Yet here he was, walking through Avaris as if he'd never been imprisoned in the first place. And all the while Pharaoh's palace was growing all too large and near.

They came close to the gated wall that surrounded Pharaoh's palace, and Joseph saw as he'd often seen from the prison wall that the "great house" of Pharaoh was actually a complex of several "houses." There were massive stone buildings, gardens, courtyards, pools, and porticos such as nothing he had ever before seen. Potiphar's estate, which had once seemed so large, paled in comparison to this vast, royal residence.

Aten, however, barely paid attention to the magnificence before them. He led Joseph up a ramp which cut through the thick, surrounding enclosure wall, and four guards bowed as they passed by.

The first inner part of Pharaoh's palace which Joseph saw was a huge antechamber with a floor of glazed, blue tiles that stretched into a long, central corridor. Aten led him down this corridor past decorated pillars and elaborate murals, and Joseph suddenly realized the room at the other end was the throne room of the king. Joseph sent a silent prayer heavenward as his stomach began to twist and churn.

"The great pharaoh, Khyan, has heard of your ability to interpret dreams," Aten said, finally announcing the reason for this sudden excursion into freedom. "You are to bow before him when you enter the throne room, and you are only to speak when he commands you to do so. Do you understand?"

Joseph nodded. That was the only thing he could do. His vocal chords had temporarily ceased to function.

Aten pushed him insistently through the door, and Joseph suddenly found himself in a large crowded room. At first he was surrounded by the buzz of many voices. Men of different ages and stations filled the room, and they were clustered in large and small groups conferring and disputing with each other. On a raised, stone dais, a tall, stern-looking man slumped forward in a white chair with arching armrests carved in the form of sacred ibis wings. Between his thumb and index finger, he was rubbing the end of a false beard, and he was gazing into empty space with glazed, troubled eyes. But the man straightened himself and fixed his dark eyes on Joseph the moment he noticed him enter with Aten.

"My lord," Aten called out. "I have brought the man called Joseph to present himself before you."

The room fell immediately silent. It was an unearthly silence, and Joseph felt the weight of a hundred or more eyes falling upon him.

"Come forward," Pharaoh said, watching him carefully. "Approach my throne."

Joseph did as commanded then dropped to his knees and bowed low before the pharaoh.

"You may stand," Pharaoh said after Joseph had remained in the same position for several long moments. "Arise and stand before me."

There was awkward silence for what seemed like an eternity. But finally Pharaoh opened his mouth once more to speak.

"I have dreamed a dream," he said. "I have dreamed a very strange dream, and there is none here that can interpret it . . . " He paused, and his eyes swept the room. It was an icy, accusing stare. Apparently the other men had been summoned to this room for the same reason Joseph was now here, and all of them had failed. "I've heard say of you," Pharaoh continued, "that you can understand a dream to interpret it. Is this true?"

"It is not in me," Joseph answered. "But God shall give Pharaoh an answer of peace."

Pharaoh smiled. Whether he was pleased by the certainty in Joseph's voice or amused by the brazen boldness of his quick answer, Joseph couldn't be certain. But now was not a time to be timid.

"Very well," Pharaoh said. "Listen to my words, and give me your God's interpretation. In my dream, I stood upon the bank of a river and seven fat, well-favored kine came out of the river and fed in a meadow. Seven other kine came up after them. But these were poor, very ill-favored, and lean. Nothing I've ever seen in the land of Egypt could be compared to how bad they looked. And the lean, ill-favored kine ate up the first seven fat kine." He paused here and his face contorted as if he were remembering a horribly gruesome sight. But he didn't wait long before continuing. "Even though they had eaten these seven fat kine," he said, "it wouldn't be known that they had. They were still as ill-favored as they had been at the beginning of my dream. I awoke at this point, but I soon fell back into a troubled sleep, and a second dream came to me.

"In this dream, seven ears of corn—full and good—came up in one stalk. Then seven more ears which were withered, thin, and blasted with the east wind sprang up after them. Just as the bad kine had devoured the good kine, the thin ears devoured the seven good ears. All this I have told my magicians, priests, and advisors, but none of them can give me a satisfactory interpretation. What do you say? Can you interpret my dream?"

There was no hesitation in Joseph's response. This interpretation came to him as clearly as if he were reading it from a book. "Both of these dreams are one and the same," Joseph said. "God has shown Pharaoh what He is about to do. The seven good kine are seven years, and the seven good ears are seven years. The dream is one. The seven thin and ill-favored kine that came up after them are seven years, and the seven empty ears blasted with the east wind will be seven years of famine. What God is about to do, He is showing to you. There will be seven years of plenty throughout all the land of Egypt, and after them will come seven years of famine. All the years of plenty will be forgotten, and the famine will consume the land. The people will forget the plenty because of how grievous this famine will become. For this reason, the dream was given to you twice. It is because the thing is established by God, and God will soon bring it to pass."

He stopped speaking now and did his best to steady his unstable legs. The words were not his—they had come directly from the Lord—and he had been physically drained by the spiritual power that had just swept through him. He wasn't the only one affected. The entire room was dead silent, and he could see that all assembled were dumbfounded—the pharaoh most of all. Khyan looked even more troubled than before, and Joseph decided he should say more.

"Let Pharaoh do this," he suggested, completely forgetting Aten's orders about when to speak and when not to speak. "Appoint officers over the land, and set aside one-fifth of the land during the seven plenteous years. And let them gather all the food of those good years that come, and lay up corn under the hand of Pharaoh, and let them keep food in the cities. That food shall be for store to the land against the seven years of famine in the land of Egypt so that the land does not perish through the famine."

Pharaoh was silent, and Joseph waited. Whatever the reaction of the king, Joseph had said all that God would have him say. He didn't doubt that he had delivered the appropriate message. He didn't doubt that the interpretation was true.

Khyan kept his eyes lowered for several long moments. He seemed to be pondering all that Joseph had just said, and it seemed to be stirring around inside his soul. Finally, he looked up and swept the room with his gaze.

"Can we find such a one as this is?" he said, his voice commanding. "Is there any man in all Egypt like this in whom the Spirit of God is?"

A murmur went around the room, and Joseph saw heads shaking in agreement. What Joseph had said was not just good in the eyes of Pharaoh, it was good in the eyes of all his servants.

Pharaoh now focused his eyes on Joseph, and a faint smile parted his lips. "Forasmuch as your God has shown all this to you," he said, "there is none in my kingdom so discreet and wise as you are. I shall place you over my house, and according to your word shall all my people be ruled. Only in the throne will I be greater than you."

There was a collective gasp, and Joseph himself felt dizzy. Now he knew he was hearing wrong. It almost sounded as if Pharaoh had just released him from his captivity. As if Pharaoh were making him a ruler over Egypt!

"See," Pharaoh continued, waving his hand around the room and over the heads of the shocked men around them. "I have set you over all the land of Egypt. You interpreted my dream when the wisdom of my wise men failed me. For this I shall make you my second in command. From henceforth you are chief vizier over all Egypt, and your word shall be as law." With all the wise and powerful men of Egypt watching, Khyan arose suddenly from his throne, strode down the steps of the dais, and removed a scarab ring from his finger. "Let this be the symbol of what I have done," he said, taking Joseph's hand and sliding the ring onto his finger. "Let every man bow the knee before Joseph as he would bow before me. Let every man know that Joseph is chief vizier of all Egypt."

The faces in the room were filled with stunned disbelief. But no face appeared more stunned than that of Joseph. He was free. He was finally free!

Chapter Notes

The term *kine* is an archaic word for "cow." *Kine* is the word used in the King James Version of the Bible and has been used in this chapter to stay as close as possible to the original wording of that translation.

THIRTY-THREE

THE THREE-LEGGED TABLE CRASHED to the ground, its contents littering the stone tiles of the floor, and Neferset stared up at her husband in surprise.

"You've destroyed us!" Potiphar bellowed, his face red with rage. "You have destroyed us both! You and your lying tongue! You've sentenced us both to death!"

"What are you talking about?" Neferset stammered. She rose from her chair, a look of righteous indignation on her face, but she took several nervous steps away from her husband.

"I was in Khyan's throne room today," Potiphar said. "He summoned all his advisors and wise men there to interpret a dream. And do you know what happened?"

"How could I possibly know what happened?" Neferset demanded, jutting out her chin and lifting her head. "I have nothing to do with the affairs of Pharaoh. Half the time I seem to have nothing to do with the affairs of my own husband."

"I'll tell you what happened," Potiphar said as he slowly stalked Neferset around the room. "None of Khyan's people could interpret his dream. None of them could satisfy his questions. But one of his servants met a man in prison. A man with the favor of a God. A man who could interpret dreams. Would you like to know what happened when this man was brought before the pharaoh?"

"Why don't you tell me," Neferset said haughtily. The initial outburst from her husband had frightened her, but her usual demeanor of bored disdain was now beginning to return. Potiphar was powerful, but the laws of Egypt protected her if he chose to lift a hand to strike her. Let him try that. Let him try that and see just how powerful she could become.

"I will tell you," Potiphar said in a low, rumbling voice. "I am telling you. And when you've been told it all, you'll have a harder time keeping that smug, self-confident smile on your lips."

She didn't know why, but something in her husband's voice sent a cold chill through her body, and Neferset was no longer concerned about what he might try in his anger to do to her. Something far worse seemed about to be revealed.

"The man from the prison interpreted Pharaoh's dream," Potiphar said. "He interpreted it so well that everyone in the room marveled at his wisdom. And there was none as pleased by his interpretation as Pharaoh. In fact, Pharaoh was so pleased that he put his ring upon the man's finger and made him chief vizier over all Egypt. You know this man, Neferset. And I'm certain he remembers you."

"W-who was this man?" Neferset demanded. "And why are you telling all of this to me?"

"I'm telling all of this to you, because the ruin you've brought upon my house is about to be completed. You brought the wrath of a foreign God upon us, and now the servant of that God has power to do with us as he will. Bow low when the new vizier rides by in his chariot, my wife. Bow low while you still have a head to bow. The new vizier of Egypt is Joseph."

Neferset stared at Potiphar, and horror filled her eyes.

"But he . . . he is dead! You told me yourself that . . . " She stopped, shook her head, and stared at Potiphar again. "Are you telling me he's still alive? Are you telling me you didn't execute him when you had the chance?"

"I'm certain you have nothing to fear," Potiphar said, becoming suddenly calm. "I'm certain Joseph's own guilt will protect you from him. He was guilty after all. Wasn't he?"

Neferset felt the blood drain from her face. Her husband's eyes pierced through her, and she was certain he could see the blackness of her heart. She was doomed. Her own wicked injustice was about to return upon her. And, unlike Joseph, there was no god to save her.

"The most curious thing happened today," Setmosis said as he absently rolled a grape around the edge of a serving platter. "I suppose you've heard rumors by now about what happened at Pharaoh's palace today."

Asenath, Netchem, and Ari said nothing. Of course they'd heard. The entire city was buzzing about it. There were stories of a potential war with Thebes, talk of palace intrigue, and even a rumor that Pharaoh had appointed a chief vizier. But no one knew exactly what had happened. No one, that is, except for those who had actually been called before Pharaoh. And Setmosis was one of those men.

"We've heard lots of things," Ari said, watching her husband as he popped the grape into his mouth, chewed it, and leaned over the small table to search for another. "But it seems that you want to make us die of suspense. Quit eating those grapes and tell us what happened. The girls are bursting with curiosity, and they can't wait any longer."

"*They* can't wait?" Setmosis asked, twisting a second grape teasingly between his fingers. "Or is it *you* who can't wait?"

Ari tossed a grape at him, bouncing it squarely off his nose, and he finally laughingly relented. "All right," he said, setting his own grape on the table and leaning back in his chair. "I'll tell you exactly what happened. We were called to the temple to interpret a dream. Pharaoh was troubled by two particularly vivid dreams that seemed to have special significance, and he called upon our skills as priests and magicians and wise men to give him their meaning."

"That's all?" Ari demanded. "All of this has been about a simple dream? We all have dreams, and we don't disrupt the workings of a kingdom to have someone put our mind at ease."

"You haven't let me finish," Setmosis replied. "This story becomes more and more curious as it goes along."

"Then tell us. What happened next?"

"We spent nearly the entire day at the palace, attempting to interpret what he told us. We gave every explanation we could think of, but none of us could satisfy him. In all honesty, I must say that none of us could really satisfy ourselves either. It was the strangest thing. All the images of his dreams were symbols familiar to us, and when the dream was finally interpreted, we all recognized the genius of the interpretation. But, at the time, it wasn't so clear. It was as if our minds were clouded. As if one of the gods were preventing us from knowing the secret of Pharaoh's dreams."

"But it was interpreted," Ari said, nodding. "Who gave the interpretation? Was it a priest? A royal advisor?"

"No. It was a convict from Pharaoh's prison."

All of them stared in surprise, particularly Asenath. A strange feeling began to stir inside her, and she gave her foster father her complete attention.

"When none of us could explain the images of Pharaoh's dream," Setmosis continued, "Pharaoh's chief butler stepped forward. He claimed that one of Pharaoh's prisoners had interpreted his dream and the dream of a former chief baker when the two of them had displeased Pharaoh and were locked up in the prison. Pharaoh immediately called for this man, and he was brought before us."

"Who was this man?" Netchem jumped in, voicing Asenath's own question. "What was his name?"

Setmosis closed his eyes and tried to remember. "His name wasn't Egyptian," he replied. "I can remember that much. He was 'apiru, not Egyptian. And the name sounded vaguely familiar to me. I believe he was called Joseph. Yes, that's it. Joseph."

Asenath grasped the sides of her chair to prevent herself from falling off of it. She was suddenly, unexplainably, dizzy, and all the blood drained from her face. Netchem cast her a surreptitious glance, but neither Setmosis or Ari seemed to notice how his last statement had just affected her. She suddenly had a million new questions of her own, but her lips couldn't move to voice them. She listened in rapt silence as Setmosis described Pharaoh's dream and all the events leading up to the prisoner being brought out of the prison. She listened for any clue that would confirm this prisoner to be *her* Joseph. And, all the while, her heart hammered in her chest like the hooves of war horses before a battle chariot.

"Pharaoh has commanded that all citizens of Avaris assemble along the royal boulevard tomorrow," Setmosis said after completing his long narrative of the day's events. "Khyan was so pleased with this man that he made him chief vizier over all the land. We are to gather so that the new vizier may be presented before us."

For the first time now, both he and Ari seemed to notice Asenath, and the looks on their faces turned to looks of concern. "Are you feeling all right?" he asked.

"Yes," Ari said. "You don't look well, Asenath. You're very pale, and you've hardly taken a thing to eat tonight."

"I'm feeling a little lightheaded," Asenath quickly replied. "It must be all the excitement of the day. I think I'll go and walk in the garden for a while. That should make me feel better."

"I have something else that should make you feel good," Setmosis said. "With all the information I could choose to give, I forgot one of the most important things. This news is specifically for you."

Asenath looked at him, uncertainty etched across her face.

"I spoke with Pharaoh about your many suitors," he said. "Pharaoh has agreed that he must soon make a decision about which of them will be your husband. I've convinced him that Senmut is the best candidate, and Pharaoh will be calling you to the palace soon to make it official."

It took all the will power she possessed to keep the horror she suddenly felt from showing on her face. One day earlier, she would have passively accepted this. But one day earlier her heart hadn't desperately grasped onto the possibility that Joseph might have somehow been miraculously resurrected from the world of the dead.

"You no longer have to agonize over your future," Setmosis continued. "You will soon be married to a fine man—a loyal nomarch—and your days of captivity will be at an end."

"Th-that's wonderful," Asenath stammered. "Thank you for telling this to me. Now, if you'll excuse me, I really think I need that walk in the garden." She stood up, turned, and walked as if in a trance away from the table. She was only vaguely aware of Ari's quick gesture for Netchem to follow. They probably believed she was ill and worried that she might stumble and fall on her way out. Only Netchem could know the true source of this sudden, mysterious illness, and Netchem said nothing about Joseph to her parents as she silently followed Asenath from the courtyard to the garden. It was fortunate that she came. Asenath's strength gave out the moment they were away from Ari's and Setmosis' watchful eyes, and her knees began to buckle beneath her. If not for Netchem's quick hands, she would have toppled to the earth.

"Thank you," Asenath said, smiling weakly as Netchem helped her seat herself on one of the garden's stone benches. Her head was spinning and her body swayed even after she was no longer standing, but after a few moments some of her strength finally began to return.

"I can't do it," Asenath whispered as Netchem sat on the bench beside her. "I can't marry Senmut."

"But you love him," Netchem said. "You can't let what you've heard today—"

"You're wrong," Asenath interrupted. "I don't love him. There's only one man I've ever loved, and, until today, I was certain that man was dead."

"You don't know that he's not. For all you know, Joseph could be a common name among the Hebrews. There could be a hundred other Joseph's. A thousand. You can't let a name without a face destroy your happiness."

"I haven't been happy since I found Joseph's name on the prison list of the executed," Asenath said. "My heart hasn't even begun to entertain the hope of real happiness until today. You have to help me, Netchem. You have to go to your father and convince him to once more petition Pharaoh in my behalf. It was a mistake for me to even begin to consider that I could be married to a man other than Joseph, and it would be unfair for my husband to live the rest of his life under the shadow of my love for Joseph."

"Don't be hasty about this," Netchem cautioned. "You don't even know yet who this Joseph is. What if you see him tomorrow and don't recognize his face? What will you do then? Are you prepared to throw the rest of your life away for the memory of a name?"

"I don't know if the new vizier is my Joseph or not," Asenath replied. "If he isn't, my heart will break again. But I can't marry. Whether Joseph lives or not, I can't marry any man other than him. You're now married to the man you love, Netchem. What if he doesn't return from the trip your father sent him on to Thebes? Could you marry another man if you thought he still might live?"

Netchem shuddered and then she angrily shook her head. "You're talking nonsense," she said. "It's the shock of hearing that name again. That's what's doing this to you. Tomorrow, when you see that this is a different Joseph, you'll regret everything you've said to me today. You'll come back to your senses and be grateful that Senmut is to be selected as your husband."

"No. No matter what happens tomorrow, it won't change my mind or my heart."

"We'll both arise early tomorrow," Netchem said. "I'll go with you, and together we'll see. If this man really is the Joseph you love, I'll go to my father and do as you ask. If he's not . . . " Netchem stopped and shook her head in frustration.

"If he's not, I still won't marry," Asenath insisted. "I'll go to my grave alone. That is my wish."

"You may not have any say in what you do," Netchem said. "Your wishes may not matter to Pharaoh."

"Then I'll deal with that when the moment arrives."

"You'd risk the wrath of Pharaoh?"

"What can he do to me? What can he do to me that's worse than what he's already done? I'd rather be dead than married to someone I don't love."

"Don't say that," Netchem said. "Wait to see what tomorrow brings. Then we'll talk about this again."

Asenath tiredly nodded her head and sighed. It was going to be a very long night. Perhaps the longest one of her life.

THIRTY-FOUR

JOSEPH FELT CONFUSED when he opened his eyes. He wasn't greeted by the depressing stone walls or the oppressive darkness of his prison cell, and he wasn't sure for several moments where he was. He found himself staring at a soothing, blue ceiling, and he felt the wooden headrest of an actual bed at the back of his neck. It wasn't until he felt the heavy ring of Pharaoh on his finger that it all began to come back to him—Pharaoh's dream, the throne room, his appointment as vizier—the events all came rushing back at him. But had it really happened, or was this all just a pleasant, waking dream?

"My lord? Are you awake?"

Joseph placed his feet on the foot rail at the base of the sloped bed and sat up. One of Pharaoh's servants was standing nervously at the bedroom door, and Joseph stared at him.

"Forgive me for waking you," the servant apologized, "but Pharaoh requests your immediate presence at his stables. It's time for you to make your appearance before the people."

"Of course," Joseph said, trying to make sense of what was happening. "Can you show me the way?"

"Yes. But first Pharaoh has asked me to give you these." The servant extended his arms, and Joseph looked to see that he was carrying white garments of fine linen—a tunic, a *shenti*—and a broad leather belt.

Joseph nodded and accepted the garments. The servant then left the room, and Joseph hastily dressed himself. When he was ready, he stepped out into the narrow hall where the servant was waiting for him.

"This way, my lord," the servant said. "We must hurry."

Joseph followed him through the narrow hall and out into a broader, tiled hall that was a gathering place for guests of the pharaoh. It felt strange to be treated with dignity and respect, and it was still difficult to accept that this wasn't just a dream. His mind was still in shock from the swiftness of everything that had happened. One moment he had been a prisoner and a slave—the lowest of all men in Egypt. Now he was chief vizier. Only God could work a miracle of this magnitude. It made his heart swell with gratitude and joy.

The stables were at the far end of the palace complex, and Joseph's nose told him which way to go the moment they stepped out the back entrance of the building. The pungent odors of horse hide and manure were all too familiar to him, and his mind was immediately flooded with memories of his service to Potiphar. He almost felt as if he should grab a shovel or a bucket and go to work. But menial labor of that type would have been inappropriate for a chief vizier. He shook his head again at the thought. How could a Hebrew slave go from servant to master in the space of thirteen years? How could a Hebrew do that in a thousand? Only God could accomplish such a thing, and the glory would go to Him.

Pharaoh and Potiphar were waiting before the stables. Teams of white horses had been harnessed to Pharaoh's first and second chariots, and a third chariot was near at hand for Potiphar. Pharaoh had a smile on his lips. Potiphar's face looked drawn and pale. As he approached, Joseph could see a tense glimmer of fear in his old master's eyes. It was obvious that this was going to be as awkward for Potiphar as it was for Joseph.

"Joseph!" Pharaoh called out, moving forward and warmly clapping both hands on Joseph's shoulders. "I slept the sleep of a baby because of you. Your interpretation of my dreams has finally put my mind at ease."

"The God of my fathers has accomplished that," Joseph humbly replied. "As you know, however, there will be much work ahead to prepare your land for this famine."

"Of course. But as long as the right man is working on the solution, this land will survive. Potiphar has informed me that you once served him. He tells me that if any man in all Egypt is qualified to prepare for such a famine, you are that man. As one of your first duties as vizier, the power over these preparations will be placed into your hands."

Joseph nodded then glanced over at Potiphar in surprise; but Potiphar wouldn't return his gaze.

"If you are to be a vizier," Pharaoh said, stepping back and looking Joseph over with a critical eye, "you need to look the part. The new clothing I sent to you is a beginning, but it still needs something more." He stopped speaking, turned to one of the servants who stood at a respectful distance, and clapped both hands. Immediately the servant moved forward and handed Pharaoh a large golden chain. The chain attached itself to the tips of the spread wings of a gold and lapis scarab—an unmistakable symbol of power and authority—and Pharaoh took this chain and fastened it around Joseph's neck.

"You are now the second most powerful man in all Egypt," Pharaoh said, his voice filled with sudden gravity. "Serve me well and as long as I am Pharaoh no other man shall remove you from your place."

Joseph bowed and Pharaoh motioned toward the chariots. "Come," he said. "It is time to present you to the people."

As Joseph moved to Pharaoh's second chariot, he passed near Potiphar. Something told him Potiphar wished to speak, and Joseph slowed his steps.

"My wife fled from the house in the night," Potiphar said, still not looking into Joseph's face. "There was fear in her eyes when I told her you were appointed to be vizier. There was also guilt." He was silent for several moments and seemed to be waging a mighty battle within himself. Finally, he looked up with agony in his eyes. "I beg your forgiveness, Joseph. I have wronged you. In my pride, I thrust you into prison for a crime you didn't commit, and I . . . I beg you to be merciful to me . . ."

Joseph stared silently at Potiphar then surprised him by clasping his hand while placing the other hand on his shoulder. "I've already forgiven you," Joseph replied. "I forgave you long ago. A man can't live his life in bitterness. It was God's will that it happen, and God has blessed me for enduring it faithfully. I bear no grudge against you."

"Thank you," Potiphar whispered. "You're a greater man than I. But rest assured, when my wife is found, she will bear the full penalty of her crime against you."

"I don't seek or desire vengeance," Joseph said. "Not against your wife and not against you. My only desire is that you know in your heart that I sinned neither against you or my God. I wish for you to be able to call me your friend."

Potiphar tried to speak, but his voice cracked and he merely nodded.

Pharaoh, who was now in his chariot, glanced in their direction to see what was holding things up, and Potiphar made a quick, silent gesture that they should get into their own chariots. Joseph stepped easily onto the platform of Pharaoh's second chariot and, a moment later, they all were rolling toward the palace gates. Just inside those gates, they were joined by several more chariots—soldiers of Pharaoh's royal guard—and they made an impressive procession as they moved to the great boulevard before the palace. One of Pharaoh's servants immediately called out and announced the king's approach to the throngs of waiting people outside.

"*Suten net, Khyan-meri-Set! Ankh! Utcha! Senb!* The king of the South and North, Khyan, beloved of Seth! Life to him! Strength to him! Health to him!"

A roar of cheering voices greeted them as they rolled beyond the gates. Joseph hadn't seen a gathering this large since Pharaoh left those many years ago for Thebes. Everywhere he looked there were people—young and old, slave and free—and he didn't know how to react until Pharaoh slowed and pulled alongside his chariot.

"The people are here to greet you," Pharaoh said, smiling. "Wave to them."

He did as told, and the roar of the crowd intensified. But things quieted when Pharaoh raised a hand above his head.

"Citizens of Avaris!" Pharaoh called out. "People of Egypt. From this time forward a new name shall be known throughout this land. You shall know the name of my *tjaty*—my chief vizier—and you shall bow before him as you would bow before me. If he issues a command, it is yours to follow. If he makes a decree, it shall be as if it came from my own mouth. Until this day he has been known as Joseph. Joseph the *'apiru*. Joseph the Hebrew. Joseph the slave. But, henceforth, he shall have a new name that you may know his power. The name I give him is *Zaphnath-paaneah*. Bow the knee before him!"

Pharaoh flicked the reins over the backs of his horses and started the procession forward again. Before them shouts of "Bow the knee!" echoed through the streets and, like a wave rippling across a glassy sea, the citizens of Avaris went down on their knees. It was an awesome sight to behold. A sight that would make most men swell with pride. But it humbled Joseph. Who was he that his God should shower such favor upon him? Who was he that all Egypt should bow down before him? He was only a simple man. Only a servant of captains and prison keepers. But Pharaoh took him along the complete length of the boulevard and back again, and every knee bowed in submission.

His eyes swept across the mass of faces. There were too many of them for his brain to register it all. But a hopeful heart searched for one face in particular—one face that he hadn't seen for far too many years. Perhaps she had promised herself to the nomarch named Senmut. Perhaps even after all this she still couldn't be his. But Joseph yearned to see her face one more time. He would give away all the power in Egypt to once more behold Asenath's lovely face.

If she was in that crowd, his eyes couldn't discern her, and soon his chariot was rolling back through the palace gates. His head was spinning from all that had happened, but his heart was breaking from what hadn't.

"Are you all right?" Potiphar asked when they returned to the stables.

Joseph didn't answer. He just gave a wistful smile.

"You'll soon grow into this appointment," Potiphar said. "You always rose to your challenges in the past."

"Yes, I suppose your right," Joseph said. "With God's help, anything is possible."

Asenath felt sick to her stomach as she waited with Netchem in the crowd that had assembled before Pharaoh's palace. She hadn't eaten any breakfast before leaving the house—she was too nervous for that—and now she felt weak and jittery.

They had come to the palace gates early so that they could secure a good place at the edge of the royal boulevard. But the mystery of what had gone on in Pharaoh's throne room had so excited the imagination of the populace that many had arrived even before them. Netchem turned to Asenath and voiced what they were both now thinking.

"We should have gone with Father and Mother to stand with the priests before the temple. It will be a miracle if we manage to see the new vizier from here." She craned her neck once more to try to peek over the crowd then looked again at Asenath and touched her shoulder with a comforting hand. "Don't worry," she said. "Somehow we'll see him. Even if we only catch a glimpse, that will be enough. Then you'll know."

Asenath nodded, stood on her tiptoes, and attempted to look

across the crowd herself. But Netchem's first statement had been right. It would be a miracle if they saw him. It would be an even greater miracle if he saw her. They could try to force their way through the crowd back to the temple, but they would probably never make it there in time. The sun was already up, and Pharaoh could come out of the palace with the vizier at any moment. A few unchecked tears clouded her vision as she tried again to look over the heads and shoulders that blocked her view.

"They say the new vizier is a powerful magician," a woman next to her said to another woman. "They say he is a *neferty*—a prophet— from a distant land, and that the gods commanded him to disguise himself as a servant in Pharaoh's court until the time was right to reveal himself."

"That's not what I heard," the other woman replied. "He is the great god Seth himself, come to earth in the form of a man to destroy all those in Thebes who have blasphemed his name. He is about to send a great famine upon Egypt, and only those who have faithfully served him will survive."

"You're both wrong," a third woman said. "I know for a fact that he is neither of those things. He was a slave in the house of my master, and he was cast into prison because my mistress falsely accused him. I myself helped the mistress flee in the night because she feared his retribution."

Asenath felt a tingle of excitement pass through her body and she strained her ears to hear more. But the conversation was drowned out by a sudden roar that arose from the crowd. The mass of humanity surged forward several cubits as Pharaoh and his vizier appeared suddenly at the palace gates. A palace servant called something out to announce Pharaoh's approach, but the noise was so deafening that Asenath could hear nothing but the excited roar. It remained that way until Pharaoh lifted a hand above his head and stilled the masses.

"Citizens of Avaris!" he called out. "People of Egypt . . . "

Asenath fought once again for a better view; but, even as tall as she was, she wasn't tall enough to see clearly past the men in front of her. She had to keep bobbing from side to side, and could only catch a vague glimpse of the tall, dark-haired man in Pharaoh's second chariot. She balled her hands into small fists and fought with discouragement and fear as it became more and more obvious to her that this day would pass without discovering for certain if Joseph still lived. She didn't even listen to what Pharaoh was saying, and she was almost beside herself with despair when cries of "Bow the knee!" began to ring out around her. The crowd went to its knees and suddenly she could see.

Her heart leaped within her, warmth flooded her body, and she tried to take a few steps forward; but Netchem quickly grasped one of her hands and pulled her to her knees.

"You must bow down," she said. "Pharaoh has commanded it."

"It's him!" Asenath hoarsely whispered. "It truly is Joseph! I've seen his face!"

"Are you sure?"

"The image of his face is etched upon my heart. I see it every time I close my eyes to sleep at night. How could I not recognize him when I saw him?"

Netchem looked unconvinced, but she nodded her head in resignation. "Then I will go to my father," she said. "I'll try to convince him to speak with Pharaoh again."

Asenath flung her arms around Netchem and embraced her. Tears of joy were flowing from her eyes. "He's really alive," she sobbed. "His execution was all a lie. He was in the prison all these years, and I never even knew it."

Netchem's eyes shifted nervously back and forth between Asenath and the street. They should be bowing respectfully like all those around them. It would be an affront to Pharaoh and his new vizier if they didn't. But Asenath didn't care whether or not she was seen. She hoped that Joseph would see her and come across the crowd to take her hand. He was alive and she loved him and that was all that mattered. Let the world see her happy tears. Her heart had never before been filled with such joy.

Chapter Notes

1. In the Egypt of Joseph's day, the penalty for a crime was typically much more severe for a woman than it was for a man. The ancient Egyptian story "The Tale of the Two Brothers" gives an account of a crime remarkably similar to that of Potiphar's wife. In this story, the wife of a man named Anupu (Anubis) attempts to seduce his younger brother, Bata. When Bata refuses her advances she becomes afraid and plots to destroy him to cover up her misdeed. When Anupu returns home, his wife deceives him into believing that Bata made inappropriate advances toward her and that he beat her to frighten her into silence. Anupu at first tries to kill his younger brother; but later, when the truth of the matter is revealed, he puts his own wife to death and throws her body to the dogs. It wouldn't be difficult to imagine Potiphar's wife taking flight if she were facing such severe consequences.

2. In Jewish tradition, the name *Zaphnath-paaneah* is said to mean "he who reveals that which is hidden"—a fitting name for one such as Joseph who had power to interpret dreams.

THIRTY-FIVE

$\mathcal{S}$ETMOSIS STARED AT HIS DAUGHTER, a look of pure bewilderment on his face, then—slowly—he shook his head. "This is an unexpected surprise," he mumbled. "Are you telling me that Pharaoh's new vizier is the very same chief steward Asenath taught at Potiphar's estate?"

"Yes. That's what I'm trying to tell you, Father."

Setmosis shook his head again, paced the room, stopped and stared at her. "In love with him? You're telling me she's in love with this man?"

"Yes. Isn't it wonderful?"

"*Wonderful?* It's the farthest thing from it!"

"I-I don't understand," Netchem stammered. "He's chief vizier over all Egypt. What could be more perfect for Asenath than that?"

"Yes," Ari, who had been listening quietly up until this point, chimed in. "Why is this such a bad thing?"

"Under normal circumstances," Setmosis replied, "I would be thrilled to hear that she had fallen in love with a vizier. But these aren't normal circumstances. This man has risen out of obscurity to total power, and he's risen much too fast. One who rises so fast is likely to fall just as swiftly."

"But you were there when he was made vizier," Netchem

protested. "You said yourself that Pharaoh was pleased with him. He wouldn't be vizier if he didn't have Pharaoh's favor."

"Yes. He has Pharaoh's favor today. But what about tomorrow? Or in a month? Or in a year? He gave an artful interpretation of Pharaoh's dream, but dreams and men can be manipulated. Even if Joseph lasts the seven years of so-called plenty, what do you think is going to happen to him if no famine materializes in the eighth year? I'll tell you what's going to happen. Pharaoh will see him for the pretender he is, and he'll be cast right back into that prison he came from. Where would Asenath be then? Who would protect her and care for her?"

"Why are you suddenly talking this way?" Ari asked. "One day ago you were as amazed by his interpretation as everyone else in that throne room. You said it was a good interpretation."

"It *was* a good interpretation. But that's all it is—an interpretation. And the art of interpreting is a subtle one. The interpreter must be careful about what he says. He must state things in such a way that, if necessary, the interpretation can later be manipulated to explain the events no matter which turn those events have taken."

"Are you saying that priests use trickery when they interpret dreams?" Ari asked, her mouth falling open in dismay.

"I'm saying that priests use wisdom when they interpret a dream. Joseph didn't use wisdom. He gave an interpretation that fit all the symbols of the dream, but he didn't leave himself any avenue of escape."

"Then maybe that's why Pharaoh was pleased with his words and not with yours," Ari said, narrowing her eyes. "Maybe he was impressed by the young man's courage."

"Courage? Since when has foolishness come to be equated with courage? It's wisdom that will keep a chief vizier in office. Not courage."

"Joseph does have wisdom."

Everyone turned in surprise as Asenath suddenly entered the

room. She had been hiding in the darkness of a nearby corridor, but could no longer listen to this in silence. She cast Netchem a quick, apologetic glance then faced Setmosis with flames of indignation burning in her eyes.

"Joseph is the wisest man I've ever known," she said. "His wisdom is not the wisdom of men—it is the wisdom of his God. He trusts his God and his God upholds him in all that he does. He won't fall suddenly from glory as you claim he will. He'll be the brightest star in all Egypt."

"He will be a falling star," Setmosis said, returning her stare with a steady gaze of his own. "And who is this God that Joseph can trust in Him? Gods are fickle beings. They put one man in power one day and another the next. Who is Joseph that he should be any different from any other man?"

"It doesn't matter," Asenath said. "I love him. Even if he were to fall from grace, I would want to be right there at his side falling with him. My greatest desire is for my life and my fate to be sealed to his."

"You will not marry this artful pretender," Setmosis said, holding his jaw now in a firm, straight line. "I forbid it. I've already told Pharaoh what is best for you, and this new turn of events changes nothing. You will marry Senmut. And someday you will actually thank me for it."

"You're no different from my own father," Asenath said, her voice trembling. "You do what's best for you and claim it's what is best for me. Are all priests the same? Do they all treat women like playing pieces in an invisible game of *senet*? My father talked the same as you the night he locked me in my room and informed me that I'd soon be taken to Thebes to be forced into a marriage with Prince Sebekamzaf. He said it was for my own good. He said I would be grateful someday. You and he are just the same. I despise you both!"

Angry tears streaked her face. She turned and ran from the room, bitter sobs catching painfully in her throat. Where was justice? Where was mercy? There was none for her. She had been robbed of them both. Even after all she and Joseph had been through—even after Pharaoh had lifted him above all Egypt—they were still to be kept apart. There was only one hope now. She could only hope that Joseph still loved her and that his God would help him find a way to free her from Pharaoh's decree. Other than that, there was no hope left to light her soul.

"He's been vizier for only two days, and already he works as hard as ten of my regular advisors." A pleased smile was spread across Pharaoh's face, and he enthusiastically thumped Potiphar on the back. "During his first day in office he inspected all the royal granaries, met with the royal architect to start building more, and calculated the total number of *setjats* of cultivated land around Avaris. This all raises one very important question in my mind."

"What is that, my pharaoh?"

"What on earth possessed you to throw such a man into my prison? You've never answered that question. Was he not as diligent for you as he is for me?"

"He was the best steward I ever had," Potiphar replied, "and my properties suffered for his loss. It . . . it was a mistake to put him in prison. It was all a terrible misunderstanding."

Pharaoh watched Potiphar, waiting for more. He had the power to command Potiphar to reveal what had happened. He had the power to discover all the sordid details of Neferset's treachery and Potiphar's decision to listen to her words rather than follow his heart. But today Pharaoh decided not to press the matter. Instead, he just shook his head and laughed.

"Well, whatever happened between you two, it was your loss and Egypt's gain. Zaphnath-paaneah is going to make my job half as difficult and save Egypt from starvation in the process."

"If anyone can accomplish such a feat, it will be him," Potiphar agreed.

"I've commanded him to accompany me on my royal hunt tomorrow," Pharaoh said. "He has a plan of organization to prepare for the famine, and he will present it to me then. That will take care of one problem; but I still have another one that finally needs to be resolved, and Zaphnath can't help me with that."

Potiphar winced. It was uncomfortable to hear Joseph being referred to by this new name Pharaoh had given him. It made Joseph truly sound like a vizier, and it reminded Potiphar of how the roles of master and servant had so abruptly been changed. But he did his best to hide this discomfort from Pharaoh. "What problem would that be?" he asked, trying to match pace with Pharaoh as the king strode purposefully down the palace corridor.

"The problem with Potipherah's daughter," Pharaoh said. "It's a problem I know I should have resolved long ago. Potipherah has been pressuring me for years to either release his daughter to him or choose her a husband. Now I'm even being pressured by Setmosis. He came to me this morning to say the girl needs to marry and to remind me that Senmut is the best choice. What do you think?"

"About Senmut?"

"About the entire situation."

"Senmut is a loyal nomarch," Potiphar said. "His allegiance to you can always be trusted. He would be a good choice."

"Yes, he probably would. But still . . . " Pharaoh stopped in mid-stride and stared thoughtfully at the ceiling. Potiphar watched nervously as Pharaoh stood for several long moments in this attitude of thoughtful meditation, and then Pharaoh looked back down and walked again. "You're probably right. You and Setmosis are both probably right. I need to make an announcement soon and put this problem behind me. With Potipherah's daughter safely married to a man who won't cause me trouble, our wayward high priest won't be quite as potent in his political aspirations. A pharaoh has to watch out for the priesthood of Egypt, Potiphar. They're as self-serving and self-important a group as you'll ever find. Sometimes I even question Setmosis' motives. He himself is a man who has always proven to be loyal, but I wonder what's in it for him to have Asenath married to Senmut."

"He has watched over the girl for many years now," Potiphar said. "Perhaps he is just looking out for her happiness and best interests. He probably feels like she's his own daughter by now."

"I suppose you could be right. In any case, this will wait no longer. Let's see if we can find Aten. I want the girl and all her suitors to be brought before me after my hunt tomorrow. Her future will be determined then."

Potiphar nodded and followed as Pharaoh once more changed his course. The past few days had been a whirlwind of events. And the whirlwind had apparently lost none of its force.

Chapter Notes

Senet is an ancient Egyptian board game similar in some respects to our modern game of backgammon. Each player had differently shaped pieces and used a form of "throw sticks" or dice to determine the number of spaces a piece could move. It was evidently a popular pastime, at least among the wealthier classes of ancient Egypt. *Senet* boards and pieces—some of them elaborately crafted from precious materials—have often been found in the tombs of important Egyptians.

THIRTY-SIX

IN EARLIER TIMES, the river valleys and delta marshes of Egypt teemed with wild game. Boggy thickets of papyrus and reed were home to large flocks of marsh birds. Trees, grass, and scrub brush along the Nile's banks provided fodder and shelter for the many species of deer and gazelles that roamed there. There were predators as well such as the ever present hyena, the elusive leopard, and the mighty lion. It was a paradise for ancient hunters.

Egyptian civilization had grown since then. Fields now covered the banks where wild grass and trees had once grown. Cities encroached upon the ancient hunting grounds of the lion. But there was still game to be hunted, and the hunt was now the special privilege of Pharaoh and Egypt's ruling elite. Joseph, the newest member of this group, was receiving a quick lesson in how it was done.

"Have you ever handled a bow and arrow?" Pharaoh asked as the beaters walked before the hunting party, pounding and prodding the bushes to drive out wild game.

"I used to carry a bow with me when I watched over my father's flocks," Joseph replied. "But many years have passed since then."

Pharaoh made an abrupt hand signal to one of the porters, and the man hurried forward with a bow.

"Here. Take this," Pharaoh commanded. "We'll test your skills and see if you hunt wild beasts as well as you interpret dreams."

Joseph accepted the bow and hefted it in his hands. It was a magnificent weapon of wood and horn and sinew—the type that had made it possible for the early Hyksos kings to conquer and subdue Egypt. Twice as strong as a regular bow and possessing a much greater range, it was truly the tool of choice for a Hyksos warrior or a royal hunter.

"Get him a full quiver of arrows," Pharaoh said to the porter. "And tell the rest of the attendants to stay close at hand. I have a feeling it's going to be a good hunt. Zaphnath brings luck to me, and I'll need plenty of arrows."

The porter nodded and moved away. Pharaoh then motioned to his Master of the Hunt to lead the party out onto the open plains.

"You said you have more definite plans about how to manage the collection of grain," Pharaoh said. "Tell me what you've come up with so far."

"In your throne room, I suggested that you appoint officers over the land," Joseph said. "I believe you should appoint officers on several levels. There should be overseers of nomes who report directly to an administrative center in Avaris. Under these men there should be officers appointed over individual cities with scribes and overseers of fields to help and report to them. Each city will need extra granaries—I've already talked with the royal architect about that—and assessors will need to measure the boundaries of all the fields so that the overseers of the fields can accurately estimate the yield of each harvest. If you do this and collect a fifth part of each harvest, there will be enough grain when the famine descends upon us."

"I will leave the management of that to you," Pharaoh said. "Choose the men you think will best serve as officers and pay them a fair wage. Do you have any particular men in mind?"

Joseph hesitated to answer, and Pharaoh noticed his reluctance.

"Is there a problem?" he asked.

"Two of the men I'd like to set over the nomes are currently in the employ of the captain of your guard," Joseph said.

"And Potiphar is in my employ," Pharaoh easily replied. "Tell him which of his servants you want and give him fair compensation in return. The welfare of Egypt comes first. When the famine comes, we will all be making sacrifices. It won't hurt Potiphar to make some of those sacrifices now."

Joseph nodded, but he was still uneasy about it. Potiphar had already lost his wife. How would he feel when he found out he was about to lose Pekhti and Khep as well?

"Where is that porter?" Pharaoh asked, glancing impatiently around. "We're bound to stir up some game soon, and he still isn't back with that quiver."

As if in answer to his question, the porter came running up to them and handed a quiver to Joseph. Joseph thanked him and turned his attention to the grassy area before him.

"Be alert," Pharaoh whispered. "I often find hyenas in this area. If we're lucky, we might even spot a lion."

Spotting a lion didn't sound anything like luck to Joseph. He'd dealt with lions while tending his father's flocks, and it was never a pleasant situation. Why a king—even with a hunting party this large—would want to go out and find one of those dangerous animals was difficult for him to understand, but he moved cautiously forward with the king.

"I hunt to relax," Pharaoh confided in a whisper. "These hunting expeditions don't last long, but they're my only escape from the problems of ruling a kingdom. The problem is simple on a hunt. You identify your prey and you put an arrow through it. The politics of government aren't so simple. Some problems have to be dealt with delicately. Some solutions are years in the making. Take my problems with Potipherah for instance. Have you heard of him?"

Joseph nodded. Pharaoh had his complete attention now.

"Potipherah is the high priest of On," Pharaoh continued, "and I brought his daughter here nearly thirteen years ago to discourage him from forming alliances with my enemies. This afternoon I must announce my choice for the husband of Potipherah's daughter and I still don't know exactly who I should choose. It must be someone entirely loyal to me. Someone who can't be manipulated by the priesthood of Ra. Do you have any suggestions?"

Joseph moved his lips to speak. He knew a man who would be loyal to Pharaoh. He knew a man who would give everything to be able to call Asenath his wife. But Pharaoh laughed and spoke again before Joseph could form a reply.

"Of course you don't," Pharaoh said. "I can't expect you to have the solution to all my problems. You've only just barely been made vizier. But I'll find someone. Perhaps Setmosis and Potiphar are right. Perhaps I should marry the girl to that Senmut fellow."

"Why don't you allow her to choose for herself?" Joseph spoke before he thought and realized too late that this brash outburst might anger Pharaoh. But Pharaoh just smiled.

"You have the uncanny power to interpret messages sent by the gods," Pharaoh said, "and you have a remarkable gift for organization. But you'll soon learn that dealing with the priesthood of Egypt is a much more complicated and dangerous matter. The priests have power that even I can't completely control. I control Potipherah only so long as I control the fate of his daughter. I must be absolutely certain that my control over his daughter extends even into her marriage. Only then can I assure myself that there will be no revolt in On."

"What if you could control the priests?" Joseph asked. "What if I could find a way to subjugate them before you?"

"My friend," Pharaoh said, patting Joseph on the back. "I doubt that even the gods could accomplish that. But if you *could* do such a thing, I would give you anything you desire."

A faint smile crossed Joseph's lips. There was only one thing he desired, and his mind was racing furiously to find the means of giving Pharaoh what *he* desired. It was a seemingly impossible task. If given an entire year, Joseph would be hard-pressed to come up with a viable plan. But God, who knew all things, could do it. If ever Joseph's fate must be put into the hands of the Lord, now was that time. The Lord had rescued him from the hands of his brothers. It was the Lord who had finally removed him from Pharaoh's prison. The Lord could help him now. He just had to have faith.

Asenath trembled with fear, her heart feeling as if it were about to break within her, as she walked the long, dark hall that led to Pharaoh's throne room. There was no hope left for her now. All the doors were closed. All options were gone. In the end her own father had lost, but she hadn't actually won. She would be separated forever from Joseph, and she was absolutely powerless to do anything about it.

She'd considered falling to her knees before Pharaoh the moment she approached him. She'd thought about pleading with him to spare her from a loveless marriage. But now that she was here, about to stand before him, she realized she was too frightened to do even that. So she stepped into the imposing throne room with her head lowered and with her eyes and face drained of all life and emotion.

"Asenath, daughter of Potipherah," Pharaoh said as she entered the room. "Come and stand before me." There was a strange smile on his face. He smiled as if he were pondering some private joke, and it made her angry that there could be mirth in his heart when he was about to take all joy from hers. "I assume you understand why you have been summoned here today?" he said.

Asenath nodded. She knew why she was here, and her body went cold as she contemplated it. Setmosis, Ari, and Netchem were waiting nervously in the crowd. Her father and mother along with a delegation from On were watching solemnly from the opposite side of the room. And, lined up along one side of the throne, were her suitors— all those men who had petitioned Pharaoh for her hand in marriage. But she wouldn't look at any of them. She wished to be swallowed up by the earth and never be seen or heard from again.

"These men have come here seeking to have you as their wife," Pharaoh said, "and I have the difficult job of deciding which one will be your husband. They are all great men of Egypt. One is a nomarch.

Two are the sons of royal advisors. The rest are men of similar accomplishment and wealth. But the question still remains. Which one should be your husband?" He placed his fingers over his chest and drummed them against each other as if he were lost in deep thought. Asenath wanted to scream, but she couldn't even twitch a muscle.

"Your foster father has given me his recommendations," Pharaoh said, nodding his head at Setmosis. "I have also listened to the desires of your own father. And each of your suitors has given me a petition of his own. But one thing still hasn't been considered. Do you know what that is?" He paused—it was a long pause—and Asenath allowed her eyes to flicker up from the floor to look questioningly at him. "No? Then I'll tell you what it is. The one thing that has never been considered is your own feelings on the matter."

Asenath's mouth dropped open. This was entirely unexpected. But she still couldn't seem to control her vocal chords well enough to speak.

"What are your feelings?" Pharaoh pressed. "Is there one of these men you prefer above the others? Is there one you would rather spend the rest of your days with? If you have anything to say, now is your chance to speak."

She opened and closed her mouth several times. How was she supposed to begin? What was she supposed to say? She wanted to tell him that she desired none of these men—that she loved only one man and that he was Pharaoh's own chief vizier. She looked suddenly around the room at all the faces watching her. At her mother. At her father. At Setmosis and his family. But there was one face missing. And now her mind was clouded with a new question and with new, unanticipated fears. Could it be that Joseph didn't know what ordeal she was passing through today? Or could it be something else? Could it be that he didn't care? She shook her head, confused, and tried not to burst into tears.

"You have nothing to say?" Pharaoh asked. "I would have expected that you would have strong opinions on such a matter as this."

"I . . . I . . . " She clenched her fists at her sides, blinked away the tears that had finally managed to well up in her eyes, and shook her head. "I love none of these men," she managed, in a hoarse whisper, to say. "I love another man."

Setmosis, who was standing off to one side, stepped forward, his face a picture of dismay. But Ari held him back, and Pharaoh ignored him entirely.

"Is this man here today?"

"No."

"Then how do you know that he loves you?"

"I . . . I don't know," Asenath quietly admitted. "At least not anymore."

"Then I have made my decision," Pharaoh replied. "Come forward and kneel before me."

Asenath's legs obeyed the command while the rest of her body lost its power to function.

"The man to whom I give you must be loyal," Pharaoh said. "He must be a man of such integrity that his word can never be doubted. Above all, he must be one who can never be swayed by the political ambitions of your father or by the ambitions of any other priest or prince." He cast meaningful glances at both Potipherah and Setmosis then fixed his eyes once more upon her. "There is only one man in all my kingdom who fits these qualifications," he said, "and I give you to him now. Arise Asenath, daughter of Potipherah."

Asenath did as commanded and got shakily to her feet. At the same time, Pharaoh motioned to one of the guards at the back of the room. The guard disappeared into the corridor for a few moments, and a confused murmur swept across the room. Asenath herself stared at Pharaoh, perplexed.

Pharaoh said nothing, but there was a kindly look on his face, and he motioned for her to watch the corridor. Hesitantly, she turned her eyes toward it.

The sound of approaching footsteps came to her first. Then she saw movement in the darkness. Her heart, for some reason, began to hammer wildly within her and her arms and hands shook. When the owner of the footsteps strode into the room, a startled cry of joy leaped from Asenath's throat.

"Joseph!" she exclaimed. "Joseph! Joseph!"

"What are you waiting for?" Pharaoh said when he saw that she still stood, frozen to the spot. "Go to him. Go to your husband."

Setmosis gasped. Netchem gave a surprised cheer. Potipherah and his wife stared in stunned silence. But Asenath saw and heard none of this. Everything else and everyone else ceased to exist. There were only her and Joseph, and she rushed across the space that separated them to collapse with sobs of joy into his arms.

"Let my decision be known," Pharaoh said, standing abruptly and casting a fierce glance around the room. "And let there be no misunderstanding. I give Asenath, daughter of Potipherah, to my loyal servant, Zaphnath-paaneah. My word is unchangeable. Asenath is his."

Asenath covered Joseph's lips with warm kisses and pressed herself into the protective warmth of his arms. "Don't let go of me," she murmured. "Don't let me wake up and find that all of this is just another dream."

"This is a dream," Joseph said, a huge smile covering his face. "A dream come true. This is a miracle that only God could provide."

"Then let me serve your God forever," Asenath whispered. "And let all our posterity serve Him as well."

Joseph held her tighter. The long ordeal was finally over, and an even longer life together awaited them. No one had ever told Asenath that a heart could be filled with such joy. But she probably wouldn't have believed them even if they had.

CODA

. . . I have gained the mastery over that which
was decreed to be done unto me upon earth . . .

The Book of Coming Forth by Day
Chapter LXVIII

CODA

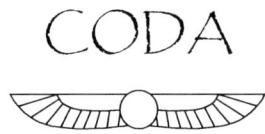

Asenath moved another one of her *senet* cones off the board, placed a slender hand against her enlarged abdomen, and tossed the throw sticks again. "Three," she said, smiling, as she finished tallying up her throw. "That gives me one last move, and then it's your turn." She moved her last piece to the *nefer* square and looked back up at Joseph with teasing eyes. "You'll need incredible luck if you want to beat me now. You still have six of your spools on the board, and I have only one cone remaining."

"It will take more than luck to beat a *senet* master like you," he said, smiling. "It will take a miracle."

"Then there's still hope for you," she replied with laughter in her eyes. "Miracles seem to follow wherever you go."

"God has been very merciful to me," Joseph admitted. "He blessed me with you and now He is blessing our marriage with a child. I have much to be thankful for." He reached out to place his own hand on top of the hand Asenath had put on her abdomen, and he gently patted it.

"I was beginning to wonder if we would ever have children," she said, looking momentarily away. "I was on the verge of giving up hope when this happened."

"You know better than to give up hope," Joseph said. "After all

398 Alex G. Chappell

we've gone through together, you should know that where the Lord is involved there's no such thing as a hopeless situation."

"You're right, of course," Asenath said, closing her eyes contentedly as Joseph stood up from the *senet* board to rub her neck and shoulders. "You're always right. So tell me this. Is this child going to be a boy or a girl, and what shall we name it?"

"Don't you remember your dream? You are to bear two sons. And I think we shall name the first son Manasseh."

"Manasseh?"

"It means 'forgetting,'" Joseph explained. "Because God has made me forget all my toil and all my father's house. Only the love He's placed in my heart for you could accomplish such a thing as that."

"You've never really told me how you convinced Pharaoh to give me to you instead of to one of my other suitors," Asenath said. "Every time I ask you about it you just smile and change the subject. Are you ever going to let me know what happened that day?"

"Isn't it enough just to know that God worked a miracle in our behalf?"

Asenath tilted her head back to scowl up at him, and Joseph laughed.

"All right," he relented. "It was simple really. Pharaoh said he would give me anything I asked for if I could tell him how to control the priests. I gave him the answer to that problem, and he rewarded me with you."

"And what was the solution you presented to him?"

"I showed Pharaoh that he already possesses all the power he needs to control the priests.

There is a portion of land given to each temple to sustain the priests and the temple herds. If the priests ever offended Pharaoh, he could immediately take this land away from them. This would cut the priests off from a significant portion of their wealth."

"But would Pharaoh ever really do this? Would he ever dare to take on the priesthood in such a way?"

"Would your father or any of the other priests dare to find out?"

Asenath smiled. "My husband is a wise man," she said. "Pharaoh is fortunate to have him for a vizier."

"Pharaoh is not nearly as fortunate or blessed as I am," Joseph said. "Look at the beautiful wife I have. Look at my magnificent house. A man could wish for no greater wealth than this."

"You still think I'm beautiful? Even when I look like this?" Asenath waved a hand at her abdomen and grimaced.

"Especially when you look like this," Joseph answered.

Asenath took his hand off from hers and kissed it then replaced her smile with a more serious look. "How is the harvest this season?" she asked. "Is Pharaoh's dream still coming to pass? Is this harvest as bountiful as the previous ones?"

"The earth is bringing forth by handfuls, and I'm laying up food in each city from the land that lies around it. When the famine strikes, the storehouses will be full. The grain we've gathered is as plentiful as the sand of the sea, and I long ago left off numbering it."

"And will it be enough to get us all through the seven years of famine? I don't want my child to starve."

"God will preserve us, and God will preserve Egypt," Joseph replied. "You needn't worry about having food to eat. There will be enough for Egypt and enough for many of those in the lands around us. But it will come at a price. Many men—your father and Setmosis among them—no longer believe in my interpretation of Pharaoh's dream."

"Even after such unprecedented seasons of harvest?"

"The nature of man is to find other explanations for God's miracles," Joseph replied. "But there will be no doubting the dream when the famine finally comes. Empty stomachs and empty treasure vaults will make believers of even the most skeptical critics."

"You won't let the people starve will you?"

"No. Even if they lose the ability to purchase from Pharaoh, I will still find a way to feed them. But the days ahead of us won't be pleasant ones. Even with God's forewarning, it will be a time of tribulation."

"I don't care," Asenath said, pulling Joseph's arm tightly against her with both hands. "I have endured worse. As long as I don't have to be separated from you again, I will have strength to make it through."

Joseph smiled at her, but there was a distant look in his eyes, and Asenath thought she knew what was on his mind. Despite what he had said a few moments earlier, his heart still yearned for some news of his family. Responsibility to Asenath and to Egypt kept him here, but she wondered if he wouldn't have left in search of them if not for that.

"God will protect them," Asenath said. "He will prepare a way for them to survive just as He is preparing a way for us."

"I believe that He will. I just wish I had some way of knowing where they are. I wish I could share my good fortune with them."

"Even your brothers? Even after what they did to you?"

"If we desire God's forgiveness for our own sins, we should be equally willing to forgive others. I forgave my brothers long ago."

"Then I suppose I should thank them if God ever wills that I meet them," Asenath replied.

"Thank them?"

"Of course. If not for what they did, I would not be your wife. They were instruments in God's hands whether they knew it or not. They were instruments in bringing you to me."

"You have a point," Joseph replied, looking down at her with a tender smile. "And for that and many other reasons, I wouldn't change a single event of what happened. I don't regret for a moment what I had to pass through to be with you, and if I had to do it all over again, I would. But I can't help but hope that I'll have the opportunity to be reunited with my family before this life is over. I can't imagine what sorrow my father must have passed through, even though the Lord gave me great blessings of joy because of it."

"If he could see you now," Asenath said, "I imagine that he would be filled with great joy. And pride as well. You have brought honor to his name. You have also represented your God well, and He has honored you because you honored Him."

"How could I do any differently? He has always blessed my life."

Asenath stared thoughtfully at her husband. Not many people would consider sorrow, servitude, and imprisonment to be a blessing. But somehow Joseph had always managed to look past the moment and allow his faith to guide him through. She could learn from that example.

Everyone could learn from that.

"Are we going to finish our game?" she asked, after he had remained silent for some time. "Or are you ready to concede defeat?"

"Defeat?" Joseph asked, laughing. "I don't know the meaning of that word." He leaned over Asenath, kissed her on the forehead, then moved back to his place across the table from her.

She had married a remarkable man. Joseph's faith and virtue never ceased to amaze her. But the most remarkable things were yet to come. Somehow she believed that.

List of References

Achtmeier, Paul J., ed. *Harper's Bible Dictionary*, San Francisco: Harper and Row, 1985.

Bains, John and Jaromir Malek. *Atlas of Ancient Egypt*, New York: Facts on File Publications, 1980.

Bains, John and Jaromir Malek. *The Cultural Atlas of Ancient Egypt*, New York: Checkmark Books, 2000.

Beitzel, Barry J. *The Moody Atlas of Bible Lands*, Chicago: Moody Press, 1985.

Bietak, Manfred. *Avaris and Piramesse: Archaeological Exploration in the Eastern Nile Delta*, London: The British Academy, 1986.

Brewer, Douglas J. and Emily Teeter. *Egypt and the Egyptians*, New York: Cambridge University Press, 1999.

Bright, John. *A History of Israel*, Philadelphia: Westminster Press, 1981.

Budge, E. A. Wallis. *Egyptian Language: Easy Lessons in Egyptian Hieroglyphics*, New York: Dover Publications, 1983.

Bunson, Margaret. *A Dictionary of Ancient Egypt*, New York: Oxford University Press, 1995.

Chisholm, Jane and Anne Millard. *Early Civilization*, London: Usborne Publishing Ltd., 1991.

Church Educational System. *Old Testament Student Manual: Genesis–2 Samuel,* Corporation of the President of the Church of Jesus Christ of Latter-day Saints, 1981.

Clayton, Peter A. *Chronicle of the Pharaohs: The Reign-by-Reign Record of the Rulers and Dynasties of Ancient Egypt*, New York: Thames & Hudson, 1994.

DeLuca, Araldo and Kent R. Weeks. *The Valley of the Kings*, New York: Friedman/Fairfax, 2001.

deVaux, Roland. *The Early History of Israel*, Philadelphia: Westminster Press, 1978.

Dumelow, J.R., ed. *The One Volume Bible Commentary*, New York: Macmillan, 1978.

Edwards, I. E. S. *The Pyramids of Ancient Egypt*, New York: Penguin Books, 1985.

Freedman, D. N., ed. *The Anchor Bible Dictionary*, New York: Doubleday, 1992.

Gordan, Cyrus H. and Gary A. Rendsburg. *The Bible and the Ancient Near East*, New York: W. W. Norton & Company, 1997.

Hayes, John H. and J. Maxwell Miller. *A History of Ancient Israel and Judah*, Philadelphia: Westminster Press, 1986.

Kamil, Jill. *The Ancient Egyptians: Life in the Old Kingdom*, Cairo: The American University in Cairo Press, 1996.

Kemp, Barry J. *Ancient Egypt: Anatomy of a Civilization*, New York: Routledge, 1989.

Landes, George M. *A Student's Vocabulary of Biblical Hebrew*, New York: Charles Scribner's Sons, 1961.

Levenston, Edward A. and Reuven Sivan. *The New Bantam-Megiddo Hebrew Dictionary*, New York: Bantam Books, 1980.

Ludlow, Daniel H. *A Companion to Your Study of the Old Testament*, Salt Lake City: Deseret Book Co., 1981.

Malek, Jaromir. *In the Shadow of the Pyramids*, Norman: University of Oklahoma Press, 1986.

Millard, Ann. *The Atlas of Ancient Worlds*, New York: DK Publishing, 1994.

Odijk, Pamela. *The Egyptians*, Englewood Cliffs: Silver Burdett Press, 1989.

Petersen, Mark E. *Joseph of Egypt*, Salt Lake City: Deseret Book Co., 1981.

Redford, Donald B., ed. *The Oxford Encyclopedia of Ancient Egypt*, New York: Oxford University Press, 2001.

Rogerson, John. *The Cultural Atlas of the World: The Bible,* Alexandria, Va.: Stonehenge Press,1992.

Rohl, David M. *Pharaohs and Kings: A Biblical Quest*, New York: Crown Publishers, 1995.

Shafer, Byron E., ed. *Religion in Ancient Egypt: Gods, Myths, and Personal Practice*, Ithaca: Cornell University Press, 1991.

Silverman, David P., ed. *Ancient Egypt*, New York: Oxford University Press, 1997.

Sternberg, Meir. *Hebrews Between Cultures: Group Portraits and National Literature.* Bloomington: Indiana University Press, 1998.

Strouhal, Eugene. *Life of the Ancient Egyptians*, Norman: University of Oklahoma Press, 1992.

Wilkinson, Toby A. H. *Early Dynastic Egypt*, London; New York: Routledge, 1999.

About the Author

ALEX G. CHAPPELL is an educator, author, and student of foreign languages and cultures. He graduated from Brigham Young University in 1995 and currently teaches in the public school system. His diverse interests in the areas of language and literature have led him, among other things, to a study of biblical and modern Hebrew and ancient Egyptian. *Joseph and Asenath* is his third published novel.